Shimoni's Lover

Also by Jenifer Levin

Water Dancer
Snow

SHIMONI'S LOVER

by

Jenifer Levin

Harcourt Brace Jovanovich, Publishers

San Diego   New York   London

Requests for permission to make copies of any part of the work should be mailed to: Permissions, Harcourt Brace Jovanovich, Publishers, Orlando, Florida 32887.

Library of Congress Cataloging-in-Publication Data
Levin, Jenifer.
Shimoni's lover.
I. Title.
PS3562.E8896S5 1987   813'.54   87-211
ISBN 0-15-181990-4

Designed by G.B.D. Smith

Printed in the United States of America

First edition

A B C D E

For Mom and Dad. Gwynne and Edie. Jamie. James.

For Sarah. DeLynn. Joyce, Tom,
and Elizabeth Patricia.

For Grandma Diana. And in memory of Paul, Ida,
Jerma, Annette, and Dick.

For Joe and Robin.

For Michael and Steven.

For Jim Skofield
and
For Glenn Person, Ironman.

For Warren and Tina. Terry. Max. Roger.

And thank you, B.J., for your help and faith.

For Avi, Ruthi, Nadav. For David, Melech Ha-Pardes.
And Russian David. And Rosetta Dave. For Grace,
Matt, Blitzstein, Jacqui, Captain Shipwreck, Mi-Wa,
Itsu, Stella, Light Horse Harry, Benji-ji, and Philip of
Zambia. For Ziona Aleph-Bet.

For OJ and Chloe.

Most of all, for Rachel.

Prologue

ON RAFI'S FIRST DAY OF BASIC TRAINING HE WOKE AT 3:45 A.M. TO *the sounds of boots stomping, wood crashing, and a large object hurtling past him to smash against the barracks' concrete wall. He sat in the dark, rigid with terror. Around him half-naked recruits slid from their bunks in panic. Someone produced a flashlight. Someone else had the guts to shine it at the long, heavy corpse slumped near a row of footlockers, and one frail kid—a mama's boy from Netanya—actually screamed. Just then the door was kicked open and lights went on. Sergeant Major Gavon stalked in followed by three jeering lieutenants. In the sudden flood of light it could be seen that the corpse was a collection of cloth-stuffed pillows tied together with rope. A few sheepish chuckles sounded. But the sergeant major wasn't smiling.*

"Idiots! Sons of whores! You think it's fun-and-games time, don't you? Stand at attention and shut up!"

Everyone did.

"These are Lieutenant Nachmani, Lieutenant Avrami, and Lieutenant Stein. They're your commanding officers. If any of you pathetic fools think this is a party, maybe, think again. This is the army. You are soldiers. One day you'll probably fight a war. Some of you may live, if we're lucky enough to teach you how. But the rest of you will

die—that's a promise. You will all *look straight down into the stinking mouth of pain and death many, many times. And your mothers won't save you then. So. Kiss your childhood good-bye. Say good-bye to all the good, civilized things you always did in that good, civilized world you always thought you lived in. From now on, you'll do what these nice officers tell you to do. That's all. I'm finished. Get your fat asses into clothes."* The sergeant major suppressed a grim smile. *"Ah. I almost forgot."* Blinking in the cruel light, Rafi could see the corners of his mouth twitching beneath his enormous mustache. Finally it broke through, displaying Gavon's crumbling front teeth and pink tongue, an expression of pure evil. *"Good morning,"* he said, and winked. Then he stormed out the way he'd come, leaving them to dress with savage speed under the jeering stares of Nachmani, Avrami, and Stein.

Outside, a bonfire was going. Groups of other recruits, already dressed in ill-fitting uniforms, were working to keep the blaze alive, breaking rotten beams into pieces, crumpling stacks of newspaper, tearing filthy old clothes apart, crushing cans, and throwing everything into the hot orange flames. Those not occupied in this way had been ordered into a large circle and were marching around and around the perimeter of the bonfire, chanting numbers. One, they chanted, two. Then, more rapidly, one-two-three-four. One. Two. One-two-three-four. *Again and again.* Firelight flashed across each sweating, bewildered young face. It was the dead time of night, when stars had faded. The sky was a solid, lightless black, and against the backdrop of black rose enormous curls of smoke. Flames from the bonfire shot up high, a lonely collage of fevered light in the dark, rocky expanse of desert that stretched everywhere around them. Rafi stumbled from the barracks with the others, still tucking in the tail of his olive-green shirt. Heat blasted his face and chest as he stared at the fire before him, some men cracking wood and shredding garbage to keep it ablaze, the other men circling, circling, in a dazed chanting march. But his back and neck were chilled by the cold of the desert night. It occurred to him then that there was not much of a real choice here—freeze or baste—and someone else would dictate which hell you went through. It occurred to him that there was to be no more pleasure in his life from now on. The middle road of comfort had been denounced and stuffed in an inaccessible coffin. The things he loved were suddenly banished.

Lieutenant Nachmani was walking past, surveying them all with cold blue eyes.

"All right. You. And you. And you, and you, and you, and you too—all of you, fall in and march."

They did, dispersing into the vast circle of men marching around and around the fire, feet stuffed into stiff new boots, sweat beginning to stain the chests and backs of their uniforms.

"Louder!" shrieked Nachmani. And the circle of marching men chanted: One! Two! One-two-three-four!

"Louder!" he howled. Behind him, Avrami and Stein were laughing.

One! *Rafi yelled.* Two! One, two, three, four! *The flames made each sweating face over again into a mask of shadow and yellow light. He marched, toes banging the hard leather of his boots until blisters rose and he began to limp. They marched on in the dark, minutes passing, then an hour, and still they marched until their chanting grew hoarse. Here and there, groups of recruits who weren't marching splintered wood against the hard ground. Once in a while something inside the vast blaze exploded—a can, an oil-drenched cloth—and the loud pop punctuated the perpetual boom and crackle of the blaze itself.*

One! *they yelled, in pain.* Two! One, two, three, four!

If you fell out of step, Nachmani saw it and jumped up and down in a rage, screaming insults. Avrami and Stein merely looked on laughing. Glancing at them through the rivers of sweat pouring down his eyelids, Rafi wanted to vomit. But a senseless necessity kept him moving. They stopped for a few seconds, once, when two men fainted. And again when there was nothing else left to throw into the fire, so the stokers were ordered to fall in and march with everyone else.

At dawn they were still marching.

There was no breakfast. They were ordered to continue marching in a circle around the diminishing flames while Nachmani, Avrami, and Stein sipped coffee from steaming mugs, ate eggs and bread and olives from plates prepared by Stein's driver as they stood joking among themselves, threw uneaten crusts to the ground, watched the stumbling circle of fatigued men chant hoarsely before them.

Stein's driver was a pale, undersized Russian with simian arms and a walleyed stare. All three officers abused him horribly, keeping him running here and there with incessant demands, calling him Dog, Pig, or Fish-Eyes. When the sun had burned away every trace of nighttime cool, he was forced to scurry around and construct a lean-to for them out of canvas and aluminum poles. They lounged on the shaded ground beneath it, tossing olive pits at the marching recruits. By midmorning the fire had smoldered to nothing. The sun beat down from above, unsheltered by clouds. The desert sky stretched blank and white in all directions. Around and around they marched, the Russian screeching laughter as he crouched sweating in the sun right next to the lean-to, echoing his three masters like a demented mascot. By noon, more than a dozen had fainted and been carted off to the base infirmary.

They were allowed to sit, then, in a miserable huddle around the ashes of the fire. Stein's driver had been sent away again, and now returned at the wheel of a truck. Hopping and babbling, he rolled from the back of it huge canisters filled with water.

They became, suddenly, a hysterical group of deliriously energized bodies, stumbling and crawling over one another, grabbing other men by the throat and throttling to keep them from getting to the water first. Rafi avoided fists and elbows, climbed over a pile of struggling bodies, and fell in the sand before a metal spigot. His eyes were red, his face filthy and unshaven. His feet had stopped hurting and were merely numb. With a final burst of strength he wrenched himself to his knees and fixed his mouth against the spigot, turned the knob and sucked and sucked. Lukewarm water gushed down his throat. He gulped like a pig, not caring that it ran over his chin and neck, swelled in his mouth like a bursting dam and filled his nose, threatening to drown him. He gulped, gagged, and swallowed more until someone kicked him in the thigh and several pairs of hands dragged him off the spigot while other desperate men fought to take his place. Some guy backhanded him across the face and he lay there in the sun, sand crusting the dark curls on his head, his nose streaming blood, exhausted and sick, blissfully filled with water.

Instead of lunch they were marched single file, past rows of barracks and dismal concrete buildings, to the other end of the base. Desert

4

stretched before them, unbroken by any hint of civilization. There were gray dunes scattered with ash-white rock, a pale horizon that at first was indiscernible, so easily did sky blend with earth. Look up and you'd see the searing glare of the sun. They were at the edge of a huge rock quarry. Below, boulders crumbled into the ground.

Lieutenant Avrami strutted back and forth in front of the long row of men standing on the quarry's rim. He was an Iraqi Jew, and had the twisting alleyways of old Baghdad in his soul, carrying with him always the deathly dry heat, the rot, the ancient cruelty of ancient and unchanging places. His eyes were dark and glittering. His smile showed teeth of sparkling white—two of his uppers were pointed like a canine's, dagger-tipped, as if to tear meat apart. He alone looked comfortable beneath the unmasked sky. Like it, he was savage and exposed.

"Now you will go down into the wadi," he commanded, "and you will separate the pebbles from the rocks. When you're finished, you will put the pebbles into these sacks"—the demented Russian driver had brought a pile of thick burlap sacks along—"and bring them up here." He paused, the glittering animal eyes passing along each face as he stalked back and forth. "Well, what are you waiting for? You have your orders. Go and do it."

On trembling legs, dozens of young recruits slid down the sides of the wadi to stumble among stones and boulders beneath the desert sky. Rafi tied a white handkerchief around his head. At the quarry's edge, Avrami looked down and laughed and laughed.

They scurried clumsily around the rocks, like injured ants. One by one, burlap sacks were thrown down to them until each man had one. The sacks were large, rough enough to scratch the skin. They worked feebly, their hands caked with dust and blood.

After a while someone else fainted. The Russian driver threw down filled canteens. Jumping to catch one, Rafi nearly broke his wrist. But he caught it, crouched to claim it, strapped it around his shoulder with the furtiveness of a thief. His lips were cracked dry, his limbs trembling with fever. He glanced around, expecting a blow to fall, someone to fight him for the water. But it seemed enough canteens had been thrown to them, after all, and every man had one. The recruit who'd fainted was revived.

The sun blazed. By two it was still high in the sky. By three, a slight breeze had begun to blow. Sand whipped their faces. The burlap sacks got heavier. Above, the three officers stared down at them grinning, munching falafels and drinking from thermoses. They were clustered under a large white umbrella held aloft by the driver, who'd discarded his army cap for a pale sombrero made of straw. Holding up the umbrella, he sweated and smiled.

Slowly, the sun's fierceness began to diminish. Slowly, they filled the sacks with dusty gray pebbles. They worked on in a shivering, methodical way, sipping water now and then, fearfully glancing up at a subtly changing sky and the three officers above who watched them like wolves lying in ambush. Rafi blinked to make sure he wasn't hallucinating. Lieutenant Avrami had stepped out from under the umbrella and perched at the wadi's edge with a megaphone in one hand.

"Okay, very good. I see you know how to work."

Every recruit stopped to stare up. The voice crackled against the increasing wind, sand rattling into the mouth of the megaphone like static.

"But who told you to stop working? You do what we tell you to do. I tell you to continue. Good. Now. In ten minutes, I will signal you all to stop and to bring the pebbles up here."

It hurt to bend down again, to feel the dust caked against each scratch and moist scab, feel the sharp edges of rock tearing at sunburnt skin. The handkerchief Rafi had tied over his head was stiff with dried sweat. Each time he bent down his back made a creaking noise, like an unoiled hinge about to come undone. Every motion blended into the larger all-encompassing pain, enveloped them all. Rationality told him this was only some kind of crazy test. But fatigue and hunger said that this was an endless hell, and there was no way out. This was the army. This would be their fate every day for the next three years or more: this mindless, endless hell, lived out under the pitiless gaze of men as superior to them as gods. He shut his eyes and clutched at the dried ground for a few more tiny rocks, dropped them into the nearly full sack, heard them clink against granite and clay. Now the wind had whipped up strongly, and sand was blowing everywhere. Suddenly a voice cracked from the sky.

"Very good. Stop. Stop! Now, bring the pebbles up here."

Slowly, they began to clamber up the crumbling sides of the quarry, burdened by the filled burlap sacks that clattered against rock still embedded in the earth. Rafi joined the struggling columns of young men. He glanced once in a while, as he crawled upwards, panting, at a face struggling next to his. Bearded, covered with dust and sores and sweat, not a single face around him appeared youthful any more. Exhaustion and fear had written new lines everywhere. He noticed, here and there, a wisp of gray hair on some kid's shiny dark head. They'd been bled of their youth in less than a day. The process of aging had irrevocably begun. The new lines, he knew, would not come out.

Finally they'd made it, and stood at the wadi's edge with the sacks before them. One to each man. Each man covered with white dust that clung to his saturated uniform, making him look like a life-sized cookie doll rolled in flour. Only the bloodshot eyes peering out seemed alive. Empty canteens swung loosely on their shoulders. Lieutenant Avrami remained apart from the other two officers, who watched, leering, from under the white umbrella, sipping from a bottle of Carmel red. Avrami began to strut again, back and forth in front of the line of panting, dust-caked men. His shallow eyes glittered over each face like the passing twin lenses of some ancient camera. He clasped both hands behind his back, his face began to soften, to calm, and his mouth curled in an almost charitable smile. Then he turned suddenly and kicked a burlap sack filled with pebbles over the quarry's edge. Rock rattled on rock. There was a terrible clatter and spew of pale dust as the bag opened and tore and spilled, pebbles bouncing back down to the bottom of the quarry. Avrami wheeled around again. The smile hadn't left his lips. His voice was nearly gentle.

"I said bring the pebbles up here," he said calmly. "I didn't say bring the sacks also. Just the pebbles." He walked along the line of incredulous men, kicked each burlap sack over the edge of the wadi, watching each spill out its contents in a stream of rock and dust. "Unfortunately, you didn't learn yet how to listen. Go down there, now, and do it again."

The driver gave a long laugh, like a high-pitched siren.

By seventeen hundred hours they were ordered to abandon their task. They climbed back up the sides of the wadi and marched across the base the way they'd come.

One, *they sang with cracked throats.* Two.
One. Two. Three. Four.
They dragged their feet along the desert.

From the mess hall came sounds of clattering utensils. Then, across the windswept darkening sky, the faint smell of food. Cooking vegetables. Sesame paste. Fresh bread, maybe? The smell of roasting meat— chicken? Could it be?

Filthy, salivating, they stood outside the mess hall and peered through windows at the crowded tables where officers dined. The driver was sent in and returned with three platters balanced on his hands and arms. They watched, blinking back tears, as Nachmani, Avrami, and Stein ate in a leisurely way, tossing bones full of chicken meat away, laughing as the Russian chased down particularly meaty pieces and attempted to catch them before they hit the ground, stuffing them ravenously into his mouth. They watched as they heard the sound of scraping chairs and officers filed from the mess hall, stopping to belch, pick their teeth, scratch their bellies, chat and laugh with one another, examining humorously out of the corners of their eyes the lines of waiting, famished, filthy recruits, nodding occasionally at Nachmani or Stein, slapping Avrami on the back and sharing a secret joke.

The sun began to go down. The sky darkened, streaked with a single bright bloody color just above the horizon. Now the wind was fierce, howling desolately across the sand. Rafi looked up once and a spasm of pain shot through his neck. The sky was lavender and, straight above, he could make out the glimmering of a single star. He shivered with cold. Something threatened to break in his chest. He was, for a moment, horribly homesick. But he fought back the feeling and, beneath dust, his face was devoid of expression. There would be no more joy in life. He would never experience a familiar comfort again. The world was cold now, utterly changed. Drool slid down his chin at the heartbreaking odor of food.

"*Now!*"

Avrami's voice cracked through the megaphone with the violence of a bullwhip.

"Listen carefully, now! You will all enter the mess hall, and when dinner is brought out then you will eat. But I must tell you something first. There are fifty-one of you, standing here. However, there are only forty-eight meals. So three of you will probably not eat tonight." He paused. They could hear the laughter in his voice. "Unless, of course, you fight for it. So go ahead. Good luck!"

They spilled through the mess-hall door like madmen caught in a tidal wave.

Chairs crashed. Tables were overturned.

Stacked neatly on two large carts were plates piled high with food. Forty-eight dinners glistened under the ceiling lights, and fifty-one wild animals in the tortured bodies of men raced howling for their share.

Rafi was a small man. He'd spent a lot of his life looking up at things, trying to see past the shoulders of others. A double panic gripped him now. If he couldn't get there first, his dinner would be taken. The world was not made for small men. Especially here. A larger man would obtain his share, would knock him to the floor with simple, superior strength. He'd go hungry again, wither away—he and two other men unlucky enough to be too slow, too small, too gentle. He clung with savage instinct to the back and shoulders of a tall boy. His fingers clutched dark curls of hair. The kid was heading for food and, like an infant, Rafi rode him.

Boiled chicken and stewed tomatoes. Fried potatoes, swimming in oil. Balls of mashed fried chickpeas. Oranges and olives and mounds of bread. Tureens of soup that swirled a muddy brown color and smelled faintly of beef. There were fistfights over the pickled eggplant. Crouched in a corner, Rafi stuffed food into his mouth with his bare hands, ripping it with his teeth, sometimes catching his tongue or a finger between teeth instead of the food, swallowing almost without chewing. He heard a chorus of grunts and snorts and screams of frustration. No one could eat fast enough, it seemed, to be satisfied. Until he glanced up, potato dripping down his chin, and scanned the ruined mess hall to see that Avrami had lied. Every man was eating with great slopping noises.

There were fifty-one dinners, after all.

Lieutenant Stein had removed his hat and was walking slowly among the overturned tables, stepping around the figures of men gorging themselves, once in a while stopping to look at something or someone. His driver followed like a deformed little dog. The driver had also removed his hat, and carried it in both hands like a straw basket, as if he was begging for alms.

Without his hat, Stein no longer looked young. His hair was thinning and streaked with gray. His eyes, when they passed over Rafi's face, looked tiny and desolate.

Slowly, the sounds of eating died down. Fifty-one plates were scraped clean. Second helpings were served. There was suddenly plenty of everything. Juice flowed from aluminum pitchers. Baskets of bread and pails full of gravy were brought from the kitchen. For dessert there were fresh apples, steaming coffee, sugary tea, a thick spongy cake layered with plum jam and almond slices. Then more was served—grapefruit, oranges, pecans, fresh-baked chocolate squares. Laughter began to sound out. Men returned, slowly, to kindness. They became human beings again. Napkins were requested, faces wiped clean. Cigarettes were lit and shared. There was, slowly, a restoration of calm, of peace, of good feeling. No one noticed the machinery being set up at one end of the mess hall. Stein's driver had lugged it in, wires and extension cords winding from thick metal cases. Suddenly, the room went dark.

There was silence. Then one naked wall was lit with a large rectangle of blank light. Into the vacuum flashed a full-color slide, blown up larger than life on the screen the wall had become. It showed black, decimated remains of buildings in the background. In the foreground were bodies. Or, rather, pieces of bodies: a hand here, a foot and leg there, rocks blown out of the ground and covered with dark red entrails mingled with odds and ends of clothing, a part of a hat, the sleeve of a shirt, a laceless shoe. Rafi heard retching sounds as someone in back of him began to throw up dinner.

"This picture was taken in Kiryat Shmonah," came the voice of Stein, "after the PLO lobbed rockets in over the border."

There were more full-color slides, larger than life: the remains of a bus blown apart by a terrorist bomb, an old rabbi with his hand blown off, the remains of a woman's skirt, of a baby carriage, a grocery store reduced to shattered glass and blackened corpses, a child's face scarred for life, the broken bleeding body of an infant clutching the broken bleeding body of a puppy, both dead and beyond pain. A terrible rage gurgled in Rafi's throat—at the pictures, at the violence, at the officers who were showing this to them after their meal, at the hands that had steadied cameras at these scenes and, one after another, recorded them all. Nausea swept him. For the first time in his life, he wanted desperately to kill.

Murmurs began to sound around him, mutterings of hate. A blood rage was beginning to stir. Fingers that did not know how to shoot were itching for triggers and guns. When the larger-than-life, full-color image of Arabs beaming happily out at them in enemy uniform flashed on the wall, there were cries of anger. Plates and cups went flying against it.

The next image that flashed was of several Syrians spattered into the mud, their skin blackened and torn, their torsos riddled by machine-gun bullets. And suddenly Rafi found himself in the center of a tornado of sound—cheers, wild screams of joy and fury, a rhythmic clapping of hands and stomping of boots, boots and jeers. He was pulled to his feet by the whirlwind of movement. Against his will he found himself clapping hands. Against his will, he was screaming for blood.

This image remained on the wall longest. Then it was removed, and the rectangle of light became blank and empty again.

Another slide flashed before them. Several more bodies in uniform, also torn and scattered into the mud, broken with machine-gun bullets, skin blackened, entrails spilling. These bodies were in Israeli Defense Forces uniform. The hand of one still clutched an Uzi grip. The faces were oddly undamaged, and terribly young.

In the mess hall there was absolute silence. The image vanished and the rectangle flashed blank again, then disappeared. The ceiling lights went on. The projector's whir stopped. Striding slowly back and forth in front of the wall, Stein clutched his officer's hat in both hands and seemed lost in thought. He paced there, back and forth, for many minutes. Watching, they were all oddly uncomfortable and all, somehow, ashamed. There was the shuffle of many feet as some sat and some remained standing. After a while the lieutenant stopped. He glanced up at them with a kind of surprise, as if realizing for the first time that he was not alone.

"Relax," he sighed.

Everyone sat.

His eyes, twinkling tiny and sad, seemed a father's eyes. The set of his mouth was almost weak. Or perhaps it was merely gentle. Looking at him from the middle of the pack of dirty, tired men, Rafi couldn't tell. But the eyes flickered over them all with sorrow, and when Stein smiled it was a weary smile. It was the weariest smile Rafi had ever seen. There was something familiar about it, too. He was reminded suddenly of the General. Then, of Shimon.

"What you just saw," said Stein, "are true things. Not particularly pleasant, but true. Such will be your life from now on: sometimes unpleasant, but always true. There will be times when things don't make sense, maybe, but you'll do these things anyway. There will also be times when you'll want to stop and hide somewhere, or sink into the earth and die. I assure you, there's no place on earth where anyone can hide any more. And, as you see, death is a revolting alternative. The truth is that we'll all die one day anyway. I give you a choice right now: either die in the revolting, violent ways you just witnessed, or learn how to kill your enemy so you can go on and live a longer time, marry and have children, maybe, enjoy things a little, and die in a bed somewhere. Such are your real choices, gentlemen—there aren't any others. What you need to do now is to proceed. We are here to teach you how. You must learn to defend yourselves and to protect the things that make a long life worth living. To do that, you must learn to kill. You are now ready to learn to kill. We'll teach you that, also. Or maybe I should say this: we'll teach you how to use something you already possess. Because the knowledge of how to kill is deep inside each one of you. The trick is to be selective about employing this knowledge." Stein smiled then, gently, tiredly. "So. Now. You're dismissed. I think you'll all sleep well tonight."

The Country

THE COUNTRY: A SEA OF FACES AGAINST A BACKDROP OF OLIVE GREEN, a perpetually moving colony of kids in uniform, lieutenants who barely shave, sergeant majors with baby fat. They should have issued whole platoons Clearasil with their ammunition. Each bus stop is a caucus of adolescents in military stripe. And they are always going on leave, returning from leave, heading for basic training, deliriously chanting in forced-speed marches across the desert. Everyone has been in the army, or is going into the army, or returning to the army. There are soldiers in every family. Soldiers fill the bus stations, the cafés, fill the roadsides hitchhiking with their Uzi submachine guns and duffel bags. Sometimes, in this ocean of children's faces, you see the face of a man.

Beyond the faces, a landscape forms. In the north, branches of kibbutz apple orchards brush over the border into Syrian air. Broken granite clutters the red dirt of mountain fields. There are pine forests, pine needles blowing in wind, the sound of thin streams against rock, groves of cypress trees and, perched on top, an occasional gray dove. To the north is Mount Hermon, peaks snow-covered even in summer. South of that is the Kineret, sunk in mist. This is the Middle East. But, deceptively, it seems removed from the hot decay of the East—things grow here, smell fresh here, seasons change here. Still, a few hours by jeep bring the banana groves and flying roaches of the Galilee. A few more hours and you reach desert, foothills, more desert. Rumors circulate about hikers who curled into sleeping bags at night and were covered by sandstorms. Later their dried bones are found, crumbling in perfect fetal position. This is still East enough to feel ghosts drifting down on you. To understand that Western modernity is perhaps nothing but a passing phase, insubstantial as dust.

But in the midst of understanding you hear something: some soldier and his woman, locked in a lovers' argument, their speech rising in harsh angry musical cadence and sinking to guttural reconciliation. Then an explosion—fighter jets on training maneuvers, breaking the sound barrier. Modernity comes rushing back and the argument screams to another confused crescendo of rage and sex, youth, war.

Mayan Ha-Emek

BACK THEN, A COUPLE OF YEARS BEFORE THE WAR, JOLIE HAD thought of herself as an egg left frying too long—hard, homely, browned and curling at the edges. The truth was that by the time she reached Israel she'd been traveling so long she'd nearly forgotten America, and the West—or at least blotted out their memory with heavy doses of exhaustion, sensory overload, and a touch of emotional instability exacerbated by the reality of being a stranger in strange lands. Sleeping on a beach in Eilat one night, she woke staring into a flashlight. Then into the barrel of an army-issue automatic.

They were two soldiers, kids really, assigned to beach patrol. Rumors were circulating that terrorists from Jordan had just landed.

"Your identification."

She handed them her passport. Above, the sky was spectacular. The Milky Way stretched out in a long line, white-blurred, littering the night with sparkling light.

"Your identity card, please."

"Come on, pal. Do I look like a terrorist?"

Later they took her to a place near the back kitchen of some beachfront hotel and smoked opiated hashish from hand-rolled cigarettes. That was when the Milky Way blurred completely until it became everything there was. Until there was no night any more. Only light. She woke up in the front seat of a rickety pickup. Bright sunlight whizzed by, and desert, and a pure raw heat blew through the half-opened windows.

"You feel better?"

She blinked at the driver, who was grinning like a monkey. He was dark, and slight, and looked like an Arab boy. But he'd spoken English to her with a thick Israeli accent. English, she thought, yes. Something in her throat ached. He was grinning, brushing thick black curls from his forehead with a vaguely feminine gesture.

"Too much drugs." He winked. "You were going the wrong way."

"Was I? Where?"

"To Egypt."

She craned her neck and frowned into the tiny car mirror. Sunburnt skin, brown hair frizzing around face and shoulders. The lips were dry. She looked older than she was, would never be pretty. And there were those twin streaks of yellow in her eyes—a definite warning signal. She sighed.

"Well, thanks." Her head hit the vinyl seat cover. "Thanks for the lift."

"*Thanks for the lift,*" he mimicked. "For the *lift.* It's a great language, you know, English. I'm glad you're American. I thought, when I saw you first, that you're Russian or Turkish. But this is luck."

"Luck?"

"Sure." He swerved around a pothole. Air danced across the white desert in waves. "For me, a free English lesson. I'll go to America soon, New York City, maybe. And leave this stinking country for good." He laughed. "*For good,* right? I said it right?"

Jolie nodded. Her temples throbbed with heat, with hunger, with a kind of loneliness she could not identify. And *too much drugs.* It occurred to her that she had no money.

"Where are we going?"

"To Mayan Ha-Emek. It's a kibbutz. I live there. Maybe you should live there, too. You're a Jew, yes? So. It's better for your health than Cairo."

She slept again, and when she woke they were bouncing uphill over dirt and worn rocks, winding through pines, past olive groves. The smell of citrus fruit mixed with cow dung blew in at them on an evening breeze. Ahead were the settlement's buildings: a dining hall, garage, clinic, post office, and rows of identical boxlike homes stretching across the grass.

He was feline, graceful, but for the sudden little movements he made sometimes that betrayed real anxiety. He kept moving from one seat to another that night in his little place, unable to settle comfortably. The truck had been borrowed from the kibbutz garage—for personal business, he said—and what she saw now was really all he had. It wasn't much. A couple of chairs, a table. Some pots and pans in the sink. A used sofa in the little front room that doubled as a fold-out bed. But there were photographs everywhere, on the walls, on the tattered rug, sticking out of crevices between sofa cushions. And on a shelf, emerging from heaps of rolled film, a camera. His own, he said. He'd worked for a while as a photographer's assistant in Tel Aviv after getting out of the army. Then quit and returned here, to the place of his birth, where he worked each day in the carpentry shop.

"A stupid mistake," he muttered.

"The job?"

"No. Coming back here."

He showed her some prints he'd assisted with. Not very good, really: bad models in tasteless clothes. Then he showed her things he'd done himself. These were more interesting. He had a lot of ingenuity with light and shadow, a good eye for unusual faces, objects, angles. Jolie noticed that, as he handed them to her, his fingers were shaking. She peeled one print away from another and stared. It was a shot of a slender blond teenager, entirely naked, sitting on cushions with one hand cupped beneath his genitals.

He blushed. Then plucked it out of her hands. She buried her disappointment—although why she should feel disappointment, she didn't know—and shrugged to make it easier for him.

"So you like men. Big deal."

"Big deal. *Big deal.* I *love* that. Your language, it's wonderful." He slipped the photograph shyly away, sat cross-legged near her on the rug. Then, solemnly, but with a kind of irony, he offered his hand. "But don't have the wrong impression. I don't think I'm really homosexual. Not *completely,* anyway. My name is Rafi. Rafi Kol."

"Jolie."

"*Jolie.* That's French, yes? It means *pretty.* "

"Yeah, well. So I don't fit the name."

"You're not so bad."

"Oh, come off it. I woke up one day and realized I was never going to be tall, pretty, and blond. Since then America and I have gone our separate ways."

"That's why?"

"Why what?"

"Why you left there?"

"Well, part of it."

Now he was cocking his head in open imitation, grinning like some devil. "Only part of it? So?"

"So. It's none of your business, smart guy."

He fed her bread and cheese. She washed in his tiny bathroom, standing on the dirty towel she'd been carrying in her knapsack since Ankara. She rinsed her hair, watched dirty suds stream into the sink, scrubbed until each strand was clean. Then she looked into the wall mirror and saw water running down her face, onto her shoulders and breasts. Drops trickled from her scalp to her eyes, mingled there with tears. She wondered why she cried. Exhaustion, she thought. And some kind of despair. She was too old to be traveling around like this. The same face sobbed back at her: mid-twenties, worn and sun-burnt, still homely. By the time she'd dripped dry, the tears had stopped. Her clothes were dirty and smelled bad. And it was disgusting, she knew, to throw filthy clothes over a clean body, but they were all she had.

Rafi sat on the sofa bed smoking a cigarette. Every once in a while he'd flick ashes onto his blue jeans.

"You'll travel here, too, for a while?"

"Nope. I need to find a job."

He rubbed ash into a denim kneecap with a slow, meditative motion. "I'm thinking about your situation. I think I have the problem to your solution."

"You mean the solution to my problem."

"Exactly. Let me show you more pictures."

He took out an old folder filled with snapshots. Pictures of Mayan Ha-Emek. *Mayan Ha-Emek.* She repeated the name several times, out loud. He told her she had a gift for language, like himself. That soon, although he didn't know why she'd want to, she'd be speaking Hebrew well.

She glanced through photos of olive trees, grapefruit orchards, cotton fields like wafting clouds under an oriental sun. There were old tractors being repaired in the oil-splashed garage, and those box-style dwellings filling the settlement center, and there were people, too. He was, he said, the third of four sons. He pointed out some dark-haired young men.

"My brothers."

"Who's the handsome one?"

"Shimon. He's the oldest—a soldier, in paratroops. A big hero, you know. He was wounded in the last war, but they'll promote him to lieutenant colonel this year. He's a smart man, my brother. He studied at the university in Jerusalem. They wanted him to stay and be a professor. But he went back to the army, he likes it so much." He shrugged, a strange expression on his face: wry disdain mixed, oddly enough, with awe. The expression made him look even younger, innocent, vulnerable. She realized how well formed his face was. Boyish, bright, handsome in a very non-Western way. But his appeal scared her, too. She looked back at the pictures. Another brother glowered back at her in black and white.

"And this one?"

"Nadav. He's the next after Shimon. Also a paratrooper. And the kid there—that's Michael. He's too young for the army, but already he wants to be like the other two. You see? A family full of heroes."

"Were you in paratroops?"

He laughed.

He'd decided long ago, he said, that military life was not for him. His was a soul that needed to breathe free. A circle wouldn't fit the space cut out for a square, he said. As a matter of fact, he'd decided long ago that the entire country was not for him, either. One day he intended to fly away.

He squatted on the bed then, made wings of his arms, flapped them and emitted cawing sounds. Jolie realized that, aside from the guttural quality of his speech, there wasn't much of the *Israeli* about him. He moved, instead, with the nervous grace of an Arab boy. She recognized his point of view immediately as that of the perpetual outsider. And his yearnings were for things American. The music, the TV, the language, L.A. and Lincoln Center, he told her ecstatically, and the Rocky Mountains—his list of desires went on forever. He had a sense of destiny about it: he was meant, he said, for America.

"I'll go to New York City and live in Brooklyn at first. I'll drive a taxi. Then I'll make enough money to buy a good stereo, and maybe another camera."

"Great. You have a goal."

"Yes. Also—"

"What?"

"I'll become a great photographer."

"Great? Or famous?"

He grinned slyly. "Ah. In America, those things are the same."

Then he showed her more pictures.

"My mother."

It was a dark, wide-eyed face. Regal bearing. There was nothing European about her at all.

"She's beautiful."

"She was once. A Moroccan Jew. See, I'm half Arab myself." He chuckled. And rummaged through the snapshots until he came up with one of his brother Shimon, and another woman—this one young, and dark as the Casablancan night, her eyes glittering with a beauty that was somehow both haughty and vulnerable. "Here's Shimoni's woman. Everyone's waiting for them to marry, but he keeps her to himself. No one here has met her even, Shimon just shows photographs. Maybe she doesn't exist." He tossed the photo into the folder and closed it. He was smiling now, a little bitterly.

"Your father's alive?"

"Yes. Also in the army. He's a general."

But there were no pictures of the General, and Rafi seemed anxious to let the subject slide.

He told her he could probably find work for her at Mayan Ha-Emek. They'd give her a room and food to eat. Provide work clothes. Cigarettes were free. And anyway, he said, he hoped she'd stay a while. She could give him free English lessons. Maybe they would really like each other. He was a kind of misfit here, he told her, blushing a little, and was always hungry for people to talk to. Especially people from America.

That's how she came to Mayan Ha-Emek.

She worked as a volunteer at first, living in a room with two girls from Soviet Georgia who stole from everyone and were visited each Shabbat by a crowd of brothers, cousins, and boyfriends picking their teeth with switchblade knives. After a few months of this, it was decided at a general meeting to pack the Georgians off to an immigration absorption center in Bet Shean. They left, taking dozens of watches and rings with them.

She shared the room then with a succession of volunteers

from a variety of countries, none of whom stayed beyond a month or two. After a while she was given a tiny place of her own. She learned the art of bargaining with Sasha Levy, who was in charge of supplies. For a pack of foreign cigarettes he'd come up with a brand-new mattress, or effortlessly move other mountains aside.

Later, if asked, she'd reply that she'd come to Mayan Ha-Emek not for a noble idea, but to escape her former life. The details were unpleasant, she'd say, and at any rate unnecessary. If you proved yourself a good worker the people of Mayan Ha-Emek were unlikely to require a song and dance.

They liked her because she did the work of a man, lifting metal scraps and piling rusted parts, operating a spot-welding machine in the little steel factory they had there. She wore protective headgear and massive gloves, while all around metal was rearranged with a deafening screech, sparks shot to the ceiling rafters, and master welders huddled over assembly stations in flaming pockets of light. It was the one place in the settlement where they hired help from outside. The screamed conversations of Arab laborers added to the general din.

They liked her, too, because she was the first female Rafi Kol had demonstrated noticeable interest in. He visited her in the evenings and sat with her at breakfast. They were seen walking together once, hand in hand, laughing over some shared private joke. It was common knowledge—also, at first, cause for celebration—that his evening visits to her room sometimes lasted until morning.

The people of Mayan Ha-Emek had never understood Rafi very well. With his fluid limbs, slight stature, remarkably youthful appearance, he was monkeylike despite the good looks. Growing up, his nickname had been The Comedian. It fit, even though all the genuinely funny things he said tended to go unappreciated—unappreciated, at least, until the American girl showed up to appreciate them. The truth was that he was full of unhappy and sometimes desperate yearnings. An outsider herself, she seemed to understand this about him. God and genetics had given him the physique of an agile young court jester. Rafi did his best to juggle all the conflicting matter inside himself. At times, though, it tore him from the inside out. The chasm between what he wanted to be and what he actually was threatened to engulf him. Then his behavior became a mocking satire, alienating and insulting. On Mayan Ha-Emek, where group cooperation reigned supreme over individual eccentricity, this behavior had sealed his social doom. Rafi fought back with mimicry, at which he was extremely gifted. This made everything worse. But he was just what he was—he couldn't help it.

Still, Jolie's arrival was changing all that. People were willing to let bygones be bygones. Their little romance was bringing Rafi into the folds of social normality more and more with each passing day, smoothly paving the road that led back to complete community approval. So what if she's not much to look at, they said. At least she has the right equipment. And he's twenty-four now, it's time for him to stop dancing around and get serious already. It's time for him to be a man.

Jolie's facility with the language grew. She went with Rafi for tea and cakes to the home of his mother, Yael, one Shabbat. She even became quite friendly with his brother Nadav, who'd finished his years of army service as a lieutenant in the paratroops and was always being called back for reserve duty. In fact, her friendship with Nadav was another great key to her acceptance on Mayan Ha-Emek. Nadav was a great favorite there. A real man, they said, his father's son. Almost as good as his older brother, Shimoni.

Jolie fell into knowing Avi Zeigler the way you fell into knowing everyone, sooner or later, on Mayan Ha-Emek. They passed each other on the way to and from breakfast, lunch, dinner. After a while, he nodded.

Communal meals took place in the dining hall, a vast space of long tables, metal folding chairs, plates and bent silverware and vats of food. The windows stretched from waist-height to the high ceiling. They were open in warm weather, and birds flew in and out. Standard fare was tomatoes, olives, bread, cheese, green-yolked eggs, and a thick dark unidentifiable jam that clung to the knife. On good days there was schnitzel.

Zeigler would sit across the table from her sometimes when Rafi wasn't there, both of them silent, and they'd eat. He was a young man sunk in obesity, with thick glasses and short blond hair. Once in a while he'd glance up. Jolie would look back. After many days of this he spoke.

"What's new?"

"Not much," she told him.

"You're Russian or Turkish?"

"American."

"American? But you speak so well."

It was a compliment. He added to it by offering a bowl of olives. When she declined he dumped the entire contents on his own plate and began to eat with methodical speed, piling pits neatly alongside his fork. The olives were green. The pits had a yellowish tinge. Swallows soared through the windows, looped delicate flight lines close to the dining-hall ceiling.

After that she would drop by his room sometimes in the evening. They'd drink tea and talk. His parents had come to Mayan Ha-Emek from Poland, he told her, where they'd met as displaced persons just after the war. Both were originally from Germany and had been married before, and both had lost their spouses and children in the camps. They were old now. Avi was their only child.

He spoke excellent schoolbook English but preferred Hebrew. Sometimes, their conversation drifted to the topic of Rafi, or of Nadav. Or of their older brother.

"You know what they say about Shimon, the idiots? That he eats fire."

"Well? Does he?"

He laughed.

"But Nadav's a man who feels. He's serious about things." Zeigler waddled to the burner where water was boiling for tea, poured out two cups. "And Rafi feels, too. Even though, personally, I don't like him. He's sensitive. But he uses people in bad ways. This you need to know."

"Why, Avi?"

"Because maybe you love him. I'm not saying you *love* him—I'm saying *maybe.*" In the pale light he beamed, vaguely embarrassed. "The pain of his life, and of Nadav's life, and Michael's too, for that matter, is that they're not Shimoni."

"Shimoni? Why?"

"It's hard when your brother's such a great hero. Then even if you're a hero yourself, you don't look so good when fools compare. Here, take this tea. You want sugar? No? Okay."

At these times there was something very sad about Zeigler. She'd want to reach across the space between them and touch him. But she rarely did. His fat repelled her. She smiled instead.

"You know, Avi, I think you read too many old psychology books."

"Sure. It's the national pastime."

"So?"

"I'm not saying you do," he muttered. "But maybe."

The first time she saw Shimon in the flesh he was trudging along the road to Mayan Ha-Emek, frayed knapsack like a tired hump between his shoulders. He'd been at the university in Jerusalem for several months—the army had given him extended study leave—and he'd hitched home for an overnight visit. She was traveling back from the steel factory that evening in one of the settlement supply trucks, an aging monstrosity covered with flapping canvas. To the west, twilight dulled the sky.

"Shimoni!" yelled the driver, jamming brakes. But Jolie knew somehow who it was before she heard the name. He climbed quickly into the back of the truck and gave a single shrill whistle for the driver to go ahead. In shadow, she saw his face. He'd been awake a long time. The lips were set in a permanently weary half-smile. Ah, they seemed to say, what do you know of burning tanks and shattered flesh? What do you know of death, my child?

His eyes were a surprising brownish green, thick-lidded, reserved, mildly mocking. The face was stony and rough-cut, with an unfinished quality, and his curly hair was thick, his coloring darkly Moroccan. He had the solitary, uncomfortable look typical of soldiers in civilian clothes.

The truck was filled with Arab men, the floor cluttered with cigarette ends. He paused, hands on hips, surveying. They rumbled around a curve, then the taillights flicked suddenly on. *I know,* she thought, *he is looking for another Jew.* When his eyes met hers he ambled over, a little bowlegged for balance, and pointed to the space of floor next to her.

"Somebody's sitting there?"

"No."

"Good," he said, and dropped the knapsack there to claim it. Then he went to pull canvas flaps aside and talk through the cab window to the driver. She watched him disappear behind workers' shoulders, cigarette smoke, into shadows. His knapsack smelled of dust and damp books, old clothes, smelled pungently of male sweat. It said what his weary young face said: that he had seen a great deal, and was no boy. There was in him, she realized, in the smell of him, not a lingering hint of anything ridiculous. She realized this with shock. He was Rafi's brother after all, flesh and blood of The Comedian. Then she leaned against a frayed knapsack edge and, for a few seconds, fell asleep.

When she woke he was sitting there cross-legged, eating shelled peanuts from a small paper bag. It was past sunset. The truck had slowed, detouring to a bus stop along the main road, and around them men were close against each other, shoving to get out and catch the bus and go home for the night. He glanced at her calmly, the lizard pools of his eyes cool and distinctly uncurious. In the crowd of moving men he was absolutely still. After a while the truck emptied.

"So," he said, "Rafi told me he'll marry you."

He offered the bag. Jolie saw that his fingers were thick and calloused, his arm muscular. Dark hair peppered the wrist bone. The driver whistled back to them, the truck turned again, heading for Mayan Ha-Emek. She plucked out a few peanuts, and they ate in silence.

Jolie and Rafi were married on a hot autumn day in the settlement dining hall. Rafi wore a pressed shirt and a brand-new pair of American blue jeans. Jolie dressed in similar fashion. Tables and chairs had been folded and stacked at one end of the room, and there was a buffet of cakes, cheese, fruit, bread. The entire kibbutz turned out. Yael stood by the side of her youngest son, Michael, for much of the ceremony, a peculiar smile on her face which Rafi, in his way, would later describe as *dazed*. Nadav came back early from *miluim*—reserve duty. Everyone thought that Shimoni would manage to get away from his duties, too, but at the last minute he called and said it would be impossible, his battalion was scheduled for training maneuvers in the Golan. He asked to speak with Rafi personally. But it was the last minute, and Rafi couldn't be located.

For a while, rumors flew everywhere that the General himself would actually appear. A bunch of kids even perched in trees overlooking the uphill dirt trail that ran from Mayan Ha-Emek down to the main road, eyes feverishly scanning the road, the trail, the fields, for some sign of him. *Idiots,* other kids whispered to them, *don't you know he doesn't always come by the main road? They say that sometimes he just appears. Like a spirit. Out of the air. That he never wears his uniform, but dresses like an ordinary man, in work clothes. You can't predict when he'll show up. Nobody knows his movements. Nobody can. It's a matter of national security.*

In the end, though, these rumors proved false. It was just a normal wedding on Mayan Ha-Emek. The rabbi was brought in from Haifa—an old man, nearly blind and a little forgetful, who took a long time to complete the service. When it was finally over, the back of Rafi's shirt was soaked through with sweat. But he was smiling fiercely, proudly. As if to proclaim that, yes, the things he'd spent years outside of, all the things he'd mocked and mimicked, were really the things he'd wanted, too, and wanted badly, all along. And Jolie seemed lit by an inner flame. It was a kind of radiance, of trust, of hope, and in its glow she appeared, briefly, to be almost pretty.

Rafi and his new wife moved into a slightly larger place on Mayan Ha-Emek, a place reserved for couples.

No one can tell, sometimes, what causes a thing to fall apart. Sometimes no one can tell what causes a thing to be together in the first place. The country, for instance. Or a marriage. Motives may seem muddied, reason extinct. Sometimes the truth will be obscured. And sometimes the truth will be so obvious that its clarity is painful.

After a week of marriage, Rafi and Jolie began to fight. Everyone heard, of course—homes were close together, the walls thin. When they argued in harsh low tones, though, the words were indistinct. Only one word leaped out, immediately recognizable, said over and over again in Rafi's voice: *America.*

With each passing day, Rafi became increasingly unreliable. He began to show up late at work, to skip meals in the dining hall. The unreliability crept up on everyone stealthily. It seemed to take even him by surprise, so that when two days of his absence from work were pointed out to him by the secretary he reacted with sheepish amazement. "Absent?" he said. "Was I?"

Then, suddenly, he was gone, and one of the pickups from the kibbutz garage was gone with him.

He returned the next day, accompanied by a Swedish boy with white-blond hair and pale drug-glazed eyes. Rafi himself was drunk, the floor of the pickup littered with bottles of Macabiah. Someone got him to the clinic before he threw up. Someone else got the Swedish kid down to the main road in time for the bus to Afula. Everyone was in a mild state of shock and shame. No one was surprised when, late that night, Rafi and Jolie had another fight—this one longer, and much louder, than what had gone before. This time, everyone heard. The things that they yelled at each other were humiliating. Things no one wanted to remember, although few would forget. But for some reason the words that rang most clearly in everyone's memory afterward, and seemed, somehow, to be the most obscene of all, were his raw and violent plea:

America!

Take me to America!

I want to go to America!

Then there was the girl's voice, drained and ragged with tears.

One of them slapped the other. It was impossible to tell, from the sound, who had struck the blow, and who received it.

A month after the wedding, Rafi disappeared again and took another truck with him. He was gone this time for several days. They were about to notify the police when he showed up again, drunker than before, the pickup weaving crookedly into the garage, a fender and both front lights smashed. It was night. Zvi Avineri was in the guardhouse and radioed the other guards. Word spread quickly. By the time Rafi'd lurched across damp grass past the carpentry shop and up the steps to the little home he shared with Jolie, a small crowd had gathered.

It didn't take long for the yelling to begin. The language was more abusive now than ever before, and they were both screaming as loudly as they could. Terrible things were said. There were the sounds of slapping again, and grunting, cries of hate and frustration. Then he was dragging her out the front door and down the steps. He was yelling at her to get out in Hebrew, English, French, and Arabic. Ripping at her hair. Until she stood and tore away from him, faced him as he staggered in front of her, then kicked him, hard, between the legs. Rafi folded like a puppet. For the first time in many minutes there was silence, a heavy, dangerous silence filled only with the intermittent sounds of her breathing. She muttered an obscenity in Arabic, and kicked him again. This time it sounded like something inside him had broken. He rolled on the grass in a wiry lump of agony, open-mouthed, dirty-faced, sobbing.

It was Yael who came to the rescue finally. Oddly enough,

though, it wasn't Rafi she folded in her arms but Jolie, speaking in hushed tones, leading her slowly away. Shlomo Golinsky, the work manager, showed up in crumpled clothes he'd hastily pulled on and helped the damaged Rafi to his feet, walked him toward his own house, took him inside, shut the door firmly behind.

Rafi spent several days after that in the clinic. He was bruised and shamed. One of his ribs was cracked.

Finally, Jolie visited him.

No one heard what was said. There wasn't any shouting this time, or pleading. No insults, obscenities, recriminations, or physical violence. They spoke in private for a long time. They separated by mutual agreement, and the next day Rafi left for Tel Aviv.

After that, Jolie moved to a smaller place for single adults near the volunteers' quarters.

She had never been fully accepted on Mayan Ha-Emek, in the social sense. There was her odd choice of a mate, for one thing. And if people were grateful to her for leading Rafi along the path toward normalcy, they also blamed her somehow when he took his final detour. She was a reminder of things that no one wanted to think about. With Rafi gone, few had more to share with her than the necessary courtesies. She socialized mostly with Zeigler, who by their standards was another outcast, a fat ridiculous boy grown into a fat ridiculous man. And, when he was back from *miluim*, Nadav would sometimes visit her in the evenings.

But they admired the way she worked. With Rafi gone, her whole purpose in being alive now seemed to be soldering steel, oiling metal, stacking welded pieces of machines still unborn, living to work among the Arab men who came each day to the factory of Mayan Ha-Emek. Hers was a job shunned by all, and Shlomo was grateful to her for filling it. When Rafi left for good, Shlomo began to stop by the factory sometimes to talk with her, grinning encouragement, shaking his head.

"I think you're crazy."

"Why, Shlomo?"

"You stand apart always, strange and alone."

He was right about that, she thought. Nevertheless, she realized that in his fatherly way he liked her. And she worked so well that no one had any choice but high praise. She's crazy, they'd say, but so what? See how she works. They'd shrug, smile. And leave her alone. A kind of hope had fled from her life. But she knew of nowhere else to go. When the war broke out, she stayed.

No one thought the war would come when it did.

Everyone thought it would come, of course, but not that day. Still, memory deceives. Looking back, it would seem that everyone had known all along. You could count the omens. Enumerate the long, heated days of a summer filled with portent. And ordinary acts, remembered, took on the gleam of significance.

She remembered, for example, a morning in early August when she'd walked to the kitchen to take her turn peeling potatoes. On the way she'd passed Yudit Spira sweeping her front steps with an ancient broom. Above them, birds flew. There were delicate tufts of cloud in the sky. The birds were heading north.

And she remembered a morning in late August, sipping coffee at breakfast. Someone had dumped too much sugar in, which made her slightly nauseous but she continued to drink it. Zeigler sat at the table. He took several pieces of bread and offered her the basket. She buttered a piece. "So." His voice was matter-of-fact. "If there's war, you'll go back to America?" "No," she said, "I think I'll stay." His blond eyebrows arched in surprise.

None of those incidents meant anything. Because they happened when they did, though, in retrospect they seemed unmistakable signals. In retrospect, every step and every breath, every bite of food, every word, every dream, led inexorably to

31

war. Until she'd ask herself: How could we *not* have known? How, when everything pointed to it—the day, the hour, the minute—how was it possible to be surprised?

Because we *hoped*, some inner voice would say. We hoped otherwise.

Nonsense, she'd think. Nonsense. We knew it would happen—yes, *that* morning, *that* second. We knew all along.

Before dawn that morning she'd been awake, listening for something. Gray light glowed around the edges of the window shade.

She thought of Rafi then, and of Nadav.

She thought of Shimon, up north in the Golan, stationed with his battalion. He'd spent the night strolling among tents, maybe, checking up on things. Or studying newly issued navigational maps by the light of a kerosene lamp. The lives of men were his responsibility. He carried that weight alone, she thought, there in the north at night, using the hours when others slept to walk, study, worry. He was worried about war.

Maybe he leaned over once, to warm his face in the lamp's heat. Maybe shadows jumped across his cheek and jaw, broad forehead, across his eyes. His eyes were like his mother's, Moroccan eyes, almond-shaped. What shone in them was the harsh clear light of doubt. Or sorrow. Maybe.

It was the worst war, burning savagely through all the months of autumn and on into winter, draining people of idealism or mercy, filling children's eyes with the fire of death. It left men broken in ways they had never imagined they could be broken any more. The sky above northern settlements was lit nightlong with search flares. In settlement chicken coops roosters began crowing at dark hours, falsely signaling dawn.

During the war, even Rafi came back to Mayan Ha-Emek when he had a day or two of leave. At night he'd sleep with his head on Jolie's lap. Sometimes he fell asleep without bathing. His uniform stank. His face was smeared with grime. In his sleep he ground his teeth. Or sometimes cried out in fear.

Two months into the war, her hatred of him vanished. They became friends. Maybe, she thought, that was what fate had always intended them to be. The war had filled her up—there was no more room inside for despising him. A terrible clarity possessed her. After all, she knew, the only real lies were the ones you told yourself. And the outcome of her marriage to Rafi had been as predictable, in its way, as the outbreak of war.

Yes, you knew, she told herself.

You knew all along.

The Hospital

LATER, IN THE HOSPITAL, THEY'D REMEMBER THE SOLDIER BROUGHT in from the north.

Physicians on emergency wards see terrible things, especially in time of war. Mortar shells and napalm wreak horror. The human body can be so wounded, so twisted, that it seems as if some madman had desecrated a fine image set on canvas.

But sometimes you see a sight beyond description. Then the core of something is revealed: all layers stripped away, a squirming kernel of betrayal left that at once destroys belief in the purpose of things. And you hear, for the first time, the single, lightless scream of the world.

It was early March. Outside, Haifa was chill and green, the sky a cloud-studded panorama broken by shadows of fighter and reconnaissance planes.

They heard he'd been pinned beneath a fire-bombed tank. The following explosion had thrown him many meters, alive and on fire. The man was totally burned, a quivering mass of raw tissue. He spent three days dying in specially isolated quarters on their ward. There was nothing to ease his suffering. Every once in a while, he screamed the name of a woman.

The staff took turns looking in on him. Several experienced the same odd sensation: a realization that between them and the skinless body glistening there in agony passed a sort of understanding. They realized he was doing his best to hurry, screams hoarser, breaths quicker and harsher every hour, like a runner straining through the final stretch. He was trying his best to die.

They could hardly wait.

On the second day, a woman came to the hospital inquiring about Lieutenant Colonel Shimon Kol. The situation was explained to her: he was isolated to minimize risk of infection. Even his own family had been advised to stay away, and had done so. But she would neither give her name nor leave. Finally she dozed in a metal chair. Her head tilted back against the blood-splashed walls of the corridor.

She had straight, thick black hair that fell to her shoulders, its darkness streaked here and there with delicate lines of gray. In sleep, her face was young; the burden of experience left it. The lips were full and mouth wide, mildly petulant, eyelashes long, and nose long and fine. Her skin was dark—the corridor fluorescence failed to drain it. It was the face of some favored member of a sheikh's harem.

On the evening of the third day, a doctor paused in the middle of a busy round to shake her awake.

"That's it," he said. She nodded and thanked him.

Then he called after her down the sweaty corridor in a rapid dialect she could not identify. She turned and met his eyes with a tired expression.

"I only speak Hebrew."

"Ah," he said, disappointed. "But you're from Morocco, yes? I know a face like that anywhere." And he pointed to his own.

"My parents were. Long ago."

When the elevator came he found himself daydreaming, nearly crashing into a cart of plasma substitute as he tried to memorize her beauty.

Downstairs she waited in line at one of the administrative desks. She waited a long time. When she got to the desk she asked if there were papers to be filed. Official papers, certificates of some sort? But no one understood. Papers, she kept saying, numbly, somewhere there must be papers. They were beginning to think she was crazy when a Yemenite girl in army fatigues approached, her fine-boned, dainty dark body looking ridiculously young and frail in the uniform's baggy folds. After hearing her story, the girl patted her arm kindly. Certificates? A shame she'd waited so long on line for nothing.

"The army takes care of that."

"The army? Of course. Thank you."

She turned, and for a moment everyone thought she'd fall. But she hitched her shoulder bag higher and began steadily walking. She didn't stop this time, or look back, just kept walking toward the busy hospital doors, then disappeared through them into the twilight.

Lieutenant Colonel Shimon Kol died in the first week of March, a day before his twenty-ninth birthday. He was given a hero's funeral with full military honors. His brothers were present, all but the youngest in uniform. Nadav, himself wounded at the front, had come on several hours' leave from a Tel Aviv hospital, his right arm and hand set in plaster and strapped to his torso. His mother was there, standing silently at the edge of the grave. His father made a rare public appearance—also in uniform, which was rarer still. Medals hung from his chest, and in the cold Jerusalem sun they gleamed. Beneath the brim of the General's hat were black glasses that completely obscured his eyes. There was a big security force and a huge crowd. But the woman who'd waited alone in the hospital was nowhere to be seen.

Three weeks later the war ended. Its conclusion was another feeble treaty, engineered by more powerful nations.

The Boy's
Returned Home

THE DOCTOR BEAMED BACK IMPERSONALLY. NADAV WAS GRATEFUL. After seven operations things were utterly matter-of-fact between them, a series of delicate business transactions requiring patience, skill, and an absence of messy emotion.

"I still feel my fingers sometimes."

"Yes, well, that's normal."

"And numbness still, up to the elbow."

"Don't worry. Nerve cells take a long time to heal. Some never do. We changed things around in there—" he motioned at the arm—"and built new highways, my friend, altered some old routes, yes, and swept up a lot of rubble. It takes time for the pavement to settle, okay?"

"Sure. Okay."

He swung the duffel bag in his left hand, nearly upset a passing cart stacked with blood pints. The orderly pushing it gave him an evil stare.

An i.v. trolley slid by, attached to a man in a wheelchair with casts encasing both legs. He wore mirrored sunglasses. One of his feet was missing. When he stopped, the trolley and chair collided gently.

"What's new?"

"I'm leaving, Yoram."

"So soon? You'll waste a couple of whorehouses, I hope."

"Actually, no."

"What are you saving it for, Nadav, your wedding night? Listen, do me a favor. When you feel better, go find a girl with nice tits and give her at least one good fuck for me. Send me the rest of your fingers as a souvenir. Where's your home, anyway?"

"Mayan Ha-Emek."

"Nice place?"

"It's all right."

"Well, kiss your little kibbutz sisters, okay? They tell me I'll never dance again."

"So? They tell me I'll never play the piano."

"What a shame. And you, a general's son. God bless you, boy. God bless you."

Nadav set his bag down, offered his hand. Yoram shook it. Behind the mirrored lenses his face was very pale.

"Come visit some time, Yoram."

"Sure. I'll run there."

He was wheeling vigorously away, i.v. squeaking along behind.

The elevator kept Nadav and the doctor waiting. Neither spoke. Things were suddenly awkward between them. No more surgery, examinations, chart readings, physical-therapy sessions to assess—there was nothing left to bind them. When the doctor glanced his way kindly, Nadav's skin erupted in chill sweat. But he gave the man a fixed, impassive grin.

The elevator opened and people spilled past: nurses, medics, visitors, everyone in some kind of uniform. You could smell perfume, the scent of a woman's hair. The odors mingled, tantalized, vanished. Nadav felt his nostrils flare uncontrollably, still trying to catch the scent as doors clanked shut again and this time he was inside, alone with the doctor in a close metal place that smelled only of sweat, going down.

"Mayan Ha-Emek." The doctor mopped his face. "A kibbutz, isn't it? My wife had friends from there, I think." The elevator lurched. Ground floor. They stepped out, both relieved. "So, this is where I leave you, my friend. Don't let me see your face again. Okay?"

"Okay. Nor my hand."

"Even better. You'll get used to things, you know. Time takes care of pain. In the meanwhile, you have your home to return to."

"Yes."

"You have your Mayan Ha-Emek. And you have someone, maybe? Some girl who loves you? Never mind, Lieutenant, it's not my business to know. Go, be well."

"Thank you."

"For what?" Down another corridor, the doctor turned and waved.

Nadav dodged visitors heading in, out, the evening heat wafting with them. A woman in a wine-red head scarf, her old face streaming with tears, passed by. For a second their eyes met. And he felt how tired he was, how weak and close to oblivion. He wanted to kneel and lay his head between her thick breasts, hear her sing Moroccan lullabies.

He dropped his bag on the admissions counter and leaned across, sweat in his eyes, grinning for the chubby-faced army nurse behind it. "Be a good girl, Dalia, and get me a driver."

"Nadav. You're leaving us?"

"Going home."

Her mouth crumbled with tenderness. "Forever?"

"Until the next war. They're creating a special unit for guys like me. Now listen, sweet Dalia, my home is Mayan Ha-Emek. North of the Jezreel, south of Kineret. Call someone, some nice officer maybe, and get me a driver. And a glass of water too. Water first. I'll love you the rest of my days."

The night was hot, summer tilting into autumn, first stars already out. The driver's name was Zvika. He was young, undersized, and there was something wrong with his mouth. The teeth curved jaggedly inward.

"This month, it's September?"

"Yes. September the fifth."

"And what time?"

The kid shot him a nervous stare. "Twenty-one hundred, sir."

Nadav tossed his bag inside the jeep. "You don't have to call me sir, okay? Relax. Just drive to Mayan Ha-Emek. East, east, and north of Afula."

Zvika nodded miserably. He had an agonized, sweating look, twisted lips turned slightly, like a dog who'd been hit too often.

They skirted Tel Aviv and headed east, past suburbs where the shrubbery was barren yellow. Hitchhiking solo, grouped at bus stops by the roadside, soldiers moved or waited, going on leave, returning from it, duffel bags slung over one shoulder, weapons over the other, boots glowing dust in the dark. Wind cooled his face. If he let himself, he'd hear a brass band in mourning, notes echoing against the stone of hills. They'd stood in a neat line, the three of them. Facing them across the rectangular hole in earth, his father. The uniform fit him still. And he'd thought: *General, you're in good shape for your age.* Thought: *I need new boots, the right one has seen its last polishing.* Nothing else. Cool spring sunlight shone. The sky above Mount of Olives was blue, without a single cloud.

They said you were pinned beneath the tank tread even before it became flame. And in the explosion the ground blew out, throwing you many meters, a crushed human matchstick. They said that you rolled over, alive, burning. That afterward you lay there wide-eyed, staring at the sky. Spent three days dying in a Haifa emergency ward. Skinless. Shivering. Nothing eased the pain. No visitors allowed. Delirious, you did not understand. But kept screaming the name: Miriam. Over and over. Miriam. That was all. That single name.

Stories. All hearsay. Still, you never knew.

"A year ago—remember? Nothing but convoys on this road. When we went north they came out from every moshav to watch. There were people crowding the hilltops. You remember?"

"Yes, sir."

"I think of it sometimes and I want to vomit."

Zvika's dog eyes examined him, now, in sideways glances filled with pity. Nadav wanted suddenly to ask forgiveness. There was camaraderie between them, here in the night, a grim camaraderie of the injured and the maimed. This kid had suffered it all his life, with undersized body, tortured mouth, and now, in the gentle pity of his eyes, you recognized superior dignity. Smells of rotting vegetation blew by. Zvika patted a breast pocket.

"Want a cigarette?"

"Thanks, no."

"There's time to sleep." The slurred voice was soft. "A lot of time. Don't worry, sir. I'll take you there."

Nadav shut his eyes.

She had a dark and violent beauty, a slim Moroccan face with eyes the color of opals. Her skin was burnished, her hair black. She wore it sometimes gathered loosely on top of her head. The underside, she claimed, bore a streak of premature gray. But he'd never seen it. Or seen her, really—not in the flesh, anyway, only in photographs. But Shimon had. Because Shimon was the one who'd seen her naked, night lamp gleaming along her breasts and thighs. When she turned in the direction of his voice, light must have seethed from her. She was his, everyone would know it. You'd know it, maybe, by the way he spoke to her in company, his voice deferential, the way he stooped to pick up an odd stone from the ground for her examination, a pretty stone, the way you did for a girl. On leave, she was the one he went to. Even if just to fall asleep in her bath. The fate of battalions was his responsibility. A heavy thing to bear. *This is Miriam,* he'd say, taking out a photograph, *Miriam Sagrossa,* his voice caressing the words. Women had always been his when he wanted them—he was handsome, a rising star, scholar, soldier. *Shimoni,* they called after him, their eyes teasing. But for Miriam Sagrossa he'd written secret poems. You'd smell her flesh in a room, maybe, sweet, pungent musk, a woman scent, a smell of the East. The name he screamed when his skin was gone: *Miri!* he screamed, *Miri! Miriam Sagrossa!* Three days dying, his body set on fire. *Miriam.*

Nadav woke to colder air. The road was deserted around them, shadows of pines rose against the darkness. His fingers hurt and for a second he thought he had them all back again, then realized he was shuddering, deep in his throat stifling horrible sounds. He realized his eyes were dry like fever, and in his corner of the jeep he strangled back sobs, not for his fingers but for Shimon.

They passed a grapefruit orchard, then a vineyard. Zvika lit a cigarette. It dangled from the concave mouth and he puffed industriously, intent on the road, on gracefully ignoring whatever private pain the jeep contained. There was birth, and death, and a thousand torments in between. Sandwiched between torments, an occasional joy, a kind word. Fragile strings led you on to the next brief worthwhile moment. This he'd learned at an early age. Sometimes, loneliness was the greatest kindness. He granted it, now, to the officer beside him. Those in upper echelons had a longer way to fall.

They passed the vast edge of a harvested cotton field. The road turned to dirt.

"One kilometer," said Nadav, "and left."

Zvika watched the stark bobbing of headlights on dirt and stone. Groves of pecan trees swayed in wind, pointed uphill to a shrill sparkle of stars. Light shimmered across the sign. KIB-BUTZ MAYAN HA-EMEK, it read, but some of the letters were gone.

"Stop. Never mind. I'll walk."

"Sir?"

"Nice night." His legs quivered when he stood, caked in his uniform's tired sweat. He wondered how he'd look—like some drifting spirit, maybe, let loose to haunt the earth. The jeep idled. Nadav lifted out his duffel. "Keep driving. *Sir.*"

Maybe the sad young face blushed. In the dark he couldn't tell.

"Okay," Zvika blurted.

"I mean it, my friend. Keep driving well. You understand? Don't stop."

Leaning out of the guardhouse window, Yossi Spira thought he saw a ghost. A moment later he was sure of it. His heart pounded violently. He was an old man, a staunch socialist, the kind whose passions had irrigated the desert, slain enemies with bare hands, fathered children even he did not know about and seen them off to war, but there was enough of the Polish shtetl in him still to contain a spark of mysticism. The ghost he watched approaching up the dirt road to Mayan Ha-Emek wore a paratrooper's uniform but carried no gun. He was of average height, with thick dark hair curling around the rim of his beret. The guardhouse light carpeted the ground for many meters. In light and shadow the ghost moved forward, and when he lifted his head you could see the eyes: large, dark, almond-shaped. Breath rattled in Yossi's chest. His thick, knotted fingers froze on the sill. And tears swelled from a nearly forgotten spring bubbling deep in the vestiges of his childhood. If the dead had risen, surely the End of Days was at hand.

It burst from his lips, half ecstasy, half terror:

"*Shimoni.*"

The ghost headed his way, walking with a man's weight. Stony soil crunched up against the soles of its brown paratrooper boots. It stopped there in the light and faced Yossi, half smiling.

"What's new, Yossi? I look so bad?"

"Nadav!"

Yossi controlled himself. The shaking in his chest quieted, he breathed again, forgot about miracles. Then he reached to give the soldier's cheek a rough pat.

"Good. You're back."

Nadav dropped his bag and squeezed the old man's thick shoulder. It was strong and muscular still, a bear's. Men like Yossi Spira had torn life from a callous, dusty earth. They'd worked in sun and storm and swamps swarming with malaria.

They'd danced away demons, created nations, dragged women to their beds with the finesse of wild boars. In old age, their bodies remained staunch as tree trunks. But their comprehension had softened, their capacity for suffering decreased. The loss of sons ripped their guts apart. Squeezing their shoulders, you'd maintain a gentle touch. You'd recognize fragility in them, and in yourself, a terror of death and pain. A part of you would hope to live so long.

"How are you, Yossi?"

"Okay."

"And everything?"

"Everything's okay. We lost on the cotton. Shlomo says the factory may turn us around. So. Things are getting back to normal, maybe."

Nadav chatted with the old man patiently. Yossi's hair was wiry gray, sprouting along his neck, lone strands curling from his ears. He caressed one of these strands between thumb and forefinger, and told Nadav months' worth of mundane details.

Nadav kept walking uphill, past the carpentry shop, garage, olive grove, and laundry, toward the core of the settlement. It was after midnight. Rows of identical little box homes stretched outward like tentacles from Mayan Ha-Emek's center. This center consisted of the dining hall, clinic, the nursery and children's quarters. You could smell pine needles, faint traces of dried honeysuckle, the earth's dampness. The houses were dark.

His boots crushed wet grass. Once, he saw a glowworm. He walked to the midpoint of a row of homes, approached his own place slowly.

The door was closed. The two wooden steps sagged. When he set foot on the first step it creaked, sharp and dry, long unused. At the door he paused. Then he dropped his bag and turned and jumped down the steps. He walked swiftly, boots sliding against grass with a wet rushing sound. Nadav walked with head down, hand in his pocket, the hair curling from the rim of his beret heavy with sweat, though the night was cool.

Zeigler slept in baggy cotton underwear and nothing else, his stomach a swollen heap peppered with wiry blond hairs, belly button poking out. He'd fallen asleep reading, so the bedside lamp was still on and lit the window shade's edges with a dull glow. He'd forgotten to take off his glasses. One of the black stems was held together with an old piece of masking tape. Behind thick lenses, his eyelids were very small.

Light rapping on the window woke him. For minutes the heavy body was motionless. Then Zeigler sat up, and the bed squealed. His belly bounced over the stretchable waist of his underwear.

Zeigler's abdominal region was a thing apart, taut, omnipresent, with a life of its own. It heaved now as he shoved glasses back up his nose with a brisk, impatient motion, and leaned across the bed to lift a window shade.

The reading lamp reflected blinding circles against glass panes. Shimmering vaguely in the circles of light was a face, one hand raised next to it in greeting. The face seemed to float, and for a second Zeigler thought he was seeing things. But he wiped his nose with the back of his hand and scowled, dropped the shade, went to open the door.

"So. It's what I thought."

"What, Avi?"

"That you'd come back this week. I have a friend who works with computers. We accessed all hospital discharge schedules the last time I was called up. There was your name, in little green letters. Everything's done by computer these days. Come in, Nadav. I'm happy to see you."

Zeigler's place had the heavy odor of bachelors' rooms. Water dripped in the narrow shower stall. The sink contained a single coffee cup. There were chairs, a sofa bed, a wooden bookshelf along one wall jammed with texts, and, on the bedside table next to the reading lamp, a small stereo with smaller speakers. Stacked against the table, a few records—Zeigler's pride and joy. Mozart's *Requiem* was outermost. He sat on the bed again with a great creaking sound. Then he looked up at Nadav, his little eyes curious and grave.

"How bad? Let's see."

Nadav pulled his right hand from a pocket, held it out in the glare of light. Zeigler pushed the glasses back up his nose and leaned forward for inspection. Then he whistled, long and low.

"A new variety of hand, my friend."

"Sure. You know the army. Soon they'll make all hands this way."

Zeigler motioned impatiently and Nadav sat in the armchair.

"Seven operations, they told me."

"Who told you, Avi?"

"The computers."

"Of course. So. Do you know what *everyone's* doing?"

Zeigler shrugged. "No. You know why not?"

"Why not?"

"Because I don't so much care what everyone's doing. Most people are very little, Nadav. Their lives are boring. They catalyze and endure a series of predictable motions through space—we call that *time*—and then one day they die. So what's to know?"

Nadav felt his face crack in a teasing grin. The sudden expression was almost painful. It had been so long. Then he thought for a moment he'd cry. But there were no tears, after all, just the aching flesh of his face. Just this stale air, this room. He and Avi. Like always.

"But if—if you *wanted* to know. About anyone, any of the little, boring people. Then you could?"

"Maybe." A smiled flicked Zeigler's mouth. "I suppose so. I found out about *you*, didn't I?"

"Son of a bitch."

"Yourself."

In the pallid light, they beamed at each other.

Zeigler had the face of a benign chipmunk. It was capped by fair hair cut very short. His ears were dainty, nose small and upturned, and he had full, soft lips you'd expect to find overlapping a mug rim in some German beer kellar. His fat was heavy and solid but had a rounding effect, the dark-framed glasses added a comical touch. All this hid a mind quick as a set of piranha's teeth. Nadav remembered fat Avi Zeigler, growing up with his group in the children's quarters, waddling to class, exiled from play and sports—an outcast, the butt of jokes. But he could, at will, shove the absurdly thick glasses up his nose and wheel to face a tormentor, smiling his sweet German smile, firing off some well-placed comment that seared his tormentor's soul. Nadav had been his only friend, which no one understood because Nadav was a popular enough kid, good at sports and a hard worker, good in school. Fine things were expected of him. Maybe even great things, as with his brother Shimon. Zeigler was obviously headed for a life of obesity and oblivion. So everyone was surprised—everyone but Nadav and a few teachers—when their group turned eighteen, enlisted, took the military's battery of tests, and, after the results came back, there were suddenly strangers appearing at Mayan Ha-Emek, reluctantly showing official credentials when pressed, asking to see Avi Zeigler. They were all surprised—except for Nadav and the few teachers—when that group of kids returned from basic training. Most were in regular army uniform, heading for this or that base, some pointed toward further training in artillery or tanks, a few, like Nadav, survivors of commando basic training, proudly wearing the boots and beret of the elite and earmarked for Officers School, like Shimoni before them. Avi Zeigler alone returned in dark business suit and tie, carrying a briefcase. A small wallet in his vest pocket, when opened, identified him as a member of the military. It was set in cloth backing and bore a special seal. Zeigler was headed for Officers School, too, but of a different kind.

Now and then, you'd see him waddling up the road to Mayan Ha-Emek, home for a few days on leave. He always carried the briefcase. On the way uphill, his big shoes churned

47

up clouds of dust. By the time he reached the dining hall his glasses would be specked with dirt. He'd have the same smile on his sweating face. He never spoke of his duties the way other young recruits did, but if asked always gave this reply: *I work with statistics,* he'd say, *and logistics. Sometimes, computers.* The smile was serious, courteous, implacable.

Often a phone call would come, partway through his leave. And Zeigler would return to his room, peel off work clothes to dress again in his dark business suit. Often he left in the middle of the night, walking downhill past the guardhouse, waving once, briefcase in hand. At the bottom of the hill a car would be waiting, lights off and engine idling.

Nadav remembered one night waking at 3:00 A.M. to soft knocks at his door. Zeigler was standing there in suit and tie. There were no stars. Nadav blinked away sleep, rubbed an unshaven cheek, about to say something, but Zeigler raised the briefcase in warning and silently stepped in. They stood facing each other like two shadows. Zeigler wasn't smiling. *Because you're my friend, I'm telling you. The situation's deteriorating. It will blow. Tomorrow. You're going north. Be ready for anything.* Behind thick lenses, the little eyes glittered sadly. Nadav searched them for further clues. It occurred to him to ask: *My brothers? What about my brothers, Avi?* But the eyes warned him—certain limits had been reached, maybe breached. Zeigler had given all he could of the truth. *Okay,* he said then, *I'll see you,* and waddled off into the night. Nadav watched until the pale, bobbing head was swallowed in darkness. Then he boiled coffee and switched the radio on softly. He was cleaning his rifle when the call came, just before dawn. By sunrise they were on the road everywhere, heading for their units. At noon fighter jets ripped the sky, traveling north. And he'd thought of Shimon.

"You want coffee?" said Zeigler.

"No thanks."

"Cake maybe? No? You should eat something. They say that hospitals make you lose your appetite. Piss in your veins and shit on the plate."

"It's true."

"See? The computers tell me everything." Rolls of thick belly unfolded as he stood. His flat feet creaked across the floor. "I know. We'll celebrate. You want wine? Red Carmel, half a bottle left. It's from last Passover."

"No thanks."

"Jews are lousy drinkers. Statistics prove this, you know. From Renaissance Rome to the Warsaw Hasidim—either we barely touched the stuff or it knocked us flat with vice. We're an addictive people."

"Your computers tell you that?"

"No. History tells me that." Zeigler patted his chest. "My heart tells me that. I look around me, I look inside me. For some things you don't need computers. What about brandy? Here's a bottle, unopened even. Sheva Sheva Sheva, the brand of the land. Tell me, it's true what they say? The anaesthesia is worse than the surgery?"

"In a way. You throw up afterward, sometimes. It depresses the system." Nadav took off his beret, set it on a knee, wondered why he felt so chilly when his hair was soaked with sweat. "Let's have brandy."

Zeigler poured into two chipped teacups. The brown-tinged liquid swirled whirlpools before settling. *Everything formulaic,* he thought. *Nature, time, the human body. Brandy.* He sat again facing Nadav, bottle on the floor between them. Then the slender, clean strand that was Avi Zeigler fell through rolls of bodily substance until there was nowhere else to fall, until the slender, clean strand was obscured and anchored firmly. He raised his cup.

"To you, my friend."

"To me? Why?"

"Well." Zeigler's round face teased. "Because you're so ugly that the women see you and head straight my way."

"Avi, you're a bastard."

"And it's a good thing, too. Growing up a bastard, you learn at a tender age. To you, my friend. Because you returned."

Nadav raised his cup. "And to you. Because *you* returned."

"To all of us who returned, then."

"Yes, yes."

"To our brave boys who survived."

Light drops of brandy spattered Nadav's beret. "To survival."

"I'll drink to that."

Fire choked Nadav's throat. He bent over coughing. The lamp flooded his face, and Zeigler noticed a vein at his temple throbbing visibly. He reached for Nadav's shoulder but pulled back. And hoisted his cup again.

"Quick, now. The second sip is easier."

It was. The fire had mellowed slightly and rolled down with a shudder. This time he could feel it ooze into his blood. Then came a rush of vague warmth. He took a third gulp, longer this time. It was easier still.

"To you, Avi."

"We already drank to me."

"We did? To your mother then."

"Okay. To all our mothers. It's so hard to have heroes for sons."

The teacups were drained and Zeigler refilled them. Nadav felt his veins and skin opening warmly. Heat caressed his stomach. He took a long gulp this time, eager for more, shut his eyes and red dots sprouted against the lids. When he opened them, lamplight flashed across Zeigler's glasses.

"Anyway, Avi. How's my mother?"

"Sad. Alive and sad. She works hard every day. She's one of those women"—sweat appeared on Zeigler's chin—"who look more and more lovely when they age, and they seem to be filled with sadness no matter what. I think life is difficult for her. But I can't be sure because she's not confiding in me, or anybody else. What can I say? It's hard to have heroes for sons. Right? Right."

Nadav grunted. "Well? And my brothers?"

"Rafi's a schmuck."

"You think that's news?"

"No. And Michael went to Officers School. He's the next

great lord of hosts, they say." Zeigler refilled their cups. His hand on the bottle left a sliding imprint. "Be aware of something, Nadav—you hurt people. When you refused to see anyone, when you didn't answer letters. Myself, I don't criticize it—I think it's your right, I think it's a man's right to be alone when he suffers. But other people think of themselves. They feel offended. They feel they're a gift from heaven to you in your time of need. They know about suffering, too, and they want to bring you into their tight little circle of suffering. You know Mayan Ha-Emek. One big happy collective of courage and virtue. Communal agriculture at its finest. So be aware. You want some more? Yes? Good. Let's drink to that."

When they raised cups, Nadav's hand shook. He felt nothing but sunlight inside him, though, his body suited to the armchair with perfect ease. "To Mayan Ha-Emek."

They drank.

The flame ran through him. It made him wonder why he'd ever been afraid of anything. Brandy soaked into his knee. He finished it quickly, savored the bitterness turned sweet inside, licked final drops from his lips. There was nothing he couldn't do now, nothing he could not confess.

"You know something, Avi?"

"What?"

"I don't care about women any more. No dreams even, nothing."

"Nothing." Zeigler belched. "So. Maybe that's normal."

Nadav laughed.

"Maybe it is, Nadav! Who knows? Anaesthesia—" He slapped a hand to his mouth as another burp shook him. The round face was suddenly very pale, and behind glasses his eyes had a desperate look. Zeigler stood. "Excuse me."

Nadav leaned back into his chair while sounds of vomiting echoed from the bathroom. He tried grinning again. This time there was no pain at all, no threat of tears. He balanced the soft beret on a finger and twirled it around. Zeigler was having a bad time of it.

"Avi. You want help?"

"Go to hell."

The revolting sounds continued.

He planted the beret firmly on his head and stood. The place was swimming in shadows, sprayed with light, the door far away, but he had no trouble walking there. The bottle sloshed gently, and he held it by the neck like a dead chicken.

"Avi. I'm going now."

"Good, so go." Tired breaths rattled through the bathroom door. "A man has the right to suffer alone. I said that, didn't I?"

"See you later."

Zeigler's coughs had a filthy sound. "Fine. Leave this to me. My noble war effort."

The stars had faded and the night turned gray. Nadav's hair curled stiffly against his forehead. He lurched ahead with long strides, listened to the rhythmic splashing of brandy inside glass. His right hand hung free in the dark, and when he swung his arm the rush of cool air on flesh was unaccustomed, raw. He hummed bits and pieces of an old song they'd chanted during basic-training speed marches, when desert blazed all around. Water was gone after the first ten miles. After twenty you could hear men dropping behind you, hollow metal thudding against khaki, flesh, earth. You stopped sweating. Moved your legs more and more stiffly, chills jetting through you like desire. Above sand and mountains, the air wavered. Officers roared by in jeeps, laughing, shouting at stragglers. You stopped feeling your blisters and wove from side to side, still marching, still keeping the pace, blood bubbling in your eyes. Sunlight burned down.

Jolie wasn't surprised when the door crashed open. Nadav brought in a cool smell of the night, and the smell of brandy and sweat. He fell sideways, sprawling on the bed.

"Here I am, the boy's returned home. Give me a kiss."

She turned on a lamp and went to close the door. She was wearing an ancient undershirt that ended at her knees. Nadav whistled.

"Nice tits."

In the lamplight she could see him, shoulders slumped against the wall. He'd pressed the bottle of Sheva Sheva Sheva to his chest and his beret was lopsided, his uniform rumpled. He'd lost weight. This gave his dark face a sharper, ravaged look.

"Here. Here!" He waved the remains of his right hand wildly. "See?"

She sat next to him on the bed and looked closely. "I see."

It was half a hand really, at the wrist end of a surgery-scarred arm on which hair was just beginning to grow back. The hand was discolored, mottled like a newborn's. Much was missing—sheared off sharply and cleanly, the last two fingers gone. Thumb and forefinger were stiff but nearly intact. A third digit next to the forefinger had been sutured back on. This one was slightly swollen and had no nail or visible joints. A thick red scar attached it to the remainder of the hand. There was no knuckle. The digit had to it, though, a kind of purity: it was bright, fresh pink and smooth. When you touched it the sensation was satiny, like touching an infant's skin. There was something repulsive about it. Also, something vaguely alluring.

"You like it?"

"Sure."

"Then kiss it."

Jolie lifted the hand in both of hers and kissed it. He watched with a fixed, violent grin. Then she pressed it to her cheek. The thumb and forefinger throbbed. The third digit was silky, like rose petals. After a while he shut his eyes. His breaths were calm and slow, but the hand gripping the bottle was pale with tension. When he looked at her again he wasn't grinning.

"She didn't come, you know. She didn't come to the funeral."

"Who, Nadav?"

"What's-her-name. Shimoni's woman." He shrugged. "You want a drink?"

"No thanks."

"You sure? Okay. But for me, yes." He took a swallow.

Brown trickled from a corner of his mouth. He watched her watching him, a fierce amusement in his eyes. "Something happened, I don't know what. I can't fuck any more."

"Get some rest. You'll be okay."

Against her cheek, the hand was very cold. "What do you know? You're a woman. You're not a man, you're a woman."

This was true.

"Anyway"—he tilted the bottle to his nose—"I'll drink to you. To you, my friend. I missed you. I'd fuck you if I could."

"Thanks. Thanks a lot."

"Please. You know what Avi says."

"What?"

"My mother's sad, he says, and people are hurt." He tried to wink. For a second, his eyes were unfocused. "So I'll drink to them. To all the hurt people. Also to you, because you know about things. I don't know how, but you know. I'll drink to you and to my mother. I think I'll sleep here tonight."

Brandy soaked the crumpled front of his uniform. His ruined hand went slack, eyes closed, head rolled against the wall, and she thought that was it. But when she placed his hand back on the bed his eyes opened.

"And to her," he said softly.

"Who?"

"To Miriam Sagrossa."

She caught the bottle before it fell.

She took off his boots, belt, beret. Then pulled a blanket to his chin.

If you listened at night, you could hear the real sounds of Mayan Ha-Emek. Cows in the dairy, acres away. Night insects. A bedspring squeaking next door. Sometimes it squeaked in rhythm. Then the sounds became faster, louder, and at the end of it you'd hear a moan. You'd hear dogs trot over grass, pants, whimpers. Children in the children's quarters giggled or cried in their sleep. After summer, the pines swayed in the wind. Men home on leave dreamed of terrible things. In the day they wandered from work to the dining hall, worn smiles on their faces. Sometimes, deep in the night, they screamed.

Jolie took another blanket and sat in the armchair. She read a book, dozed off and on. Nadav slept with his mouth open against the pillow. This gave him a childlike appearance. But the rest of his face was strained and gray.

She listened then, expecting to hear it: the sound guards listen for after midnight, something that rings of trouble and terror and sends primitive blood pounding through you. It never came that night. Still, she waited. Saying, *Yes, my friend, yes, I know that sound. You hear it shrill up from the black pit waiting at the end of hope, and you hear it shriek with your own voice when you've jumped down deep and pulled the lid shut overhead. Then even when they break through to pull you out, rescue you, comfort you, and speak of healing, even when you talk again and smile again to please them and their love for you, things are not the same. You know too much about the dark place. The single, lonely scream it makes. The fragility of the layers of life, layers that obscure this sound—which is composed of your own voice, and the voices of others. You talk again. You smile again. But you are not laughing.*

Everyone thought Nadav would visit his mother immediately. Or stop in to see his brother Michael, who was home on leave from Officers School. Instead, he stayed at Jolie's place another few days. She and Zeigler brought him food from the dining hall. Like thieves, they stuffed hard-boiled eggs and cucumbers into their pockets. No one thought it strange when Zeigler waddled from dinner with extra pieces of schnitzel wrapped in wax paper.

In the end it wasn't they who betrayed him, but old Yossi Spira and the duffel bag left on the sagging front steps to Nadav's room. By noon of the first day, everyone knew. They also knew that Zeigler had been sick drunk the night before. And Jolie endured raised eyebrows and questioning leers at every meal.

In her room Nadav made a pig of himself, consuming all they'd filched from the kitchen, spreading his boots, socks, and underwear around, neglecting to shave, listening to the radio or sleeping when he wasn't eating. The duffel bag remained on the steps to his own place, unmolested. Dew soaked it each night. Sun dried it in the morning.

Through all this, his mother Yael moved with dignity.

She was a sad, silent woman these days. Vestiges of her original beauty still clung to her: a sensual mouth, gestures of fluid grace, ebony eyes swimming in sorrow and understanding. The General, consumed by government and military matters, had rarely been there with her. She'd borne four sons. Now there were three. Nadav's boycott of social responsibilities was something she didn't interfere with. She was used to being deserted by her men.

Finally, Michael Kol approached Jolie at lunch. He'd spent the morning pruning grapefruit trees, and pieces of twig were stuck here and there in his curly black hair. He was nineteen. She didn't know him well. Like Shimoni and Nadav, he was of medium height and powerfully built, but the oriental was missing in him. His jaw was a solid, square European one, his eyes pale blue, almost gray, his father's eyes.

"Peace."

"Peace, Michael."

"Please tell my brother I'll visit him tonight. I have to leave in the morning."

"Okay," she said.

"Thank you."

"It's nothing."

He blushed and nodded. It was early autumn, and hot. The dining-hall windows were opened wide. Outside, flies danced on flower petals.

When he heard, Nadav grunted and ate half a loaf of bread with eggplant sauce. He sat for a while, listening to the evening news. Then he showered and shaved. He combed his hair. He dressed in clean shirt and blue jeans Zeigler'd brought from the laundry, changed the sheets on Jolie's bed, and folded each blanket neatly. He set his boots outside the door, dirty socks stuffed into them.

"I'll see you," he said.

They heard later that he'd walked directly to his place. That he'd responded politely to several greetings along the way. Rivkah Fishbaum, going on ninety, said he stopped to help her carry a bag of oranges to her door. Yudit Spira corroborated this. Yudit even invited him to tea, and Zeigler reported later that their conversation was brief but to the point.

"Welcome back, Nadav."

"Thanks."

"You should visit your mother. But come for tea tomorrow."

"Okay," he said.

He was seen picking his duffel bag up from the steps and entering his place without hesitation. Soon, a light went on inside. In an hour Michael stood at the door and paused before going in.

Later Zvi Avineri, Hava Golinsky, and a few others who'd grown up with Nadav appeared at the door. Later still, music was heard blasting from the radio inside, mingled with many voices. There was also laughter.

Yael had trouble sleeping that night. After two o'clock she wrapped herself in a cool white cotton robe. She went to the kitchenette and boiled coffee, sat in the front room's big armchair with the steaming cup cradled in her hands. She felt a dislocated weariness brought on by lack of sleep. The coffee cup seemed weightless, the familiar objects of her home suddenly made strange by the dull lamplight. Sounds were amplified: insects singing, grass brushed by a suggestion of breeze, a pair of lone feet walking past outside, the shoe soles sucked by dew. For a moment, she thought a child's voice had called her name. She wanted to stand but lead flooded each limb. Then she relaxed, filled suddenly with peace.

The spirit of Shimon Kol entered through an open window. He settled in a chair facing her. Yael smiled.

"Shimoni."

"How are you, Mother?"

"Okay." She felt the dryness of her eyes. "I'm always okay,

son. When you died, a light inside me also died. Since then I don't look for happiness, or reason. And life is easier that way. Well, so. So I'm always okay now."

They were silent for a while, an easy, familiar silence. Cows groaned in the dairy, many fields away. Yael heard the faint tap of her fingers against the rim of the coffee cup.

"I try, Shimoni. But I can't put your death from my heart. Four sons. You can almost expect that one will die in war, these days. Still, I don't really believe it sometimes."

"I know what you mean."

"It's like a cruel dream that doesn't end. Or maybe everything that came before, maybe that was the dream. And this now, this pain that runs on forever, is what's real. But I wonder—"

"Yes?" he said softly.

"What's it like to be dead?"

"Ah. Not so bad! The only difficult thing is that no one can touch you. That's not so bad for me, you understand—but for the living it causes suffering. When you're dead you don't care."

Yael nodded. "Just like that, yes. That's what I imagined. But the *dying*, sweet boy. Was it very bad?"

"No," he lied. "It was soon over."

Wind blew in from outside, bringing the smell of earth and darkness.

"When a child dies, it's a reversal of nature. Parents are meant to die first. A child's death is such a terrible thing that no one ever tells you it's possible in a lifetime. And if it happens, you want very much to die too. You desire death the way a starving man desires food. Because it would be so easy—"

"Yes," he whispered gently.

"So easy, to slip peacefully into death instead of living the cruel dream that life will become. Still, you live."

"For as long as you can."

"You live because you can't help it."

Yael felt herself wrapped in a sunlit glow. Her head, heavy, sank surely to her chest. Softly, she dozed.

She dreamed of her eldest son. In the dream he was a flame flickering at her ear. But the touch of the fire caused no pain.

Sleep now, Mother. Live to a hundred and twenty. You think sometimes the will to love is gone. But still you possess it, even after the light inside you dies. You open a door and there it is. Lips of flame kissed her forehead. *I'll see you.*

When Yael woke it was almost dawn. The cup of coffee was still cradled in her hands, the liquid lukewarm. She blinked. A young man sat on the sofa facing her, forehead framed by shaggy dark hair, observing her sadly with his large Moroccan eyes.

Shimoni, she whispered.

But it was her second son Nadav—tired, maimed, alive. A tear stained her cheek.

"Hello Mother," he said, and reached to take her hand.

A Man in Limbo

A FEW HUNDRED METERS FROM THE TURNOFF TO MAYAN HA-EMEK was a bus stop. Nadav walked there early that morning with his brother. Michael's boots were freshly polished. The tassel on his beret bounced as they walked, an Uzi swung from one shoulder, a bag was slung over the other. Nadav wore jeans and a work shirt. His old tennis shoes flopped in the dust of Michael's boots. Sun was burning moisture from the trees.

"You'll talk with Shlomo today?"

"Maybe."

"Then tell him that it's true about the oranges. If we expand the orchard they'll do better than grapefruit. Soon no more government loans to cover bad cotton crops, maybe. Tell him, Nadav. He'll listen to you."

"Okay. I'll talk to him."

He glanced at Michael. The uniform, weapon, gear all seemed so familiar, but at the same time far removed from him now, by more than hours or days. He felt light and insubstantial walking next to his brother. A civilian.

And he was daydreaming, remembering things from years

back: one long-ago Purim. In the dining hall each class of children had put on a show. They'd spent hours painting masks, coloring posters with crayon to be hung on the walls. That night they'd brought a dozen candles to each long table. Shimoni and the older boys had lit them, one by one, until the dark room glowed with specks of light. But Michael had escaped from his group and followed them all evening, a lonely little toddler begging to be picked up and tossed in the air, his pale-eyed face filled with longing, until finally Shimon lifted and tossed him. Saying, *Look, look, see the lights. For Esther, who killed a great enemy. And saved us so we live today. See the little fires of light and war.* He'd tossed him up high, making the solemn face giggle.

Nadav wiped a sleeve across his forehead. Sunlight shot through the pines.

"Tell me, Michael. Did you ever hear from her? Shimon's old girlfriend?"

"No."

Nadav sought out the pale eyes but they avoided him, staring straight ahead.

"No letters? No explanation?"

"Listen. More than a year with Shimoni and she doesn't come to the funeral, she doesn't write letters or even meet any of us. Nobody knows anything. To me, she's a whore." The young voice was flat and bitter. "So there's nothing to say. Let's forget it, all right? Let's forget it."

They reached the main road. A sign pointed to Afula, in the other direction to Jerusalem. The bus-stop marker up the road glinted bright white sunlight. Fields spread around them: orchards, groves, bare cotton stalks waving darkly in the wind. Michael held up a forefinger.

"Chamsin. Chamsin's coming."

"It's the season."

"Yes."

"How's the General?"

"I missed his visit. He was here last month—"

"I heard."

"You should call him, Nadav. Call Jerusalem. You know what he said? When you refused to see anyone?"

"What?"

" 'Leave my son alone,' he said. 'Leave him alone. I understand.' "

Dust flew in their eyes. A bus appeared far up the road, heading south. For a second Michael looked very young to Nadav. Both of them seemed slender and insubstantial somehow, figments of the same past memory, small enough to blow away with the sand. Nadav jammed his hands in his pockets.

"I thought of something this morning. You remember Purim, maybe fifteen years ago? You ran away from your group and followed the older boys. They were lighting candles. You remember? Shimoni picked you up and threw you in the air. You laughed so hard you couldn't breathe."

The pale eyes searched his until they remembered, and smiled. Michael gripped Nadav's shoulder. His hand was large, the fingers brutally strong.

"Sure I remember. But *you* threw me in the air, Nadav. It was you."

The bus screeched up to them, windows slathered with dust. Through the dingy glass you could see the shadows of kerchiefed heads, children's heads, sky-pointed rifle barrels, officers' hats, the shadows of men standing.

"Something I know, Nadav—just one thing. About Miriam Sagrossa." The door swung open, and Michael's boot clumped on the first step. "With Shimon's things, there are a couple of letters from her. A Tel Aviv address. That's all I know." The bus driver shouted at him to hurry. Michael grinned, an expression soon gone. "I'll see you."

The bus left in a haze of fumes.

Nadav knocked on the door to the General Office and went in. Shlomo was sitting on the edge of a messy desk, papers in hand, running another hand through what remained of his hair. He looked up when the door opened and nodded, smiling.

"So. Michael left?"

"This morning. Listen, my friend, the experts say that oranges will do better for us than grapefruit. Please consider it."

"I'll consider it." Shlomo raised both eyebrows in mock surprise. "So sit. I also listen to experts. They tell me Michael's going to be outstanding cadet at Officers School. The next Shimoni, they say."

Nadav sat in a chair with a woven straw bottom, felt it sag beneath him. There was a large screened window to one side of the desk. Honeysuckle brushed up against the screen. There weren't any buds now, but in the spring they bloomed sweetly and filled the office with inebriating perfume. This complemented the running inside joke among kibbutz members concerning the sobriety of every work manager who occupied the office. *No wonder he assigned me three weeks in a row to the turnips. He's making wine in there. The founding fathers were drunk too, maybe—a glass of beer, a whiff of honeysuckle even, would do it. Weizmann, Ben Gurion, Herzl. Especially Herzl.* He grinned back at Shlomo. For a minute he'd felt surprisingly at peace.

"The next Shimoni? Maybe. But for me, no. And I'm glad."

He'd said it calmly, without bitterness. Then it echoed in his head and he winced slightly. Almost like something Rafi would have come out with. But when he glanced at Shlomo he found the kind eyes smiling back at him, anything but appalled. Nadav swallowed away the sudden lump in his throat.

"I mean," he said softly, "that my days of war are obviously finished." He held up his right hand like a burnt offering. As if to say: *See, this is why, only this.* But it felt like a kind of lie. He searched the feeling uneasily. It *was* the real reason, wasn't it, his ruin as a soldier? But he couldn't avoid knowing that he'd held out the hand to Shlomo almost triumphantly. In explanation, yes. Also, in a kind of relief.

Shlomo grabbed the wrist and examined his hand briefly. There was a wry expression on his face. Then he released it and shrugged. "Welcome home."

"Thanks."

"For what? I'm going to give you some choices, my friend. First, let's dispense with the work details. We're low on manpower. You have some special job you want to do? Something you prefer? Or if the hand limits you—"

"I'm not limited."

"Good. Then you have any work preference? No? Even better. I go crazy sometimes, trying to fit all the prima donnas into their job of choice. So as long as you don't care, you can work in the sugar beets or the steel factory. In the sugar beets you crawl around all day in the dirt—"

"Sure, Shlomo, I know."

"And in the factory there's your sister-in-law. You'll be the only other Jew. Maybe you don't want to work with so many of our Muslim and Christian fellow-Semites."

Nadav shrugged.

"Good. So work in the factory, all right? The truck leaves from the dining hall every morning at five-thirty. You can get some breakfast before you go. Give it at least a week or two before you complain, okay?"

"Okay."

"Fine. Now. Tell me what else you want to know. You were gone a long time, there's plenty of gossip. But I heard Yudit Spira invited you for tea. Maybe you want to wait until then to know it all."

"There's so much to know?"

Shlomo flicked papers out of the way and settled farther back on the desk surface. His long, thin legs dangled over the edge. The wry look remained on his face. Nadav realized it was almost always there. It had been there ever since Shlomo was sent to the university in Jerusalem, at his own request, to study history. His studies had been successful. He could have had a teaching post, maybe a professorship in time. But he'd chosen to remain at Mayan Ha-Emek instead. To know history, he'd said by way of explanation, was pointless after all. People did not learn its terrible lessons. Teaching it was, therefore, an act of futility. He preferred to pick pecans or shovel cow manure. At least those actions served a necessary function. And, while performing them, he would be among friends. Now he examined Nadav's face, the way he examined everything, as if dusting it. His long thin legs swung like a child's.

"Dodi Kinderbach left his wife."

"I heard."

"You heard? Well, so, maybe there's not much gossip to tell you. Maybe you heard everything already."

Shlomo's eyes were evading his now, and Nadav leaned forward to tap Shlomo's knee with his good hand, coaxing. "Listen, Shlomo. Something's happened that nobody's telling me. I thought maybe it's something with my mother, but she's okay. And Michael. My father's all right too, yes? So tell me—what's it about? Something with Rafi?"

Shlomo's cheek and eye spasmed. Then he stared back at Nadav. "It's just rumor."

"So?"

"I heard he's planning to leave the country. And not for a vacation. He wants to emigrate."

Emigrate. The word sounded odd to Nadav, stilted and uncomfortably formal. Then he felt something crushing the center of his stomach. When he spoke, his voice echoed harshly back to him, strange in all its careful, fixed calm.

"I'm not surprised. He's always saying he wants to leave, Shlomo. He said it first years ago, he's still complaining today, it's nothing new. He's living the city life these days and maybe that's putting ideas into his crazy head. But tell me, how often does Rafi do what he says he'll do? I can count the times"—he grinned cruelly, felt himself begin to sweat as he held up his right hand—"on *these* fingers, my friend. That's the truth."

"They say this time he's serious."

Birds scuttled alongside the screen on the outside sill with pieces of dried grass in their beaks. Once he'd watched them for nearly an hour, building a nest on the outer ledge of a classroom window at Officers School. The sunlight had streaked his desk, laid golden stripes across his notebook, the pen poised in his right hand, all the fingers attached and whole, and not a note was scribbled that day anywhere on the blank, beckoning page. He'd watched the birds at work. And missed an important introductory lecture on heavy artillery. Later he'd had to copy another man's inadequate notes. Remembering made him smile now, softly, a little sadly. He looked back at Shlomo.

"Little Rafi. Maybe he will, this time. Maybe he's serious."

"You shouldn't feel angry, Nadav."

"Me? You talk like he already left. Tell me, you know when he's planning to go? And where? To America, of course?"

"Of course."

"You know any details? No? I'll find out, then, I'll ask people. Maybe I'll visit him myself. If either of us can stand it."

Shlomo smiled tentatively. He reached into his shirt pocket for a cigarette, lit one, and blew gray smoke with a contemplative look. "You know, Nadav, I'll tell you something—not to burden you, but because you have a good heart. I don't blame those who want to leave this land. You're surprised? Don't be. Sometimes I have terrible thoughts. These thoughts I have, maybe they shouldn't be said out loud. But sometimes I think that a hundred years from now this sad little country of ours will be nothing but a nice idea someone once had. To keep it a reality requires more and more fuel, like an oven that must be perpetually stoked, except that in this case the fuel is blood—blood and bone, and the flesh of our children. Such is the price we pay, when we stay. And the cost keeps rising. Is it worth it?" He paused, smoked. When he began again it was with absent-minded quiet, as if speaking to himself. "Well, no man can determine the value for another man. He can only try to see if what *he* gets back from the land is, to him, worth all that he puts into it. Life takes pieces from you anyway, even if you live a long time. *Especially* if you live a long time. What is anybody, when he dies as an old man, but a diminishing sack that contains some kind of spirit? And this diminishing sack asks itself, as it dies: *Was it worth it?*" He looked at Nadav, smiling in a bitterly amused way. "In a few years I'll be an old man myself. And I tell you, I still don't know. I know only that social ideals are rarely realized in history. I know that, in history, there are no straight paths, only endless detours. And we rarely learn from the past, so a path may repeat itself—or then again, may not. Who knows? I go to sleep each night wondering if the sun will wake me up or if I'll wake up instead to witness the world's end. Inside me, I think, are equal measures of hope and despair. If the measures weren't equal, I would end my life. There. I've said it. And it's true. But you know something? It seems that my destiny is to exist in this constant *balance*. My son, I'm a man in limbo. Each book I read teaches me more, and all the knowledge of the universe can't resolve my dilemma. I hope that in my old age—if I live so long; if any of us do—I'll grow to accept the existence of the dilemma itself, and the insolubility of it. Also, then, the limbo. Then maybe there will be a little peace in my life. I don't mean peace in the external, social sense of peace among men or an end to the wars, but peace that is emotional, peace that grows out from inside a man. Maybe our dream of Israel will live. Who knows? But how much will she be worth if her shell exists without the core of the dream? I don't know that, either. See? Knowledge gives you *nothing.*" He watched the cigarette burn a long, long tip. He watched ash fall to the floor. Then he stubbed it out on the sole of his work boot, tossed it into a wastebasket, and the wry expression returned to his face. The sad eyes looked into Nadav's. Then winked. "That's my annual university lecture, son. Are you hungry? Good. It's almost time for lunch. I heard there's fish—but maybe not, Namit Kinderbach told me this morning, and for all I know she's thinking of a lunch seventy years ago. But we can go and see, yes? We can go and see."

Yudit Spira

YUDIT SPIRA WAS AN OLD-TIMER, ONE OF THE FOUNDERS OF MAYAN Ha-Emek. She'd come to Palestine at the age of sixteen with a Zionist group from Kishinev, back in 1920. Her name then was Davidoff.

She had not found the new life kind. But she had found it preferable to the old world she'd left, where blood would suddenly spatter the winter snow, where days ended quickly and spirits wandered across the gray horizon, and people ate dirt when they were hungry enough. Compared to that, her group's rations of rotting tomatoes and stale bread seemed pretty good.

They worked twenty hours a day, trying to drain the area of swampland in the northern part of the Jezreel Valley designated for their new settlement. Some died in the attempt—of malaria or other diseases. They were joined by a group from Poland. One of the newcomers was Yossi Shapira. When he immigrated he changed the last name to Spira. He was also young, a crude, strong, handsome man, and several of the new settlement's first-born were credited to him. In those days he and Yudit Davidoff had a son, who died after three hours of life. They married soon after. And waited fifteen years for another child. The second was also a boy, who lived to fight several wars and then die, in the Golan Heights, a month before Lieutenant Colonel Shimon Kol.

This confirmed Yudit's long-held view that life was a matter of absurd chance and the perpetuation of the species essentially meaningless. She never expressed it as such. Her cynicism was of the quiet kind. Through it all, she'd never quite lost her sense of humor, or her ability to puncture Yossi's occasionally overblown ego with a single statement of fact.

Back in the old days, Yossi liked to lecture younger men, *we worked from dawn until midnight, and then—do you think we ate and slept and listened to the radio? No! Men were men then, not like these young softies today. We worked from dawn to midnight and then we danced! We danced, you hear? We danced out of joy.*

Nonsense, Yudit would say calmly, *as soon as we could we stopped working and went to sleep. If anyone danced it was because they had fever. They couldn't stop themselves. They danced madly, then they died.*

"Nadav, it's good to see you. Sit. You want coffee? Or tea?"

"Coffee."

"Nes or Botz? Wait—I know, *Botz.* You're like Shimoni that way, he always wanted Botz. And some of my cake too, yes? Good. Sit down, Nadav. What are you standing for?"

Nadav sat. It was one of the better homes on the kibbutz. A nicer sofa. An extra armchair. Two rooms and a bathroom instead of one and a half rooms. A heater for winter—electric, not kerosene—and a big window fan for summer. The older members got the best facilities. By the standards of Mayan Ha-Emek, Yossie and Yudit lived in a sort of palace, and knew it. Their bearing had become, with the years, almost regal. Mayan Ha-Emek belonged to everyone who lived there, but they and the other old-timers had an extra stake in it and the young ceded them their territory without complaint. That was what it was, they knew, to grow old on Mayan Ha-Emek: the longer you were there, the more it took from you and the more it was supposed to give you. The older you got, the more you could run amok. But no one ever asked Yossi or Yudit if Mayan Ha-Emek had turned out to be worth what they'd paid for it.

For a while, it had looked as if Yudit would become fat in her old age, a dowager queen. But when her second son died, all that changed. She seemed, for a time, to wither. Eventually she recovered some of her royal bearing, but it was much mitigated. Her gait was choppy now instead of flowing. Her features had a sharpened, feverish look.

"Yudit, how are you?"

"Who's complaining? Am I complaining? No. Now, have some cake. Here's the coffee. With milk. That's the way you drink it—see, I'm not so old I don't remember things. I remember what I need to remember. What's wrong with you, Nadav? You're not hungry?"

"I'll eat."

"He'll eat. When the End of Days arrives, he'll eat. Eat, my child, what's wrong with you? You think I'm so young I can wait until then?"

Nadav stuffed a hunk of cake into his mouth, swallowed without tasting it, and grinned back at her. "It's delicious."

"Have some more."

He did, and this time swallowed too much at once. A gulp of coffee saved him from choking. A second gulp soothed his throat. Yudit settled in a chair facing him, relaxed, her face mellowing with a hint of radiance as she watched him consume things. Nadav downed more coffee and belched.

"Excuse me!"

"For what? That means the food's good. Okay, show me. I want to see your famous hand."

Nadav held it out. Her eyes flicked over it disinterestedly. Then she sighed and waved it away.

"A shame. But you're alive and you have your mind still, that's the important thing. Does it hurt you? No? Good. Tell me, was it awful in the hospital? I heard they gave you seventy operations!"

"*Seven*, Yudit. I had seven operations."

"Well, see! That's not so bad!"

"Probably not."

She shook her head, poured a tiny bit of coffee into a cup for herself, added a few drops of milk. "It's good you're home again."

"Yudit, are you sure that's all you want? Here. Let me pour you more."

"No, no, no. For me, this is fine." She shook a finger at him and he set the pitcher down. She was stirring the coffee wildly, as if the milk would never blend. The spoon scraped the cup's sides, rang against it with high-pitched pinging notes. Above the noise, she raised her voice almost to a screech. "You visited your mother finally?"

"Yes."

"Well, good! Your mother's a good woman. And beautiful, still. When she first came here, I'll be honest, Nadav—between you and me—I had my doubts. Speaking Arabic and Ladino and who knows what else, it was hard to see such a woman settling down, but believe me, she's made herself one of us. And you boys—the cream of the crop!"

He placed his left hand gently on hers, stopped the frantic stirring and rattling. He gently removed the spoon from her fingers and laid it on a napkin. Then he seized the cup and lifted it like an offering. "Here, Yudit. The coffee's excellent. Drink."

She did. He watched her sipping, birdlike. The old lips trembled tentatively on the rim. Each swallow was tentative, too, almost fearful. She blinked at the taste. He watched. The action consumed her entirely. A quiet melancholy gripped him.

"Yudit, I want to ask you something. You know about some of the new kibbutzim in the movement? You do, don't you? You know anything about Ramat Alon?"

She hesitated, steadying the cup against the platter and setting it down. "Ramat Alon?"

"It's a little place. In the Golan."

"Ramat Alon. Ramat Alon. Wait. Wait. Ramat Alon, yes. It's a little place. In the Golan."

"Yes."

"So? They evacuated it during the war. Afterward they had to rebuild some things—they had to rebuild the dairy. And their apple orchards were ruined."

"That's all?"

"What do you want, my boy, a novel? It's a little place, that's all. Just a little place. Why? You know someone there?"

He shrugged. "Shimoni talked about it a lot. He said it was a good place, he said it was—what's the word?—*enchanting*. But I never saw it."

"Well, go and visit. I don't like it so much there in the north; it's too cold. But maybe that's because I'm old. Go, visit, get away for a day or two, have some fun. Fun you can have when you're young. Although when *I* was young, there wasn't any such thing. I'm glad it's different nowadays. But why did we work so hard and suffer so much? *So things will be better for our children,* we said. I'll tell you something now, my boy: we were idiots to think that way. People work for themselves. We work because we have to work, because it's a necessity to work like it's a necessity to eat and to drink and to sleep at night. Don't look for other reasons. To think that there are other reasons—that's as stupid as planning for the future. What if there's no future to plan for? But when you're young, you think the future will always be there, you think time and life last forever. Well, who knows? Eh? Who knows? I'll tell you, I don't even know what I'm saying any more. That's how old I am. You want more coffee? No? Why not? I made so much! You want something else to eat?"

Nadav reached to pat her hand again. There was a bright, unhealthy glaze to her eyes.

"Yudit, Yudit, I have another question. You heard anything about Rafi?"

"Listen, Nadav, it's time for my nap."

"One more question, Yudit, that's all." He spoke softly, pleading. "Tell me anything you heard about Rafi. Tell me if it's true."

"You know what they told me? I mean the doctor last time

he came here. They told me I have to go to Afula for a hearing aid."

"A hearing aid." He sighed and squeezed her old hand, once, then let it go.

"Yes! A hearing aid! You believe it? But maybe it's true, Nadav. Maybe I'm older than I think. That's what life does. Your body grows old, it betrays you. The cruelty of it is that, in your heart, you believe you're eighteen always. Listen, it's time for my nap. I think it's time for my nap."

He stood. "I'll help put these things away."

"What? You'll help? Don't be ridiculous, Nadav, it's my pleasure, you're my guest today, and besides I'm full of energy. You go now. Go visit your friends. Go see the girls! I'm glad you came—it makes me feel young again, a young man like you spending time with an old lady—"

"You're not so old, Yudit." He leaned down clumsily and kissed her cheek. She blushed then. And firmly lifted the platter of cakes in both hands, heading for her tiny kitchen. In her eyes flashed a brief warning: she would not answer the question. He closed the door gently behind him when he left.

Working

ZVI AVINERI WORKED IN THE GRAPEFRUIT ORCHARD ALL YEAR round, except during cotton season. Every morning he drove one of the pickups downhill, past the turnip field and sugar-beet field, the dairy, olive grove, and chicken coop, across the main road and past the loop that swirled off toward the fish pond in one direction, the steel factory in the other. The back of the pickup was filled with workers carrying long burlap sacks and pruning instruments. Half the workers were kibbutz teenagers, released from school for part of the day. The other half were volunteers. They came from everywhere—Britain, France, Holland, Japan, North and South America, even Germany—and in return for room and board, free soap, free cigarettes, and a small monthly stipend, worked picking the fruit of Mayan Ha-Emek.

During the war no one drove the pickup down to the grapefruit orchards any more. The women walked, pausing at the main road while jeeps and supply trucks and battalions went by. Every few minutes the air was punctured by the sonic boom of fighter jets flying overhead.

When the fighting ended Zvi came back, and immediately resumed his morning drives. He looked the same as before, a willow tree of a young man with thin lips and aquiline nose and round brown eyes, but his hair, once dark and rich, had turned completely gray.

Sometimes after the war Jolie took long walks at night. Sometimes in the starless part of night she'd see a black shape rumble by along the downhill road: a pickup truck, lights off, tires squealing gently on the earth. If she walked far enough she'd see it heading for the grapefruit orchard. She'd see it drive around the orchard's overgrown perimeters, lights still off, engine chugging more and more frantically as it drove faster, around and around in an automotive St. Vitus's dance, the turns shorter, choppier, brakes shrieking in warning, a barely contained merry-go-round of petrol fumes and dumb grief. Sometimes a pale shadow would show in the window of the driver's cab. A flash of gray hair.

Mornings, if there was no one with real status who needed a ride, she'd sit in the cab with Zvi. He'd nod at her and smile briefly.

"So," he'd say, "what's new?"

"Not much."

He'd look out the window and back to make sure everyone was on board. Then he'd start the engine.

"Tell me. You don't mind working there? At the factory?"

"No."

"And them. You don't mind working with them?"

"It's okay," she'd say.

They were silent.

One morning, though, Zvi broke the customary silence and talked, and Jolie, surprised, simply listened. Sitting there as the truck bounced slowly around rocks, she got the feeling that he wasn't speaking *with* her or *to* her so much as *at* her—she was the backboard for his words, spoken, after all, to no one but himself. Sometimes, when they were growing up, he said, they'd gone on field trips, their whole class, and several of the

75

older boys would lead them. If they were lucky, one of the leaders would be Shimoni.

They would have followed him anywhere. *Anywhere*, Zvi stressed urgently, his eyes flickering absent-mindedly over the pickup dashboard and the road—so absent-mindedly that for a moment Jolie was afraid. But the pickup stayed on route, as if it knew the way regardless of its driver. *Anywhere*, Zvi was saying, through ravines and wadis, up the sides of ancient hills that once had been mountains. He and Nadav and Hava Golinsky had stuck pretty close together. Once in a while, at Nadav's insistence, Zeigler had joined them. They'd gone on excursions through the Jezreel and the Galil, down into the Judaean Desert. Once, in the desert—this was the summer before Shimoni went into the army, and he and all the older boys were their big heroes—they'd met up with a youth-camp group and decided to camp together for the night. Two fires. Many sleeping bags. Cucumbers, apples, bread, tins of fish and chocolate spread, jam, here and there a forbidden cigarette. Canteens sloshing water. Adolescent voices singing, off-key, into the cold desert night. They were flanked on one side by a great wadi, on the other by crumbling foothills. Above them the sky was moonless and spattered with brilliant white stars. He had sung into the night with everyone else. Sometime during the evening, he'd put an arm around Hava and she'd snuggled against his chest. Nadav's eyebrows had arched in surprise but he'd said nothing.

Zvi remembered more: in the light and shadow of twin fires, a wrestling match between Shimoni and a youth-camp leader, a guy named Uriel Lucero. They'd sweated and heaved against each other, twisted arms against spines, torn each other's shirts off, grunting, laughing, while everyone cheered them on. And in the end no one won. They'd called it a fair match and a tie. So all the kids cheered, but for some reason, he remembered, they were all a little disappointed, too—they'd wanted Shimoni to win. Still, he said, that night marked the beginning of a friendship between Shimoni and Uriel Lucero. They were exactly the same age. As it turned out, Lucero would volunteer for paratroops too, would attend Officers School at the same time as Shimon. There, they'd recognize each other immediately.

Once, Lucero had come with Shimon to Mayan Ha-Emek on leave, and they'd all recognized him: a slender, strong guy, noticeably older than the first time they'd seen him. His parents, he told them, were Iranian Jews. He had skin the color of honey, jet hair cropped close to the skull, features that were delicate for a man. But he had a big, broad, man's mouth, and perfect white teeth, and the girls on Mayan Ha-Emek had fluttered around him and Shimon like moths around twin light bulbs. That was the night when Zvi and Hava and some of the others from their class sat with the two soldiers in the dining hall. Lucero had told them a story of the time he'd hitched a ride back to his training unit, somewhere in the Negev. The driver had let him off at the wrong place. And he was new to that part of the country. So, in twilight, he'd set out along the road alone. He'd run into a Bedouin herding some goats. They'd talked. Lucero was excellent at languages, spoke fluent Arabic. The Bedouin had invited him to share a fire and coffee, and Lucero, chilled, lost, had accepted. Throughout that long night, whenever he began to doze, he'd seen out of the corner of his eye a movement: the Bedouin, still smiling gently, reaching for a knife. Then he'd snap awake and point the tip of his Uzi straight at the man's heart. This went on until sunrise: the Bedouin watching him, hand ready near his knife, Lucero smiling back at him and cradling his Uzi. In the morning they had both stood and half bowed to each other, and the Bedouin made coffee. They drank it, then went their separate ways. But Lucero stood there in the road and watched the Bedouin's back until it was out of sight in a haze of morning heat. Until the tinkle of goat bells had vanished. Then he'd hitched another ride and found his unit without trouble.

There was a lesson to be learned from this, he told them: an enemy was always an enemy. Survival meant knowing who your enemy was. Being vigilant always. Being willing, at any second, to kill if necessary. Never thoughtlessly. Never without real cause. But you had to be willing, and you had to be trained to do it if the need arose, and your enemy must know that. Listening that night at the dinner table, Shimon had nodded gravely. And, taking their cue from him, the rest of them had too.

The pickup bounced to a stop at the factory gates. Zvi blinked suddenly, as if the stop had surprised him. He turned to Jolie, large eyes fiercely sad.

"You see. It's good to be careful. You, too."

Jolie said nothing. There was a strange look on his face. The voice was strained, the eyes a little too bright.

"I mean," he continued, "when you work with them. They smile and say nice things. It wouldn't take too much, maybe, for one of them to pass as one of us. But I see what they want, and I've seen the things they do—and, believe me, there's nothing in their hearts but murder. They don't want peace. So why should we? When you work there—with them—remember. You're American, you're not expected to know these things. But I'm warning you now because I think of it and worry about it every day."

Shoukri Afafa and his brother Zaki were welders. They worked at the factory for pay, came on time every morning carrying their lunch in paper bags, got a lift to the bus stop on the main road every evening.

The spot-welding machine was situated near the assembly station where Shoukri worked. Jolie and he had a friendly relationship on the job, taking breaks together, talking. On her first day there, he'd taken her for a Russian. When she told him no he'd decided she was a Turk, then ignored her for two weeks. Jolie was sure she'd insulted him somehow. But during a morning break he'd approached her again warily, work helmet under one arm and his gloves thrown into the shell of it.

"Excuse me, you're Turkish?"

"No, no."

"But your eyes. And the bones of your face—"

"A few ancient relatives were, maybe, but none of importance. I'm American."

"Really?"

"Yes."

"The Turks are no good."

"You're probably right."

He smiled suddenly, a broad flash of ivory across the soft dark face. "Excuse me, but you want some coffee with milk? And I have sweets too—my wife baked them, they're delicious. Please. You speak Hebrew very well. This is my brother Zaki."

Zaki was a slender, handsome boy who spoke little, listened to everything Shoukri said, and smiled or nodded sometimes in agreement.

Shoukri smoked two cigarettes at every break, plucking them from a half-crushed pack he kept in the big breast pocket of his factory uniform. Each pack was made of thin paper and bore a picture of a palm tree beneath the Arabic brand name. In the few lovely days before chamsin the three of them sat together outside the factory during breaks, sipping coffee from plastic cups, gloves and helmets beside them on the grass.

"It's not a bad place, this country." Shoukri lit a cigarette. He took a few puffs and blew out the wooden match, reinserting it in the tiny matchbox he carried with him. "At times I believe there's hope for us here. That's why I stay. At times I believe my children will be able to claim what belongs to them, and live in peace."

Jolie put herself on guard. But he smiled sweetly.

"Please understand, hostilities shouldn't come between us here. We're all workers. My children are Israeli citizens. If you know the history of the land, you know that Arabs and Jews have lived here in peace before—but only when the Arabs ruled. I know sometimes the rule was harsh, but then, those times were harsh and savage times. We're both ancient peoples, yes? We're both ancient peoples full of ancient rage. Maybe we have real hatred for each other in our hearts. Maybe. But you know what I think? I think the powerful men of the West see us all as a lot of oriental fools. I think they want to convince you Jews that they accept you as part of the power structure of the West, so they can use you to get rid of us. And then, wait—they'll get rid of you Jews. This is your vulnerability. You all want to believe that the white Christians of the West love you and accept you. But the truth is they never will. The truth is they will always have only contempt for you in their hearts. Unless their own property or money is involved, they will never lift a finger to save you. Arabs know all this. We know not to be vulnerable to the white Christians of the West, not to pretend intimacy with them, we know it can only lead to disaster. You Jews become nationalists here, just like the ones who most badly oppressed you. This will be the death of your culture. This will be the seed of fatal disease that spreads through all the houses of Israel."

His cigarette had burned almost to the end. Miraculously, the long gray tip hung there until he flicked it off. Beside him Zaki was silent, staring at the ground. Jolie sighed.

"Will you be better if you come to power? Or even as good? Can you promise that? Can you promise for your people?"

He thought a second, and smiled gently. Then lit another cigarette. The first puff was a nervous cloud. The second was well formed, an almost perfect circle, white, ephemeral, dissipating.

"No," he said.

Zaki nodded slowly, his large eyes dark and sad.

After he dropped workers off at the bus stop that evening Zvi called back to Jolie to get in the cab. She did. When he shifted gears and swung the truck around they left the sunset behind, driving into the east and darkness.

"Tell me. You think Nadav's okay?"

"I think he's sad."

"But you don't think he's insane?" He glanced at her sideways. She looked back, but in the twilight his face was obscured by the spray of reflecting headlights and had a pale, formless appearance.

"No. I don't think he's insane."

"Good. That's good." A stray dog ran across the road and he barely avoided hitting it. He was silent for a while. When he spoke again his voice was flat and monotonous. "You know why it's good."

It wasn't a question.

"Because I think *I'm* insane. I think I'm insane, so it's good that my friend is *not* insane. I wish happiness for my friends, and to be insane is to be miserable for eternity, because you lose your soul. You know that Nadav's mother was mad, also? No? You didn't hear? Sure, Yael went crazy once, years ago. Just after Michael was born, she tried to starve herself, she didn't leave her room for a week. She never slept, and all night long everyone heard her singing. Then doctors came from Afula and they gave her drugs. After that she slept a lot and cried. She said she would leave the General, that she hated him. That's when the thing happened again with Shlomo and her. You didn't hear? Well, you will now. They had a thing between them for years, off and on—since before *I* was born even. They say it all ended between them years ago, and that she's recovered, too. But myself, I don't believe it. I don't believe she's the same. I know that *I'll* never be like I was. Everything changes. You never turn back. All of my future will be like this, now. You understand? I burn in the hell of myself."

It was Nadav's first day of work since returning to Mayan Ha-Emek, and Jolie climbed into the pickup after him.

Autumn was deepening. Wind and dust blew through their hair, dust settled into the burlap sacks littering the bottom of the truck. A solitary grapefruit rolled by Jolie's feet, bruised and yellow.

Nadav was ignoring her. She thought at first that he was just in a bad mood, and left him alone. Then she noticed that he shot angry glances her way when he thought she wasn't looking. The truck bumped along past the pecan and olive groves, turned off the main road alongside the grapefruit orchard. Jolie nudged the toe of his boot with her own. She lifted a handful of dust and watched it blow.

"Chamsin."

He didn't reply.

By the time the truck creaked to a stop at the factory gate, dust was blowing more thickly and breathing had become difficult. The sun overhead burned through faintly, a pale blurry ball. The wind was warmer. Nadav fished a handkerchief from his pocket and held it to his face. Jolie did the same. It was obvious, by now, that she'd given some offense.

He jumped from the back of the truck and so did she. He slammed the back shut again, then banged a fist against the truck's side, and Zvi drove off into the dust.

"Nadav. What's wrong?"

"Nothing."

"You're angry with me."

"Why should I be angry with you?" His eyes flashed furiously over the white edge of the handkerchief. His voice was muffled. "You're my good friend, aren't you? You're even my sister by marriage."

Her insides went suddenly empty.

She headed for the factory without looking back. The racket of steel on steel already engulfed her. Chamsin had started for real, and walking into the cavernous metal place was walking from a swirl of hot dust into a world of sputtering blue sparks and shrieking noise. The Arabic of working men, guttural, singsong, punctuated by sudden jokes and laughs and wishes directed to God, mingled with the sound of steel, rose to the faraway ceiling along with spirals of smoke from a dozen cigarettes. Jolie walked past the row of welders soldering radiator pipes. Shoukri lifted his face-shield and winked. His Hebrew was loud and fluid.

"Good morning, sweetheart."

"Good morning."

He laughed, a long, musical sound that echoed behind her and then stopped abruptly, echoes lost in the blast of machines.

Walking on, she realized that all the talking had stopped too.

Nadav had entered. He was passing by them, and they were watching him, examining, deciding that silence was the best policy. Nadav's work clothes marked him as a Jew.

Maybe, in other clothes, they'd have been hard-pressed to tell the difference between him and them—at first. Then it would have come out—not by speech, perhaps, but *before* speech: a way of moving, a way of standing. He was, for all his civilian clothes, still something of a soldier, treading strongly but a little uncomfortably on the earth. Now his trail was marked by surrounding silence, itself broken by the clatter of machines. He ignored the men watching him as if they were nothing. Ignored the fact that all of their attention was riveted on him in curiosity, dislike, fear and nervous caution, the lines immediately and instinctively drawn. And Jolie realized that now she too was an enemy. Of them.

Of him.

"Schmuck," she whispered, but the machines obliterated it and no one heard. He'd caught up with her. Briefly, impersonally, his left hand tapped her shoulder.

"You'll show me what to do."

"Yes."

She tossed him a clean rag. This, after all, was work. Work was important—the closest you came, on Mayan Ha-Emek, to a state of grace. For work, all other things must be put aside. So both of them did.

"See those radiator parts?" she shouted over the screech of banging metal, pointing to a pile next to the spot-welder. "They're new. They were soaked in oil to preserve them. You have to wipe off the oil."

"Wonderful. And then?"

"Then you give me two at a time. Like so, and so. I mount them on this part of the machine, you see? When there are enough lined up, I press this button. I weld each pair together in three spots on each side—here, here, and here—and here, here, here. Then we lift the welded pieces off and put them over there. Someone else solders them together for a radiator. There are gloves and helmets under that bench, in the second box. Put on ear guards now. Before you go deaf."

She put on her own, slipped her hands into the thick, harsh gloves that made them look like enormous oil-stained paws. She hit a button and the molten spot-welder plunged down against carefully aligned metal, smashed cleanly on the rim of steel. Red, orange and blue sparks streamed against her face-shield. From the perfect welded spot, smoldering black and scarlet, steam rose. She moved the rack forward once more, quickly, and the spot-welder descended again. Sparks flew toward her eyes. Steam hissed from the perfect circular burn in the steel. It was momentarily so raw, so cleanly scarred, like the delineated aftermath of a cruel, destined kiss.

Nadav worked next to her, wiping excess black oil from the smooth new parts, placing matched pieces face to face on the welding rack. Her work required constant attention and Jolie ignored him after a while. But once she glanced over and saw that the inside of his transparent face-shield was steamed with sweat. The fingers of his right-hand glove flopped with every motion, peripheral, empty.

Their feud lasted several days. Nadav remained grim and silent each morning on the way to work, hard-working and silent while there, silent and contemplative on the ride back each evening.

He wasn't talking to anyone else, either. Once he passed Jolie and Zeigler in the dining hall at breakfast, glanced at them, and continued to another table where he sat, for the entire meal, alone. Zeigler looked at her glumly and shrugged, then had an extra helping of cheese.

This was the worst season. Breathing had become difficult. Two kibbutz members with asthma were driven to the hospital in Afula for treatment. The air blew fetid, heavy, and wherever it blew it carried with it a pale blanket of dust. Grit flew into your eyes and mouth. Zeigler said he'd seen Nadav returning to his room late from solitary nighttime walks, a handkerchief tied across his face, his thick hair white with dust.

One evening she looked up from her dinner plate to see him sitting calmly across the table, munching a piece of cucumber.

"Peace," he said.

"Go to hell."

He stuffed another wedge into his mouth. "Forgive me. I was angry."

"You were angry? Well, that's news. Maybe someday you'll be enough of a king to tell me what you were angry about."

"Here." He set a slice of bread carefully on her plate, then took one for himself. "It's about Rafi. You want some milk?"

"No thanks. What about Rafi?"

"Maybe you know something and you didn't tell me. I heard he's going to America."

"That's what he says."

"He said that to you? He said that to you, didn't he. He was here, he saw you, just before I came back." Nadav downed a cup of milk. "But you never told me."

"You never asked."

"I know."

Zeigler paused and nearly sat, then saw them glaring at each other and veered away. Out of the corner of her eye Jolie watched him waddle to the other end of the dining hall. For a moment she wanted to stand and reach across the room for him. To say: *Come back, Avi. Come back, save me.* But what he'd save her from she didn't know.

She grabbed a bowl of pickled eggplant and dumped it onto Nadav's plate, then poured him another glass of milk. She plucked several pieces of bread from the basket and stacked them onto his plate on top of the eggplant. She reached for a bowl of green olives and spilled all of them onto his plate, next to the bread and the eggplant. He watched silently. Then he smiled.

"You forgive me."

"Well, you know what they say."

"What?"

"Those who deserve love the least need it the most. Listen, Nadav. If you want me to tell you something, please ask. You want to hear about Rafi's visit?"

He nodded, still smiling.

"Fine. Rafi came to see me. I made tea, we talked. He plans to go to New York City. I don't know exactly when—before next spring, he said. He's working in Tel Aviv as a photographer's assistant, he has a little apartment there, he saves his money. That's what I know."

"Thank you."

"It's nothing."

"Tell me." He picked up a fork, twirled it through the mess on his plate in a kind of fascination. "You hate him?"

"No. Not any more. Maybe I'm an idiot, but in a lot of ways I still love him—not that if *I* love him he's *not* a schmuck, you understand—but I think he's bright. When I was with Rafi, I really *laughed*, probably for the first time in my life. Rafi has a ticket to the human comedy. And for a while, with him, I had one too. He knows how to have fun—"

"Not like the rest of us boring kibbutz boys, eh?"

"I didn't say that!"

"I know. *I* said it. But it's true?"

"What is?" Jolie crumpled up a piece of the thin waxy paper they used for napkins. She was getting exasperated again.

"We're boring. We're not good jokers, we don't live thrilling lives. Like, for example, the boys in New York City. Or the boys in Los Angeles. Or the boys—"

"I'll be angry again, Nadav."

"Okay." He smiled peaceably, his voice relaxed now and almost teasing. "Okay." He crushed some bread into the vegetable puddle on his plate, hacked off a piece with his fork, and shoved it into his mouth. Calmly, he consumed everything piece by piece. When he was finished he downed his second cup of milk, then grabbed a bread crust from Jolie's plate and sopped up some oil with it, popping it into his mouth. He crumpled his napkin and tossed it into a disposal container. Then smiled at her, friendly again. "A lot of oil here, yes? Like the factory. Next week I'll ask Shlomo to assign me to sugar beets. Come and visit in an hour. Tell Avi to come too. I'll make us coffee."

Legends of the General

IN THE CHILDREN'S HOUSE IT WAS NAP PERIOD, BUT NO ONE WAS actually sleeping. Giggles sounded out. Floor cushions were tossed back and forth, streaking darkly through the slivers of sunlight that crept in around the edges of drawn window shades. Once in a while a door would open, a *metapelet* would glance around the door jamb with suspicious eyes—but at these times there was absolute silence, broken only by an occasional cough or tiny snore. Then the door would close, the sound of adult feet fade away down the corridor, and another pillow would sail through air, another laugh and hiccup be stifled against blankets, a chorus of whispering rise and mingle like the gathering of miniature clouds on a windy day.

With Nadav's return, a rumor had arisen that the General would soon visit. The rumor wasn't based on fact. No one knew what it was based on. Maybe something as simple as one guy in the carpentry shop saying to another: "Well, Nadav's back, I guess the General will show up to see him one of these days." And maybe the other guy replied, "Sure, he probably will." However the rumor had started, though, once started it persisted. A barely perceptible hum of anticipation hung over the dining hall during meals. Kids eavesdropped on their parents, the rumor splintered, became many, and some of these rumors took on the character of legend.

My father says he'll come with soldiers and spies. They watch him while he sleeps.

Why?

To keep him safe. For national security.

So. My father says it's better for national security if he wasn't so safe. He says it's because of him we had the war. Because he didn't find out about the Syrians soon enough.

That's a lie.

No it's not.

Yes it is.

No.

Yes.

No.

Yes.

Oh, shut up.

Shut up both of you. He'll come to visit, because of Nadav's hand. They gave Nadav a medal for his hand. He ran a dozen kilometers holding on to his fingers.

It's not true. He ran eight hundred meters. *Moti told me. Then he fell down and they took him to the hospital.*

He was in the same room as Shimoni.

No.

Yes, it's true, he was. Shimoni burned to death. All his skin was gone—

Shut up!

—and there was blood running out of his eyes—

Stop it! Stop it!

Shut up, Odi, you're frightening her.

All right, little coward, so I'll stop. But that's why he died, because the Syrians burned him to death. So when we go into the army we have to kill the Syrians. Then we have to get rid of the other ones—

Who?

All the Arabs, stupid. The ones here. *Because they help the enemy. Moti says it's like having wild dogs around, you never know when they'll bite, he says. He's coming back from basic training soon. He says he'll bring me a bullet on a chain, and I can wear it around my neck.*

Rakel won't allow it.

Who says?

She won't. Danit had one from her brother, and Rakel made her take it off. Then she threw it away. Danit cried.

Well, she won't take mine *off. I'll cut off her stupid toes.*

Guess what, Odi?

What?

You're shit.

There was a muffled fight with fists and pillows. Some watched gravely. Others ignored it and carried on their own conversations.

They say he's from Germany.

Who?

The General.

I heard he's from South America. From Peru. They have wild Indians in the mountains there, and he came here long ago to be a Jew. He brought Indian weapons with him, too. That's how he knew about fighting in the mountains—that's why he loves the Golan, that's why he taught Shimoni about fighting in the mountains, too, and why Shimoni loved to be there. Shimoni could kill a hundred Arabs all by himself, and when he was finished he threw them over the edge of the mountains and watched them break into pieces on the ground. He did it for revenge.

Revenge?

Sure. Revenge for what they *do. They blow up buses with women and children inside, and everyone's arms and eyeballs go flying into the air. And they set schools on fire so everyone in there dies. They never stop. That's why we're always at war. When they capture Israeli soldiers they do something disgusting—*

What?

I'm not going to tell you.

Tell me!

Okay. But promise not to scream—

I promise.

They cut off their balls and eat them.

There was silence. Then someone groaned nauseously into a blanket. And someone else whispered:

He rides in a big plane.

Who does?

The General. It's a plane that goes all around the world, it never stops flying. There are machines inside the plane. Computers. They see everything and hear everything that happens down on the earth, and they record it. The General flies in this plane sometimes so he can take a look.

They say he has blue eyes, like the sky. And his hair's turning white now, like the clouds, because he's getting old. They say that after Shimoni died he didn't want to live any more. That's when he started going up to fly in the plane—because he wanted to be away from the ground where his son died. He's up there right now, probably, looking down through the computers, and he knows everything we're saying and everything we think and feel. He looks down on us when we sleep at night, to make sure we're safe. But sometimes he gets lonely up there in the plane. Then he comes here to be with other people, on the ground.

They say he cried.

Yes. Once. When he heard about Shimoni. Because Shimoni was the best soldier ever. He was the youngest lieutenant colonel in the history of Paratroops. Except for Uriel Lucero. And both of them died. And Shimoni was going to marry the most beautiful woman in the world.

Who?

Miriam Sagrossa.

Odi was beating someone else up, slamming his head against a floor cushion.

They do it! They do! Eat your balls. Because they're all queers!

Shut up, Odi! You're the queer!

Rakel the metapelet stormed through the door then, stamping a foot until her long hair shook around her shoulders.

"If all of you don't close your eyes right now and get quiet, you can forget about your cake and oranges today. Odi, stop sitting on his head! I don't care *what* your brother says about basic training, enough is enough. If you don't lie down and be nice, I'm going to pick you up by the feet and shake you until your head spins. *I'll* show you hand-to-hand combat, my friend—and that's not a tall tale, that's a promise."

Yael was at the laundry picking up some sheets and blouses when she nearly bumped into Shlomo. Since he'd come for only two pairs of trousers, he helped her home with her load.

It was nearly dinnertime. Dust blew across the grass and flower beds. They blinked against it.

"So," Shlomo said once, "how are you?"

"Okay," she replied.

Then they were silent, walking.

When they got to her place, Yael piled more sheets into his arms and went to open the door. He stood there at the bottom of the steps, peering over folded bedding. When she turned to him in exasperation, she saw that he was waiting.

"Listen, Shlomo, come in if you want."

He edged up the steps slowly but gratefully, deposited the armful neatly on a chair. Then he glanced over at her with caution. But her back was turned to him. She was making coffee.

"You saw Nadav?" he asked.

"Yes."

"He's quite a man, don't you think?"

She didn't reply. Her hands were busy with the coffeepot, busy putting date squares on a tiny plate. For a moment, he had the odd feeling that he'd always looked at women like this: he full of uncomfortable longing, they with their backs turned to him, folding sheets, diapering babies, preparing food. The long-ago ideal of equal labor—of men and women side by side in the fields, the factories, the trenches—had given way so quickly. How soon they had returned to the mending of clothes, the tending of children, the fixing of food for their children and their men. How soon their men had deserted them, going off with other men to war.

Shlomo didn't blame her for ignoring him now. In an odd

way he'd never blamed his wife, either, when she left years ago and wound up remarried to a construction worker in Ramat Gan. She'd given him a daughter, Hava—but really, he knew, Hava had never been given to *him*. She'd been given to the *metapelets* and teachers of Mayan Ha-Emek—other women— and to her little group of peers. And in her own way, despite the dutiful Shabbat and after-dinner visits, she also did her best to ignore him. In some way he couldn't put his finger on, too, he felt it was no more than what he deserved. But his wife's desertion, even his daughter's desertion, hadn't bothered him the way Yael's did. The sight of her back opened up a gnawing ache inside him.

He sat at the little table, observing her back and his own ache. The wry smile flickered across his face. Sometimes, he thought, even his own pain seemed funny these days. He didn't know why.

"Yael."

She'd turned the faucet on full force and didn't hear him.

"*Yaeli!*"

Then she turned it off and just stood at the sink while coffee began to boil. It was clear to him that she'd heard this time, and just as clear, for some reason, that she would not respond. At the same time, he didn't feel that she hated him, or even that she wished him gone. For that reason—that instinct—his voice, when he spoke, was calm and considerate.

"Yael, tell me. You're really okay?"

"Of course, Shlomo. My sons are men now. Why shouldn't I be okay? One wants to go to America, another to Officers School, and Nadav, who knows? At least he can't fight any more. But I don't say a thing. I don't for a minute have *anything to say any more*—that's the truth. They do what they want. I get a little older. It's all the same to me."

Coffee steamed in the pot and he stood, approached her back, took courage and another step forward and looped his arms around to hold her. He pressed lips against the back of her neck.

"*Yaeli mine.*"

"Go away," she said, but she didn't mean it, and as the ache inside him swelled up and around to envelop them both, he knew that if he reached to touch her naked cheeks his fingertips would fill with tears.

Tel Aviv

NADAV HAD BEEN BACK A LITTLE MORE THAN A MONTH WHEN HE left for Tel Aviv. It was a dusty, breathless morning, and early. Ephraim Benvenisti was nodding on the windowsill of the guardhouse. He shook himself awake when Nadav went by, frowning so that the bushy thick black of his eyebrows met just over the bridge of his nose.

"You're leaving us?"

"For a few days. To Tel Aviv."

"Tell him to stay, Nadav. Tell him he's crazy. He always was crazy. There's nothing in America but dollars."

Nadav blushed.

Walking along the hardened earth, then along the main road to the bus stop, he felt himself invaded by the heat and dust, as if they had rivened him, had laid him open with a surgeon's delicate knife for all interested spectators to observe. The world was foreign to him today. When the bus pulled up he paused a moment before boarding, unsure, for a second, of how to move his feet, and when he saw that there were actually a few vacant seats he took his time getting to one. Then he sat slowly, turned to stare back at the spewing cloud of petrol that momentarily obscured a gentle roll of land, green land, far-off green mountains whose sharp peaks had long since been humbled and rounded by age and weather.

He got off at the station in Afula, stood in a long line and bought a ticket to Tel Aviv. There was some time to wait and he meandered. He couldn't get used to the slim, light feel of himself. Without boots his feet felt naked. Without a gun, his shoulders seemed to have vanished. When he glanced up at the sky a sensation shot through him like a muted electric shock. It was the sun up there, a piercing white ball of burning light, made hazy by a film of dust.

At a fruit stand he bought a small bag of dates. A soldier brushed by in front of him, asking for sunflower seeds and an orange drink, and Nadav realized he was gazing at the man's rifle and boots and shoulder stripes with a kind of longing. When he turned away the sunlight pierced him again. Dizziness rocked him.

Then he caught his breath. There she was. Standing with her back to him, in line for the next bus to Jerusalem. But why was she going to Jerusalem? He blinked away the dizziness and felt himself break into a sweat. He headed straight her way.

"Miriam!"

She didn't turn.

"*Miriam.*"

He tapped her shoulder gently. When she looked around, her dark blanket of hair shifted like a curtain. But the face staring up at him was all wrong. Too broad. Too young.

"I'm not Miriam, mister."

He blushed. "Excuse me."

"No problem."

The sun shot through him again and he shut his eyes. He found a bench, sat. Realized he was still weak. Pressing a hand to one side, he could feel his ribs clearly delineated. And on his back, and the backs of his thighs, the ugly remains of bedsores. *Go easy now, easy now, my friend. Go easy. You're all that you have, really. And there's not so much of that left.*

When the Tel Aviv bus pulled in, he stood slowly. He stepped to the back of the line instead of pushing for a better position up front, and, when he boarded, didn't elbow for a seat. Luck guided him and he got one anyway—near a window, even—so he slowly pressed the latches aside and pulled it partway down for some lukewarm air. Sitting, he popped a date in his mouth, sucked on it slowly before chewing. The taste was strange to him, sickly sweet. Sweat beaded his forehead and upper lip. And he felt, at the core of him, quite emptied out, like a warehouse no longer in use.

Easy, he told himself.

Go easy.

Then he felt like crying, but didn't.

Tel Aviv. How many times had he gone there on leave? He couldn't even count. Three-day furloughs. Most often he'd gone alone, but sometimes, especially in Officers School, with a couple of others. What were their names? It surprised him now, looking back, how few real friends he'd had in his life. Plenty of acquaintances. But friends, no. Those two in Officers School—what were their names? *Zev. Zev Gold.* And the other, the Algerian Jew, what was his name? They'd gotten along very well at the time. Yes, he had it: *Avi Castellano.* Pure Sephardi, boasted a family tree that went back to 300 C.E., or something like that. The others used to tease him about it, they'd called him Our Historic Conscience. He'd been blown to pieces, eventually, somewhere near Beirut. But the women. He'd talked about them constantly, constantly complaining that he never got enough, that there wasn't enough in the world for him anyway. He was a real machine, he'd said, he could go once an hour, all night long, the real stuff. Zev Gold would sit back laughing silently. He'd laugh so hard his pink face turned red like fresh-stewed beets, but he'd never make a sound. They'd gone off on leave together a lot, he and Zev Gold and Avi Castellano, and more often than not they'd go to Tel Aviv. Then as soon as they'd checked into one cheap room or another, Castellano was down the hall shoving simonim into a pay phone, gazing at the dozen or so scraps of paper he held in his hand with phone numbers scribbled on them, trying to remember which number he'd just dialed and which girl he was actually speaking to. Back in the room, Gold would shower and change into a clean uniform. He was always finagling extra uniforms from the supply sergeants—a real hoarder. His mother used to send him plum pastries all the time, freshly baked, boxes of them, and he was always hoarding them, too. In their room in Tel Aviv he'd shower and change, crack open a book, and read for a while. Then, late at night, go out to visit a whore. *There are certain things,* he told Nadav once, *certain things I want from a woman, that only a professional can provide.* Then he'd laugh silently, and his pink young face would turn scarlet again. Sometimes tears would appear in his eyes. Whatever it was that only a professional could provide, he never said. Nadav never asked. And while Gold and Castellano were out on the town at night, Nadav slept like an exhausted infant. He slept in his underwear, his uniform crumpled on the floor next to his bed, rifle leaning against the wall. Sometimes he'd wake, strip completely, shower, and return to bed. Sometimes he'd get dressed and go out and find some food to bring back. Once in a while he'd call someone, some girl he'd met at a supply base maybe, and they'd have dinner, and if she had a place for the night they would go there. That was nice when it happened, it momentarily warmed the deep, continual ache in his gut. But truly, for the most part, he couldn't have cared less. He was too tired. Sometimes in the middle of a groggy weekend he'd wake to hear a key in the door and someone tiptoeing in: Zev Gold. Or there'd be a pounding at the door, a gleeful baritone ripping through the hallway: Castellano, returning from another triumph. *All night, my friend!* he'd sing, leaning back against the door, rubbing a hand over his unshaven chin. *All night! The things she did! The things she did—with her mouth, even. It was incredible!* Nadav would throw something at him, a book, a boot, and go back to sleep.

While Gold sat in his corner, rocking back and forth and laughing until he cried.

The old days. Army days. Not really so long ago. But it seemed that a lifetime had passed since then—countless lives, anyway, countless deaths. It seemed to him that he'd been so young. At the time, what had he felt? He could remember only vaguely: the dull ache inside, a nagging pain mitigated only by accompanying emptiness. But at the time he'd thought he was having fun. The service, a ritual of progression into adulthood for him, for all his people. And he'd thought it difficult but at the same time quite splendid in a way. Because he was following the same path, he told himself, as Shimoni. And Shimoni would never have followed an empty path. Whatever Shimoni did became a good thing, a full thing, by virtue of the fact that he did it. He could redefine the meaning of a thing. He could show men how much they might be.

And you, Nadav? Could you?

No, he said silently, helplessly.

No.

The bus drove west, and he slept.

Tel Aviv was hotter. The Tachanat Mercazit was a mess, an aimless stew of people and buses, fumes, air filled with the smell of roasting meat, chickpeas, candied pastries. He spilled out into the mess like everybody else, moved away from the station and all its clinging chaos. On a side street he bought a map. And felt ashamed somehow, buying it—it was an admission of failure, he thought—but what exactly he'd failed, he didn't know. He reached into his pocket for the crumpled envelope. Again the longing seized him, curiosity mingled with an intense self-disgust, and he wanted to read the letter inside. But he glanced at the address instead and folded it in two, slipped it back into his pocket. Then he opened the map and found the right street. He looked on the back of the map for the bus route.

The rest of the morning and early afternoon he spent waiting in lines, buying bus tickets, changing buses, waiting again. He took the wrong bus twice. For lunch, he ate a falafel.

It was late afternoon when he walked by the place. A shabby building in a shabby neighborhood: gentle, dreary, working-class, kids storming by on their way from school. There were a few European faces among them: Russians, maybe, and a few Rumanians. But most were oriental Jews, and it was the dark Moroccan faces that caught his eye. The curling dark hair, brown eyes shaped like almonds, like his mother's, like his own—why, then, didn't he feel right at home?

He walked up and down the street twice. Then again. A kid kicked a soccer ball his way. He stopped it with his knee, then kicked it up in the air a little and booted it back.

"You want to play?"

"No," he said.

"We need another guy."

"Maybe next time."

He wandered back and forth again, pausing in front of the building with the right number on it. The sunlight began to mellow, a shadow of evening tinted the sky. And he was suddenly embarrassed. What was he doing, anyway? Drawing attention to himself, probably, the attention of any mother leaning out of any window to call her kid in for supper. He looked like a rough country guy. Some kind of prowler.

He crossed the street and went in through the door, past the vestibule and through another door that didn't lock, into the hallway. First floor. Yes. The place was close and musty, and the smells drifting around him were of cooking: potatoes, egg-plant, everything obliterated by spice clouds of ginger and turmeric. In the back, it must be, toward the end of the hall. There. The right number, yes. And all he had to do was knock.

He did.

It seemed to him that everything had fallen suddenly silent. He stood there knocking. Then realized he'd been knocking, with increasing force and loudness, for a long time.

Down the hall another door opened. A woman leaned out and stared. A feeling of hopelessness filled him. Then he stopped knocking, turned to look back down the hall at her. A chubby woman, maybe thirty-five, maybe forty. Bright-colored apron in oriental pattern. A bright white scarf held up her hair. She had wrinkling dark skin, tired eyes, tired mouth—a mother, many times over. From inside her apartment sounds spilled into the hallway: a baby crying, kids fighting, someone else laughing. Singing. And the smell of cooking food was suddenly very strong. It stung his eyes. He could feel himself salivating, and swallowed with a sick sensation. She was evaluating him slowly, with the knowing look of one who read faces better than books. Then she gave a kind half-smile.

"You're looking for someone?"

"Yes. She lives here, I think. You know Miriam Sagrossa?"

"Ah. Her. She left."

"She's gone?"

"Sure, yes. Months ago they left."

"She went with someone else?"

"Yes, of course! With her daughter. Months ago. You're a friend?" Her dark eyes took on a speculative glow. "A good friend? From before, maybe? Not like her soldier friends, I hope. Because a woman like that, she needs someone. She needs someone strong. I'll tell you that much."

A daughter.

The smell of eggplant filled him. When his voice sounded it cracked like an adolescent's.

"Excuse me. You know where she went?"

The dark head shook gleefully, tassels on the white scarf shivering like dried strands of rope. "Sorry, my boy, I don't know. She told me once. To some kibbutz, I think she said— I'm sorry, please forgive me, I don't remember the name of it. The young man who came to visit—a little man, very handsome—he was a friend of hers, I think, he would remember. But he left, too. He said he was going to America."

He nodded faintly, barely hearing her. His voice cracked again.

"You don't remember?"

"No. I'm sorry, my friend. No."

He wandered out. Their eyes met as he went past. And he saw a sort of amused pity sparking hers. He felt weightless. When he reached the vestibule he heard the door to her apartment close. The sound of it echoed behind him. Then he was outside, and it was twilight.

Rafi

HE WAS NO TALLER THAN FIVE FOOT FIVE, AND SLENDER. IN THE
swirl of luggage, moving people, steaming shish kebob on café
spits, bus exhaust, car horns, and torn tickets that made the
Tachanat Mercazit a central station of chaos, he moved with
frenetic grace, a high-strung man who at first sight looked like
an adolescent Arab boy: dark, sharp-featured, with almond
eyes. He carried a small overnight bag with PAN AM scripted
across its sides. Around his neck hung a camera encased in
battered black leather.

Rafi dodged a bus to cross the intersection. He bought a ring
of sesame bread at a sidewalk stand and bit into it, jumped a
railing near Gate 75 and cut into line between an old woman
and a kid in a yarmulke. She turned to scowl, her eyes obscured
by wrinkles.

"It's not fair."

He gave her his most radiant grin. "This is the bus to Afula?"

"Yes, of course."

"Thanks, beautiful. You want a bite?"

"Go away," she said, but the ancient eyes were smiling.

A young recruit passed by, slender, tanned, blond, half-full knapsack hanging from one shoulder. His eyes were looking for something. When they met Rafi's they stayed there for a second, thinking they'd found it, then lost confidence and looked away. He ambled to one of the station entrances, turned and paused. Rafi thought he saw the knapsack shudder.

A bus passed between them spewing clouds. When it had gone, the kid was still there. His feet, stuck in brand-new regulation boots that were probably a size too big, shuffled nervously. Again the eyes searched. They caught Rafi's and held them this time, more plea than invitation.

Well, why not? Who knows, who cares—but maybe I'll feel good for a second. Last wish granted before I go to battle again with the good people of my childhood. Look at him, waiting. So young. And a blond, too. Staring back, Rafi shrugged. Then smiled. He left his place in line, tossed the half-finished ring of bread to the street. Another bus went by coughing gray clouds, and he waited. When it had gone, so had the kid. But he knew where to look and went into the station, inched through the crowds, stepped over pieces of luggage and squirmed around the tips of carelessly held weapons. A urine stink filled the washroom. There were urinals and three stalls, a pair of brand-new boots showing beneath the door of one, and no one else around. Rafi went to the sink and ran water. *Come on, beautiful. If the bus is on time for once, I only have ten minutes.* Someone came in, used a urinal and left, and when the door was closed again he heard the stall creak open behind him, then a breath on his shoulder.

"You want a cigarette? Or gum?"

It was said in Arabic. Rafi wheeled around to see him tapping a breast pocket nervously, the words tumbling out in a clumsy way. Arabic. Well, so. He understood suddenly, and wanted to laugh. A misunderstanding of sorts.

"Don't worry, friend, I speak Hebrew."

"You do."

"Sure."

"Israeli?" It was said with horror. "You're not a Jew, are you?"

"Me? No! No. My mother's Egyptian, you know. My father's from Jordan." The lie opened up a world of new possibility to him. He was tickled—he hadn't even suspected its existence before. He patted the hard leather case of the camera hanging against his abdomen. "I'm studying photography here. At the university."

"At the university?" The kid smiled, relieved. "Me, I'm not familiar with Tel Aviv, I'm just here on leave." Sweat peppered the space between his nose and upper lip. In the dull light, Rafi could see the flesh was raw where he'd shaved. A child. And so nervous. His slim fingers tapped the breast pocket again, trembling and shy. The backs of his hands were hairless. "What's your name?"

"*Abdu*. And yours?"

"Shimon."

A wave of revulsion throttled Rafi. He felt himself sweat, shut his eyes and clutched the smudged rim of the sink. The washroom door opened and an old Hasid shuffled in, heading for a stall. The kid turned to the urinals in panic and fumbled with the buttons on his pants. Some guy in a business suit walked in, used a urinal, glanced oddly at them both, and by the time he'd left the old Hasid was shuffling out too. Then they were alone again. Rafi opened his eyes. He realized he was running cold water, leaning down to splash it over his face. A slender hand caressed his back.

"Are you all right? Abdu? You're all right?"

He straightened and turned, his face dripping water. "Sure, I'm all right." Then nausea gripped him. He forced the words out anyway. "I'm *fine*. What do you want from me?"

"I want—I—"

"Listen, my bus leaves soon. Why don't you shut up and just do what I tell you." The kid stumbled back, frightened, and facing him Rafi felt a kind of rage bubbling up inside. "Well, so, what will it be? You'll do what I tell you? Or not? *You stupid Jew.*"

The knapsack was trembling again on the kid's shoulders. Rafi moved toward him. For some reason, the kid was nodding—pale, terrified, but nodding.

In the stall the toilet seat was filthy, and with the door latched behind them the space was so small that their legs were entangled. Then the rage left Rafi and he was suddenly weak as a leaf, clutching the camera straps to keep his hands from shaking as the kid slid to his knees, looked up once in supplication, then pressed his forehead gently against Rafi's thighs.

"Please, sir, don't go. Please don't go away from me."

Something surged through him helplessly, desire and a kind of pity that swelled the front of his pants and made him want to cry. What was it for—the desire, the pity? For this blond boy kneeling in front of him? Or for something else? What filled him now felt too sorrowful to bear, too expansive—it was like a lust for everything he'd never had, all that he'd had and lost, dreamed of, wept over—a desire and a mourning.

"Please, sir."

Why does he call me sir?

The kid rolled his face against him and began to unzip his pants.

I am Abdu now. His dark little oriental, his opposite, his enemy, his slave and his master. As he is my blond German boy. And God save us both.

"Please, sir."

Sir? Sir? Why does he call me sir? That word. What is it about that word—something I just thought of now, I almost remember.

The bus door swung open. The line began to compress. He went with the spastic motion of it, shuffling ahead, stopping suddenly, finally spilling up the steps to present his ticket. He shoved his way toward the back with the grim, compact determination small men sometimes have. Seats were filling rapidly, kids shrieking and dropping things, people quarreling over who had the right to sit where, and he slid between an old man and a paratrooper to claim a place near the aisle. Sunflower-seed shells littered the floor. Teenagers stood crammed together, cracking the seeds between their teeth and flicking out the shells with a deft movement of the tongue. *No, I won't be so sad to leave. Sloth of the oriental in us—this country will never escape it. The great god of sunflower seeds spitting shells from his mouth onto all the floors of Israel. Me, I'm getting away from that shit. Going to where a half-breed Moroccan Jew is something exotic instead of a thing to cut your teeth on. Let them think I'm Omar Sharif. Or maybe a Puerto Rican.* He watched through the haze of heat settling over his eyes. The usual: fight for a seat here, fight there, clawing at a dirty window to wrench it open for whatever air the day would give. His hands were shaking. He folded them, shaking, over the camera in his lap, over the damp crotch of his pants.

"Get in!" howled the bus driver. "Move!"

"Shut up! We're moving."

"Shut up yourself."

The engine started. Petrol wafted in. The city swam before him through dirty windows, a late-afternoon mirage. Rafi closed his eyes.

He dreamed in color. Unremitting dark green, the fields of Mayan Ha-Emek. Then there were colored specks against the green that blossomed into clumps of crops, grapefruit orchards, oranges, apples, the tiny patch of olive trees, grove of pecans. The squares of brown turnip fields. Family houses in rows, the children's houses, the volunteer quarters. The dining hall where he knew every cracked plate. The dairy where he'd worked the night shift sometimes in his adolescence, hating every minute of it, hosing down the cows with disinfectant that ran light blue onto his boots. You attached milk siphons to their teats one by one, row by row, making the rounds of each stall. At the end of each round you detached the tubes one by one, sprayed more disinfectant, hosed away the slop and began all over again. The rhythm of those nights had produced in him a sort of sexual yearning. The initial overpowering disgust of smells and filth, the continual washing, disinfecting, soiling, the crap that splashed over his uniform, forced him to evolve a resignation to it all that ultimately, side by side with the hatred, became almost a joy. It was a will to do this thing, to partake of this rhythmic movement, this endless enterprise waltzing him far into the dark, milky night. Moving, bending, hosing, lifting, prodding, he'd thought of boys' pricks and girls' breasts, and of the way the backs of necks looked when you sat behind them in class. In his thoughts he leaned forward to kiss each neck. They shuddered, all the boys and girls, and turned to face him, naked.

His yearning then had been bright and poignant. Sometimes he'd worked in a state of arousal so harsh, so vibrant, that he wanted to burst out into the night. Sometimes, in a gentler state, he felt himself on the border of tears and didn't know why.

General, remember the first time I stole a cotton truck. I was four-teen. It was just after my birthday, early June, no one expected you home, as far as we knew you were in Tel Aviv, or was it Jerusalem? And I drove like a real man, away from Mayan Ha-Emek, singing folk songs and the words of American tunes I didn't yet understand but only memorized phonetically. I drove all the way to Afula. I parked at the bus station there and bought some things, a falafel, a bottle of cheap grape wine, a pack of Europa cigarettes, a box of wooden matches, a copy of the Jerusalem Post. *I sat on the hood of the stolen cotton truck and drank and ate and smoked, until I was sick and vomited into the gutter. I opened the paper across my lap and pretended to read the English words. General, there was a breeze. When it blew through my hair I lost all hope. I knew that if I ran away you'd find me no matter how far I went. I drove back to Mayan Ha-Emek later that night in defeat. I remember the stars. Cotton trucks in the garage there look strange after the harvest, dirty white strips hanging from them. Did you know I saw you first in the headlights that night? You were like a ghost. Walking slowly up the road. A ghost coming out of the smells of the night, reminding me of my lost freedom. In the headlights of my stolen truck I saw a ghost, and the ghost was you. But I thought you didn't see me and I drove quickly past you up the hill. I parked in the garage. Sick, shaking, humiliated. I failed after all. Failed again. To run away. But I parked properly and I hung the stolen keys back on the wall there. Then I turned around and in the entrance to the garage was the ghost. You, in civilian clothes, a briefcase in your hand. The pines swayed behind you. Between the pines stars shone.* Go to sleep, Rafi, *said the ghost.* There's work tomorrow. *Then you turned and walked away, farther up the road, to mother's place, knowing I would obey. You could turn away with ease, certain in that knowledge. That I can never get away from you. Or from my people. And you know what I dreamed that night? I dreamed of the stars. I dreamed each star was a drop of blood. I held each drop in my hand and blew until it turned to fire and the fire to gold. I dreamed I was a general of Israel, leading men to battle. Bending over their burnt bodies on the fields where they lay dead. Kneeling down to kiss the tender backs of their necks. I woke up coming all over the sheet and blanket. Enough for a million babies, General. Enough for all my people, for all my brothers. Maybe even for you. In the morning I went to mother's place and there you were, awake as always, but nothing was said of the night before. It's strange, isn't it? Two ghosts meeting in the dark of Mayan Ha-Emek, and in the day they become two men, father and son, afraid to meet each other's eyes. Me, always your great disappointment. But maybe you need me now. I don't know—do you ever need anyone? You didn't then. Shimoni was still alive.*

Rafi opened his eyes. Twilight pressed on the bus, the road. Soldiers were hitchhiking everywhere. The land was wrapped in a deepening orange glow, tinged by darkness.

He smelled the fields of kibbutzim they passed. In the aisle next to him stood a woman—eighteen, maybe—in basic-training drab. Her black hair was tied beneath her cap. Her fingers and hands were absurdly dainty, poking from the dull-green sleeves. But beneath it all—he could smell it and it filled him like the aroma of a poppy field—she wore a foreign perfume. He shut his eyes again. He imagined her with nothing on but the perfume, her nipples brownish pink and pointing out toward him. It occurred to Rafi to open his eyes and look at her. But somehow that seemed a violation. He wanted to preserve the perfection of the moment, as if it were a photograph. To remember her this way, always, this girl he didn't know, leaning down toward him, naked, her nipples stiffening with desire for him. Her legs spreading, slowly, like petals, bird wings, waves of the sea, revealing the secrets of the universe. For him. And all the people of Mayan Ha-Emek gathered in a vast circle to watch, applauding. Bending over him as he lay there on a field of battle. His neck arched upward, revealed. He would die with a permanent erection. Preserving perfection—his own, and hers, and theirs. Somewhere in eternal memory, a photograph: of a great general of Israel. Of his father. Of Shimoni.

Of Miriam Sagrossa.

He kept his eyes tightly shut, and everything darkened as the bus creaked east. Rafi bowed his head. Her perfume rained down.

The dark face at the window startled Jolie. It pressed against smudged glass like a nightmare, nose flattening, the almond eyes narrowed to slits, a white expanse of teeth glittering wickedly out of the evening gray. She'd been reading in a half-doze, slumped into the part of Middle Eastern post-twilight that sometimes made her yearn to blend with the night. But she went to the window and opened it.

"Rafi. It's you."

"Hey. Speak *English* to me. Soon I'll be American."

"You're a creep, you know that?"

"Sure, I know." Then he was inside, grinning in that nervous, almost cockeyed way he had. He tapped the camera swinging from his neck. "See, I bought it. Pretty groovy, huh? Far out."

"Rafi, nobody talks like that."

"They don't?"

"They don't. Not even on TV."

"You gotta be pullin' my leg."

Jolie sighed. "Look, have a seat. Do you want some tea or coffee?"

"*Have a seat. Have a seat. Look, have a seat.* How's that? That's okay? It is? Good. No, I don't want tea and I don't want coffee.

I don't want cake or bread, either, and you know what I don't want more than nothing?"

"What? You mean *what you want least of all*—"

"Yes! Yes. What I want *least of all*. *Least of all*. Well, guess what I want least of all?"

"What?"

"Eggplant. Least of all in all the rest of my life I want to not eat eggplant. I mean to eat it. I said it wrong?"

"Actually, that's pretty good. Just forget the double negative."

"Ah. I like that—*pretty good*. *Pretty* good. It means good *and* beautiful?" He was cross-legged on the bed, fingers fidgeting with the camera strap as if playing a stringed instrument.

"It means *sort of* good."

The grin fled. His forehead wrinkled in worry, but then the smile returned and he shrugged. "Pretty good, then. Pretty good? I don't know, English is like the rest of my life, maybe. Nothing makes sense, but it still goes on and on. You know what I could really go for? A couple of beers."

"How's Tel Aviv these days?"

"Fuck Tel Aviv. How are you? You're still surviving among all the great Zionists of my childhood? The *real* men and *real* women?"

"Everyone thinks I'm in love with Nadav."

"The idiots!"

He laughed. Then she felt a little insulted. But he didn't notice, and talked enthusiastically.

"All these good-hearted Zionists who approve of you so much just because you're a good worker will throw you down the shit hole without a second thought if they ever discover that you have an original thought in your head. You know why? Because they never thought about making their own choices. They feel so self-righteous to be *real* men and *real* women, making more Jewish babies for Israel. Don't fool yourself, my friend! I grew up in misery here—I *know*."

Jolie looked at him cautiously. But maybe, she thought, it was possible to build a society of *real* love, and true acceptance, somewhere. She didn't know how to explain it aloud. It wasn't all that clear to her in words, really, she just knew what she felt. And maybe it all had to do with finding the perfect balance in life, between work and love, between male and female. On the other hand, maybe something was wrong with her. At her age, and after all she'd been through, she was still mostly untried and inexperienced in matters of love. The truth was that she didn't really believe in the value of sex—sometimes, it seemed, it wasn't the best way to know someone else. To know their essence. What made them human. Maybe at the root of things there was no sex, no personality, either—maybe there were only *souls*. Without so-called cultures. Without names, even. She guessed she didn't know very much about souls. But, she realized now, she wanted to find out.

"You think things are simpler than they are, Rafi."

"And you, of course, you *know* the way things *really* are. So tell me, what do *you* think?"

"I don't know. I think there's truth somewhere, maybe. Maybe sex isn't that important?" She avoided his eyes, expecting scorn. But he was listening with a look of gentle amusement. He made a clicking sound with his tongue.

"My friend, sooner or later you will just stop worrying about that transcendent shit and fall in love again."

Jolie bristled. "*Again?* Why? You think you were such an expert at love?"

"No."

He sulked. A familiar mixture of guilt and compassion stirred her.

"Rafi. Talk to me."

"I'm nervous and sad, I don't know why."

She thought he'd cry. But he just looked glumly at her, until she forgave him everything and winked. Then his face brightened. He smiled slyly. "My *beloved* wife. Tell me, Nadav's here?"

"As a matter of fact, no. He left this morning to visit *you.*"

Rafi's hands, playing with the camera strap, froze for a moment to fists. When he spoke again it was in Hebrew.

"Then he knows."

"About your plans? Yes."

"But he left today? So he won't be back tonight, yes? You think maybe not?" His face smoothed again. The flicker of a smile returned, but his coloring was pale. "Because I should see my mother tonight, anyway—I mean, alone. I want to tell *her* myself, first. It's important."

His fists had clenched on his knees. His face had a petulant little-boy's look. But there was sweat on his forehead, and Jolie could feel his beginning panic. It reminded her of the first time they'd tried to make love. She didn't want to think about it and excused herself to go to the bathroom. When she came out he was taking off his pants. His mouth had set in a grim, determined way.

"Rafi, what the hell are you doing?"

"What do you *think?*"

"Oh, no."

He fingered the waistband of his underpants then and paused, a little crestfallen. The jeans were bunched around his feet on the floor. "What do you mean, *oh, no?* You used to *love* it!"

Jolie waved a hand, dismissing him. Then she sat tiredly and examined him standing there in his underpants, relieved to feel not a twinge of desire. He seemed so childlike tonight. And it was time for the truth. Realizing that, she also realized that even if she had been capable of feeling desire for him now, or in the past, things really were over between them. This was a relief. Nevertheless, it left her sad somehow.

"Listen, Rafi, it's time for the truth—okay?"

He put his hands on his hips. "Okay."

"The truth is that I never *loved* it—I mean, I never loved *it.* I only loved the *idea* of it. And the reason I loved the *idea* of it was because we hardly ever *did* it. It was all a great fantasy in my head."

He sat on the edge of the bed. His eyes avoided hers for a while, then gazed back at her sharply. "And me? You think you loved me? Or was I a great fantasy in your head, also?"

"I don't know."

She thought she saw him cringe. Then his cheek rippled in a flutter of nerves, and she was immediately sorry she'd said that. Still he kept looking at her, and his eyes had softened to an expression of mild humor. "Well, so. I think we should do it, anyway—once and for all."

"Why?"

"For old time's sake."

They both laughed.

She watched him sitting there, his shoulders a little bowed. There was something gentle about him now, and also, with his pants bunched around his ankles, something a little ridiculous. It brought out the tenderness in her. She had a sense that if she reached out now, right now, to touch his back, kiss his cheek, tousle his hair—if she could make any kind of contact at all— then he'd respond naturally, easily, fully, as he never had before. Yes. It was that. That reaching out. More than the other thing of his liking blond men, some kind of preference or biological need. That preference and need might have coexisted with a genuine love of her, she thought, a love of her that in time might have grown to be both emotional *and* physical, if only they had let it. But they'd never succeeded in really loving each other. Instead, they had let everything in the world flood in between them: Israel, America, greed, social expectation, loneliness, sexuality, stupidity, fear, looks, self-deprecation, Mayan Ha-Emek. And now, when for a few brief moments there was real opportunity, maybe, she was letting it go by. She was letting it pass, quite consciously. Aware of the depths of her own masochism and passivity. She had spent a long time punishing *him* by continuing to absorb his punishment of *her*. Because he'd wanted America. And she'd wanted a husband. All in the way of attempting some fantasy notion of marriage. How pathetic, she thought. How ridiculous. How wasteful.

Rafi thumbed open the waistband of his underpants and gazed down.

"It doesn't *look* queer."

Then they laughed again.

He pulled his jeans up and zipped them. He looked at her a little oddly, gently, eyes narrowing in genuine inquiry.

"Tell me something. It was never good for you?"

"It was never long enough."

"Ah. Maybe you should have told me."

"Sure," she sighed, "maybe."

"Maybe I would have tried to be better."

"I don't think so. You didn't really want me. Only America."

The flutter ran up his cheek again. Then he nodded. "Yes," he said, "that's true." And then, softly, "But why wouldn't you take me there?"

A single tear dripped along his nose, fell to one leg of his blue jeans and left a splotch. She looked for more but there were no more coming. She stood and walked over to him and sat next to him on the bed, and for a while they just held hands.

"I'm sorry," he said.

"Okay, Rafi. But forgive me, too. I wanted to be a bride and you wanted an American passport. Somewhere in there we forgot about love. Or even affection."

"It's true. But tell me why—"

"Why what?"

There was an edge of sly mischief in his voice. "Why I should *forgive* you."

She slugged him in mock anger, he began to tickle her, and they wound up laughing again.

Jolie fixed him tea then, even though he didn't want any. And they talked. Or, rather, he talked while she listened. This seemed to calm him. Rafi was a man who lived on the energy of his own nerves. Maybe that was why he was so slender—his insides had stretched him tight over a network of red-hot wires, burning away complacency and any hint of contentment. Despite all they'd been through, the feverish, unfocused yearning inside him touched her. He was a foreigner here, just as much as she was. Maybe more.

As usual, when they talked, he brought up his army days. Unlike Shimoni's, his own military career had been marked by a notable absence of heroism. Jolie still didn't know all the details—he never told everything, just spoke of his own horror obsessively. Military life had marked him terribly, had offended him right down to his core. There was something in him still that squirmed at the memory of it.

But he couldn't stop remembering.

All the days of mock hand-to-hand combat came back to him. The hours of fear under bleached desert sun. Once, toward the end of basic training, Sergeant Major Gavon had ordered him into hand-to-hand with a frantic, panicky kid named Yitzhak something-or-other—he forgot the last name—a fellow-malingerer. And each of them tried hard to make it appear as if they were busting each other's guts, hearts, kidneys, ripping out each other's eyes, when in fact the thought of any of it terrified and revolted them. There was the moment when a sudden terror took its turn in Yitzhak's heart and Rafi found himself struggling in the harsh, unyielding grip of a man gone insane, a mama's boy transformed under pressure into a demon of murderous rage. It was rage at the acts they were ordered to pretend to perform here, in the desert, under the gaze of a sadistic drill sergeant. Rage at their own humiliation. Rage at the terror itself. In that moment, pretense became reality. Rafi found himself dodging real blows. He found himself coming back at the boy with kicks that, had they landed, would have killed. He knew then that he was fighting for his life. This was no longer a rehearsal, but the real thing. The flat of his hand burned sharply as he slammed it into the boy's face once, twice, again.

When Gavon took mercy and ordered them at ease, the other recruits chuckled and glanced away with discomfort. But there wasn't the usual applause.

They were given water. They were given kerchiefs to mop up their blood. Yitzhak's nose was broken and wouldn't stop gushing. In the infirmary, his lip required several stitches.

They avoided each other in the mess hall that night, and every day thereafter. Not that they'd been friends before—not really. They'd met near the latrines a couple of times, late-night rendezvous, impersonal release. Still, something between them had been spoiled. Any possibility of comradeship was dead. They'd seen too clearly the deadly nature of their own untrustworthiness and terror.

Sergeant Major Gavon seemed slightly regretful, too. Sometime later that night he approached Rafi with an apologetic smile lurking beneath the absurd extremities of his mustache. He patted Rafi on the back clumsily, inquired as to his welfare. *A good show*, he said. And squeezed Rafi's neck. One hand passed gently over his crotch. At this, chills spilled down Rafi's back and vomit rumbled in his belly. But Gavon was oddly tender, fumbling through a pocket. *Good fight*, he kept repeating, embarrassed, obviously ashamed. He stroked Rafi's back and shoulders, ran a trembling hand through his hair. They were between the latrines and the barracks. There was no one else around. Stars glittered down in the darkness, wind swept sand into miniature desert cyclones. Gavon reached out with the gift he had in his hands. *Take it*, he said, his usually booming voice dry and gentle. *Please, kid, take it*. Rafi did. It was a candy bar.

"They say the army makes children into men, but they're wrong. It makes children into apes. It makes assholes think they're real cowboys."

"You have something against cowboys, Rafi?"

"No. As long as they're American."

He crouched on the bed, knees pulled tensely to his chin.

He'd made money playing cards with drunks on the fuel-supply base where he'd spent his years of service. The gambling that went on at that particular base was notorious and highly illegal. Men went into heavy debt sometimes, tangled with the wrong people. There was theft and violence. Sometimes, suicide.

Soldiers who wound up on fuel-supply bases weren't exactly the *crème de la crème*. They weren't in the same class, for instance, as Nadav, or Michael, or Shimon. They were, instead, the flotsam and jetsam, the ones for whom no other solution—

except maybe discharge or prison—could be found, and other solutions were unfeasible unless a man's character was truly desperate. Everyone had to serve.

Rafi wound up among them. It didn't surprise him. He'd been a misfit all his life. Like any intelligent misfit who was also a survivor, he found his own way to make the best of it, and he got out while still in the money. All profits went to fulfill a long-cherished dream. Discharged finally, and, somehow, honorably, he paced the streets of Tel Aviv in search of a good used-camera store.

Inside one, his dream waited: an ancient Canon, abused old zoom lens thrown in for good measure, a battered leather case. He handed over worn shekel notes, fingers trembling. That was the beginning of his final break with Mayan Ha-Emek, he knew, and with everything it represented. In a way, it was the beginning of his final break with Israel too—although he didn't know that yet. He would have to fail at marriage to know that. But this was a gift he'd given himself, this camera: his first real possession. For days he wandered the country like a tourist, traveling everywhere by bus, the camera strap pressing into his shoulder.

At first he was afraid to use it. When he finally did his hands shook, his skin erupted in sweat, images blurred before him. Peering through the tiny hole through which he could now observe a cruel and ridiculous world, he made light bend, vanish, reappear and freeze.

"That's when I *knew* something." He stopped grinning and stared past Jolie, out the window at the night, nodding. For a reluctant second she loved him again, and felt her own voice warmed with tenderness.

"What, Rafi?"

But he just kept nodding, watching something she couldn't see, a suddenly gentle smile on his lips.

"Mother, you look tired." Rafi sat on the small sofa's edge. It was his third glass of tea that night, his second piece of cake. He imagined the tense grin on his face and had to stop himself from laughing. Instead he choked down a hot swallow. *Not just tired, half dead. Sorry, that's not fair. But how long do you plan to suffer the indignity of it, woman? Slogging through each day on this godforsaken piece of land with the same dull souls, waiting for your great military leader of a husband to show his face once in a while—his aging face, and maybe his aging cock too, if you care any more, but you probably don't. Sorry, that's not fair either. I'm an asshole, I can't help myself. You were so beautiful when you were young, Mother. Like a delicate Moroccan doll. What did he use you for, the great boor? A nice ornament to drag to public occasions. Just like Shimoni and his own little oriental display piece. But maybe he got more than he bargained for. History repeats. He learned from the General. Your good fertile Eastern ovaries to bear Father's children. A warm place to stick it in when he felt the need. Did you ever enjoy it and did you ever protest? Did he do it more than four times, anyway? I'm a shit, I admit it. Sometimes I want to cut out my own tongue. Here I am, and lucky for the whole misbegotten family, and for the country, too—a native-born scapegoat. Let's face it, it's either me or the Arabs. I who live while real men suffer and die.*

"I'm not so tired."

"Ah." Rafi crossed his legs. His sense of humor was rapidly deserting him, and the evening was still young. He was right in the middle of custom now, and this was one of the customs of Mayan Ha-Emek he'd always loathed: this habit of evening visiting, sitting, gulping endless cups of a hot beverage and stuffing various kinds of cakes or breads down your throat. It was the community's way of socializing. In the evening, every evening, you were either entertaining guests who'd walked in without knocking—knocking was considered rude, since it assumed the existence of aloofness or formality—or you were barging in on someone else. It was the only real way of reestablishing contact outside of work, breakfast, lunch, dinner, or general meetings. It was the way to keep abreast of gossip, or to spread some yourself. It was one of the main reasons why there were seemingly few secrets on Mayan Ha-Emek. In the eyes of Westerners, privacy here was close to nonexistent.

Actually, there *was* privacy. But it consisted of elements

different from those that constituted privacy in the West. Here, what was truly private was more elusive and self-contained. Visible emotions weren't easily evoked. Display of affection was kept to a bare minimum, as was display of anything, for that matter. And the life of the heart, they would tell you if pressed, though barely expressed outwardly, held full sway. It was the unspoken inner reality, they'd tell you, that made up the genuine underlying truth of life in the community. The idea that only the visible, the spoken, the outwardly demonstrated, constituted *reality*—this was an illusory Western concept anyway, they'd tell you, and carried little weight on Mayan Ha-Emek.

Rafi would have said they were hypocrites. *You have your own illusions,* he'd have told them, *your own set of appearances to maintain, your own set of social standards to uphold.* And he'd have preferred almost anything to the continual sensation he had whenever he returned for a visit, the same sensation he'd experienced throughout all his years of growing up, that he was being stoically measured, picked apart, judged unworthy, and unceremoniously discarded, all in inscrutable silence. Sometimes it seemed to him that what he longed for most was simply overt *reaction.* It was the one need that, in all his young life, had gone most unmet. He'd spent tortured years trying to provoke it. A lot of negative reactions, he told himself, were better than none at all.

"I heard that Nadav's back."

"Yes."

"You saw him? He's okay?" He bit off a large hunk of dry cake. *Maybe talk English to her, idiot. Then we'll really be totally incomprehensible to each other, but at least there will be a perfectly good reason for it. What can I do for you, Mother, to make everything bad go away, all the pain, all the years? Your sons are either dead heroes or trying to become one, or else they're fools like me. How can I give you back your beauty, your hope? Despite youth and marriage and the miracle of life and all the rest of that, see, things always result in disappointment and grief. Me, I'm just trying to run away and maybe earn a small chunk of happiness. Or peace.*

Or at least some money, eh?

But Yael leaned forward in her chair, and the expression on her face surprised Rafi. He swallowed as if swallowing lead. Her face was suddenly radiant. But whether it shone with joy or anguish he couldn't tell. It was merely the sudden surge of emotion that changed her features instantly, revealing a core of youth and beauty that seemed to linger always beneath the surface, and her eyes sparked brightly. They were the eyes of a woman filled with passion and dreams. Watching, he could barely tell what emotion gripped his own soul—ecstasy? terror? Then he realized that his mother was looking straight at him. The pity he'd felt for her dropped from him like molting skin. What he saw in her eyes now was a piercing mixture of pity and understanding. The pity wasn't for herself, but for him, and he knew then that she saw him clearly, that she had been a full-grown person with her own life long before she'd borne him, had made her own choices and decisions, had lived with the consequences. He felt color drain from his face.

"Listen to me." Her voice was commanding and gentle. "You think, Rafi, that I want to sit here to watch the time we have together now waste away with stupid words? Don't ask me about Nadav. He's a man with his own pain and his own life. You're curious? Then ask *him*. But for now, tell me this: tell me about your own life and your own pain. You're going away soon? Yes? I heard about it, you know—everyone heard, and why should it be such a great secret? You care so much what fools will say? You think I'm not glad for you somewhere inside that you're leaving all this craziness and war and death, that you're going to do what you *need* to do, finally? You think because your own choice is different from another's that I won't respect it? How? You're part of my flesh. And maybe we don't have much time together. Who knows when I'll see you again? So please, let's not be stupid now. Don't be so afraid, Rafi. Just be the man that you are. Tell me what's in your mind. Tell me what's in your heart."

She sat there waiting. The glow lit her face. And now what he saw in her eyes were the beginnings of tears. He set his glass down. There was a terrible dryness in his mouth and throat, he tried to cough it away but couldn't, then couldn't look at her any more and bowed his head. He understood for the first time that he was afraid. Understood, for the first time, the enormity of what he was going to do. He glanced at her quickly again. Twin bolts of love and fear streaked through him. He covered his face with both hands and cried suddenly, silently, rocking back and forth like a child.

No News Is Good News

NADAV SPENT TWO NIGHTS IN TEL AVIV, FINDING HIS WAY TO A CHEAP hotel where water leaks stained the room's sink brown. He moved in a kind of dream. Soldiers rattled through the corridors day and night. Sometimes he woke in a sweat to hear hoarse baritone singing echo drunkenly through the door. He must have eaten, too. Later, though, he didn't remember. He felt weak and desperate. In a fit of black anger once, he called Rafi's number, but no one answered. He'd written down Rafi's address, too, and went there one morning. No one was home. The next day he checked out of the hotel and decided to leave. But a last black streak of anger seized him. Riding it like a wave, he went into a real restaurant and ordered a meal. Fish, potatoes, vegetables, salad, soup, plenty of bread, a glass of milk, two desserts smothered in syrup and cream. When it was over he had just enough for a bus ticket and felt much better than he'd felt in months. It wasn't to the Tachanat Mercazit that he headed, but back to Rafi's apartment. This time he knocked with force, calling out his name. After a while the door opened.

"What's new, Rafi?"

"Nothing."

"You know what the Americans say: *If there's no news it's the same thing as if there's good news.* Something like that."

"*No news is good news.*" Rafi sighed. "Come in."

Nadav stepped across the threshold. Three cardboard boxes sat in the middle of the front room. The window curtains were pulled aside, and sunlight flooded through. Nadav leaned back against the door, heard its shutting click sound hollowly around him. But he gave his brother a bright grin.

"Leaving?"

"Sure. On vacation."

Nadav sat on a box. "Vacation?" He saw Rafi staring back uneasily. "Where to?"

"Who knows? It's a free country, we can go anywhere, right? I hear Cairo is nice in the winter."

Nadav was on his feet clutching Rafi's shirt front before he could think, rattling him back and forth like a boneless sack, wanting suddenly to strangle and destroy. This close he could see Rafi's forehead sprout sweat, his eyes panic as he tried desperately to pry loose. But Nadav realized that somehow, with a kind of sick courtesy, Rafi was avoiding pushing at his right hand—afraid, maybe, of damaging it. Or maybe just afraid. Anger left him then and a feeling of nausea flooded in to take its place. "Bastard," he said, but it lacked force. He shoved Rafi against a wall and let go. "You disgust me, you know."

"Sure, Nadav, I know! You're such a big commando, guys who don't like getting killed deserve your disgust. Well *be* disgusted if you want. Because *I* want to be a living man much more than I want to be a dead Zionist. Anybody who feels differently should stay—right? You agree? *Good.* So let *me* go. Be glad there'll be one less coward around to stop the rest of you from being such great heroes. I'm leaving in the spring. I'm going to New York City. And you won't stop me."

"Fine. That's fine." Nadav reached into a pocket, tossed

some shekels at his brother. They fluttered to the floor. "Go ahead, since you're the poor suffering artist among us, and buy yourself something to eat. I know it's hard to work and fight with everyone else when you have such a sensitive soul. But to each according to his need. Maybe they won't feed you enough on the plane. So buy yourself a falafel or something, Rafi. Buy yourself a Coca-Cola."

"*Go to hell.*" Rafi kicked at the colorful notes. But his eyes glittered tears.

The final images Rafi took with him from his last year in the East, he was determined, would be as Westernized as possible. But Nadav had come to talk, so Rafi did—knowing that the final images he'd leave with would be internal and not tangible, after all, knowing they'd be, irrevocably, images of the East. It was Shimoni his brother wanted to talk about. And behind the dead shadow something else: the woman, Miriam Sagrossa.

"I heard she has a child."

"A daughter," said Rafi. "It's true."

They sat on cushions on the floor, cross-legged, sipping the warm remains from a bottle of grapefruit juice.

"How old? And how do *you* know about it?"

"Four years old. Because I went to visit one day, that's how. I introduced myself. It was about a month after the funeral. I thought maybe she needed something—money, who knows? *I* didn't know. But Shimoni seemed to care for her, so I guess I thought she was worth a visit at least. I went back a couple of other times, too. We didn't talk much—she didn't have so much to say, not exactly the verbal type, not *her*. I lent her some money once. It wasn't much. I don't expect to get it back. I asked was there anything else I could do, and she said no. She said she wanted just to go far away somewhere, where no one knew her—she was depressed, not in the most cheerful of moods, my friend, and who was *I* to cheer her up, eh? But the kid is pretty. Also very strange, a little crazy maybe, who knows? No one told me who the father was. But she has an

Indian name. Quite a little potpourri of a nation, aren't we? Shimoni's daughter she isn't." Rafi laughed. "Gandhi's, maybe."

Nadav gave him a warning look.

They rattled down dirty cement steps at twilight, took a walk up narrow streets suffocating in heat and car exhaust. They were within walking distance of the Tachanat Mercazit and could hear the rumble of a hundred buses. Bread vendors yelled from sidewalk stands. Nadav stopped to buy a bag of figs.

"Want some?"

Rafi took one. The flavor burst open in his mouth. Dried sugar. Punctured seeds. It filled his senses now, poignant and sweet. He swallowed.

"You know, Nadav, I didn't really like her so much."

"Who?"

"Shimoni's *woman*, of course. Miriam *Sagrossa.*"

Nadav was chewing and paused a moment. When he looked at Rafi there was distaste in his eyes. "You didn't like her so much? Well. So tell me why."

"I don't know." Rafi watched him carefully, cautiously chose his words, unwilling now to tempt a fight between them. But caution made him clumsy, and he found himself blurting out something close to the truth. "Maybe it was something as little as—as stupid as something like, maybe—I don't know, Nadav! Maybe the way she *smelled!* She had the smell of—of a *woman*, and she wore this kind of perfume that left its aroma in a room, even after she was gone. Do you know how women smell when they're not teenagers any more? When they've had a child or two, maybe?" He blushed bright red. "Anyway, I'm an ass. I don't know what I'm talking about. Maybe it's just that I was afraid, too, being there with her. After all, Shimoni is dead— what was there to say? And I'd never met her before in my life. So I sat there in her sad little apartment, making jokes like an idiot, and once in a while the kid would throw something at me, or want to play, and I'd bounce her on my knees, great father figure that I am. I think"—he reached carefully into the bag for another fig—"I think she used Shimoni, maybe. I think she had reasons of her own."

"Reasons?"

"Sure. Listen, Shimoni obviously wasn't the first for her, right? Well, I think he won't be the last one either. I think maybe she kept looking for something in him that she didn't find." Rafi picked seeds from his teeth, watched his brother gazing at him now with a wary but hopeful expression. It had opened the gates to some sort of bridge between them, this matter of Miriam Sagrossa.

"I thought maybe that she was always *looking* for something," Rafi insisted softly, "for something in her men. She isn't yet satisfied."

"Yes? What, then? What do you think she keeps looking for?"

"Who knows? Maybe for something simple, maybe for something difficult. For a superman, some genius who was also strong. Or maybe just someone who would stay alive a while."

It was after dusk and street lamps glowed overhead. Buses packed with civilians and soldiers roared by. The roads around the station were crammed with market stalls selling shish-kebab, sesame, peppers, cheap cologne. Nadav blinked, taking it all in. The city overwhelmed him. He was filled, all at once, with a vision of his own smallness. *You aren't much of a sophisticate, after all, Kol, are you? Not much of an educated cosmopolitan, not a man of the world, a fighter and scholar rolled into one, like Shimoni. You're basically just a country guy who thinks he's been around, a kibbutz boy in awe of the noise, the people, the lights. Where were your eyes and ears every time you were on leave in a city, stumbling around at dawn? Didn't you see the confusion of it? Civilization? Your own blood, everywhere, all colors and languages, what little Rafi calls a* potpourri, *yes. And what are he and I then? Put us in robes and burnooses and we're a couple of Moroccan Jews wandering through this* shuk. *Ancient and modern combined to create chaos. You've been unconscious too long. Even this schmuck of a brother sees the world more clearly than you.*

Tell me, Shimoni—it seems you were a man of many secrets—but how did you see it?

127

"Nadav." Rafi tapped his shoulder. "You're okay?"

"Sure. I'm thinking."

"About the woman?"

"About Shimoni."

Rafi plucked the empty fig bag from him and tossed it to the gutter. The problem with the dead was that they occupied your living thought. Planted themselves there, tormented you with loss until through memory they became something other than what they really had been. Heroes. Demons. Saints. Giants. Still, you missed them.

They walked a long time. Night speckled the sky with a thousand stars, but the stars were obscured by streetlight. Car headlights glowed into store-front windows on Disengoff. Between intermittent rays of shadow, people walked, sat at café tables, stopped to gaze at window displays. Rafi bought a falafel. Shredded cabbage and crushed chickpeas mingled on his tongue. He waved the falafel at his brother, feeling suddenly, terribly homesick.

"You want some?"

"No. Thanks."

"It's good. You're sure? Okay. You know, I think it's not only Miriam who searched for something. I think Shimoni used her, too—"

"*He* used her?"

"Listen, Nadav, he knew many women, he wasn't a fool. I think he wanted someone beautiful to come back to sometimes, a woman he could show off in public when he needed to. But she had one little problem, see? Like a child—a child that wasn't *his*. He was a career man—"

"Sure, I know." It came out resentfully. "I *know* he was a career man, Rafi."

"Okay, good, we both know. Well, a career man needs to be hard, right? Especially in paratroops. It's no place for soft hearts."

Nadav grabbed the falafel from Rafi and took a large bite, forced himself to swallow. His eyes stung bitterly.

"Shimoni was *hard*." Rafi waited for the falafel but Nadav

doggedly consumed it. He wandered to a food stand and bought another, smothered it in onions and tahini, then spooned pickled eggplant on from the condiment tray. The first taste made him homesick again. Nadav had already finished the other, crumpled the wax paper, and tossed it to the sidewalk.

"He was a *sensitive* man too, Rafi. He was educated, he had respect for civilization. He talked to me about poetry sometimes." Nadav glared down at him. "*He* knew what he was fighting for."

"Sure, Nadav. But fighting was the work he *chose*. Listen, this is how I see it: there are different kinds of men in this world. Some endure the army as a duty, they even succeed there, but when the duty is done they leave—like you. Others are filled with nausea every second of every day. The army spins around them in a bright white heat of cruelty and death. They can't succeed, they barely function, they're glad to escape the insanity of it, even if it means being an outcast among their own people. Well, we all know that *I* am such a man. But there are others, a few maybe, who find in all the discipline and violence something that to them is *life*. They see a meaning in it. They see in it their own purpose, they commit themselves to it, they become our leaders and our generals, and if they get killed at a young age they become our heroes. Does that sound familiar? Maybe a little like Shimoni? He *liked* it all, Nadav! He really liked it!" The falafel dropped from his hands. "Listen, maybe you don't believe me, but I admired the man. He did more in his time than most men ever do. He had a good mind, a good heart even. But war was his job! He was hard at the core, he was hard like stone. And I miss him in a way that hurts—I miss him like you miss your fingers. I loved my brother, Nadav, but I never for a single minute worshiped him. That's why I'm leaving here, and I'm not coming back. *That's* the difference between you and me."

Then he grabbed the front of Nadav's shirt and pressed his face against it, and in the passing lights of Disengoff he stood and cried. After a while Nadav put his arms around him. He felt foolish and out of place at first, as if he were a father, Rafi his son.

They walked some more that night. Sea wind blew east from Jaffa. The air became cool. Sidewalks were crowded now, café tables sloppy with cups and pastry crumbs, every seat occupied. *It's a little like New York, maybe,* Rafi had told himself, hopefully, *crowded, unplanned, worldly.* But the thought of a new land made him afraid now.

Nadav wondered if things would be difficult for Rafi in New York City. Momentary compassion swelled in him. His little brother, this slight man beside him, flying off to another land. What would happen to him there? How would he make his way?

But he remembered the fast tongue, quick grasp of language, and gift for mimicry, the old Rafi sneer. The schmuck would be all right.

"You think it'll be strange, walking along some street and knowing that most of the people around you aren't Jews?"

"I'm going to *New York*, Nadav. They're all Jews there."

"It's not true."

A small group of Hari Krishnas went past, dots on their foreheads, pastel robes flowing, tiny ponytails of hair sweeping their necks. Rafi glanced up at him and grinned wryly.

They made their way back to his place. From the street the apartment's windows looked dark, vacant. Inside, Rafi lit a candle to save on electricity, poured a glass of wine, and, when Nadav refused it, kept it for himself and poured his brother some juice. They sat and talked more, mostly about America.

"What'll you do there?"

"I don't know." Rafi sighed. "Photography, maybe. That's what I want. Maybe someday there I can do what I want." *Or love who I need to love,* he thought. But didn't say it. "Listen, Nadav, maybe I shouldn't ask you this."

"You shouldn't ask me what?"

"All right, I'll ask. You won't stay on Mayan Ha-Emek, will you?"

"Why?"

"I want to know."

"Okay. I'll tell you the truth. No. Eventually, I don't think I'll stay."

"*Good.*"

"Why? Why is that *good?*"

"Because Mayan Ha-Emek is old, it's an anachronism, and you—you're young. You should go to new places and do new things. Listen, Nadav, I know you don't respect me much, but a lot of people feel like I do, and the truth is I like holding my own money in my own hands at the end of every week, even if it does all get pissed down the toilet at tax time. So I'm not much of a socialist, eh?"

Nadav smiled uncomfortably.

"The truth is that kibbutz life was a cute little experiment once, but it doesn't really make sense in the modern world, you know? I'm not going to let some committee tell me what to do with my life. I like to have my own say, my own little apartment, and no one listening through the walls—what about you? Maybe you want to try that someday, too? A little *autonomy.*"

"Well, sure."

"There, you see? I said it." You could almost hear Rafi's grin leering through the shadows. "And something else, as long as I'm such a courageous Lion of Judah tonight."

Despite himself, Nadav smiled. "What, Rafi?"

"What'll you *do* now? For yourself, I mean. What are *your* plans?"

Nadav raised his right hand until it loomed large against the flickering wall, a distorted shadow beyond life-size. If he moved the thumb and stiff forefinger apart, then together, it looked like the head of a silently barking dog. He let the hand fall to his chest. There was still a damp spot on the shirt there where Rafi had cried.

"The first thing I'll do is find her."

"Find *who?*"

"Miriam Sagrossa."

Rafi could feel his heart thud slowly. What he wanted to say now he'd never say. He closed his eyes and saw himself: a small figure roaming through some endless airport looking for the right gate but never finding it, suitcase in one hand, aging Canon around his neck, a foreigner in every land. Always in transit. He'd see things no one else saw, record them, maybe, for posterity, but remain always apart. He too would search, would wander all his life—but would he know, himself, what it was he searched for? For peace? Or love? And wasn't Nadav lucky in a way, to have at least something that embodied what *he* searched for now: a vision, an illusion, a woman? Even if she belonged to another man, or to many men. Even if one of those men was his own dead brother. Let him discover what he thought he wanted. And let him have her, his Miriam Sagrossa.

"Listen," Rafi said at last, "she told me she was going to Ramat Alon. It's in the Golan, north of Zfat. Who knows if she really went there? But that's what she told me. So go and see, Nadav. Go and find her." *And I'll stay here, right here. Because I can't leave yet. Spring is too soon. I understood tonight that I am not ready. I'm still afraid. To leave you all. To free myself.* Rafi sighed. There were tears in his eyes. "Go and find her."

Ramat Alon

RAMAT ALON WAS JUST OFF THE ROAD LEADING DOWN TO ZFAT. Farther north, cypresses clustered thinly along slopes of rock. Granite fields and red dirt surged upward. The route twisted in a spiral, passed through sparse pine forests, wound up the sides of ruined mountains pointing to the sky.

The bus let him off down the road, and Nadav hitched a ride with a guy driving a dusty, rattling little pickup. A few bruised apples rolled noisily in the back. The guy was a few years older than Nadav, a well-built man with a raw blond face and thick forearms. After noticing Nadav's maimed hand he didn't look at it again.

"You're going up to the kibbutz?"

"Yes."

"Then you're in luck. You're visiting someone?"

"Yes. Miriam Sagrossa."

There was an awkward silence. Nadav felt himself being examined in sharp sideways glances. Then the driver said, cautiously, "You're a relative?"

"No. An old friend."

"Ah. So tell me, friend—you have a name?"

"Nadav."

"Nadav." He shrugged himself then, and smiled briefly, as if relenting. "Nadav. Well, I'm Schindler. Yitzhak Schindler. I'm the assistant secretary here. If you're staying overnight, let me know. I'll arrange a room."

They turned onto a dirt road sheltered by pines. The chill of autumn was harsh here, and Nadav rolled his window up as they slowed to a stop at the tiny settlement guardhouse. A man leaned out, wiry and dour. One arm sheltered an Uzi. He nodded at them.

"Peace, Yitzhak."

"What's new?"

"Not much. Kobi Becker says he'll leave if you don't reassign him to the carpentry shop."

"I'll talk to him." Schindler sighed, then motioned toward Nadav. "He came to see Miriam Sagrossa."

"So? She's here."

"You know where?"

"Maybe in the laundry room. Maybe going to eat, it's almost dinnertime. So go ahead."

He waved them past. Nadav noticed one rugged hand wrapped around the Uzi grip, thumb thick and knotted like the limb of a tree.

They drove farther, uphill through the pines. A smell of cow dung blew into the pickup, and there was the odor of chicken feathers and crushed apples, sawdust, machine oil. Nadav thought he heard cows mooing. Then the sound of children laughing. Like Mayan Ha-Emek, only smaller—but he felt he'd crossed some kind of border and fallen into foreign territory. Everything had a strange quality, the sounds, the smells, the texture of the air. He felt himself an outsider. Then the pines receded and the road ended abruptly.

There they were: children. Holding hands, peering between adult legs, round eyes searching out their own parents among the stream of men and women heading for the dining hall from work. Children clung to the cloth of trouser legs. Family time would extend through mealtime.

Yitzhak Schindler stopped the pickup. He and Nadav got out on opposite sides and stood there a moment. Very different men, but both had been through the same wars. Maybe that was part of the reason why, different as they were, the children enchanted them both, and they stood there watching fixedly. Nadav noticed the slight bulge of belly that rounded out Schindler's pullover. He looked down with sudden, senseless desperation, was relieved to see that he had none himself. Beyond the horizon sunset gave the white strips of cloud a red-tinged look. A boy went by, eyeing them sideways.

"Adi, you know where Miriam Sagrossa is? This guy says he's a friend."

A dark pair of eyes looked Nadav up and down, flickering mistrustfully. Then the kid pointed to the dining hall. Starlings soared around the windows, and Nadav was reminded of home.

"Let's go," said Schindler.

They joined the flow of people headed along the stone-lined paths. Bright ceiling lights gleamed through the dining hall windows. As the sky outside darkened, the entire building took on a glow.

Nadav would remember it later: the pines, the windburnt faces, a mountain horizon before winter, cold sky changing into twilight, the settlement ringing with sounds of utensils. He'd remember the smell of cooking. But most of all the light—it was warm and golden, seemed almost tangible, and it seemed to him, also, that he'd begun to move slowly, walking with the flow of unfamiliar people in work clothes holding children's hands, very slowly, as if in a dream. He'd recall it the way you recall dreams. The way a man will say to himself, speaking of a dream: *I walked slowly along a simple dirt path toward this place of light.*

The food's good tonight, someone behind him said, it's chicken.

Before they'd reached the dining hall a man came over to speak with Schindler. Then Nadav was alone. He followed the flow inside.

There was a table in one corner, at the end of a row of tables. A boy leaned over it, talking to a woman who sat there next to a very young, dark-haired, dark-skinned girl. Then the boy glanced up and pointed at Nadav. Nadav looked briefly at first, avoiding her eyes. Just enough to see her and to know it was she, thick black hair falling past her ears. Even from far across the room her face was a tawny rose color that seemed to give off heat. He felt a hand on his shoulder and jumped a little. But it was Schindler, squeezing his shoulder and grinning in a hard, anxious way. Schindler waved at her. When she nodded in response he released Nadav's shoulder.

"So. There she is. Enjoy yourself, *old friend.*"

Nadav ignored him. Then Schindler drifted away somewhere and he was alone again, staring straight ahead at the only corner of the big, crowded, bright-lit room that mattered. Automatically he moved forward. The woman watched him approach but remained still.

"How are you, Miriam?"

He stretched out a hand.

Yes, there was a streak of gray in her hair. It was unnoticeable at first, streaming around the side in a single thin strip, fading before it reached full length. And she was still young, yes, but from a distance had appeared much younger. Close up, there were lines visible on her face, across the forehead, around the mouth. What he was fixated by, though, were her eyes: large and curving slightly up at the outer corners, shining blacker than two washed olives. They met his only briefly before darting to his neck, his chest, and finally his hand. He followed her gaze and realized with horror that he'd offered the maimed right hand. He shoved it in a pocket and quickly held out his left. But she didn't take it, only touched it briefly and withdrew, then looked steadily up at him again. Faintly, she nodded.

"Miriam, we never met. I'm Nadav. Shimoni's brother."

The dark eyes examined him. "Yes," she said, "of course, I saw you in photographs. Nadav. How are you." But it wasn't a question and invited no reply. She inclined her head toward the child sitting next to her. She was small, and actually very pretty. Her skin was darker than the average Moroccan's. Her hair was silky black, and fell short of her shoulders. The mouth was broad for a child, the lips full, dark eyes large and round. She was toying with a piece of tomato on her plate and didn't look up.

"My daughter Rana, Nadav. Look, Ranit. You remember Shimoni? Shimoni's brother is here."

The child glanced up then. It seemed, he thought, that she'd taken him in in one quick glance, and with a touch of scorn, before staring down at her plate again.

"Ranit." Miriam caressed her hair. "You want to say hello to Nadav?"

"No."

"But I want you to, sweet one. Say *peace, Nadav.*"

"Peace, Nadav."

He felt his cheeks redden. His own words came out with an attempted lightness that fell flat. "Peace, Rana. What's new?"

She shrugged. Then she squirmed quickly out of the chair and away from Miriam's caress, running off into the dining-hall crowd. At the other side of the room a metapelet caught her, lifted her in both arms and carried her to a table where only children sat. Nadav watched. He could see, from across the room, that the girl was struggling to get away. But he turned back to the woman. "Well, so, Miriam. What's new with you?"

"Nothing," she said. Her eyes flew over his face again with weary curiosity, a quick examination that left him feeling momentarily stripped to the bone. Then he was afraid.

Her eyes were more afraid, gleaming back at him. He thought for a moment she'd cry. She didn't. This surprised him. She bowed her head in a gesture almost of submission. But it wasn't him she was submitting to, it was something else, and he stood there looking down at her for what seemed many minutes, seeing her head bowed in gentle sorrow. What surprised him most was her silence. That, and his own complete ineptitude in the face of it. What he'd come for, he didn't know.

After a while she looked up.

"You ate something?"

"No."

"Please. Get some food for yourself. And please sit here if you want. I know you traveled—you traveled a long way."

Wind blew down from Mount Hermon. It whipped the pines and the sides of houses. Their walls were so thin you could hear cups rattle through them. You could hear coffee being poured, faucets gushing, people making love, and arguing, or sobbing. Sometimes a laugh would ring from several houses away. In that way it was just like Mayan Ha-Emek: there were no secrets here—at least, few thought there were. And it was here Miriam had come to, here she'd brought her child. He felt betrayed somehow, as if his whole way of life had denied him knowledge of her secret on purpose. A child. How was it possible that Shimoni hadn't told him? That some sort of rumor hadn't reached him? But the woman wasn't married. So whose child was she?

By now, she was asleep in the children's quarters. And Nadav drifted through Ramat Alon feeling exhausted, detached from the earth, following Miriam to her home. She'd invited him for tea after dinner. In the dark they walked, pine needles crunching like whispers underfoot, whispers punctuated by brief pauses during which the wind rapped trees and walls. Three wooden steps led up to her door. A single bulb, encased in frosted glass, was fixed above the door front and lit each step dull yellow. Inside, this light infused the room with a subtle glow. Nadav tried to make out her face in shadow. Then she switched on a lamp and he looked away.

He'd tried to catch her eyes several times during the silent meal of chicken and vegetables. Once, he'd glimpsed them through a haze of steam rising from her coffee cup. They'd returned his gaze with a sorrow so vehement he'd immediately stared down again. Now she motioned for him to sit, turned to the kitchenette to boil water for tea. She served it in glass cups with sugar, offering nothing else.

Once in a while Nadav spoke briefly, clumsily. He found he didn't have that much to say. He thought he'd come to talk about Shimon. Now he realized he couldn't even conjure up an image of his brother. It had been replaced by an image of Miriam's strange little daughter, and the question that burned his tongue most—*Whose daughter is she?*—was the one he would not ask. He mumbled things instead, told her a little about the funeral. About his brothers. About Mayan Ha-Emek, and being back in civilian life. Her questions were few and polite. Almost as inane, he thought, as his own talk. When really he'd have liked to tell her how haunted he was by death, how tired he had been of duty and of pain, how he'd wanted to share it with her somehow, thinking that she too must feel something of what he felt, must mourn the losses he mourned, would mirror the past for him in properly radiant colors. That she could not, and that he could say none of this, lent their conversation an air of strained apology and futile anticipation. She was still in a state of mild shock, he thought, from seeing him so unexpectedly—a man who, after all, she'd known only through photographs. Nadav was disappointed. Also, somehow, ashamed.

When their tea was finished they sat in silence. Nadav felt his own weariness and felt hers, too. And he felt himself to be oddly useless. Here, he'd done it, the thing he knew he'd feared all along: he'd come up to Ramat Alon and was sitting talking with Shimoni's woman. But Shimon was oddly absent from this place.

"You'll sleep in one of the volunteer's rooms?"

"No, it's okay. My things are back at the dining hall. I'll sleep on the grass, in my sleeping bag."

"You'll be okay?"

"I'll be okay."

"Good," she said, "I'm glad you came," but it wasn't true.

Then she took the empty glass cup from him and put it into the sink along with her own. She ran water. He watched her for a while in silence, until he realized she'd been at the little sink for a long time and was washing both cups feverishly, over and over again. Her shoulders were rigid, like a dam holding back a flood. Terror shot through him and he stood and quickly stepped to the door.

"I'll go now."

He knew she'd heard him even though she didn't respond. For an awful moment he waited, dreading that the dam would break, that it would happen before he got out the door and yet somehow willing it to happen because then, if only he had courage enough, he'd hold her. But the dam was rigid and the flood never came. He left.

He walked across the grass of Ramat Alon. Somewhere a shutter flapped in the wind. It was time for the night milking shift, and in the dairy cows groaned.

Whose is she, Miriam? Not Shimon's.

Well, whose?

To the north Mount Hermon loomed dark and silent, sending its chill creaking through all the trees below. He found his things just where he'd left them, outside the main doors to the dining hall. It occurred to him to spread his sleeping bag on the grass right there. But he slung everything over a shoulder and headed back toward the home of Miriam Sagrossa. He didn't know why. He didn't particularly want to be near there. He didn't even care if he saw her again. But every piece of ground he came across along the way proved somehow unworthy—too rocky, too hard, too soft, too low. And when he found himself in front of her place again, he was tired of walking and figured that sleeping there would be better than nothing.

He spread the sleeping bag. He sat and took off his boots, his socks and jacket and thick pullover.

The light above her door was off now. Her shades were drawn. Lamplight seeped through around their edges. He sat staring at the dim light for a while, nothing in his head but a dull pounding tiredness. When it got too cold he slipped completely into the sleeping bag, cradled his head on his knapsack. In a couple of minutes the lamp was turned off. All around him, homes were dark. Everyone was sleeping. There was no moon. Nothing but stars. He held his right hand in his left, rubbing it absent-mindedly.

A sound shattered the dark. It was a single cry, like a sob, ringing from behind closed doors. Not quite a sob, but a wail. Not quite a wail, but a terrible female sound that echoed harshly in the wind and was over as quickly as it had begun, a lament sprung from nowhere, ending abruptly. It made his flesh prickle. He recognized something in it, without reason, without knowledge. It was as real as blood, as ancient and inevitable as death itself, then gone.

Nadav lay without moving in the dark. He knew with sudden clarity that the sound was hers. And that she was beautiful, beautiful beyond what he'd imagined.

When he stopped trembling he slept, fingers still curled around his scarred right hand.

When Nadav told Schindler he'd like to stay a few days and work, Schindler nodded and said to come see him later. So Nadav took the morning off. He was surprised to see Miriam heading his way at lunch, and even more surprised when she offered to show him around.

She spoke little. A few facts were dropped here and there. The child was a problem. There had been something wrong with her emotionally since last year, no one was quite sure what. Not that she'd ever been quite like other children—she'd begun to walk much later than normal, begun to talk quite late too. Doctors had been consulted. There was a lot of traveling involved, to Tel Aviv, Jerusalem, Haifa, and a lot of tests had been taken. Results were inconclusive. But the girl was strange, and incapable of relating successfully to the other children.

Some time in the afternoon they wound up in one of the playrooms in the children's quarters. It was nap period. Miriam's daughter was the only one not sleeping. She'd dragged her blanket down the hallway with her, entered one of the bright-colored, toy-filled rooms, and when they found her she was sitting there alone surrounded by building blocks.

She glared up at him. Nadav crouched until their faces were level. "Hello, Ranit. What's new?"

There was an angry twitch of the nostrils. Then the lips trembled. Beyond that, nothing. Miriam knelt beside her and stroked her hair. The girl turned to her, suddenly softening. Miriam spoke then, gently teasing.

"Ranit, can you smile today?"

But she buried her dark head against Miriam's breasts, her shoulders trembling. Miriam sighed.

"Well, so, it's not a good day. It isn't easy to know, from one day to the next, what to expect." She put her arms around the child and squeezed with sad affection. "But on a good day, there's no child anywhere who's more enchanting. First they told me she was retarded, you know."

"Who told you?"

"Doctors. In Tel Aviv, and in Haifa. But then they said she was deaf. So they tested her hearing. All the tests! I can't tell you how terrible it was, all the time testing her here, testing her there, but the results came back, and her hearing is perfect. Then they said she was—I don't remember the word—she was *seized* by something, like a bad spirit—"

"Epileptic?"

"Yes! Like that. But it wasn't true. They tested her with their machines." She laughed sadly, stroked Rana's hair. "Tell me, you think that machines tell the truth?"

He sat cross-legged amid a circle of bright-colored blocks. "I don't know."

"I don't know either. But then—for the first time in a year—she began to talk again."

Rana yanked on her mother's hair. Warily she turned, still holding a dark strand in one little fist, glaring at Nadav, large eyes flooded with suspicion. Miriam kept both arms around her.

"Ranit, sweet one, you want to play? You want to play with Nadav?"

"No."

"But maybe you'll like it if you try." She nodded at an

azure-blue plastic stool, on the top of which were stacked wide colorful cards, and he reached for them. "Why don't you try?"

Nadav looked through the cards. They were picture cards of easily recognizable objects: dogs, trees, flowers, the sun, a smiling man, a smiling woman. He moved forward a little, held one out to her gently.

"What do you think, my friend? What's this?"

One by one, slowly, he went through them all. But she'd become vacant of expression, her little body still and silent. Once in a while she even seemed to doze for a few seconds, and Nadav could see her tilt slightly sideways, then right herself. He could understand why the doctors had thought of epilepsy. Petit mal maybe—he thought that was the term—but their own machines had proved them wrong.

"All right, Ranit." Miriam began to release her grip. "I'm going to let go now. I'm going to let go."

She did and the girl clutched wildly at the air, seemed for a moment to fall forward. As she did she collapsed against Nadav and gripped his right hand fiercely, clung with animal tenacity to his thumb, her eyes shut tight. Nadav felt sweat drip down his neck. But the child stood pressed against him, holding the hand. Now she opened her eyes. She poked curiously at the palm. She sniffed all three fingers like a puppy, seemed to examine them all closely and at great length, then began to make a high-pitched gurgling sound of fascination, surprise, and, if he guessed correctly, a kind of recognition. She placed her own palm over his, let it rest there. She examined the mismatched hands and seemed puzzled. Then she gripped his wrist and held up the maimed hand in triumph, excited.

"Look!"

Miriam paled.

"Look! Like *his* face."

Miriam closed her eyes in a sort of pain. But Rana continued to hold the hand up, pointing to it.

"It's like *him*, like *his* face." Then she seemed to panic. She turned to look at Nadav and dropped his hand. There was bewilderment in her eyes. "But it's not him. You're different.

Did they do the same thing to you, but only to your hand? Did they?"

He opened his mouth to say something, he didn't know what. But sweat was pouring from his upper lip and when he tried to speak no sound came out.

The child lost interest suddenly and wandered away. The slope of her shoulders seemed to him a little sorrowful. She sat abruptly in front of some toys on the floor and tilted to one side before sitting upright again. She stayed there then, unmoving, her back to Nadav and Miriam. Staring at the tiny back, he realized his shirt was drenched, realized everything about him smelled of fear.

"Ah," said Miriam, "I'm sorry."

"For what?"

She sighed. "I'll tell you the rest of the story. You want to hear it?"

He nodded. His panic was beginning to wane.

"Okay. When she began to talk again it was with the words of a child many years older, as if all this time she was listening to everyone, not saying a word, learning all the ways of adult speech in silence. But the things she said—ah, they were terrible things, awful stories she told, they were tales of horror and death, not just the make-believe of a child. So again the teachers consulted, again they took her for tests. They took her, this time, to the hospital in Jerusalem. And you know what the doctors there said? They said that she's brilliant. A genius. And also, they said—" she stared at him sadly, her mouth trembling—"psycho—psycho—something. I don't remember the word. It means that she's insane. That she believes the terrible dreams she has at night are *real.*"

"Psychotic," said Nadav, because he'd seen soldiers diagnosed the same.

"Yes," she said wearily, "yes, that's the word."

"And you, Miriam. What do you think?"

"I don't know." She covered her face and, crouching there, rocked slowly back and forth. Then she started to cry. "Please. Leave me alone."

He stood and walked from the playroom, down the bright hallway with murals of children and animals everywhere. The rest of the place seemed deserted. He found a kids' bathroom and went in. There was no lock on the door. The toilet was very low to the ground, the sink small, and he had to stoop to wash his face. He unbuttoned his shirt and peeled it from his skin. Then he hung it on a blunt-edged plastic wall hook. Half naked, he met his own eyes in the baby-sized mirror above the sink. His was essentially a tight, strong body, dark-skinned, dark-haired. It had walked more than eight hundred meters holding two severed fingers in the undamaged hand before collapsing. What was it he'd screamed on the way to the hospital? He was volunteering to go back right then and kill with one hand.

A thousand deaths, he'd yelled, *for them and all their brothers.*

Yes. Strange how it had come back to him now. It had flooded back like sheer pain the instant the child held his hand in hers.

Nadav stared at his eyes in the mirror. Arab eyes. A family trait—except for Michael. And, of course, the General.

He felt calmer now. He raised his right hand to wiggle the thumb and the stiff, pink forefinger. He turned the tap and washed his face. Then splashed cold water over his chest and arms and waited for it to dry.

Look! Like *his* face!

The other one!

Which other one, Ranit? Eyes screaming from the death mask—a soldier, my brother, or just a monster of your dreams—who is it, who? Tell me who it is. Maybe then we'll both go and find him. Because the truth's the truth and we must know it. Beyond a fire lies barren ground of ashes. Beyond the ashes, pain. Then a tunnel. Then the grief inside yourself. Then, maybe—should I even dare to think of it?—potency, love. A land of light.

But I won't even think of it.

He reached for his shirt and put it on. He felt suddenly quite weak. And wished he hadn't come up here, after all. Wished he hadn't promised the few days of work. Maybe he'd leave right now, walk several kilometers to the nearest bus stop and go back the way he'd come, all the way back to Mayan Ha-Emek. But his mind formed silent words that weren't even his. Until he heard himself say:

I will have her.

Heard himself say:

The things men want, fight for, die for—all those things I'll have. Land. A child. A woman. The light. I will have her. My Miriam, my dark, bright Miriam. My Miriam Sagrossa.

But he didn't really want her, he knew, he didn't want anybody any more, and glancing again in the mirror he laughed at the odd voice that wasn't his, then shrugged and smiled.

When he got back to the playroom Schindler was there.

Nadav watched from the doorway silently, something boiling to hot resentment in his belly as the man knelt protectively near Miriam. Rana was in a corner, her back turned to them all. But she was playing happily now with some building blocks, creating palacial structures and knocking them apart. Once in a while she sang snatches of a lullaby. The notes were high-pitched, like bird sounds.

"You're all right?" Schindler was asking solicitously.

Miriam nodded, her head about to touch his shoulder.

Nadav cleared his throat. They both glanced up in surprise. Then Schindler stood, his face slightly flushed. He grinned faintly at Nadav. But the eyes weren't smiling.

"So. It's you. Miriam's showing you the place?"

"Yes."

"You met Ranit?"

"We met."

"An unusual child, don't you think so?"

Nadav eyed him steadily. "I don't know."

Tension hung in the air. Then Schindler shrugged. His broad, flushed face took on a wry expression. "Listen, come to the General Office and see me before dinner. When you have a minute. We'll assign you to the apple orchard."

"Thanks, Yitzhak."

At the sound of his name Schindler blushed. But he flashed a joyless smile again, briefly, savagely.

"Don't mention it."

Then he seemed eager to leave, stepping quickly from the room, pushing past Nadav. Nadav stayed where he was, listening to the squeak of Schindler's shoes down the hall, listening to a door opening, sounds from outside come rushing in, then the door closing again, and behind all these other sounds was the rising, falling, birdlike one of Rana singing.

Miriam stood.

"I'm sorry I sent you away."

"It's okay."

"No," she said, absent-mindedly, "not really."

He knew then that she was listening to the singing voice of her daughter.

They spent some of the afternoon talking. A teacher came for Rana and managed to coax her away with the promise of candy. It was time, Miriam explained, for her play therapy. A psychologist from Haifa was there once each week. Several children had developed mild emotional disturbances or learning disabilities since the war. But Rana was by far the worst, the only one who never played with the others. It was because of the nightmares, she said tiredly, but beyond that would explain nothing and Nadav didn't ask.

Shimoni had liked Ramat Alon because it was small and new, she said. They'd investigated the possibility of living there. She laughed. He'd always liked the idea of *smallness*. The only way a community could remain close to its ideals, he'd said, was to limit its own size. And he'd sometimes spoken to her of leaving the army forever, to settle with her and the child on Ramat Alon. But he'd said that only in hours of despair.

"Despair?"

She nodded. "When he was tired. But he was often tired."

"He wanted to leave the army?"

"Very much."

"I don't believe you."

"It's true."

She showed him where they'd begun to dig for a fish pond. The digging had stopped—there'd been the war, of course, when everyone was evacuated and everything stopped. But she'd come to live here after that. In the summer, after Shimoni's death. After the man who knew about fish ponds had been killed in a battle near Rosh Ha-Nikrah. Another agricultural expert would have to be called in, and there hadn't yet been time to do this. She took him on a long walk to the apple orchard. They passed a small dairy, stepped out on a crumbling cliff to see the valley stretching away toward the Kineret. She pointed down at an area of plowed reddish field.

"They're putting in potatoes."

"Just this year?"

"Yes. And down there, that's the chicken coop."

Far off, he saw the buildings of a moshav. Beyond that more pines, then the green of the valley, the lake's mist. To the north were only spruce and air and mountains. Hermon. Lebanon. Tree branches on the farthest edge of the apple orchard brushed Syrian air. For a moment, looking north, he felt dizzy. He shook his head and cleared it.

"Tell me, Miriam, you like it here?"

"It's okay."

"You miss city life?"

"I miss *life.*" She smiled a little bitterly, and they were silent.

Something came to him on a breeze, dampness, the sound of running water. He sniffed the air and gave her a questioning look. She patted his shoulder tentatively. "Come. I'll show you something."

They walked uphill through groves of spruce, then down, passing grassy knolls crowned by saplings, granite cliffs, heading into sloping stretches of pine where the needles crunched gently underfoot and rivulets of sunlight shot across the ground.

It was a tiny stream, running over water-smoothed rocks and winding away downhill as far as he could see. Kneeling, she cupped water in her hands. When she bowed her head to drink, her hair fell over her face and her hands like a long dark curtain, faintly touched with gray. She glanced up at him. Her lips were wet.

"Drink. It's good."

He got on his knees, let the water run onto his hands. It was ice-cold. The raw-colored skin of his right hand tingled with pain, then went numb, but he forced the thumb to a curve and linked the three right fingers with all five fingers of his left hand in clumsy imitation of the cup she'd made, stooped down to fill the cup with water. Then he drank. It splashed on his shirt, froze his chest. He laughed.

"You know something? Gideon wouldn't choose us for his army."

"Gideon?"

"Sure. He marched all his men until they were dying of thirst, then led them to a river—or maybe it was God who made the river appear, I don't remember exactly. But for his army, Gideon chose only the men who got down on all fours and lapped at the water with their tongues, like dogs. They used to tell us this story in basic training. You know why?"

She was looking at him with an odd expression that he couldn't read. But she smiled, not bitterly this time, and shook her head. "Why?"

"Because for the war they were about to fight, the last thing he needed was men with table manners. He needed men who were desperate enough to forget about all the things of civilization and concentrate only on *survival*. He needed soldiers who felt close to the wild animal inside themselves."

Somewhere, a bird called. It was a frail sound, long and lonely. The rocks echoed it faintly, buried it slowly beneath the pine cones and the earth. Miriam shook her hands. Water sprayed his face and he licked some off.

"But you," she said, "you still remember your table manners."

"Well. Maybe I shouldn't fight wars."

"No?"

"Not for Gideon, anyway."

She led him up past the spot where the water bubbled out from underground, the land sloping up through rocks and trees to a large plateau. He saw that they'd circled around and come out at one end of the orchard. Beyond were the carpentry shop and repair garage. Then the tiny guardhouse. And beyond that the rest of the settlement living area. He'd had to work hard to climb and hike up here—it had been a long time, he realized, since he'd done any kind of really strenuous activity at all. It had been since before his stay in the hospital, months of idleness, sickness, pain that drained him in ways he hadn't even thought about, and now, standing there in the chill mountain wind, he felt how hollowed out he'd become and how far he had to go before all the hollow spaces would begin to be refilled. He realized, too, the source of the fear jetting through him: maybe all the spaces would never refill. And he'd walk through life this way, a dulled combination of apathy and pain, exhaustion, impotence. When she glanced up at him in concern, he felt suddenly old.

"You're all right?"

He nodded, wiped his face. "I became a little weak. From the hospital—" and he held up his right hand. "But tell me something."

"Yes."

"All that time you were with Shimoni. When he was away—he was away *most* of the time, yes? How did you feel, when he went away? Did you hate him for it?"

"*Hate* him?"

"Sure. Tell me, did you? I wondered about this a lot. I thought maybe you felt too much alone with him, and that's why—"

"Why what?" Her eyes were filling with tears.

"Why you didn't come. To the funeral."

Then he was sorry, terribly sorry, that he'd even thought to say it, and watching the tears drip silently along her cheeks he wished again he hadn't come, wished again he'd stayed at home, wished as he'd wished a thousand times that the world would leave him for dead. The tears dripped relentlessly across her face, into her voice. Her voice was trembling but the words were clear.

"Because I hate the *dead.* You understand? I loved a man who was *living.* I *hate* all the men who die. *Why shouldn't I?* You understand—you understand *any* of it? But tell me, that's why you came here? To ask me that?"

"*No,*" he said savagely, and heard his own voice shaking.

"No," she sobbed, "I didn't think so."

Then she was walking away quickly. She walked with her head bowed. Her arms were crossed over her chest. He turned and leaned against a plucked, gnarled apple tree, dizzy again, something pounding through his chest, alarmed at the violence swelling inside him.

He put his things in the little room he'd been assigned. Two beds were separated by a narrow space of floor. There was someone else there already, a pale, slender young man who introduced himself as Avner Galitzianer, adjusting the yarmulke held to his hair by a clip, some kind of tension narrowing the tiny eyes that, avoiding Nadav's, darted everywhere.

Galitzianer spoke with the cadence of a yeshiva boy, lapsing sometimes into Yiddishisms, which Nadav couldn't understand. His language was formal and a little archaic. Once, his eyes met Nadav's. Then he winced and turned even paler. But he spoke rapidly, as if anxious to get all the facts out of the way. He said he'd spent most of his childhood and adolescence on Ramat Alon, with his family, then gone into the army. But since the last war, he said, he hadn't been well. And he lived now in a hospital near Haifa. Once in a while he came back home to visit.

It didn't take Nadav long to figure out that the guy was emotionally disturbed. Schindler had given him a room with a lunatic. Nadav decided he could live with it for a short while. Galitzianer's bag was half open on one bed, underwear spilling through the broken zipper. Nadav threw his things on the other bed.

"Excuse me," said Galitzianer. "You're not religious?"

"No."

"Ah. Well, so, you'll forgive me—you see, I *am*. Religious, I mean—I mean, I am since the war. Religious. But let me explain: I mean religious in the ancient, in the *mystical* sense."

"Fine," said Nadav, and settled on his bed wearily, stretched out next to his things, one arm flung over his face.

Galitzianer chuckled. "I know!" he said suddenly. "You! Paratroops?"

Nadav glanced at him. "Yes, sure. How did you know?"

"Because I was there, too—"

"You?"

"Me? Yes, of course. I have a theory about the paratroops, my friend, a special theory. It's what I mean by *religion* in the ancient, the mystical sense. Commandos. Angels of the Name, blessed be He—we were His guardians. We were the *initiate*. You remember during basic training, your first night jump? You remember? I know you do—it's the kind of thing a man never forgets—we were the initiate, the special, chosen ones." Galitzianer slammed his palm against the side of the cot. The sudden sound made Nadav wince. "*And when we jumped, we fell. We fell*, my friend, like the soul of man."

Nadav sat up then and gazed at Galitzianer. Perspiration speckled the man's upper lip, making the pale, shaven skin shine like silver. The tiny eyes avoided his, darting everywhere like bird eyes gone out of focus.

"We were the *initiate*. The initiate must purify themselves. They must go through a cauldron of flame many times, they must put themselves through scalding hells, to stand in the fire of knowledge without wavering. Such things, we did. We were the initiate—you see? *God's soldiers!* We endured the crucible of fire. From which only the righteous can emerge. Does it remind you of something? Basic training, maybe?"

Galitzianer laughed. Nadav felt his stomach churn. The pale man glanced at him then, his mouth moving rhythmically like a goldfish feeding.

"You know the tale of the rabbi who entered the Palace of

Divine Knowledge before he was really ready? And his soul became scarred forever by the bright hot light of the truth he found there? And he emerged from the Palace of Divine Knowledge a madman, a man of evil? Tell me, my friend, you know this tale? The truth can make a man mad. Such was *my* initiation. I did my night jumps, friend—like you. Like others. Into the Lebanon. Over the Golan, into Syria. I saw the Other. Lucifer. I saw crushed wings of cherubim. School children dead in heaps from fire bombs—were they our bombs, or theirs? Do you know? Does anyone know any more? Children dead in heaps, in northern villages. Arab kids. Their hands were cut off. All of them. I saw a mountain of little hands next to the mountain of little bodies. All in the gray light of dawn. I wanted to die then, I wanted to poke my own eyes out—"

He'd begun to shudder all over. Watching, Nadav felt himself shuddering too. After a while Galitzianer began to do something strange: to move slowly, rhythmically, back and forth on the edge of his bed, as if at prayer. His tiny eyes shut. One frail hand moved gently to adjust his yarmulke. Afternoon sunlight faded from the window sill. A chill crept into the room, and Nadav wondered where the kerosene heater was, but realized he was sweating as he watched Galitzianer rock back and forth, back and forth. He wiped his face and stood. Then he headed for the dining hall even though he wasn't at all hungry, closing the door firmly behind him.

It was twilight, and cold. The members of Ramat Alon had set up waist-high lanterns along each path during one of the children's holidays. The lanterns were electric, bulbs shaped like miniature torches. They glowed a soft gold each night, illuminating the path to the dining hall in sporadic puddles of light. No one had ever bothered to take them down. Passing along the path, Nadav thought people were looking at him, a stranger with a maimed hand, somebody's brother from Mayan Ha-Emek. He passed from light pools into shadow, then into another bubble of gold again, feeling protected in darkness but exposed and judged in the light. It was a kind of gauntlet he was being subjected to, he thought. A way of testing any alien. Or of driving him away.

She was at a far table and the child was with her. He filled his plate, made his way there slowly, sat across from them. Rana had plucked every seed from a chunk of cucumber on her plate, piled them to one side and was busily stabbing the remains, over and over again, with a fork. He poured two cups of tea.

"Forgive me, Miriam. I was rude today."

"It's okay."

He thought that for a second she smiled. But the child tugged at her arm. She'd put down the fork and was looking at him with hatred.

"Tell him to go away."

"Ranit, no. I can't do that."

"Tell him. I hate him. I hate his hand."

"Be quiet."

Rana's face was wrinkling threateningly now. Nadav sensed a tantrum, sensed Miriam's helplessness.

"Tell him," Rana hissed, "it's like what happens at night."

"*What* happens?" he asked suddenly. She glared at him then, clinging to her mother's arm. But he could sense the threat of tantrum receding, and he spread both hands on the table now in full view. "Tell me about it."

"*He* comes." She stopped, glaring suspiciously.

"In your dream?"

"No. He really comes, walking. Out in the fields. But quietly. You can't hear him. Then he's there, where there's only the two of us, looking down at me."

"He looks down at you?"

"Sometimes he touches me, here—" she touched her cheek— "and here—" her hair. The touch was soft, he realized, and didn't seem to frighten her. "Or he carries me in his arms. He tells me not to make a sound. I don't. He has a red face—like your hand—a burned face—"

"*Burned?*"

"From the fire. And he tells me he'll come soon to take me

154

away with him. He tells me—" She stopped, her eyes suddenly vacant and shielded with a strange light.

"What, Ranit," he coaxed, "what does he tell you?"

The large eyes refocused. He saw the beginnings of a sneer settle around the corners of her mouth.

"Fuck you," she said, "that's a secret."

Then she threw a clot of cucumber seed at him. It landed on his shirt, dribbled between buttonholes to his chest. She'd run from the table before Miriam could hold her. Nadav reached for a wax-paper napkin. He mopped at the damp stain on his shirt futilely, wanted to sulk but found himself grinning instead as he turned to watch Rana race among tables, overturn a chair, elude the grasping hands of several metapelets before someone finally caught her, struggled with her, settled her firmly in place at one of the children's tables. Insane or not, she certainly could fight.

"An interesting dream, eh?"

Galitzianer slid his plate of food next to Nadav's. He'd materialized without a sound, and Nadav glanced up in surprise, saw Miriam do the same. But Galitzianer seemed cheerful now, his pallid face almost pleasant. He gave her a half-bow.

"Do you mind if I sit?"

"Please," she said.

His wrists were thin, the hair along his thin arms sparse and dark. Nadav noticed the leather-capped wristwatch. From the army, an excellent watch. Most guys never bothered returning them to supply—he'd kept one himself. Still, it was difficult for him to imagine this pale guy with the yarmulke enduring commando training. Galitzianer grinned and took a seat. When he spoke now, his voice and cadence were different, almost normal.

"So. My parents convinced me to stay a week. I heard we'll be picking apples together tomorrow, my friend."

"Fine," said Nadav. He poured more tea for Miriam. Galitzianer grabbed the pitcher then and filled his own cup, gulping it down immediately without waiting for it to cool.

"What did you think of that dream, eh?" He winked at Miriam, and Nadav wanted suddenly to crush his mad face beneath a boot. "The girl has quite an imagination. Or mental problems, maybe?"

Miriam looked steadily down at her untouched plate.

"No," Nadav said sharply. "No, I don't think so."

Staring back at him now, Galitzianer's eyes lit with interest. "You don't?"

"No, I don't." He heard himself speaking with a voice of great authority—a voice, he thought, that was surely not his own. "I don't think she's crazy. The rest of us—maybe we're crazy. Or *you*, for example." He gazed at Galitzianer with open dislike. "Maybe you're the craziest. Or the stupidest."

The guy chuckled softly. It was an unexpected sound. Now his eyes, too, had in them a strange twinkle of understanding. He blinked, embarrassed.

"Maybe you're right," he said quietly. And bowed his head at Miriam. "Anyway, accept my deepest apologies. I'm stupid sometimes, it's true. I offend people who don't deserve it."

After a while they softened. It was difficult, anyway, to hate him. He was so obviously unbalanced, and, after all, had suffered a lot. The three of them sat talking about annual fruit and dairy yield. Until Yitzhak Schindler joined them, sat next to Miriam, nodded at Galitzianer, flashed Nadav a smile filled with warning, like the gleam of a switchblade knife. Then the four of them ate in silence.

Nadav worked at Ramat Alon for more than a week, until Galitzianer's babble drove him crazy and he decided to leave. It was stupid, he thought, to stay there anyway. He'd done what he came to do. And the woman seemed ambivalent about having met him in the first place, so whether or not he'd done the right thing he guessed he'd never know. Aside from a few dinners and lunches together, he had no further contact with her. Whenever he ran into her—usually at dinner, on his way past one of the children's tables—Rana ignored him. And, for some reason, Schindler seemed a little relieved to know that he was leaving.

But it was all okay, Nadav told himself as he lay in bed his last night there, listening to the aggravating sound of Galitzianer snoring and sputtering in his sleep. It was okay, because he'd done what he'd set out to do: he'd come up here to meet Shimoni's woman. In doing so, he'd thought maybe he would come face to face with some kind of truth. But he realized that he hadn't come face to face with anything like that. Or, if he had, he hadn't recognized it as such. He'd only stumbled upon a situation that, like all situations in life, among people with their own grief, joy, loss, and trouble, was a complex one. One he wasn't really eager to involve himself with. Anyway, he hadn't even been invited to.

It was a chilly morning when he left, hoisting things onto his back and leaving from the dining hall. Maybe one of the pickups was heading for the road. Maybe he'd get a lift partway to a bus stop. He was going back where he belonged, to Mayan Ha-Emek. Yes. No matter what he'd told Rafi in some moment of false dreaming, Mayan Ha-Emek was his home—it was where he belonged, and he had no unknown woman to search for any more.

It was nearing the end of October. Back home they'd be short of men to harvest the grapefruit. And it was Michael's birthday soon, besides. Michael had mentioned something about coming home on leave around this time. Nadav wanted to see him again.

Still, he felt a little empty leaving that morning. The autumn chill whipped right through him. Or maybe it was just that he was still a stranger here—maybe that was the emptiness. He'd be glad to be on familiar ground again. It was early, and a lot of people weren't awake yet. He didn't look back at the little volunteer's shack where he'd spent the week. No one would be waving except Galitzianer.

On Leave

"YOU KICK YOURSELF OUT OF THE PLANE, LIKE THIS—" MICHAEL pushed himself back from the dining-hall table with both hands, allowed his chair to tilt precariously, then right itself— "and there you are, out in the air, the wind is screaming past you, it's completely black because it's night, and you're falling down, down, so fast you barely feel it. It's true what they say—you hardly know you're falling until you're nearly at the ground."

Intent young faces gazed back at him. Their forks were set on plates, their hands clenched the table in suspense. They were members of the same class, all of them seventeen. Next year they'd go into the army.

"That's why you have to count to yourself, very carefully. So you'll pull the cord on time. It's like this: you're falling through the night air, counting. Then suddenly you pull the cord, and for a second you feel it won't work, it can't *possibly* work. And then the miracle happens. The parachute opens. You're floating. But you keep counting. Because you want to curl up with your knees right against your chest, before you hit the ground. A lot of guys get hurt coming down. There are plenty of broken legs and knees and ankles, my friends, because they don't hit right and roll."

"Were you afraid?"

Michael smiled. "I don't know. My heart was pounding so hard it was all I felt. Then you feel—it's hard to describe! You feel excited, and alone, but still part of a great thing. Because there are other guys there too. It's black night. So you're together with them but still you jump out one by one. You're alone in a way, yet still part of a group of special men. And you *want* to jump. In that moment, you want it more than anything. You feel—"

"Afraid," said Nadav, coming up behind them and placing a hand on Michael's shoulder. A tray of food balanced on his other arm. He grinned down at his brother. "Afraid, but you don't want to admit it at the time."

Michael frowned. Then the pale eyes filled with warmth. "Nadav! Sit. Sit and talk."

"Okay, but not about night jumps. I'll be airsick."

Some of the kids sitting there laughed gently.

After dinner they went over to Michael's place so he could drop off his duffel bag. The room was dusty and barren, but a fresh pair of trousers and a clean-pressed work shirt were folded on the bed.

"I brought them over from the laundry this morning. We wear about the same size, yes?"

"Sure. But I'm okay in my uniform for now."

Nadav shrugged.

They went to his place then, stopping to say hello to people along the paths lined with stale autumn bushes. Inside, Nadav turned on the heater and lights and made coffee. Michael settled in an armchair, watching him.

"You look healthier these days."

"I'm okay."

"Your hand is healed?"

"Sure, as much as it ever will. Sometimes, though, I feel the lost fingers hurting. The doctors told me it's natural."

"Ah."

"Here's some cake. Yudit Spira made it—especially for little Michael, she said. So eat it, please."

Michael grinned and pulled off a piece with his fingers. He was licking prune filling from his hand when Nadav turned and sat near him, leaning forward almost conspiratorially.

"Rafi's going to America."

Michael paused, hand to mouth. Then swallowed and tore off another piece of cake. "Tell me something, Nadav. He's really queer? He likes men only?"

"For sex, yes. I think so."

"He married Jolie because he wanted to try it with a woman, then? Or he just wanted her to take him to America?"

"Maybe for both reasons."

Michael chewed cake slowly, meditatively. The coffee was beginning to heat and he sniffed the air with appreciation. Then gazed directly at Nadav, his blue eyes hardened.

"Well, so. Let him go. We don't need his kind."

Nadav sighed. "What kind do you think we need, Michael? Only the perfect, maybe? Only the brave? The ones who'll make more babies to populate development towns?" He settled back in his chair, a kind of desperation in his voice. "Do you ever think that maybe, just maybe, there will someday be a stop to all the wars? And that then, maybe—well, what do I know, really?—but maybe then we'll all have to sit down with each other, all the Jews, the religious, the socialists, the Moroccans and Americans and Europeans who came here to be part of a Jewish state, and we'll finally have to make peace among *ourselves*? So, who will there be to help us make such a peace then? Who, when we're all trained not for peace but for war?" The coffee bubbled with a light, insistent sound. Nadav shook his head. "But I'm not an educated man, really, so what do I know? Still, my mind is changing these days. What I think sometimes, now, is that we really do need *everyone*, we need that everyone should stay, especially the ones who don't fit in so well now, maybe! Because maybe *they're* the ones who will know how to be—I don't know—men of peace?" He stood, a little uncomfortable under his brother's intent gaze. "Well, so. I don't even know what I'm talking about. Forget it."

Nadav went to get the coffee. As he served it he noticed that Michael was staring at him cautiously, the blue eyes blank and round. Then he blinked, looking up at him with sudden affection.

"Nado, Nado, tell me—you're really okay?"

Nadav switched on the radio softly. The evening news was over and gentle pop melodies were playing. He sat again, took a few bitter sips before replying. Then sighed.

"Listen, Michael, I should tell you. I finally met her."

"Who?"

"Miriam Sagrossa."

He watched Michael's face for a sign of distaste or surprise, but there was none. "I went looking for her, actually. To Tel Aviv first. She wasn't there. She moved to Ramat Alon—"

"In the Golan."

"Yes. You knew?"

The white face blushed then, eyes sought an escape, but finally Michael set his coffee down and faced him fully.

"No," he said, "I never knew."

They were silent then. Nadav made more coffee.

Later, he walked Michael back to his place. Their breath blew white around them. At the door, Michael patted his shoulder. "Nado. You remember one time when Shimoni came home on leave with Uri? Uriel Lucero?"

Nadav nodded. He remembered the two of them: dark, handsome, strong, fresh from Officers School. Polite, well-formed young men with eyes too old for their faces. The girls had surrounded them like hungry, chirping birds. Uri Lucero had been Shimoni's best friend and fellow-cadet, the more smooth-featured of the two. Michael nodded too now, remembering. He squeezed Nadav's shoulder warmly.

"I knew then that that was the way I wanted to be—just like them. They were like two kings, Nadav, you remember?"

"Yes, sure."

"I thought then that if I could do the things they did, I'd be just like them someday. And I prayed—" In the dull outdoor light, Nadav thought that Michael blushed. But he wasn't sure. "I prayed to a god I didn't even believe in. *Let me grow to be such a man*, I said, *and I'll fight in your name forever.* You see, Nadav—it was everything I wanted. I knew it then." He faced Nadav and put both hands on his shoulders. For a moment, Nadav had the strange feeling that Michael wanted to kiss him. But the feeling passed and they just looked at each other, a little uncomfortably, with remote affection. "Well, so. Maybe I was just a stupid kid. I'm glad you went to see her, Nadav—Miriam Sagrossa, I mean—that's the truth. But I'll tell you, I'm not ready to talk about her yet. I don't understand certain things. I don't know why she didn't come to the funeral. Maybe women like her are dangerous in a way, you know? They lack loyalty."

"Well," said Nadav, "maybe."

"You'll come to see Mother tomorrow? Good. Because I have to leave after Shabbat, so maybe we can get a truck. You can drive me to Afula."

It wasn't Nadav who drove the next evening but Michael, heading carefully down to the main road, turning right for Afula. It had begun to drizzle, and when Nadav glanced at the rear-view mirror he saw headlights beaming hazily from the damp fog behind. Michael noticed them too, looked over once at Nadav and continued driving. The mirror kept reflecting two bright eyes of light, always behind, maintaining an identical pace.

"You think he wants something?"

"Who?"

Michael's chin jutted toward the mirror. "The guy behind us. What do you think? It looks like Arab plates, eh? Nazareth?"

"I can't see exactly."

Michael pulled to the side of the road. Behind, the beaming

headlights also pulled over. Amid the gentle swell of the drizzle they could hear another motor idling. Now, just behind them, the license plates could be seen: Nazareth plates, yes. An Arab's car.

Michael opened his door a little and turned to Nadav. There was an odd excitement in his eyes. In the shadow his face was split by a foreign grin, and when he spoke his voice was hoarse.

"Okay, Nado. Come and watch if you want."

Something rumbled inside Nadav, a strange kind of fear. But he felt himself move almost unwillingly. They both stepped from the car.

Through the fog Nadav watched a figure approach, could hear the scrape of shoes against pavement and roadside dirt. The man was young, dressed in trousers and a V-neck sweater. Was there a smile on his face? Nadav couldn't tell. He heard the man's voice then, a muted inquiry: flowing Hebrew with a distinct Arabic cadence.

"Excuse me, but your tailpipe's smoking. Engine trouble?"

With one motion Michael doubled him in half and broke his nose. Blood spurted darkly to the road. Fog covered it. The man collapsed on his side in a fetal position, moaning.

"Tell them!" hissed Michael. "Tell your friends and all their brothers!" He shoved a boot against the man's chest, stepped on it once, twice, then just stood there with hands on hips staring down. "You should stay inside after dark, my friend."

The man was silent then, breathing heavily. Something spread from his face to the roadside sand. Nadav stared at the fallen figure. Then found himself reaching, in slow motion, as if his body was not his own, reaching down with both hands to offer help. Michael grabbed his arm.

"Let's go. He'll be *fine.*"

Meekly then, like a child, Nadav allowed himself to be led back to the truck. Behind them they could hear the man move a little and moan. Dirt shifted. Maybe he'd eased himself to a sitting position. But before Nadav could turn to look he was in the truck again, the engine was still running, and Michael was in the driver's seat pressing the gas pedal until they sped back onto the road and through the night, the tag-along headlights left far behind.

"Bastards," spat Michael, "you can't trust a single one of them. *They* should be dead, my friend. *They* should be maimed. Not you. Not Shimoni."

No one should be maimed, Nadav thought. But fear froze his throat—was it fear of his own brother? Or of something in the night itself? He didn't know. He only knew that the spasms squeezing his belly were real. *No one should be maimed. A hand, a face—I know the life of the maimed, my friend. And I wish it on no one. Not even an enemy.* He said nothing.

They'd reached the bus station in Afula before his stomach calmed. But numbness gripped him now, a fumbling, mechanical numbness. It was the numbness, he thought later, and not his own will that allowed him to reach for Michael's hand before the right bus appeared. That allowed him to press the hand harshly, firmly, with his own undamaged left one, and wish him a safe trip back. Then he remembered Michael's birthday. Two days from now. His brother would be twenty years old.

"Happy birthday," he called after him, into the damp and fog. His voice echoed back to him meekly. He thought then that, from the line of people waiting to board the bus, Michael turned and smiled broadly, and waved.

Michael's Birthday

IN HIS CUBICLE OF A ROOM AT OFFICERS SCHOOL, MICHAEL SLEPT through midnight and the first day of November was over. The second day was his birthday. He'd been born just after 3:00 A.M. Maybe that was why his breath came quickly now as he slept, his eyes rolling wildly beneath the lids, dreams causing sweat to speckle his forehead. Sometimes he seemed to speak, lips moving, forming words that never sounded. Once, he moaned.

The second day of November had begun, and for a few hours spirits from Mayan Ha-Emek rummaged around in Michael, giving him uneasy dreams. He woke at three o'clock and sat in the dark, sweating and afraid. By instinct he reached for the bedside lamp and turned it on. Dull golden light illuminated part of the room. In a chair facing the bed sat his father, watching him, in full uniform. His chest was like a wall devoted to the hanging of medals, and when he breathed the medals rose and fell, glistening in the light.

"Sir?"

It had come out of his throat faintly. Michael calmed his breathing. He tried to calm the beating of his heart.

The General looked at his son. Their faces were similar,

European, pale-eyed. The way he looked now was the way his son would look, if he lived as long. He sighed. It was a short sigh, barely audible.

"Today is your birthday. Congratulations."

Michael pulled the blankets to his chest, wiped his forehead. "Thank you."

"Please. I remember when you were born. I was in conference, a sort of emergency meeting—well, never mind. A telephone call came. I was allowed to take the call, and that's when I learned I had another son. Congratulations, they all said. What do you think happened then?"

"Sir? I don't know."

"I continued with the business at hand. It was important. It took several hours to conclude. Many things were at stake— lives—but I shouldn't speak of this. Forgive me. Security regulations. Just after dawn that morning I got a car and a driver and ordered him to drive as fast as he could. We broke all speed limits, we almost crashed a dozen times—our people never learned to drive too well. I arrived at the hospital in Afula by late morning. You were early. They had you incubating under glass. Your face was bright red and your hands curled to little fists, you were sleeping, your lips sucked at the air, there was no hair on your head at all. Congratulations, the doctors said, he's a healthy little man. I saw your mother then. She was very tired—it was a difficult delivery for her, she suffered a lot of pain. I held her hand and sat by the side of her bed, but I don't think we spoke much. How's everything? she asked me. Fine, I said, you should sleep now, you're tired. When she fell asleep I still held her hand. It seemed necessary. I knew then, somehow—I think we both knew—that this was the last child for us. The nurses threw me out of the room soon and told me to go home, and one of them took me for another look at you in the little glass incubator. A real beauty, don't you think? she said. I didn't reply. Most parents think their infants are beautiful, but the truth is that a newborn is odd-looking, almost ugly. I was happy that day but inside me there was also a sadness. I can't explain it. You'll have children someday and you'll feel this sadness, too, and there will be nothing to do for it. I went downstairs to the first floor of the hospital and sat in a chair and fell asleep. When I woke up it was late afternoon already. The driver was still outside, waiting. He was hungry and thirsty. Duty makes men do strange things—some will be obedient even if it means their death. That's something I never want you to be. Always choose life, even if you must betray an order. Survival is your life's theme, you understand? When I woke up that afternoon I felt an aching in my throat. There were tears on my face. It was the first time I had cried in—I don't even remember how long—twenty years? More. So. That's what it was like for me, the day of your birth. The next day I went back to—never mind—to the place I was before. I didn't see you again for many months. Well. Just about now, it was, yes. The minute of your birth. Congratulations."

"Thank you. You look tired. You traveled a long way tonight?"

Outside, desert wind shrieked. Silence crackled between them. It was a long silence, not entirely comfortable, rimmed by the dim yellow light. Michael realized he could probably count the times he'd seen this man in the flesh. And never before on his birthday. Still, this was his father. The General. Sitting there, he seemed out of place, too big for the room, weighed down by the decorations tacked to his breast. And Michael wondered, vaguely, why he'd appeared in uniform. It was something the General rarely did. He always traveled incognito. The last time he'd appeared in uniform was at Shimoni's funeral. But he hadn't really seemed comfortable in it. Now his pale eyes met Michael's, unblinking. He didn't acknowledge the question.

"Today you're older. Old enough to be an officer. Maybe I know what you're thinking. You want to be a career man, too."

Michael nodded. Beneath the blankets, his legs were trembling.

"I thought so. Well, you're a man. Men do what they need to do. But some men need to do different things, too. Remember that. You'll be very strong, I know, they can make you into a killing machine, and you'll feel your own great power. But always remember that a single piece of tiny metal can end that power—you understand? So have respect for men who make other choices. Your brother Rafi, for instance. Or even, for instance, your enemy. I know it's hard to understand. Just remember it for now. The understanding will come later."

"Yes, sir."

"What I want to say to you now are some difficult things. Wait until you're older to understand. What I want you to remember is that your enemies, the ones you'll have to fight and kill, are not inhuman. They aren't monsters or vermin, but men—men who love deeply, who have passionate beliefs, who worship their gods with humility. They have loving wives and beautiful children who suffer terrible things in war. They're men like you. Like me."

The General sighed. Michael thought he'd heard a hoarseness in the sigh, the beginning of tears. But he realized he was mistaken. It was just the sound of wind. His father continued.

"You'll hate your enemy. This is unavoidable. It's even desirable sometimes. You shouldn't stop yourself, ever, from hating or from loving. Those are the feelings of a human being. You'll have to kill your enemy, and do a good job of it. But to kill your enemy, you must never forget his humanity, his similarity to yourself. Remember: never lose sight of the enormity of your crime. Because it is a crime, even though it's a necessary one—a crime of human enormity. Every war death is a murder. A soldier who fights becomes a murderer. That's the way it has to be. So. Only if you remember the enormity of committing murder can you remember the enormity of what you *protect* by committing murder: your own beliefs, your own gods, your own world and women and the children who come from the seed of your body. A soldier protects what he loves when he murders the enemy who wants to take it away. A soldier fights and kills to preserve the love inside him. I don't ask you to understand it now, but just to remember. Only if you remember can you remain a human being. Only if you remember can you remain a man. To kill instead of being killed is to save your people from extinction. Well. You're old enough to begin to live with these things. Maybe you're ready—you think so? Are you ready to begin?" The General looked at his son. Pale eyes burned back at him from the young face, lit with a deadly fire. He noted that the trembling of his son's legs had stopped. Like this, they stared at each other. Until the General smiled—a slash of white across the lined, rough-cut face—and slapped both hands down against the arms of the chair. "Good," he whispered finally. "Then begin." And, standing, bent to kiss the top of Michael's head.

They talked about a lot of things then. Michael relaxed. He sat up in bed while his father sat easily back in the chair, and heard his own voice ringing softly but surely, telling his father things he'd always wanted to tell him. Asking him questions, seeking advice. He had a few confessions to make.

Once, he'd struck an old man. A Hasid who'd scolded him in the streets of the Old City, months ago, when he'd gone to Jerusalem on leave.

It wouldn't have bothered him usually, but he was tired that day. When the spit flew his way Michael turned, hand automatically seeking his rifle grip. Then he'd looked with disgust and disbelief from the old Hasid to the glob of gray spit on his boot, and back. The old man's black overcoat swayed around his knees like a filthy robe. He was all black and white: the coat, the vest and hat, the scuffed shoes black, the thin socks he wore a dirty white, his face and hands pale, flabby, stark white like a plant denied sunlight, and his hair, too, was white. But when he grimaced and hissed his teeth were yellow.

"*Criminal.*"

Michael glanced down once more at the boot. Then at the Hasid again, but it wasn't the old man's face he saw now, only a speck of decay on one of the yellowed teeth.

"You spit at me?"

"Of course."

"Of course?"

"Tell me, my boy." A stark white hand curled, vaguely beckoning. "Why do you engage in criminal activities?"

Michael stepped nearer. Later he'd tell himself that he should have just shrugged and gone on his way. But he was so tired, the ancient cobblestones of the narrow street so shadowed and sad in the evening light—it had been as if a great weight planted itself on his chest, so that he had trouble breathing. The steps he took toward the old man were difficult ones. Something snarled up inside him and fought there, making his heart pound in a terrifying way. His hand gripped the rifle so hard that the skin hurt. But the old man was beckoning, yellow teeth displayed broadly in a grin that was half reprimand, half welcome.

"Tell me, my boy. Tell me why? You think the Holy One, blessed be the Name, meant you should dress up like the soldiers of the goyim? You think He meant you should become goyim in Palestine before He decides it's time to create again an Israel? Before He decides to gather the Righteous Ones before him, in the *real* Israel, at the End of Days?"

He was speaking partly in Hebrew, partly in Yiddish. Michael didn't understand it all. But the raw sense of it was clear. Still he approached slowly, trying hard to breathe. The glob of spit on his boot had seared a hole in his mind somehow. And something was escaping through the hole, he knew—but telling it all to his father, later, he had no real idea any longer of what it was he'd lost. He could only repeat, in a mildly astonished way:

"You spit on me."

"Tell me, tell me—you think it's right? You think what you're doing—dressing like the goyim, denying that Shabbat is sacred, going with all kinds of women—sure, I know what you soldiers do in your idle time, eating *trafe*, making Jews goyim in the eyes of the world, *in the eyes of the Holy One, even!* and forgetting the laws of the covenant, the promise every Jew made with Him—you think all this is good? You think the

Holy One, blessed be He, meant you should do all this? And call it *Israel?*"

The two upper front teeth in the old mouth were blunted, one cracked nearly to the gum. Michael was close enough to see. He could see the stains on each tooth, could smell them: an odor of decay, unwashed onions, meat ground to dead pulp. Maybe, above the mouth, was a pair of eyes flashing darkly, ironically amused at the ignorant young soldier approaching. Maybe the eyes were one more sign of life beaming from the ash-dead face. But he didn't look for them. He saw only the old mouth, heard the ring of disgust that came with the words, along with some strange kind of triumph. *You spit at me,* he wanted to tell the mouth, but the words wouldn't come any more. He stopped where he was, looking down at the man. He realized how tired he was. How very, very tired.

Maybe, he told his father that night, it had happened because he was so tired. He didn't really know.

"You're young," the old mouth said. "You're young, you're just a child. Listen—can I tell you something? Myself, I have two sons, thanks be to the Holy One, two men. Did they fight in your army of criminals? No! We made sure of that, we sent them to yeshivot in France, they did with their young lives what men are meant to do. What is that, you ask me? Well, to *study,* of course. Because that's what men are supposed to do. To study and to sing the name of the Lord *only.* To dance the Name, the Name alone, His only. *Not* to dance with the whores of Babylon. *Not* to sing with the voice of the goyim."

Something had cracked across Michael's eyes then, a stream of sparks that immediately vanished. Then he thought: *Shimoni.* And didn't know why. What was it Shimoni would have said now? And what would Shimoni do? But he didn't know. What had his brother been to him, anyway? More than ten years older, more a legend, maybe, than a flesh-and-blood brother, someone he rarely saw. A handsome man, they said. Strong and brawny and, when he walked, full of the sun. He was tanned, you could see the muscles move along his arms and legs. *He* was a man, not like this talking maggot before him now. A *man*, not a voice, not a row of decaying teeth, clothes stinking of unwashed flesh. What had his brother been to him, anyway? Well, a legend. And a man. A man with color in his flesh. With a smile. With a cock. A man who held guns and knew how to use them. Held women and knew how to please them. He'd led other men and known how to save them. He'd known when it was time to kill. And had he known, too, when it was time for him to die? Or had death just crept up on him one day in the form of fire, suddenly there, roaring and yet insidious as a sudden glob of spit, smearing the fine picture of his youth and manhood. Michael stared down at the jabbering mouth. Then he released his grip on the rifle and his shoulders sagged. What could you do, after all? The enemy wasn't only outside borders. It was inside too, in the cities, the temples—a festering core of ancient hysteria that could burn right through modern steel, send its tentacles of rust and decay shooting into everyone's soul. The mouth was spewing Yiddish, and he raised a hand as if it was some foreign object, then sent it slapping across the thin lips and yellow teeth so hard that the lips split and blood began to dribble. The old man shrieked, like a shocked animal. Then he cowered, shoulders rising up around his bleeding face. Michael hit him again.

"*You maggot. You Jew. Good men died for you.*"

Somewhere, water ran over cobblestones into a sewer.

"*You spit at me? You maggot. You Jew.*"

Then he was running, bumping into the wooden corners of canvas-covered market stalls, dodging a loose goat or chicken, heading deeper into the Old City, and all the time the image of the cowering old Hasid with red dripping across the yellow of his teeth spread through his system, a tiny core of nagging rot and self-hatred. He shouldn't have hit him, shouldn't have hit another Jew—and an old man, too. But the need to kill was welling up inside him. He wanted it desperately. For himself. For all he'd been through, or would go through. For Shimoni.

"*Good men die for you.*"

He stopped running and just walked quickly, words mumbling from his lips.

After a while he followed an Arab kid along the crooked sidewalks. The kid pushed an old wooden cart filled with goats' heads and sacks of figs. Smells came to him: sugared fruit, spices, dead flesh. The Old City stone was warm from a sun just vanishing. Shops were closing now, canopies tied over the open-air stalls. It was twilight, and he followed the rattling wooden wheels as they bounced on stone. The aroma of hashish came to him, smoked in basement cafés through hand-blown glass pipes.

Michael turned corners and skirted the Via Dolorosa. He passed through the Armenian Quarter. Small lamps glowed between shutters. He followed a tiny alley winding through rows of doorways. Blue doorways. Green doorways. Sacred colors to ward off the Evil Eye. Then doorways colored only drab. He stopped in front of one. Evening chill had settled. He gave three raps and waited. Three raps again. Then he gave the door an impatient rattle and stood there, still waiting, silent.

"What do you want?"

It was a woman's voice, sounding from the other side.

"I want to see Shara."

There was a pause. The words came back half Ladino, all petulance. "Listen, muy señor mío, already it's Shabbat. Que vergüenza! Go home to the mother of your children."

"I have no children," he called patiently, "and my mother is far away. I want to see Shara. Tell her, señora—tell her, por favor, that a friend is here. My brother sent me."

"Ah. Estimado señor. And cómo se llama?"

"Shimon."

Something echoed from streets away. He swayed slightly, his eyelids rolling down like dust down a hillside. Time compressed and expanded. Maybe he waited seconds, maybe hours. His knees quivered wearily. When the door opened he drifted in on a gust of evening wind, past curtains dividing rooms, past open rooms where lamps gleamed or candles flickered, and he was climbing worn stone stairs to the second floor before he actually felt the soft hand on his arm and turned to look at her face. It was a dark face, the eyes large and shaped like his mother's. Like Miriam Sagrossa's. Candle shadows shifted across her forehead. The cheeks and lips were utterly smooth.

She guided him through thick hanging curtains to a small room lit by a single white candle. The room had no windows. Her eyes examined him sadly.

Shimon. You're a soldier.

Yes.

And what do you want tonight?

Perhaps to sleep.

There was a bed with white sheets and a tapestried pillow. He sat on its edge. Candlelight shot grotesque shadows across the floor, the sheet, the pillow.

To sleep?

Maybe. I don't know. I kill men. It's my job.

Somewhere far off, a dog barked. Darkness jumped on the walls. She sat next to him, hand on his knee.

Kill?

With my bare hands, sometimes. Soldiers know how to do these things. Not once but many times. Many men. And I think of it often—

Yes. Digame, is it guilt you feel now? Or maybe regret?

No, no, not guilt, not regret. Only sadness. I feel it all around me. I feel it in my hands when I kill a man. Not guilt, or regret, but a sadness. The same sadness others feel. The sadness of the world. And I'm tired now—

Yes.

I'm so tired.

Lie down on the bed. Duerme. I'll tell you stories to make you dream. Our mothers are from the East. But our fathers wandered far, to the West, and when they returned they brought the blood of the West to us. In the West, men steal dreams and hide them from their children. Our people become lost there, without dreams, without God. God speaks to us in dreams. How does a Jew know God, if not in dreams? And East is the place of dreams.

Wax dripped to the clay candleholder. The flame sizzled and leaped, blue at its core.

Look at my eyes, Shara. What do you see?

I see fire in your eyes. Cold fire, devouring the earth. And death.

Still?

Wait. No. Now, only sadness.

Verdad?

Sí. And a weariness of things. Sleep now, little boy. I'll hold you while you dream.

Pulling her down beside him, he moved the folds of her blouse apart and rolled his face in soft brown belly. He breathed her flesh, sweat and perfume, grape wine. He slept with her breasts brushing the hair on his head, his mouth crushed against her belly.

Michael dreamed of stars. Constellations shot across the gentle dark flesh he breathed. He saw the sparkle of a million stars over bleak desert. Her breasts sheltered his ears. *Oye,* they whispered, *listen.* He listened to the dream, to his own feet crunching sand, looked up at the icy glitter above. Comets shot from his fingertips. He sprayed a ladder of comets across the sky. Then he stared up again, and what descended from darkness beyond the stars was a single figure, clothed in flame. His father.

Querido. Little boy.

Half awake, he sucked a dark nipple until it hardened in his mouth.

This is your first time?

There's money in my shirt. Take what you need.

Sometimes during the night he felt himself pause, glance at the wall and watch his own shadow there, larger than life, hunched like a moving spring over the shadow body of a woman. He smelled her and the sharper scent of himself. His thighs poured sweat, slipping against hers. The first time he was too urgent. He entered her with a heavy, desperate thrust that was suddenly broken, and then he was spilling everything into her with a long shudder of surprise, stifling the sounds that burst from his throat. But the second time was effortless.

The candle burned low, wax piled around the rim of the clay holder. He saw his shadow move with methodical grace against hers, against the sheet, the bed, the wall.

What a man. What a good man you are. My love. Querido. You're the best man ever. The best lover. Better than the others. Better than them all.

Better.

Better.

Yes.

He closed his eyes and imagined her dark hair streaked with gray. Her hair spread against the tapestried pillow, the dark strands become rivers, his fingers clutching at her strands suddenly in flame, the sky above them stars, beyond the stars a vast unyielding night. His hands were Shimoni's hands. Hers, the hands of Miriam Sagrossa.

Ah. Yes. Close now. Finish now. Finish now. Finish. I feel it.

No. No. Not yet.

Finish.

I'm the best, you understand? Better than them all. Better than my brother. I'm going to live.

My love.

I'm going to live, you understand? I don't want to die!

Finished.

I'm going to live.

When he came it was sweet and silent, almost controlled, a long, slow ecstasy. Sweat dripped to the bed. The candlelight shivered on the wall, raising larger shadows.

He slept on top of her, without thinking about whether she lied or not, took drugs, stole his money. Michael slept without dreaming this time. There was no more Shimoni, no more Miriam Sagrossa. No stars jetted along his spine. No sand crunched beneath his toes. There was no ladder of comets stretching up from the desert, no creature of fire descending.

In his bed at Officers School, he hunched into the blankets and couldn't meet his father's eyes. Embarrassment shook him.

How could he have told his father everything? There was something obscene about it all.

But the General sat quietly and didn't seem at all surprised. After a while, a faint smile touched his lips. Then he stood, motioning briefly at Michael.

"Come with me. It's time for us to go."

"Sir? To go where?"

"Hurry now." Impatiently, the General frowned. "There isn't much time."

Michael stood, naked. The blanket fell from him to the floor. For a moment he was ashamed. But the General didn't seem to notice. He held out a hand. Sparks shot from it and became long fingers of flame. Suddenly, in front of them, a ladder of flame formed. Michael saw that there was a ragged hole in the ceiling of his room through which the ladder stretched, burning. Through the hole he could see the desert sky, white stars glittering. When he held a hand to his own mouth in shock, he saw that his hand was burning too, everything radiating and sparking in a molten five-fingered torch. He tried to scream but no sound came out. Then, beyond his will, he was following his father. They were climbing the ladder of fire, breathing thickly in unbearable heat. He saw that his father had become the flame creature of his dream. That he himself—his entire body—had also become flame.

They climbed for minutes, then for hours. He lost track of time. He forgot that he was in agony, forgot that he was no longer breathing, just moving, up and up, a burning shadow. Around them the stars seemed very close—no longer shimmering lights, but raging orbs of white and red. Below stretched the desert. But as they ascended farther the desert receded, faded. Looking down he saw oceans, vast green stretches of rain forest, mountains, specks of gray that were cities. Then even those receded and the earth below was nothing but a bright floating globe, shooting a single tentacle of fire up into the heavens. On the ladder Michael swayed dizzily. His father caught his arm.

"Seven more steps, now. Just seven. Come with me."

Michael counted the steps. He let his father pull him up by the arm, felt his burning feet stumble over each rung of flame.

Then the ladder disappeared and they were in a large room. The walls were stark white. Around them, machinery whirred. Computer display screens lit with shifting lines of numbers and letters, codes flashing across each boxlike screen in red, green, auburn. They walked silently by rows of bright metal and plastic. The room stretched everywhere, the machinery ran automatically, and Michael was aware that all around them blinked the noiseless crimson lights of surveillance cameras.

He followed his father along one row of beeping, blinking machinery. At the end of the row sat a man, hunched over a computer screen, his back to them. He wore an olive-green uniform.

Approaching, Michael could see past his shoulder. Red lights blinked across the screen. He saw that the lights were numbers forming a circle. The circle was a clock with no hands. The numbers changed rapidly, clicking away seconds and milliseconds.

Without turning, the man spoke. His voice rang forcefully, a hollow baritone.

"It's you again."

"Yes," said the General.

"Well? What now? You brought me another one?"

"My youngest son."

"Ah. That's good. Wait a second, and I'll check the clock— his name is Michael, yes? And today is his birthday."

"That's correct."

"I never forget," sang the hollow voice. "Not the smallest detail."

Then they were silent while he touched keys, fed figures into the computer. The blood-red clock on the screen kept clicking numbers away. After a while it stopped and the numbers froze.

"Here it is," rang the voice. "The day of your birth. And the day of your death." The chair swiveled and he turned to face them. "Do you really want to know?"

Michael stepped back in panic, crushing against his father. The face he stared at was a mixture of ash and desert. The eyes were hollow, gaping black holes. The mouth grinned and displayed a vast darkness swirling with stars.

"*Do you?*" howled the voice. Then, above his head and all around, Michael heard a wild and horrible laughter.

He realized he wasn't standing any more but had sunk to his knees on the floor. He was bowing very low, his forehead brushing cold metal.

When Michael woke he was covered with sweat. His blanket had fallen to the floor.

It was early morning, and alarm clocks all along the corridor were beginning to sound. In the east, a white dawn spread. The bedside lamp was on, the notebook he'd been studying the evening before cracked open beside it. He took a few minutes to calm his breathing, dimly remembering that he'd had strange dreams. Then he remembered: today was his birthday. The second day of November.

Michael glanced once around the room, at the closed door, locked from the inside, the closed window. He was quite alone.

Cootie

THERE WERE THREE TELEPHONES ON MAYAN HA-EMEK. ONE IN THE General Office, one in a boothlike shed outside the clinic, which was midway between the General Office and the dining hall, and a third in the home of Namit Kinderbach. Namit's arthritis was so bad that sometimes her food was taken to her. The phone had been installed by general agreement. Her daughters, all married and living in Tel Aviv, called her several times a day, and no one begrudged her the special privilege.

When anyone else wanted to call somewhere outside the kibbutz, they used the phone near the clinic. This was the one that rang, too, whenever someone outside was trying to get through. When it rang, whoever happened to be passing by would pick it up. Private love affairs had thus become public knowledge. The best way to live on Mayan Ha-Emek was to have no secrets, or else to keep a secret buried so deep inside that even death would not release it.

Nadav headed for the phone one night during the second week of November. Sometimes the clouds overhead shifted, and a star showed through. The pointed tips of pine trees moved darkly against the sky. He'd pulled a sweater on over his shirt. Every night after work and dinner he showered, laid out fresh work clothes for the next morning. But tonight he'd shaved, too—meticulously—and carefully combed his hair. The clothes he'd put on were his good ones. Trousers that fit well. A tailored cotton shirt. Partway through the act of shaving, he'd grimaced at himself in the small circle of mirror hung on his wall. Lather and water dripped from the razor. It was ridiculous, he knew, to be grooming himself like this in the middle of the week. All for a phone call. But something fluttered like hummingbird wings in his knees, moaned at the walls of his belly. And for the first time since coming back from Ramat Alon, he began to feel alive in some way he hadn't before.

The shed was doorless and dark. He reached for the chain that activated the bulb, and light glowed suddenly. He stepped inside quickly, afraid that someone would see—although why he was afraid he didn't know. With his left hand, he fished a scrap of paper from his pocket. With the right thumb, he dialed.

There were signals, static, more signals. The phone at the other end was ringing. And ringing. Somewhere farther north, a telephone in a similar boothlike shed was jangling in the night, the sound obscured a little by mountain wind. He pressed the receiver between ear and shoulder, listening, waiting. He waited a long time. Then there was a click. Then a rush of sound, and a clatter—the receiver on the other end being dropped, maybe. Then scraping noises, and from far away, as if through a long funnel, the voice of a man.

"Yes?"

Nadav cleared his throat. "This is Ramat Alon?"

"Yes," said the faraway voice impatiently. The voice of a young man. "Yes, sure."

"Listen," Nadav said, and paused.

"*Yes?*"

"I want to speak to Miriam Sagrossa."

The line crackled. The voice on the other end was speaking, or not speaking—it was all obscured by static. Then the line cleared suddenly, the impatient voice came through more strongly, no longer so far away.

"Wait. Wait. She's not here now. They left for a few days."

For a moment, he panicked. But he pressed on, the hand on the receiver beginning to shudder. "She'll be back soon?"

"In a few days, I said. You want to give me a message to her? I'll write it down, I'll leave it for her—"

"Yes."

"So? Tell me." Static ravaged the next words. The connection was going bad again.

"No." His tongue was dry in his mouth. "Never mind."

"What?"

"No message!" Nadav shouted. "Nothing! Thank you, thank you very much. You understand? Thank you!" And he hung up, his shirt damp with sweat. He leaned against a wall.

"No!" he whispered savagely. "Nothing! Fine! Thank you *very much!*"

Passing by in the dark, Zeigler and Jolie heard him.

They hurried along.

There were times when you stopped to ask questions. This wasn't one of them. Something in the sound of Nadav's voice had sent ice ripping up Jolie's spine. It had been like stumbling into a long-hidden cache deep in the woods, or catching a glimpse of a raw thing exposed. Immediately, she and Zeigler picked up their pace and then began to run.

They ran past the dining hall, where lights were out, past rows of the little one- or two-room houses. Finally Zeigler stopped to bend over, gasping for breath. In dull light seeping from the corners of someone's window shades, Jolie saw that he was flushed and perspiring, his eyes narrowed with pain behind the thick lenses. She knelt and grabbed his arm. Somehow, it felt easier to touch him now than it had before. After a while he straightened, pulling her up with him. He put an arm around her shoulders and they walked together, clumsily, heading for his place.

"I'm too fat," he said.

"I know."

"I'll die all alone. Inside myself."

"No, no. No, you won't."

By the time they reached his place, he was breathing calmly. His short yellow hair was ruffled by the breeze, his glasses no longer misted. He went in and turned on a light, lit the burner for tea, put on a small pot filled with water. Then he crossed the room, got down on his hands and knees in front of the bed and searched, straining, under it. His body rolled over into folds as he bent forward, his shirt catching in the creases, bulging with contained flesh, and then he pulled something out from under the bed, a hard-covered book the size of a large atlas. He sat on the edge of the bed.

"I'll show you something. This was a gift to me."

"From whom?"

"A few months ago I was on reserve duty again. I did a favor for this guy, a major. He was a student of anthropology at Hebrew University. We produced for him a map that charted the migrations of certain Mongoloid tribes back in—never mind when, back before recorded history. He supplied the probable statistics. We asked the computers for their kind help, like we usually do, and ran everything over to the cartographer. It became everyone's favorite little project."

"Everyone?"

"Never mind. The thing is that we produced a map to set the world of maps on fire. The major was ecstatic. He'll use it for his doctoral field work, he said, and if he lives through the next war and actually manages to *go* to southern Africa to study Bushmen in the flesh, he'll write a great book on the subject and dedicate it to us. Thanks, we all told him, but it would be better for national security if you just dedicate it to the computers. All right, he said, no problem. He brought everyone presents. Mine was this book. You know what happened to him?"

"What?"

"He was driving to Haifa to visit his parents one night and ran into a stalled truck. So he went right through the windshield, he broke his neck, he died immediately. I don't know what happened to the map. Probably someone found it in a drawer of his desk and threw it out, or folded it up and stuck it in a box with his other notes. Who knows? Anyway, he gave me this book."

Jolie took it from him. It was heavy, the binding thick, the title embossed. *The Races of Man,* in English. She opened it, unexpectedly delighted to read from left to right again. The pages were high-quality glossy.

"It's a nice book, Avi."

"He was a nice guy."

She settled cross-legged next to him and flipped slowly through it. He glanced over once in a while. She knew he was taking much of it in at a glance—Zeigler's memory was photographic. There were pages of charts and illustrations, flat maps of the world with different bright colors splotched here and there to delineate regions where different races had settled in significant numbers. Mongoloid, Caucasoid, Negroid, then subgroups. There were subgroups of subgroups. Mixtures of everything. Mixtures of mixtures.

"Lots of Semites."

"Sure. Down here, his wonderful Bushmen. He *loved* the Bushmen. These people he never saw were the great passion of his life. He said that evolution never occurred in an orderly way. There were always different primate groups, or tribes, living at different levels of technological complexity—what we call *civilization.* See—" he reached over and flipped a few pages—"today, also, there are thousands of variations among men."

They gazed at photographs and color drawings. Women's necks elongated by spiraling collars of bone. Lips distended with inserted studs to the size of small plates. Semite, Hamite, Pygmy, Senegalese, Australo-Aboriginal, Malayan, Polynesian, Mongoloid-Negroid-Caucasoid, Bedouin, Undifferentiated Caucasoid, Northern Mongoloid, Ainu. The religions, the languages, the combinations and derivatives thereof. Maps exploded on each page in a multiplicity of color, a hundred varying keys explaining so much that they explained nothing. The complexity, the variety, was too much. Ultimately, what they described was a great, swirling chaos, pocked here and there with tiny pools of clarity.

Hindu, the keys read, Buddhist, Shinto-Buddhist, Taoist, Confucianist, Tibetan Buddhist, Muslim (Mohammedan), Shiite Muslim, Sunni Muslim, Christian, Christian (Catholic), Christian (Coptic), Christian (Undifferentiated Protestant), Eastern Orthodox, Undifferentiated Polytheist, Tribal Totemist, Aboriginal.

"See." Zeigler poked a thick finger at the page. "Israel."

"Where?"

"That little speck of blue there. For *Jewish.*" She looked closely. It was hard to find. There was so much else surrounding, spreading, intermingling. The land was a tiny dot in a turbulent sea of other colors.

"So," he said, "the prognosis is poor."

"Tell me something I don't know."

"Sure, okay. Just so you *know.*"

They looked at more text, more illustrations and graphs. The section on language was absurdly cluttered. There were thousands of dialects, uncounted variations in dialectal pronunciation, languages spoken by only a few isolated groups here and there: Germanic, Romanic, Slavic, Sino, and on and on. Urdu. Tamil. Gujarati. Arabic. Farsi. There were pages of alphabets. Letters stood nakedly in rows of other letters, stark and stripped of the forgotten appendages that once had ornamented them, given them their pictorial meaning, now distilled to single sounds.

"You know what they say: many ancient languages are sounds defined by gesture and tonal level, the words written as consonants without vowels. Sometimes the same word means opposite things. You derive the meaning from the context."

"*Who* says that, Avi?"

"Anthropologists. The linguistical anthropologists. Hebrew, for example, is written with consonants only, it's a very ancient language. Letters, numbers—these things are the raw material of real symbolism. It's similar to the beginnings of computer language."

The flicker of a smile moved his lips.

The colors clashed, blended, danced. She ran fingers across the face of each map and key. What was the sense of a word, anyway? Didn't each word have its own supposed meaning? But didn't real feeling constantly alter the real meaning of a word? And feeling was indicated, was modified, by tone and gesture. *No,* Nadav had said, *fine, thank you very much!* whispering bitterly to himself in a lighted shed in the Middle Eastern night, and the sound had been what spurred them to flee, not the words—the sound of pain, of solitude and desire.

Zeigler's hand was spread flat out against a page in front of her. The hand was flabby, the knuckles hidden by flesh. Tiny blond hairs glistened on the flesh. Suddenly there were tears in her eyes. Colors blurred on the page, mingled in the spaces between his fingers. She touched his hand gently, and bent down to kiss it.

Autumn was going to end soon and the cold, gray rains would come. Sasha Levy handed out tins of kerosene at the supply store, and for a pack of Marlboros he traded Jolie a new heater for her old one. When she blew him a kiss, he threw in a chocolate bar.

Flowers were withering all around. The dining-hall windows were closed often now, and the sounds of birds outside seemed more remote, their chirps a little plaintive. There was damp in the air.

Nadav kept to himself these days. Shlomo had transferred him to the sugar-beet fields. Jolie saw him, sometimes, at breakfast or dinner. Once, he stopped by her place to borrow coffee. He wasn't unfriendly so much as preoccupied, wrapped in a kind of gloom no one could penetrate, alone with his melancholy.

Zeigler kept to himself a lot, too. He'd gotten into the habit of taking long walks before sunrise, and again after dinner. You could see him panting up the road each morning to breakfast. Sometimes, at night, his white shirt glowed ghostlike in the dark.

"Exercise," he explained politely. "It's good for the heart."

One night he was at her door, winter coat thrown over his bulk and tailored material peeking through here and there. In his hand, the briefcase. He held out a key.

"I have to go again. So. Here. Listen to the records if you want. You can also study the anthropology book."

He looked pale and serious, and vaguely thinner. The customary sparkle of curiosity was gone from his eyes. In its place was a deep unhappiness. Jolie stood on tiptoe and lightly kissed his cheek. She watched him waddle off into the night, an enormous figure with bowed blond head. Later, after midnight, it rained.

Life on Mayan Ha-Emek dragged through late autumn, gray and chill. Kerosene fumes spewed from the slightly opened windows. And she missed Zeigler. She realized she believed almost religiously in the power of his mind. Sometimes, remembering talks they'd had, she thought she understood him a little, had glimpses of his capacity for knowledge. That ability to separate oneself from a thing and therefore study it, then absorb it totally, so that it was no longer separate but became a part of you. All this meant that, in a sense, you owned it—the only nonmaterialistic form of possession there was. Zeigler's knowledge built on knowledge, became theory and the application of theory, became computer language, the juggling of statistics into meaningful facts and probabilities—finally, the sending of men to different fronts of a war. His mind was an ever-expanding fund. It lent him a piece of the wheel of power that determined life and death. All the while, his investment in knowledge grew. It was the only really self-profiting venture a committed Labor Zionist would condone. When she curled under a blanket in the dark, she was surprised by what she missed. Not Rafi, or even America. It was reason she missed. It was Avi.

Some nights, though, she missed nothing. On these nights, it all seemed rather hopeless.

On other nights, Jolie thought about America. She knew that, although she'd been born and raised there, she had somehow never felt *American*. And, although she hadn't exactly been *lost* there, the truth of it was that she'd been *at a loss* there, one of those misfit kids at school, not pretty enough or well dressed enough, or enough in touch with current style, to climb the social pyramid constructed by her peers. As a result she'd been a real outcast for a while—like Avi, in a way—the butt of jokes.

There was a word her American classmates had for such a person: *cootie*. A cootie was a kind of untouchable, a creature whom boys would dare each other to kiss, who bounced from taunt to taunt in a closed universe of more fashionable beings. One year, in high school, a change of hairstyle and some involvement in sports finally elevated her from those lowly ranks. It had seemed bizarre to her, even at the time, that an elevation in rank would result from such relatively minor external changes. But she'd never really recovered a deep-rooted sense of self-esteem—from then on there was always this homely little girl inside her, displaying lack of confidence at the worst possible moments. She'd had neither money nor style. In America, even at a young age, those can be everything. At least that's what she'd learned, and it filled her with a faint nausea even now: the money of it, the style of it, the loneliness.

Sometimes, thinking of America, she had trouble distinguishing memories that were real from those imagined. Sometimes all of her past, until Israel, and Rafi, seemed a quivering mass of pain and brief flashes of light. Or of doors opening to the night air. Shopping malls with display windows, the colors too bright. And lights of cars, all the cars of America, bouncing endlessly along dark highways. The cruel words of others. Phone calls never made, kisses she'd never had.

She remembered, often, an incident that occurred at a local YMCA one summer where she'd worked teaching kids to swim. One of her private pupils was a seven-year-old named Al, a red-haired button of a boy who was severely autistic. He'd enter the water only if clinging to her like a baby monkey, arms and legs wrapped around, and if she tried to let go he'd scream. The screams had a horrible quality, animal, harsh, wailing, as if some insane gremlin inside him was pushing up through his throat. Jolie hated those screams of his. One afternoon she'd faced the lesson with particular dread. The solution to her dread, she'd decided, was to *make* him swim.

The pool had been deserted except for the two of them. Water lapped gently at the pool gutters with a sound that magnified and distorted into a chorus of wet sucking, then died. When they stepped down the ladder, she could feel his fingers dig deeper into her back. She could feel the weight of him lighten as water lapped around her thighs, then waist, and both of them were floating like mother and infant kangaroo, bouncing there, gently supported. Al was stiff with fear but silent, drooling onto her shoulder strap. Until she took a breath and pushed him away.

They were chest-deep in the cloudy, rippling false blue. He tore at her suit for a hold, pinching desperately as she danced away from him in the water with evil terror pounding through her. She heard his shrieks echo in the hot, damp air, and whispered with a hypnotic ferocity that frightened her because it did not even seem to come from her: *"Swim, goddamn you! Swim!"* and he dog-paddled a few yards to the metal ladder, screaming all the time. The act of self-sufficiency had momentarily destroyed him. He'd lost all faith in her. And she'd felt, in pushing him away, that she was tearing out something from inside, then letting the rest of herself disperse, transform, float away and vanish into that vast and thoughtless country.

Zeigler was at *miluim* a long time. When he came back winter had really begun, with its continual chill and rain.

He'd lost a lot of weight. He was still a fat man, no question about it, but there was less of the grotesque about him now. When he moved, the fat he carried seemed less solid. It looked like it was disintegrating. Still there, but disintegrating slowly, wobbly and unsure of itself now, or of its hold on him. And he seemed calmer somehow.

But there was in him, in his every gesture, a deep sadness. The eyes sparked less often. His repartee had a listless quality. Avi was a man on a diet. In place of food, he'd steeped himself in melancholy.

"Avi, you look good."

"Thanks. It's not true, really. Maybe I look better."

"You feel all right?"

"Sure."

"There's nothing wrong?"

"No."

He ate vegetables and tea for dinner, and every morning took a walk of several miles. Once Jolie woke long before dawn and heard someone passing by between the rows of little houses. Lifting the shade, she saw him. He was shuffling across the drenched, sparse grass, his winter jacket like a dark cloud around him, the false fur of the collar turned up to cover his ears.

Once she went for a predawn walk herself. It wasn't her custom. Maybe there was a seed of curiosity inside, maybe she was hoping to bump into him. It would have been an embarrassment to them both. But it never happened. What would she have said to him, anyway? Something about her past?

Maybe she'd have told him that some are born more vulnerable to hurt than others. This wasn't really anyone else's fault, she thought. Destiny was destiny, genetic or otherwise. Maybe, like Zeigler—for whatever the reason—she'd been born a little too sensitive. Old hurts stuck to her like scars. Recovery occurred slowly or not at all. Society had always bewildered her, and at parties back in America she'd stayed in corners clutching a beer can in one hand as if it would save her. Rafi had been the first for her. He had not been particularly good, or kind, but he'd been the first. The only.

Maybe she could have told him. Told him that love had passed her by, and she'd let it go.

Once, during a predawn walk, she poked her head around a dim corner and saw him in front of Nadav's place. He stood there in the starless dark, looking at the door. He motioned vaguely, as if to go up the steps. As if to knock. But he didn't. After a while he turned and walked quickly away. Jolie was surprised, watching, at the speed with which he moved. It was as if he was momentarily somebody else: not plodding, weird Zeigler, but a big stranger moving with deft force—someone foreign, and a little dangerous.

She ducked back around the corner of the supply store. There was no sign of dawn. Soon it began to rain again. She spent the day working through a haze of exhaustion, and came down with a cold that lasted two weeks. Zeigler had one, too. They spent evenings at her place, flipping through *The Races of Man*, sipping tea spiked with foul brown cough syrup he'd gotten at the clinic.

"Guess what I heard while I was away? They're going to put up a statue of Shimoni near Yad VaShem."

"A statue?"

"Yes. In bronze. Someone anonymous commissioned it, but they say whoever did must have a lot of diplomatic strings to pull, a lot of *proteczia*. So now we have another burden to bear with courage: the eternal bronzed memory of Shimoni Jesus Christ Kol."

"So, the truth comes out."

"What truth?"

She handed him tissue to blow his nose. On the burner, water steamed. "You didn't like him. Shimon, I mean."

"That's not true."

"No?"

"No. I'll have mine dark, with lemon, no sugar. Thanks. No, it's not true, not exactly. Shimoni wasn't to love or to hate. The truth is, my friend, that he was beyond all that."

"Beyond *what*?"

"Beyond mere *emotions*, mere human *opinion*. Listen, it's

hard to explain, especially to an American, but I'll tell you a story. When I was a kid, our whole class used to go on field trips, with the older boys acting as counselors. And I'm sure you can maybe guess that I wasn't exactly popular with the others. In fact, they hated me. Well, I'm not sure they *hated* me, but they treated me in a hateful way, because I'm fat—every day of my life I was constantly on guard, there wasn't any rest, not even at night. I was always a good one to play some practical joke on. I was like their court jester, someone to torture when you were bored. I'm not saying this in disgust, or anger, but it's true. Well, the older boys made some lackluster attempts to stop the others from teasing me. Some of them did, anyway, and the others just let it continue—except for Shimon. He was the only one who could really make them *stop*. And you know why?" He smiled wryly, a little painfully. "He told them that *real Jews* didn't act like that. He told them that *real Jews* were strong, and tolerant of other Jews. That real Jews, having a choice to speak an insult or to remain silent, would remain silent. That real Jews would fight anti-Semites and their other enemies, but would never fight each other. Oh, he said other things. I forget all he said—which is strange, because usually I remember everything. But he delivered it all, all these little rules of his about how a Jew should be a *real* Jew, like he was giving a very stern and solemn lecture. And you should have seen all of them then, how they shut up immediately, how they *listened*, like they would listen to God. He stood there in his little campfire circle, like this—" Avi got up from his chair, sneezed, and spread his arms like wings—"and delivered Shimoni's Sermon on the Mount. Really, I'm not lying. He had everything figured out. At such a young age—what was he, sixteen, seventeen? Yes, he did. How a Jew should be. How a man must behave. And the little imbeciles squatting there in a field, listening to him, they thought they were listening to Torah, they thought this stern, solemn, handsome young kid lecturing them was Moses himself, they were in awe of him because even without killing anybody or risking his life he was already their hero. He had charisma, I'll tell you. And he used it, he used it all the time. But you know what all his charisma was really composed of? It was composed of *his* looks and *their* awe, *their* adoration." Zeigler blushed, and sat. "*Ours.* Shimoni was a composite of all the little Jews who adored him. And why did any of us adore him? Because he was everything we were told a pioneering Zionist should be. In all the important ways, he suited the historical ideal. He was such a good speaker, so good-looking, he could think, he had courage. Physically, he was strong, mentally he was hard. He could endure a lot. He could work through difficult problems. All these are admirable qualities. But it wasn't really any of *his* qualities that gave him such charisma. It was what *we* gave him that mattered—our adoration. We told him he was a hero, so he went out and became one. Shimoni did only what he was *supposed* to do, he did exactly what everyone wanted him to do. We needed a new young hero, so he defined what a hero was and then stepped right into the role. There. I said it. A terrific act, really, but an act just the same. Who was the real man behind the hero? Shimon? Shimon *who?* Nobody knows, even though a lot of the little imbeciles probably *think* that they do. Maybe *he* knew, but I'm not even sure that he did. He was too governed by the momentum of what he'd started: the legend of Shimoni, Our Great Military Hero. The Fighting Jew. That's why I say he wasn't to love or to hate. What do you love or hate, but the role itself? It's what he was. He became the role. Love *him,* the man? Hate *him?* How can you, when all there is, is the hero. Shimon the man? He never existed."

Jolie leaned against the burner and jumped back, blisters rising on her hand. To one side of it, the teakettle whistled weakly. Tears of pain came to her eyes. She held her hand under a faucet, turned on cold water and felt it wash some of the pain away.

It wasn't true, what Zeigler was saying—no, she told herself, it couldn't be. Because she'd seen the man, sat close to him. There had been tired lines on his face. A handsome, weary young man in a country of weary young men, with strong, thick bones and thick black hair. Surprising eyes—cold, watchful eyes. But very real. He'd been an emphatic presence. She'd seen him. Smelled him. Maybe Zeigler just resented what his slim young manhood had been, envied him somehow, sought now to strip him of his mystique.

But she'd known *about* Shimoni, too, before ever seeing him. Maybe that had lent something extra to the encounter. Something illusory, something that had only to do with her, and not him. Had she expected a hero, therefore received one? She still would not talk—not to anyone—about that encounter.

The blisters whitened. She fought back tears. Maybe everything Avi said was true. Shimon had been a man playing a role, thus exceeding his own personal limitations because he'd *become* the role he played. And he'd existed, really, only in the act of being a hero. A performer. Like any fictional character's, his very presence suggested the absolute impossibility of really knowing him.

Or had he been something simple, really: just a man. Just a man who had taken part in wars, been pierced by weapons, bled, been broken, healed, loved, hated, been lonely, been decorated with medals of honor, died horribly, screaming a name, the name of a woman, of Miriam Sagrossa.

The laundry machines broke down one day that month, and things backed up. By the time they were repaired, a week's worth of the settlement's sheets, work clothes, underwear and diapers had gone unwashed and unfolded. The women began to put in overtime. Those who worked at other jobs volunteered an extra hour or so to the laundry, so for a few days the place was busy around the clock as women bent, tossed, folded and pressed into the dim hours of night and morning.

Jolie did her share. She was pleased when it turned out that Yael would also be working the same three-hour shift. She'd always liked her mother-in-law. Even though she saw her much less since her separation from Rafi, a benevolent feeling existed between them. She had the sense that Yael held nothing against her.

They worked for an hour in easy silence. After a while, Jolie was surprised to hear Yael laugh. Looking up from the clean-pressed sheets she was folding, she saw Yael staring at an old work shirt, one hand over her mouth to suppress the laughter. When Yael saw her looking she dropped her hand and smiled gently, then held up the shirt for Jolie to see. It was an ancient flannel thing, crisscrossed with stitching, buttons of many different sizes and colors lining its middle.

"My husband's shirt."

"Ah."

"He wore it thirty years ago. Now it belongs to everybody." She paused, scanned the shirt carefully, as if an examination might reveal something otherwise hidden. "The first time I ever saw him, he was wearing this shirt. I was in an immigration-absorption camp near Akko. My whole family was there. We came from Morocco. When we arrived, they told us we had to be deloused. My parents were so humiliated. It was a terrible experience for them; they felt they'd lost their honor. Later, though, I saw *him*. He was walking through the camp with some military people—soldiers, officers—they were looking for someone, a man they thought was a spy for the Arabs."

She placed the shirt on top of some unfolded clothes, smoothing it gently. Watching, Jolie felt a little like an intruder.

"Did they find him?" she blurted.

"Who?"

"The spy."

"Ah," said Yael, still smiling softly, "no. Between you and me—well, I think that the spy never even existed. But Gavi saw *me.*"

Gavi. It was a name Jolie'd never heard. Yael blushed then, violently, something in her eyes freezing for an instant. But she seemed to relax, the blush faded, and she nodded quietly, as if to herself.

"Yes, that's his first name. He uses his family name, always, in public life. My husband. He was very young then, but he had a hard face, like this—" her hands formed sternly around her jaw—"and those big eyes of his, very blue, like the sky, very pale. He could stare at someone with those eyes and make them do whatever he wanted them to do, just by looking. Like a magician." Then she shook her head and shrugged, folded the shirt, set it on a pile of other work shirts. When she spoke again her voice was tired. "Maybe it's good for my sons that he was away so much. I think that for a young man it's difficult to live with the reality of such a father. It was for them, I know—for all of them. Even Shimoni." Something dried her voice then and she was silent a while, busily folding other clothes. Jolie made herself busy too, and was careful not to look over at Yael, afraid she'd see tears dripping onto pressed flannel and cotton. But when she did look there were none, only Yael's tired face and busy hands, and when Yael spoke her words were clear. "But especially it was difficult for Rafi."

"Yes, it was. It *is*."

Yael turned to her. "Tell me. He's really going to America? I know he *says* he'll go. But with Rafi, well—" she sighed— "you know, what he says he'll do isn't always what he'll *do*."

"I know," said Jolie. "I know that."

"But you think this time he'll go, yes?"

Jolie blinked in surprise. The tears were in her own eyes—she didn't know why. Then she tried to speak but her voice was gone too, and finally she just nodded. Watching her, Yael's face softened.

"Ah. Forgive me."

"For what, Yael?"

"For asking stupid questions. It's not my business to know. I'm sorry."

"Don't be sorry, Yael. I'm the one who should ask forgiveness."

"You?" The dark eyebrows raised. "And why?"

"For marrying your son. Without knowing how to love him."

"But maybe he didn't know how to love you, too?"

"Well, yes."

"Then it's not for me to forgive. It's for both of you to forgive each other. Then, maybe, you'll love. Or maybe just be able to let each other go. Sometimes that's the best thing. Not that I know from personal experience, of course, you understand—although in the past I tried, I tried many times. But it's something I don't have the talent for—to forgive—to forgive *myself.* Or to release my hold on pain that's old, that I can't heal, and to say good-bye to old feelings that keep me awake at night. I don't let anyone or anything go, not in my heart. In this I know I'm not alone. It's a thing women do. But the world is the way it is, and people don't change either, and sometimes the only way to love someone is to leave him. Or to make him leave *you.* Yes. We meet and stay together for such a short time, anyway. Then it's over. Life, I mean. We're alone in our beginning, aren't we, and alone in our end."

Later that night, at Zeigler's place, Jolie told him a little of what Yael had said. Zeigler frowned. He sipped at his coffee, lips trembling a little in the haze of steam. The lips were getting thinner too, like the rest of him, and his face was in that stage of shedding fat that made it look almost malformed: lumpy here, slender there, skin suddenly unsupported and beginning to sag helplessly. It was shocking if you weren't used to it. In fact, he was becoming healthier all the time, but if you didn't know him you might have thought he was terminally ill. It was an undefined area, this transitional one of heading into or out of life. And now that his body was diminishing, becoming more like its own real frame, the only constant features were his eyes, twinkling small, shrewd and blue behind the thick lenses of his glasses. Staring at him through the rush of steam, Jolie had a sudden and surprising image of what he'd look like thin: a light-footed, nervous man, shooting sharp facts and vaguely cruel witticisms into the air of the world. This image was mildly alarming to her. But not altogether unpleasant.

Finally Zeigler looked at her. "Listen. No matter what Yael says, the General's a great leader. He made more important decisions in his career than anyone will ever know. He did a lot to unify the intelligence community in this country. That's not an easy job, you know, not in any country. You want something else? Something to eat, some bread maybe?"

"No, Avi, this is enough for me."

"If you want something, ask. He's a real phenomenon, the General. You know that there are maybe only one or two men alive who know his real name, or where he's really from? The family name, for instance—Kol. No one knows if it's the real one. Myself, I just assume it's *not*. And no one knows where he comes from, what country he really was born in. You don't believe me? It's true. Some say he wasn't born in Israel. Apart from his wife and his sons, he doesn't have any family here—not that any of us *know* about, anyway—there's only rumor. For instance, you know they say that he drove his own brother mad during an intelligence operation? And then he put him in an insane asylum somewhere—sure, that's what they say. But no one really knows. And there's no way to obtain information like that, I can tell you for a fact. Not even with a computer." Avi's voice cracked with excitement. His eyes were blazing through the coffee steam. "I remember times when some prime minister announced that they'd captured an important terrorist, or broken up a chain of espionage agents operating here—things you don't hear about on the news very much. But, *I* know, these are the *real* things that make governments collapse or endure. So the prime minister would announce it at a news conference. Around him would be his bodyguards, and maybe a couple of cabinet members. And behind him, in the shadow somewhere, dressed in a shabby suit and tie and wearing dark glasses so no one could see his face completely—that's where the General would be. *He* was the man responsible. Next to the prime minister he was the most important man in the country. Sometimes, maybe, more important."

The window was opened a crack, and through it you could hear the shriek of wind. Air blew damply inside, mingled with the kerosene fumes seeking an exit. As if by plan, both of them coughed simultaneously and waved the fumes away.

"Because," Avi said softly, "because he knew all the secrets. And the ones he didn't know, he knew how to find. They say his men would do anything for him. That they hated him, but they loved him too—you understand?"

She nodded uncertainly.

"For him, Israel was the world. There was nothing more important than the safety of the nation. You know what else they say about him? That he could step on his own mother's face for Israel."

Jolie had a brief, horrible vision of a boot planted squarely across some older woman's kind face. Tears filled her eyes. Then she shook with sudden, anguished laughter. Glancing up Zeigler smiled faintly, but the smile vanished. His eyes were alive with both pain and enthusiasm. And she realized then that what fascinated him most was the way men twisted themselves, of their own free will—the way they catalyzed the twisting of others. Zeigler gulped more coffee and sputtered.

"I burned my mouth."

"No. Let me get you some cold water."

She went to the narrow counter, found a smudged glass and filled it at the sink. Another image bloomed briefly inside her: she would stand there always, filling a glass with cold water, adrift in sensations of dim sorrow and comfort, and Avi would be there, too. The image didn't last long.

"Here. Drink."

"Okay. You're becoming more like a real Jew every day."

"One of the perils of war."

"Ah. I'm better now. Well, so, it's true—that's what they say about the General and I'm sure it's true. He's a man with one purpose in life: Israel. Like Ben Gurion. A hard man, without any sense of humor, but probably he doesn't have much to laugh about. Anyway, it's not such an easy thing to keep this nation safe from every other nation on earth. They say the General had something engraved on a bronze plaque and hung it on the wall of his office: *If it's good for the country, it's good.* 'Don't tell me about right and wrong,' he used to say, 'if it's necessary for Israel, there's no such thing as wrong.'"

"How do you know he said *that?*"

"I heard. Listen, tell me, what do you think? You think we

can afford to sit around worrying about morals *all* the time? We should worry because a few terrorists who slaughtered children get beat up sometimes in our jails? If this was Syria, you know what we'd tell an enemy in prison? 'Too bad, my friend, but we're stringing you up without a trial, and we'll let you rot there with a sign hung on you for all to see. You think you can get off easy with us, well, you're wrong. We're not soft like the *Israelis,* you know.' That's what we'd tell him. And the General, well, he knew what to do, he knew what our enemies understand: fear. He made them afraid. With him putting a little terror in their hearts, we had some good times in this country, we sometimes had months of real peace. Myself, I don't think it matters so much if *I* condone all his tactics. Whether I'm in agreement or not, I'm grateful to the man."

He set down his cup abruptly. Coffee spilled over the rim. The heater was burning low again and he rummaged in a corner for the kerosene can. When he filled it the heater sizzled as if it would die, then took on a bright orange glow and began to burn strong and hot. He stood in the center of the room, the can dangling from one hand. For a minute he seemed to be surveying everything: the few crowded bookshelves, the few records and the little stereo, the room bare of all else save necessities. Then he nodded emphatically, satisfied.

"He used to ride in a plain civilian car. But sometimes in an army vehicle. Then everyone could see him. It must have looked strange, don't you think? A little man in his shabby civilian clothes, wearing sunglasses, surrounded by generals in uniform. And probably he had the highest rank of all. Because he fought the wars of *intelligence,* the wars for the minds and deeds and loyalties of other men. And the proof that he won more often than he lost is that the country still exists today."

"Avi. You're planning to drink the kerosene?"

He looked down and blushed. Then turned and set the can in its corner. His shirt was too large for him now and flapped around his belt, frail cotton with not so much to fill it any more. He sat on the edge of the bed and leaned forward, as if to reach her.

"Most of the time, he wasn't here. He was in Jerusalem, or maybe somewhere else—who knows? But he was always busy with his work. I know he called for Yael once a week, while Nadav and the rest of us were growing up. Everybody knows. And I know also that he wrote letters sometimes to Shimon when Shimon was in school here. Nadav told me that. Once in a while, maybe a few times a year or less, he came to visit. Sometimes he didn't stay longer than a day. He usually came in a civilian car or else in a jeep, with officers driving. You understand, most officers have their own drivers, but *his* drivers were *officers*. And there would be a few others, bodyguards, assistants, men with security clearance. They'd stay the whole time he did. They'd examine the home before he entered it, and if he stayed for the night, they slept outside around the place. Yael would step over them on her way to work in the morning. But *sometimes*—the tiny blue eyes burned—"he showed up by himself. No one ever saw him coming. You sat down to eat dinner and he was suddenly there next to you, pushing the food around on his own plate—I never saw him eat much—waiting for his wife to appear. When she walked into the dining hall he immediately stood and nodded at her. Then she would come to sit next to him. And when you turned around, he was gone. No one ever saw him go, either. It's true. For a while you were sure you'd seen a spirit. Even me, I tell you, I'd believe in them just a little at the time. But you knew that *he* was real, and that he'd really been here, because everyone else saw him too. And Yael—her expressions never changed. She always looked the way she does now. You know, how do you say it in English? *Tragic.*"

Jolie wanted, then, to ask about Yael and Shlomo, but something stopped her. It was the wind, she thought. Its howls as it banged against the window and sides of the little home were like ghosts of animals long dead. Farther north was the Kineret, farther north still the Golan. From Zfat you could look down on the lake, on a night like this, and see it enveloped in a cloud of white mist. She felt open to the winter chill now. Images were spilling in through all the cracks in her. For a second she let them, and it felt then as if spirits spilled in too with the wind and momentarily possessed her, so she was filled with visions of blood and terror, then of good things also. But what made her pause, what brought a sweet stinging to her eyes, was this vision of the valley lake, blanketed in a cloud of itself.

"She went mad once." Zeigler's voice was soft. Waves of heated air wafted past them, recoiled and liquefied against the window. Jolie could hear her own voice, low as a whisper, drifting out in a way at once conspiratorial and dreamlike.

"I know."

He smiled gently, almost regretfully. "You hear all the rumors around here too, eh? It's unavoidable. Rafi told you?"

"Zvi Avineri told me."

"Zvi? Well, so, it's true. It happened after the birth of Michael. She wouldn't come out of her home. She stayed there all day and all night, and she made up new lyrics to go with some of her favorite folk tunes and sang them as loudly as she could, all day and all night, until her voice got hoarse, but still she sang. Those new lyrics of hers—they were horrible things for a woman to say. She sang about how she would cut all her insides out, her womb and her heart, and her sexual organs. Then she would leave all her insides on the floor, and with nothing inside her any more she would be light enough to fly out the window and join the spirits of her ancestors. And she sang about how when she was gone all the people of Mayan Ha-Emek would gather up her insides and clean off the blood, and an Orthodox rabbi would bless them—her organs, I mean—and then the people of Mayan Ha-Emek would sell them at an auction in Jerusalem. She sang about this, day and night, to the tune of pleasant folk melodies. People brought food to her but she wouldn't eat, and she refused to allow anyone in to clean up the food she didn't eat. So it began to pile up and rot in her home. After a few days only Shlomo would go near her. He talked to her in a kind way and tried to reason with her, but of course she didn't listen. I doubt that she even heard him. Anyway, the next day the General came, and he arranged for some doctors to give her medication. They took her to the hospital in Afula for two weeks. When she came back she was normal." He drained his cup with a quick, harsh gulp. "No more singing."

Zeigler stood abruptly and went over to the sink and cupboards, pulled out a plate and tossed some things on it, setting the coffee to boil again. He came back, handed the plate to Jolie. For a second she thought the plate was trembling.

"Here, have some cookies. Rivkah Fishbaum made them, they're her pride and joy. Just because I'm on a diet doesn't mean you can't eat. Eat. Please. I don't even want them. To tell you the truth, I don't even feel hungry any more—"

"Never?"

"Never. At first I was hungry all the time. I dreamed of food: chocolate bars, eggplant swimming in grease, stacks of bread loaves, with a knife waiting next to a mound of butter. But I think something happened to me, in here—" he pointed to his head—"and here—" to his chest—"because I never dream about food any more. And when I'm awake, I never want it. Maybe that's because I never *dream* about it, I'm not sure."

The platter balanced on her knees. Prune squares, an old Ashkenazi specialty. Pieces of crushed pecans poked here and there from the swirls of filling.

"What *do* you dream about?"

His face paled. He swallowed nervously. Then he adjusted the glasses sliding down his nose, shoving them back up with an impatient motion, and shrugged, a false grin spreading across the pallor. "Never mind."

"Ah," she said, teasing, "now I'm curious."

But he shook his head sadly, the grin gone. "No, it's not always good to be curious. Men like the General, they spend their lives being curious, discovering everybody else's secrets. The work is so crucial, they don't have time to really develop any secrets of their own. I mean that they don't have a personal life. The nation and their duty to her is everything. There was a lot of that in our great hero Shimoni, too. Men like him, they sleep with and eat with and live with Israel." He smiled faintly, a little mournfully. "I know the cabalists say that Israel is the wife of God. But she's not a mortal wife, is she? At least not for a man of flesh and blood. I think, sometimes, it's the greatest secret of the world."

"What is, Avi?"

"The thing they call the original sin."

"You mean eating from the tree of knowledge?"

He blushed. "No. Sex."

She smiled at him kindly, remembering what Nadav had told her about him. *Poor Avi,* he'd said, *he's still a virgin.* Well, maybe for a virgin sex *was* the greatest secret. But everyone had his own greatest secret, and she didn't for a minute believe that everyone's could possibly be the same.

"You mean you think the General didn't care about sex."

"The General?" He shrugged. "No. Well, maybe—I think maybe he was too busy most of the time. Such men are different from the rest of us in certain ways. Maybe he wasn't really interested. He's a man of destiny, though. It's too bad that his worst mistake will probably be his last."

"The war."

"Of course. There wasn't really any excuse for the failure of our intelligence then, was there? And we almost lost. So I think—well, I believe that when things settle down, this year, maybe at the very latest next year, he'll be forced to resign. Even though all the official government committees exonerated him. Even though he's the best head of military intelligence in our history, maybe even in the history of the world."

"You think so?"

He leaned forward intently. "I *know* it."

"They won't forgive him?"

He sighed. "We're not a forgiving people."

Then he took the plate of cookies from her knees and set it on the floor next to their empty cups. On the little stove, coffee boiled. The bitter scent of it and the bitter smell of kerosene were the evening's only warmth. Jolie wanted, suddenly, to curl up in the chair and sleep.

"And you, my friend." His face was close to hers. "What do you dream of?"

She shook her head, suddenly afraid because she didn't know. "Avi, that's *my* secret." Then fought back the fear, trying again to tease him. "Anyway, you still didn't tell me *your* dreams. Why don't you, if you're so curious about mine? Tell me what *you* dream of."

"Of you," he blurted, his small eyes narrowed and sad.

A Nasty Cut

ONCE A MONTH, EVERY WOMAN ON MAYAN HA-EMEK TOOK HER TURN prepping food in the dining-hall kitchen. The work began at 4:00 A.M. and consisted of peeling potatoes, plucking chickens, scaling fish, boiling eggs in enormous vats, and slicing old vegetables into other steaming vats to make soup. Namit Kinderbach had once been in charge of food prepping. Unlike most of the women, who were there for their once-a-month day of service and gone the next, she had had this rear part of the kitchen for her permanent domain. Some of the old-timers still told tales of the days when Namit had ruled it with steely resolve, ensuring that none would starve while at the same time boiling, mashing, and draining the taste from everything that fed them. She was such a dedicated worker and model Zionist that they all forgave her. They'd come, over the years, to view her in their hearts as a kind of Mother Nature, bountiful yet merciless. When she became too old to work full-time and her arthritis kept her housebound, the scepter passed to Levana Benvenisti. Slowly, some changes were made. New lights and ceiling panels were installed in place of the naked bulbs that had once protruded from cement. Sasha Levy was prevailed upon to fix all leaks. The worst of the bent and mangled utensils were discarded, and after much behind-the-scenes maneuvering by Levana herself, an allotment of funds for cookware was voted in at the general meeting. Over the course of years, the food itself began to retain a hint of flavor.

Retired, Namit Kinderbach received the reports of long-time friends, who occasionally acted as spies. More than once, when Shlomo paid her a visit, she complained bitterly. She accused Levana of using ginger and turmeric. She'd heard that dates were now chopped for cooking. If it was permitted to continue, she warned him, they would all be in the grip of heathens. The orientals were worse than the galitzianers. Worse, even, than the Arabs. Because at least you could count on the Arabs to betray you, but an Arab Jew you could not count on for anything.

Shlomo tried to calm her with reason. He pointed out that Levana's lineage was both ancient and glorious. Members of her family had lived in Palestine five centuries, and could trace themselves back much farther. The blood of royalty ran in their veins. But his reasoning had an effect opposite from what he'd intended. *Of course,* Namit snorted furiously, *they always think they're better.* Who? he asked futilely, knowing the answer before he heard it: *the Sephardim.*

He couldn't bring himself to reprimand her—she was too old and frail. And she'd been the one to feed him in a most essential way, too. In the ideals of the community, she was as much his mother as any woman of Mayan Ha-Emek, and biting his tongue he tried to believe that. But he left thinking black thoughts. He left thinking that the real dichotomy of the land he loved was not so much this business of Arabs and Israelis, or Muslims and Jews, as it was the chasm that loomed between East and West—and seemed, with contact, to grow ever wider. It wasn't just a difference in seasoning of foods, but in perception of time, honor, beauty, responsibility, life itself.

Hava Golinsky took after her mother, who'd left years ago. Red hair swung down past her shoulders, shielded her bold, freckled face. She'd grown up with Nadav, Zeigler, Zvi Avineri, and the others of their age group. Between most members of an age group, special bonds existed. It wasn't friendship so much as fraternity. They shared secrets. They'd been more important to each other, in many ways, than either a mother or a father. Their society was with one another. The future of Mayan Ha-Emek was with them—with all the children reared within the bright-colored muraled walls of the infants' and children's quarters—and they knew it. They were raised ideologically. Their existence was both restricted and pampered. Maybe that was why, when they became young men and women who in reality owned nothing, they acted as if they owned everything, everywhere. Many of them were strong and good-looking. Friendship was their group ideal, but if you did not fit the mold they could brutalize you for years. They understood sharing extremely well, and were magnificent at it. Tolerance of individual eccentricities, though, asked more of them than they knew how to give, and their answer was rejection. They were fiercely proud and fiercely repressed.

Apart from her friendships with Nadav and Zeigler, and the occasional necessary greeting, question, or response, Jolie had always steered clear of them. This worked to everyone's satisfaction. Silently, they tolerated her because—even though she'd been stupid enough to marry Rafi, then compounded the error by proving incapable of keeping him—she'd stayed during time of war. If any of them had questions about Jolie, they asked Nadav. But her friendship with Zeigler stigmatized her. They'd never learned quite how to take him. Still, after all the years of scorn and emotional torment they'd dealt him, they were proud of him, too, the way a father might be proud of his son's taking a terrible beating from him without whining. He'd been run through their gauntlet, and although obviously different could be considered worthy. But he was still too fat and too bright. Nowhere did he suit the norm. He was destined to remain apart from them always, using the misunderstood reaches of his brain to seal their destinies, or to save their lives if he could.

Hava shoved potato peels into a mound with one foot. She scraped without looking, miraculously avoiding injury. Jolie peeled too, tossing each skinless spud into a large metal pot. It was six in the morning and they'd been doing this for two hours. After a while Jolie began to copy Hava, scraping away in methodical, careless rhythm and pushing the peels into clean mounds at her feet. She was not as deft, though. Blood from a dozen tiny cuts swelled on her hand. The dark trickles met and crisscrossed, drying in a pattern like veins.

Around them women were peeling, cutting, plucking, throwing food into pans and vats and plastic containers, stacking eggs in refrigerators, laughing, talking in loud whispers, smearing their linen aprons with vegetable pulp, while in the background the morning news sounded from a portable radio in Hebrew, then Yiddish, then Ladino. Hava stared piercingly. Jolie felt it without looking up. Warning signals shot through her.

"So," Hava said finally, "you love him?"

"Who?"

"*Nadav. Nadav Kol.*"

Jolie cut her thumb but kept peeling. Answers occurred to her immediately. Just as immediately, she rejected the notion of an immediate reply. *No!* she could say, *We're only friends!* But that would have been taken as a denial of truth. Here, truth was in the unsaid. She could tell Hava to mind her own business, but that would have made her an enemy, and if all her traveling had taught Jolie nothing else, it had taught her that foreigners in small societies do well to avoid making enemies. Or she could reply, laughingly, *Yes! Of course!* But then Hava might assume that she held Nadav in low esteem. That she was treacherous, because she associated with someone whom secretly she did not take seriously. That she absolutely did not love him. And Jolie realized that wasn't the truth either.

On the other hand, there was peril in waiting too long to respond. Hava would think she had something to hide. And once anyone on Mayan Ha-Emek thought that, you never heard the end of it. So Jolie kept peeling and glanced up with what she hoped was a casual smile, cutting her thumb again. Then she shrugged.

"Do I love him? I don't know. He's a good man. But I never think about it."

Around them, activity had ceased. There was no clank of utensils, no sound of food plunking against metal or laughter hushed with loud whispers. There was only the radio, morning news in Ladino cut through now and then with static. Jolie saw Hava frown. But the frown changed to a sort of smile, her eyes narrowed. Jolie could sense the spin of her mind and, behind that, the spin of other minds meshing gears, pausing in a silent community of judgment. In the background, the news ended and a very Eastern melody began. It was a folk tune interwoven with reeds and tambourines and small hand drums. From some unseen corner of the kitchen came the voice of Levana Benvenisti, humming along. Then, very softly, the voice of Yael.

Hava nodded in a kind of approval.

"Well, so," she said softly, "why don't you know? But if you're smart, you'll forget about him and consider a real prospect—like Zeigler, maybe. Why not? Plenty of men are fat, but how many are smart like Avi? Not many. And everybody has to marry."

She winked. Then laughed. Almost immediately the usual sounds resumed. Spoons fell against aluminum tabletops. Eggs were stacked, a few dropped, and the mess of mashed yolks, feathers, fat, and vegetable parings mopped from the floor. In the outer kitchen breakfast had started. The smells of frying drifted back to them, mingled with the odors of the food they were preparing and preserving, the damp scent of water and blood, clothes, soup, hair, feathers, seeds, dead flesh, living flesh, the smell of citrus fruit, coffee, the smell of women.

Levana's voice twined with Yael's and both echoed faintly through the noise and clutter. Others started to hum too now and then. Sometimes they hummed different melodies, so there was a cacophony of contrasting tunes in the air.

"Nadav's right," said Hava. "You're okay. If you want, come over for tea tonight."

"Fine."

When Hava began humming a folk song she knew, Jolie hummed along for a while. Then she got tired of it and stopped. A second later Hava cut her thumb. It was a deep cut, and Levana shuffled over with the first-aid kit. Jolie held Hava's hand steady while Levana poured burning iodine on and swathed the thumb in an impressive bandage.

Hava's place was a riot of color. She'd decorated every piece of furniture with Bedouin tapestries. The wall hangings were all large framed prints, blazingly bright graphics done in abstract, linear style. She was proud of these, and a little shy. She'd done them herself. Also, there were arrangements of wildflowers everywhere: in vases on the coffee table, on kitchen shelves, on the top of her bookshelf. They gave off a dozen different aromas. Jolie found it a little unsettling.

"Your place is pretty, Hava."

"You like it? Good. Myself, I think most homes around here are boring. People don't know how to decorate—they're afraid to be different."

"You want help with the tea?"

"No! Sit!"

"The flowers—they're a hobby of yours?"

Hava was pouring tea, and through the kettle's steam Jolie thought she saw her blush slightly, pleased. Hava shrugged. "Yes, sure. You want sugar? No? Lemon? From the time I was a kid, I loved going out in the fields and gathering them. Our class went on a lot of hiking trips. Ask Nadav, he'll remember. Sometimes the older boys took us camping. Especially Shimoni—Shimon Kol, Nadav's brother, you knew him? Yes of course, you were here, I forgot. In high school he was a youth-camp leader. One summer we went all over the Jezreel and the Galil, we went down into the Judaean Hills, and near Jericho. You were in Jericho? You saw the ruins? All the old stones, they're bleached pure white by the sun. You know they say it's the oldest town in the world? It's true. I remember the way it looked that summer. White in the sun, and the shutters of all the Arabs' houses painted blue or green. They think those colors keep away the Evil Eye. It's an interesting place to visit. The honeysuckle grows wild there. Wild. All day you can smell it, all day, and all night." She handed Jolie a glass of tea with lemon. She was staring down at her own cup and the steam blew into her face. Jolie thought then that for some reason she'd cry. But she only looked up, her freckled skin damp with steam, a quiet smile on her lips. "Shimoni was very serious with us. He demanded obedience. We knew he was a leader even then. But also we knew that he loved us, so we didn't mind doing whatever he told us to do. He was full of information, he lectured us all the time on history and geography—this part of the valley, that part of the mountain, the flowers that grew, the battles that were fought. You see, already when he was so young, fifteen maybe, sixteen, he had a serious mind and heart. Even idiots felt it. For us, he was always a hero."

She gazed at some place on the wall beyond, her eyes misty with memory. Jolie wondered why she was suddenly privy to this information. Something nagged. The name. *Shimoni.* And she realized that for all the freshness and color, Hava's place seemed a little stale. It was like a kind of altar, or shrine. As if someone had just died.

Hava set her glass of tea down, rubbed her hands together. It was a clumsy gesture, limited by the large white bandage on her thumb. "You want to see photographs?"

"Sure."

"In America everyone has cameras, they all keep photograph albums, right?" She was rummaging through a drawer near her sofa bed.

"Some people do."

"And you?"

"Me? No."

Hava found what she was looking for and pulled it out, smoothing dust from the glossy brown cover. Jolie saw the album in sudden relief against one of the walls, a dark note in the frenetic, bright-colored room. Hava pulled a chair over close. "Here. I'll show you some of our field trips." She was flipping through pages sheathed in plastic. Then she stopped, staring. She kept the album on her lap and didn't offer it, gazing down at one page for a long time. Jolie waited silently. Finally Hava turned a page, settled the open album on the arms of their chairs so they could both see.

There's something impersonal about a black-and-white photograph, a no-nonsense, documentary quality that even the most intimate of them possess. For this reason, they seem sometimes to have the authority of fact. You may get the sense, looking at them, that what they show is what actually was—when, in fact, a photograph of what actually *was* is rare. Because people hold cameras, set them at a certain angle. People decide when the image will be frozen, and, more often than not, what image to freeze. A camera can be as subjective as any painting—a tool of extension, subjective as the person using it, an extension of a single pair of human eyes, as a computer is the extension of a mind. These black and whites before them, stiff and artless, were no different. Someone had decided what images to freeze for posterity. Hava had decided which ones would be preserved in her album. The pictures she showed were just that, then: pictures, carefully selected, maybe approximating truth, but then again maybe not.

Jolie saw gawky adolescents in black and white. Pale skin, dark skin, white brimless hats, work shirts, knee-length shorts, sandals. Some were smiling. Some seemed caught off guard, and their expressions were blank. Some made monstrous faces. Zeigler was unmistakable: pallid, obese, legs swelling out of his shorts, enormous white toes overflowing the edges of his sandals, and behind thick lenses his eyes had a tense, unhappy look. She recognized Zvi Avineri and a few others.

"There, that's Nadav."

"No!"

Hava laughed. "Yes, yes, believe me. He wasn't much of a beauty back then."

It was true. He'd been a little on the gangly side, large hands and feet awkward even at rest, hair curling messily around his ears, down his neck, his mouth broad and grim. His face hadn't yet fleshed out fully, so his nose looked misplaced there.

A group shot. All of them kneeling among some wildflowers, Mount Gilboa far behind. Nadav was glaring foolishly into the camera. The almond-shaped eyes had a faintly demented look. Adolescence. Jolie laughed, too.

"So, Hava, where are *you*?"

Hava's finger strayed, pointed. Jolie glanced sideways and saw that she was reluctant.

There were a few shots of her alone, kneeling in the grass or gathering flowers. Then a few of her with Zvi, and one with her between Zvi and Nadav, all of them linking arms. She'd been prettier in those days, Jolie thought. Maturity had solidified her features, giving a face that was otherwise attractive a flat, guarded look. Hava turned the page.

"Here. Here's Shimoni."

She said it eagerly, as if offering a gift.

Jolie could see that it was so. These shots were better than the ones preceding, more carefully framed, taken with greater cognizance of light and shadow. He'd been a handsome boy, anyway. At fifteen or sixteen the physical mold of the man he would become was already there—without pimples, baby fat, or adolescent clumsiness—it was as if the lines had existed all along and, with time, merely deepened, the form settling more firmly over the years. His face was smoother at sixteen, the nose slightly rounded at its tip. He was already shaving. His hair was dark and thick, curling like Nadav's, though neatly trimmed. But Nadav, a couple of years younger, had been tossed carelessly out of boyhood into painfully unformed limbo at a time when his older brother was already a man.

There were pictures of Shimon with the group, standing behind or to one side while they sat, and others of him alone. Always, he looked straight into the camera. In more than one shot he was squinting a little, as if trying to perceive something behind the flash of light, curious, yet conscious that it would elude him. In these, he had an expression of vague worry. A few lines creased his forehead.

Hava turned the page.

"Here. He gave these to me."

The pictures spread in front of them now were of nothing but Shimon—this an older Shimon: eighteen, in uniform, a new recruit.

Even from the first he'd been comfortable in uniform. It showed on his face. He was happy singing and marching with the others in basic training. He'd volunteered for paratroops.

Flushed with strength and exultation after successfully completing his first jump.

Stiff with pride, his beret donned just so, receiving commendation as outstanding cadet at Officers School.

In several of these photos he was standing next to another young officer—a man of striking appearance, smooth dark skin, enormous eyes, glistening straight black hair clipped short, and a broad smile that displayed rows of perfect white teeth. His features were well formed, almost delicate. He was Shimon's height but slimmer. Only the arms and hands were as muscular, the shadow on his clean-shaven cheeks less distinct. In one picture they'd each flung an arm around the other, comrade-style.

"Who's that?"

"Lucero," said Hava, "Uriel Lucero. They were in basic training together, also Officers School. They were best friends. A great soldier, Shimoni said, and a genius. He also was made lieutenant colonel."

Then Jolie remembered the name. "He died in the Golan."

"No." Hava looked at her sharply. "He was wounded there, a month before Shimoni. Later, in the hospital, they said, he died."

Jolie examined each photo. Both men beamed, vital and handsome, into the camera. They seemed so easily fond of each other. They were young, and in each picture it seemed to be spring. Hava turned the page.

This was another Shimon now, older and, in the midst of

cultivating a beard, unshaven. He wore civilian clothes: jeans and a work shirt. His left arm was in a cast to the shoulder. The opposite leg was in a cast, too, and he supported himself on one crutch.

"Before you were here—you remember the war before the last, just before you came? He was wounded in battle. They thought he'd lose the arm, but he didn't. They gave him many medals. Also a promotion. But they said he was fifty percent disabled, and they discharged him. So he left the hospital before he was supposed to. He went to the university in Jerusalem. You heard about this, maybe?"

Jolie had—again and again.

"He went to study philosophy. Everyone was afraid he'd get sick and lose the leg, too. He wouldn't rest. He walked with this crutch for months and months. He climbed stairs on one leg and carried his books on his back, and he did everything with one arm. Even his father was worried. They say he visited him in Jerusalem once and asked him to rest. But you know what Shimoni told him? 'All my life,' he told him, 'I wanted to be like you. Still I want it. So how can I rest?' And they say that when he heard that, the General cried. But nobody knows for sure."

Jolie stared hard at the photographs. He'd been changed by life, yes, but the basic form was still there. His long convalescence had given him a feverish look. The eyes were weary now. Hava turned the page.

Jolie swallowed the sudden lump in her throat. The photo gazing back at her now was the Shimoni she'd known. For a minute, she wanted to tell Hava all about it. Tell everything, all of it, to another woman. But she stopped herself, and was silent.

Suddenly Hava laughed. It was a sound choked off immediately, harsh and short.

"That beard of his! Always, he shaved it after a few weeks. We teased him when he came to visit. We told him he looked like a Hasid. He laughed. 'Sure,' he told us, 'and if I study a little harder, soon I'll be worthy enough to talk to God.' He was like that, you know—he wasn't *just* serious. Shimoni could laugh about things."

She turned another page. Suddenly the cast was gone from arm and leg. He was clean-shaven again, his hair very short. His jaw was squared, the tired eyes had a hard and determined look. And he was standing on two feet. Two strong arms were crossed against his chest.

"Here. You see? You know what he did—you heard? He began to rehabilitate himself. They said he was fifty percent disabled. But when the bandages came off he walked everywhere, and he lifted weights to make his arm stronger. So after many months he was as good as new. Then he left the university. Everyone was very upset. The professors all wanted him to continue studying, they said he was brilliant. But he volunteered again for paratroops."

And was accepted. Jolie'd heard all that, too. Again and again.

Before that he'd been a leader, even a hero. But he had not yet become a legend. Legend requires some sort of resurrection, and he had not achieved his yet.

His would be made up of the stuff of long months of rehabilitation, made up of all the stuff that had come before, pouring substance into the mold. Somewhere along the line, growing up, he'd committed himself irrevocably to the military. He would be a soldier. Rejoining was his final, fatal choice. He went to it with pain and knowledge. It was, he'd decided, his destiny.

But why?

Hava's fingers wandered. They caressed photographs as if touching him in the flesh: Shimoni here, Shimoni there. Shimoni in his uniform. Another promotion. And another. Advanced officers training. On extended study leave, again in Jerusalem. Out of uniform he had a rough, distracted look. The look Jolie remembered. Back in uniform he was weary again, but obviously at ease and in his element. And she remembered that look, too. Shimoni with the troops. With the tank corps. With a battalion. Shimon was growing older. Twenty-three, twenty-four. Twenty-five, twenty-six, twenty-seven. Twenty-eight—near the end of his life—though he did not know it.

Hava closed the album. It snapped shut almost silently, plastic page covers clinging together and compressing with a dull thud. She stroked the dark brown cover.

"Why don't you keep photographs?"

"I don't know. I don't always like to remember."

"Why? Maybe that's all you'll have in the end." She stared intently at Jolie for a second, as if trying to impart something. Then Jolie understood: Hava's reason for sharing all this was suddenly perfectly clear. What better confidante than an outsider who did not matter? What safer way to unburden yourself, certain that your secret would be kept?

She didn't for a minute resent it. In her own way Hava was bluntly, utterly honest. This was a world where everything had its place, and Jolie had hers. But Hava had hers, too. And hers demanded secrecy concerning certain things. Still, a human burden borne too long in silence turns in upon itself and rots, and the rot spreads to the bearer, and so without words she had told someone—someone barely better for her than no one—in an attempt to save herself.

"Everyone thought he'd marry that woman. Miriam Sa-grossa, that's her name. They were together a long time. But he didn't."

"No."

She tossed the album to the coffee table casually. It caused the glass teacups to jump. "Me, I'm going to get married in the spring. To David—you know him? No? David Yardeni, from Tel Yonah—we know each other since army days. Maybe you'll meet him. He's all right, a nice guy. Maybe he'll come here to live, or maybe I'll go there. I didn't decide yet." Her bandaged thumb tapped the chair arm slowly.

It occurred to Jolie that listening was her passport to Hava's hard, real world. Also, having a listener was Hava's ticket of escape from all the frantic fantasies engendered by that world, by the land, the wars, the sun and wind. In this community where nothing was owned, everything shared, where nothing was private, and there were no secrets, there existed a deep-rooted human contradiction that made the foundations shaky at times—at times, a lie.

And Jolie was an outsider now only to the extent that she belonged to it all, too. She lived here, ate here, worked here, had married and been deserted here, was considered, however peripherally, a part of the substance of things. And she had her own secrets here, too. About Rafi, and herself, and others.

About Shimoni.

What were they, anyway, she asked herself, but a collective of souls? Each soul carrying with it the burden of a secret, after all. Maybe the dark, sweet secret was pain. Maybe the dark sweet secret was love. And maybe in a way, without knowing it, Hava was a self-appointed committee of one, assigned to draw her closer to the core of things.

"Think about Zeigler." The bandaged thumb stopped tapping. "I've known him a long time—all of us have—he was born here, he's not so bad. And it's obvious that he loves you. Everyone can see it."

Before Jolie left she helped Hava put a new bandage on. The thumb was raw and swollen, a nasty cut.

A Recent Legend

IT WAS DECEMBER WHEN NADAV WENT BACK TO RAMAT ALON, THIS time on personal business. He had a few things of Shimoni's—letters, a book or two, even a couple of poems in rough draft scribbled across sheets of lined paper—he thought Miriam ought to have.

He'd called ahead. He didn't want to surprise her this time. For some reason, it had taken all his will power to place the call, and he'd tried to do so several times before actually succeeding. That it had been so difficult bothered him.

The trip was long: from Mayan Ha-Emek to Afula, then to Haifa, then up north past Zfat, and the farther north they got the colder it was. He was glad for the folds of his lined winter jacket, glad for the crowded warmth of the bus. And sorry to see how few remained on the bus after Zfat.

They wound up mountains with winter fields, pines and spruce spread out below, smoke from kerosene heaters spiraling out of the windows of settlement homes. He clutched the bundle of Shimoni's things closer, feeling isolated and a little afraid. Maybe being this far north brought back bad memories. It was in the north, after all, that he'd lost his fingers. In the north, too, where Shimon had been pinned under the tank and burnt to a piece of unrecognizable tissue that would soon die. For him, for his brother, the north had been the crux of the war they'd fought. One of them hadn't survived. The bus rattled as it forged up and up. One lived, one died. Nadav wondered why. Why he, and not Shimoni? How could he have been chosen somehow for life while Shimoni perished? Yet he was glad now, bitterly glad, for his own survival. Maimed or not, he'd accept it. And there was an odd guilt in that acceptance. Maybe he should have died, too. Or at least, honorably, wished for an honorable death. But he didn't.

He got to Ramat Alon in the evening and walked up from the main road, looking now and then for a lucky pickup truck to go by. None did. His face was whipped cold and raw by the time he turned up the settlement road. He stopped at the guardhouse and the guy inside waved him on after one weary look. Nadav was wearing gloves, and the fingers of the right one flopped uselessly in the wind. He'd hitched his small knapsack over the right shoulder, cradled the bundle of Shimoni's things close to him with his left hand and arm. He could feel the missing fingers tingle as he walked now, tiny jets of pain rippling through him. How strange that pain was so much in the brain, so little in the limbs. As if it was, all of it—pain, joy, life itself, maybe—an act of imagination.

The lights of the dining hall loomed ahead. He turned toward them and went inside. Warmth surrounded him. People looked up. A couple of them, remembering him from before, nodded.

She was sitting at a far table with Rana, Schindler, and a few others. When he narrowed his eyes a little, he could see that one of the others was that crazy guy, Galitzianer. It was Galitzianer who looked up first, then grinned wildly and waved at him with both hands. Nadav sighed. He could guess that, if he stayed a few days this time, he'd be put in the same room as Galitzianer again. When he saw Schindler look up and frown in anything but welcome, he knew what his fate here would be: constant little obstacles put in his path, to dissuade him from staying. Then he saw Miriam glance his way, meet his eyes and hold them for a moment. He thought he saw her smile. Thought that, in that moment, she'd been happy, really happy, to see him.

Another strange sensation rippled up him, firming his back and tired shoulders like a slender rod of steel. He realized with surprise that the sensation was hope. He hadn't felt anything like it for more than a year. In an instant the sensation spread through him and dissipated. But to feel it again, he knew, he would stay here longer than a few days. And Schindler could go to hell.

Miriam looked at him again from across the big room and smiled, openly this time. Then motioned for him to join them.

The days became a week, then longer. Nadav stayed on Ramat Alon, working with Galitzianer at odd jobs—pruning apple trees, washing old oil cans in the repair garage—and sharing a room with him at night. He ate his lunches and dinners at a table with Miriam, joined sometimes by Rana, or Galitzianer, or more often Schindler. Once or twice Miriam invited him over after dinner for tea. He found it easier to speak with her now. When she talked, it was sadly and anxiously, mostly about her daughter. Emotionally, the child was no better. The doctors were at a loss.

Working next to Galitzianer all day, every day, Nadav found himself becoming more tolerant of the man's ways. He was regaled with inside stories about life on the kibbutz, stories Galitzianer said he'd gotten from listening through the secret invisible antennas growing out of his head. One night during the third week of Nadav's stay Galitzianer invited him for a walk after dinner, saying he had something to show him. He led Nadav along the outskirts of Ramat Alon. He knew the place well, and walked with grace in the dark.

It was cold. The sky threatened rain and was starless, tinged with opaque gray. They headed in a northern direction for a while, their noses and fingertips growing numb in the wind.

As they walked, Galitzianer chuckled sometimes—a high-pitched sound ending on a husky note. It was a knowing sound, too, as if he always expected to be ironically amused by the follies of those around him. Nadav watched him reach down for a pine cone. As they continued he began to shred it meticulously, scale by scale.

"So. Our friend Schindler doesn't like you."

It struck Nadav as a personal question. And personal questions he answered rarely, even if asked by a member of Mayan Ha-Emek. But he managed a shrug. "Maybe not."

"*Maybe* not? Listen, my friend, don't tell me you're blind to the facts. Any idiot can see that he's itching to own her."

Signals of caution inched up Nadav's spine. He felt intruded on, and a little suspicious. Still, there was a yearning that went against the grain of all his reserve—an eagerness to discuss the matter with another man. To mention her name aloud, and dance for a while around the tiny bright flame of feeling that had begun to flicker inside him. *Miriam.* His tongue wanted desperately to utter it. *Miriam Sagrossa.* Then he blushed, and was glad the night hid it.

"Sure," he said coldly, "maybe he wants to do that."

"And you? Maybe you want to do that, too?"

They'd stopped in the middle of the trail leading back to the volunteers' quarters. Galitzianer was peering at him steadily. Nadav wanted to cuff his face. But the crazy eyes glittered knowingly from shadow, the rest of the features obscured. Nadav stared back. Then he shrugged. Galitzianer's sudden grin broke up the shadows, displayed his teeth, turned the hidden face into a buffoon's mask again. Then he shrugged too, almost in imitation. "Well, there I go again, asking you personal questions, behaving like a fool. Forgive me! I'm stupid—blurting out every idiotic thought I have—please forgive me, my friend. I like you, you know. Yes, really, I do. You look to me like an honest man, an intelligent guy, too. But, listen, your personal life should be your own, eh? In my ridiculous way, you know, I was about to compliment you. What I was really trying to say was this: From what I see, I think our friend

Schindler is a dog sniffing around the wrong skirt, you know what I mean? I think she doesn't care for him at all. You know how women are. She's only tolerating him."

"You think so?"

It had come out before he could stop it. He blushed again, utterly ashamed. Still, there was a tiny part of him waiting eagerly for Galitzianer's reply. And the little man grinned.

"Sure! Sure I think so. In fact, my friend, the only reason I don't say I *know* so is that I don't have it in writing. It's an old saying, you know: don't trust a man until it's in writing, and even then, don't trust him! Anyway, it's not my concern. But I wondered—"

"What?"

"What's your connection to the woman?"

Wind lifted pine needles in a flurry around them. The lamps up ahead swayed. And Nadav could have sworn that somewhere, far off, was the dim rumble of thunder. He stooped to pick a stalk of weed, crumpled it in his hand and kept pressing on it as if it were another one of the hard rubberized objects they'd given him back at the hospital during physical-therapy sessions. He saw Galitzianer glancing at the hand. Then heard his own voice sound with bitter calm.

"She was my older brother's woman. He died last spring."

"A shame. In the war? And the child—she's his, too?"

"Yes." For a moment, the lie chilled him.

"Forgive me." Galitzianer's voice was quiet now, with genuine sorrow. "I'm an idiot. Forgive me."

They headed uphill and off the trail, skirting trees, passing north of the orchard. Another cold gust blew. Nadav felt his hair lift from his forehead and fall again. His bitterness had faded to a kind of numbness. Galitzianer hung his head as they walked, his repentance so real that Nadav felt himself fill with forgiveness. Who was the little fool, anyway, to be worthy of his anger? Nothing. Just a young man gone mad with war.

"Listen, Avner," Nadav said kindly, "it's late. Where are you taking me?"

"To spy."

"To spy?"

"Sure." Galitzianer's face brightened immediately. "To spy on a recent legend."

"What are you talking about?"

It was thundering now, far off. The sky had grown lighter, become a dull grayish silver where it outlined trees. They were heading north on an uphill grade that leveled off, gave them a shadowy view of the apple orchard and, farther south, the chicken coop. To the west were the homes, the children's quarters, the volunteers' quarters, the nursery. Windows glowed with light. Farther down, in the valley, settlement lights studded the darkness in geometric patterns, clustered together like miniature constellations, dotted the way sparsely to the Kineret—which tonight was obscured by a thick dull cloud. The land stopped suddenly, fell off to a sloping, crumbling cliff that led to another small plateau below, then to shadows of more rocks, and more, and trees. Across the chasm was another rising wall of land. On its top a small light shone.

Nadav looked around, south, west. Everywhere, one light was accompanied by a tight bright cluster of other lights that shone almost identically. But this one light shone alone. A window light, yes, he was sure of it. Galitzianer pointed. But he didn't have to. Nadav's strong suit at Officers School had been his knack for noticing small things in a terrain, things a little out of place.

Wind fluttered his jacket collar. He noticed Galitzianer smiling at him with a sort of approval.

"You see it? The little light, to the north there?"

Nadav nodded.

"Good," said Galitzianer. "You know who lives there? Maybe you heard."

"Maybe I heard what?"

"Ah, you didn't. All right, so, I have the pleasure of telling you the great secret myself. One man lives there, alone. He was a soldier. If you listen to rumors around here—and who doesn't, eh?—they say he was an officer, and he was ranked high. And in the last war, they say, he was terribly maimed, he was disfigured, and they also say that he lost his mind. But he recovered. Well, he recovered a *little*. And when he was discharged, the government arranged to give him something in return for his years of courageous service. He asked for a house and some land, far away from other people. They did what they could. Nice of them, you think? To stick him here, near the border?"

Nadav stared at the solitary light. He thought, for a moment, that a dark shape had passed quickly in front of it. The wind froze his hands.

"What's his name?"

"No one knows."

"No one?"

The pale face grimaced briefly. "Maybe some military-intelligence boys know, eh? But maybe he *changed* his name, too, I wouldn't be surprised. That's the way those things often work, isn't it? I don't know myself. But I hear—I hear that's how they work."

"It's true?" Nadav blurted it suddenly. He could feel cold sweat on his forehead. "It's true? Or just rumor?"

"Who knows? Anyway, it's a good story, eh? You should ask someone, one of my old kibbutz comrades. In fact, ask *any*one, they'll all tell you the same thing. With a few embellishments here and there, of course, you know kibbutzniks, we thrive on gossip. And this is our greatest little secret."

Nadav's panic subsided and he wanted, again, to hit Galitzianer. But the guy wasn't looking at him—he was staring out at the little light, continuing pleasantly without a hint of shame. "My brother's kids brought me up here once to see. 'There it is!' they all told me, 'That's *his* house! The guy who had his face blown off!' They told me no one ever sees him up close, he won't let anybody near him. Sometimes when the kids are bored they borrow binoculars from the General Office and come up to try and catch a look. Me, I'm nothing but an overgrown kid at heart. But these are my own, of course."

From one deep pocket, Galitzianer pulled a small leather-cased pair of binoculars. He put his eyes to them, spent some time focusing. Nadav watched with revulsion. He could see Galitzianer's face in perfect profile. The lips were apart, the teeth clenched slightly, but from the side you couldn't tell if it was a grimace or a grin. The small binoculars looked like extensions of an insect's eyes. Then the ashen face swiveled to face Nadav. The binoculars remained pressed to his eyes. Below the metal and glass, his mouth twisted in a savage grin.

"Ah! I see *you* now."

He offered them to Nadav.

"Want a look?"

"You know what you are, Avner? You're a piece of shit."

The grin didn't change. "But you want a look anyway, don't you?" One frail hand held out the binoculars, unwavering. "Don't you?"

Later he would think it hadn't been he, really, reaching to seize the binoculars with his own maimed hand. It wasn't he, he'd think, it couldn't have been—he wasn't the man who'd pressed his eyes to both lenses in a cloud of self-disgust and pity. It wasn't he, focusing on that solitary little light across the chasm of stone, seeing now, against the enlarged background of lamplight, the slender figure of a man standing, bending forward from the waist until his upper body had vanished from the window frame, then standing straight again, and again bending, over and over in a rhythmic motion. His head and face and shoulders and neck were covered by something—a sheet, Nadav thought at first. Then he realized it was a shawl, a white tasseled shawl, a prayer shawl. The man was praying. He was praying with a graceful, weaving motion, ghostlike against the light.

It started to rain.

Nadav dropped the binoculars. Water splattered his hair and back and he crushed the instrument methodically beneath the soles of his work boots, grinding them into the earth as if to grind out his own mind, his own sight. His vision of that unnamed, ruined man, praying alone in the night. The rain came down with force and he kept grinding until the sound of splintered glass was deadened by the slop of his soles in mud.

Galitzianer watched with a sorrowful gaze. Then he reached gently to touch Nadav's shoulder. Nadav recoiled. When he glanced up he saw a completely different expression flash across the little man's face, one that was sober, intelligent, deadly serious. Then the expression changed to stupid glee again. Galitzianer let his hand fall.

"What do you think, my friend? Such a man as *that*—" he motioned at the solitary light glowing from across the wadi— "is good material for nightmares, right?"

Rain dribbled into Nadav's eyes. He stared hard at Galitzianer and saw someone different again. Then he was afraid. And Galitzianer smiled.

"Tell me, Nadav. What do *you* think?"

Thunder growled from the north. The force of the rain increased and wind swirled around them, bringing with it a smell of apples crushed in bark and earth. Nadav felt immobilized, drenched with the weight of the skies. Water made both their faces shine in the night's strange silvery light. He stared at Galitzianer and his eyes narrowed.

"You piece of shit. You yid. Who do you think you are, to say such things?"

But the little man only looked back at him, mute.

Nadav turned and walked. He headed for the settlement as quickly as he could without running. Chilly water clung to his bones. He headed for the clustered pool of lights flickering between trees, stumbled over rocks and small potholes, unfamiliar with this place, wishing that he'd never come back. He paused sometimes, heart thumping like a kettledrum in his chest, and listened. He listened for the sound of footsteps behind. None came. So he kept going, wanting to be home, to be safe, to curl up into himself and forget about it all. He could feel his jaw tremble, as if his teeth were chattering.

Galitzianer never showed up in the room that night. The next day Nadav wandered in after breakfast to find the other bed neatly stripped, blankets folded precisely on top of the mattress. Galitzianer's bag was gone, so were his shoes. The place didn't even smell of him any more.

When he inquired at lunch, he was told that Avner had shown up at his brother's place the night before, sobbing and drenched to the bone, crying for his medication. He'd kept people awake all night. Before dawn, they'd driven him back to the hospital near Haifa.

Nadav looked for Miriam that afternoon. It was raining again, and cold, but beneath his coat he kept sweating. His legs were trembling in a kind of panic. He found her in the laundry folding sheets. When he leaned into the room all the women fell silent, looking first at him, then at her, then back at their work.

"Miriam."

She glanced up briefly but said nothing.

"Miriam, I came to say good-bye."

The words fell dully, surprising him—he hadn't known, until that moment, that he'd leave. *Coward*, he told himself silently, *coward, coward*. She kept folding sheets in perfect white rectangles, and didn't look up again.

"Fine," she said, "good-bye."

Her voice was bitter. He stood there, willing her to look at him once more. But she wouldn't. So he walked back through the rain. He stopped off at the secretary's office to let them know he was going. Then went to his room, gathered up his things and left.

Zeigler's Computers

WALKING UP THE DIRT ROAD TO MAYAN HA-EMEK THAT NIGHT, Nadav was certain for a while that he was going mad. Every time he glanced to the west he saw traces of smoke against the dark sky. He could smell ashes, could sense the heat of a fire.

That was the way it happened, he knew, when a soldier went insane in combat. Later the illusion of battle would sometimes remain. He'd believe that, all around him, fighting continued. That there was smoke everywhere. Everywhere bloody limbs torn from bodies, edging up like black stumps of trees from the earth. Now the memory was real to him again.

He circumvented the guardhouse, walking swiftly and without sound. It occurred to him as if for the first time that despite the presence of night guards making their rounds the settlement was open and unprotected. Any terrorist could walk in from the east. It was pathetically simple to come into the core of the place and step silently past the pecans, olives, pines, children. Pathetically easy to plant a bomb, then run away. And he wanted less than ever to see things destroyed. But there wasn't really any security in anything, these days. Not in your home, your people, your country. Not in life. Or in love itself. Perhaps there was in death. Still, he didn't want to die.

Nadav went directly to Zeigler's place. There was no ceremony in this, no thought. He felt hard and dry inside tonight. What he wanted was Avi's help: the identity of one more anonymous computerized pawn flashing across a pale green screen, capable of being shuttled from one position to another if the occasion demanded, flexible, dehumanized, expendable.

He watched his breath cloud out into the air, then opened Zeigler's door and tossed his knapsack on the floor. He thought about switching on a light but didn't, realizing his paranoia was a little ridiculous. He heard the bed creak as Zeigler sat up suddenly.

"Don't turn on a light, Avi."

"Nadav?"

"I'm here, near the door."

He waited for a response but there was none, just the sound of breathing in the dark. Nadav leaned against the door and felt his back scrape it. Across the dark, he could feel Zeigler thinking. A terrible sensation gripped him—was it possible that Zeigler was part of the great machinery he knew could betray him in an instant? And that he, Nadav, was just like the guy with his face blown off—another innocent pawn, a mere cog in the wheels? But who else could he tell his true thoughts and feelings to, if not to his best friend? And why wasn't Zeigler speaking now, greeting him, calming him? Somewhere far off, a dog barked. Nadav heard himself panting in fear.

Then Avi stood and turned on a light. Nadav stared at him, blinking. For a moment he thought it wasn't Zeigler he was staring at. It had to be somebody else, a stranger. Zeigler was half the size he'd once been. His clothes hung on him like sacks once filled to bursting, now nearly empty. Nadav propped himself against the door. He slid down it, pulled his knees up to his chin like a chastised child. The light had flooded him with a sudden sense of relief, and his breathing calmed.

"Shit, Avi. You're sick?"

"I lost some weight. I'm actually healthy."

Zeigler dragged a chair over and sat, looking down at Nadav. He was a nearly slender man now, with pale blond hair and thinning face. The eyes were no longer small or sunk in fat, but sparkled large and blue, full of an almost malicious intelligence behind the thick lenses. They stared down now devoid of humor. Zeigler handed him a handkerchief.

"Here. Use this."

Nadav wiped his face. When the sweating stopped he stood and got a glass of water. Zeigler turned to watch him, the eyes calculating. Then after a while he wasn't looking at Nadav but at something out in space that no one else could see. He smiled almost impatiently. Outside, a wind had begun to blow and rattled the windows. The light flickered for a moment.

"Help me, Avi. I think I'm crazy, maybe. Or maybe everyone else is—"

"Nadav, what is it?"

Zeigler knelt beside him, and Nadav cried on his shoulder like an infant.

On Mayan Ha-Emek, rumors had been circulating for a while about Nadav and Miriam Sagrossa. Now the truth was out about her, too: she had a child. A psychotic daughter. And no one knew who the father was.

These rumors had a fresh scent to them, like blood or spore. They cast the memory of Shimon in a somewhat sullied light— although why this should be, no one could say for sure. The result was that people became depressed by it all, their depression evolved into a sort of anger, and, even though no one would have admitted it, the anger was directed at Nadav. This meant that his friends, particularly Jolie and Zeigler, were guilty by association. Most nights the two of them sat in a corner of the dining hall at supper, alone but for each other. Everyone else except Shlomo avoided them. In a way this seemed fitting. The role of outcast was one they both played quite well.

That was when the rumors really began about them, too: the outcasts who, everyone said, deserved each other.

Zeigler left for *miluim* suddenly one night and was gone three days. When he came back he kept to himself. He was absent from the dining hall, appearing on time at work every day and then shutting himself in his room at night. Even Jolie didn't see him much. During meals she'd sit alone, or with Nadav.

About a week after returning, Zeigler invited Nadav for tea. On the way over, Nadav was afraid. He knocked hesitantly, then went in. Removed his boots and coat, sticking the toe ends of the boots near the kerosene heater.

Zeigler motioned for him to sit. It had begun to rain and the dull sound beat against the window glass, cracked by wind. Idly, Zeigler fingered the lampshade on the light near his bed —it was torn and needed repair—and poked a finger straight through one of the holes until it came out the other side wriggling like a worm. Looking at Nadav he gave a mild grin.

"So, here's the real story. I asked the computers for help. I gave them the name you mentioned—the creep with the binoculars, yes? *Galitzianer*—to see what would happen. It was a real dead end. He wasn't anywhere on the records *I* have access to. But I borrowed a friend's security-clearance codes and was able to access additional records. If they find out what I did I'll go to jail. I just thought you'd like to know, in case you doubt my loyalty—"

"I don't, Avi."

"Okay. Well, the story is this: I feed in these other security-clearance codes and what do you think happens? A regular gold mine. Well, not exactly. Your Avner Galitzianer—that's actually his real name, by the way—was with *us*. Beyond that, no information. It's all classified under even more stringent clearance codes. So what do I do? I break even more laws. I have friends in the library, I go rummaging around there one night. Off duty, too." Zeigler was playing with the lampshade again. Then he stared at Nadav, fear on his face. "With a little reasoning and mathematics, and a few lucky guesses, I put together the proper clearance codes and then it was back to my wonderful little computers again. This time a few other names came up with Galitzianer's. All listed under his personal brief. All code names. What do I do? I take another trip to the library. By this time I'm ready to run screaming at the slightest noise. I access more codes, I cover up some more of my own tracks, I feed all this into my computers once more. *This* time I get access to the personal dossiers pertaining to each code name. Except that two of these dossiers have the real name expunged." Zeigler kept playing with the lampshade holes, and Nadav wanted to slap his hand away but didn't. "You see, there were some commando raids up in the north a few years ago, still highly classified. A group of guys were involved. A few of them are still in active service, and some of them are listed as alive and relieved of duty. Honorable discharges, et cetera. But one was a *psychiatric* discharge—all this is top secret, my friend—and that one is your Galitzianer. And those two dossiers with the real names expunged, well—" Zeigler paled. "You remember, of course, the night Galitzianer was at his worst? When he took you to spy on the unfortunate man who lives all alone in that house? Well, one of those dossiers is *his*. A lot of the rumors Galitzianer told you are true: the man's an ex-commando, he was badly maimed in the last war. Very badly maimed, in fact, he doesn't have much of a face left. And it's true that he asked for a place away from other people, where he could be alone. And it's true that the government arranged it. Just for him. He was an officer. Some of his years of service were filled with risk. So they also arranged, for security reasons, to change his identity. He lives there under an assumed name. But the strange thing is this: when I tried to find him under the *code* name of the dossier, he was listed as *dead.* And so is the *other* guy. Anyway, you know me—" Zeigler tapped his forehead—"I put some facts from each dossier together, dates of promotion, citations received, et cetera. And I find something *else* strange: the same essential facts are duplicated in each file. There are even two dates of birth given in each.

234

It's as though they took the factual history of two careers and rolled them together into one. But I took these facts, anyway, and I spent a long time with another computer's data banks. The history of the nation passed before my eyes, Nadav. It's a good thing you're sitting down. You're ready for this, you think?"

"What, Avi?"

"One of those guys died in the last war. Well, probably." Zeigler laughed suddenly, harshly. "The other didn't. The thing is, Nadav, that one of those guys is Shimon. The other is Uriel Lucero."

Kessem the Magic Cat

BACK BEFORE THEIR ARMY DAYS, ZVI AVINERI AND HAVA GOLINSKY
had a thing going between them.

This was unusual, and, in an unspoken way, against all tradition. Boys and girls growing up together in the same age group
on the same kibbutz rarely became involved with each other
intimately. It would have been considered almost the same as
brothers and sisters mating. There was an unstated sort of
incest taboo against such involvements. Rarely, of course, they
did happen. It was love in a glass fishbowl, with an audience
that never left and never shut its eyes. But there was nothing
to be done by the audience, really, except to let the thing run
its course.

The affair between Zvi and Hava ran its course inside a year.
During that year they came back from a group field trip to
Jerusalem with a kitten some Arab kid had sold them for a few
shekels. The cat was a short-haired, off-white little creature
with copper eyes. Hava raised it in the group house she shared
with several other girls, but since she and Zvi were always
together, they considered that the animal belonged to them
both. Zvi named him Kessem—because, he said jokingly, the

cat was the reincarnation of a wizard who'd dabbled too much in black magic, and been reborn in an animal body as fit punishment. During the year of their love affair, you could see the three of them, Zvi, Hava, and Kessem, walking everywhere together. The cat was a very friendly one, and was trained nearly like a dog. His tail was always held high as he trotted along behind them.

When Hava broke off with Zvi, the cat stayed with her. When she went into the army, she left it with her father. But when she came home on leave, Kessem sensed her arrival sometimes before it actually occurred, and would stand outside the door to her place meowing in anticipation. When she did arrive, he rubbed smoothly up against her legs, getting hair all over her uniform. Sometimes, when Zvi was home on leave, Kessem spent the night at his place instead. He'd curl up on the top step when lights went out, and, if it wasn't mating season, sleep.

For Hava, the affair was over after that first year. But for Zvi, love lingered. Maybe it wasn't love so much as passion. They'd come to each other virgins. He remembered the intimate details of their love-making, even the first clumsy, sweet, painful moment of penetration, in such a way that chills rippled his spine at the memory years later. Maybe it wasn't passion so much as a kind of nostalgia. Once he'd been a willowy thin boy with no scars on body or soul. In those days he'd believed in eternal life, perpetual arousal, and the mystical nature of physical union. Secretly he'd been a sensitive boy. Secretly, too, in a community of Labor Zionists, a few Revisionists, and even a disgruntled Marxist or two, he'd found himself praying to God. God's reply came whenever he nestled in the thick red hair of Hava's head and body. All this he kept to himself. But it formed the nexus of his nostalgia. And increasingly, with the years, nostalgia became his prime reason for continuing to exist. He told himself, crouching night after night in a border trench covered with netting against the flies, that once he had loved someone.

Sometimes during their army years Zvi and Hava wound up at Mayan Ha-Emek on leave at the same time. Sometimes they wound up spending the night together. For Hava it was an expression of friendship and regret, a pleasant release from the tensions of military life. For Zvi these times were terrible gifts, like ephemeral, bright-colored balloons filled with foolish hope and wounded love. But the cat was happiest during these nights, curling up outside Zvi's place, or Hava's.

That winter, Zvi gravitated toward Nadav in a friendship that, increasingly, seemed to arise from need. Something in Nadav's nervous manner these days touched him. Looking into the anxious, haunted eyes of his friend, Zvi saw himself.

It's said that King David's first-born son, Amnon, fell in love with his half-sister Tamar, Zvi told Nadav, over tea, one especially cold night. *He pretended to be sick one day, and asked that she be sent to his bedchamber to feed him. She appeared in her robe of many colors—that was the proper dress for a virgin—and she brought a lot of cooking utensils, and while she was baking little cakes for Amnon he ordered all the guards and attendants from the room. Then he asked Tamar to come close to him and feed him with her own hand. But instead of tasting the cakes he raped her. When he was finished he immediately became filled with revulsion and self-disgust. Also a loathing for her. The hatred, it's said, far surpassed his love. In disgust and humiliation, he drove her from his bedchamber. Tamar was deceived, abused and discarded. She tore the many-colored robes she wore on her body, covered her forehead with the ash of mourning, and wandered through the royal palace lamenting. She was quite insane. Her brother Absalom tried to comfort her, but she was beyond the reach of human voice or reason. Even King David was revolted by what had happened. But Amnon was his first born. And Tamar was only a woman, after all. So he didn't do anything about it. A while later, Absalom took matters into his own hands. He convinced his father to let Amnon accompany him and some servants on their annual sheep-shearing expedition. When Amnon was drunk with grape wine, out there in the fields, Absalom ordered the servants to hack him to death with their sheep shears. They did.*

While he recounted this old tale, a strange look settled on Zvi's face. The look was eerily familiar to Nadav—one he'd seen, in the hospital, on the faces of men who did not expect to live. For a moment, staring back at Zvi, he was afraid. But he didn't know what to say or do. And after a while the look went away. Then they sat in silence, finishing their tea and cake, until it was nearly time for bed and Nadav left.

Later that night, alone, Zvi went over the tale in his mind. Sitting in front of his kerosene heater, he rocked slightly back and forth. In the dark his stark gray hair glowed. Why he'd spoken of that legend tonight he didn't know. He only knew that it reminded him of a chunk of his life that had long since been lost. Somehow, he thought, youth had been taken from him. The loss had always felt like a violation. His youth had been taken from him by war, by pain, by the passage of time.

Zvi heard scratching at his door and opened it. The cat stood there, back arched, shivering, thin, lame. There'd been something wrong with him for months. Recently a livestock veterinarian had visited the dairy and Hava'd asked him to look at Kessem afterward. What the outcome had been Zvi didn't know. He and Hava rarely spent time together these days, unless it was with a group of others from their class. Sometimes they ate dinner together, or once in a while visited each other for coffee. But aside from old inside jokes that dated back to school days, they had little to say.

Kessem's pinkish skin was showing through his coat. Zvi snapped his fingers, coaxingly, and the cat stumbled inside.

Zvi took a towel from the back of a chair and knelt to rub the animal dry. The eyes gazed at him in hopeless pain, a grateful flicker shining through. Zvi rubbed him thoroughly, then reached for the only other towel in the place and rubbed him down again.

"What's with you, Kessem?"

The cat meowed faintly, still shivering. He tried to lick his paws.

Zvi filled a bowl with water. He pulled a tin of stewed

chicken from the cupboard and opened it, dumping the contents into another bowl. Then he set both bowls on the floor.

"Kessem, come here. Eat."

The cat wandered to the bowls and sniffed, then sat, shivering. He looked up at Zvi. Again a faint meow sounded. But it seemed, to Zvi, that the sound came from somewhere else: not from Kessem but from the room itself, or the night, or the rain. Or else, he thought with real horror, maybe it had come from inside *him*. Maybe it had, and he was too insane to realize it. He knelt on the floor then, a terrible fear rumbling through him. Gently, he stroked the animal's head and neck. His long thin hands were shaking.

Zvi went to Nadav's the next evening, but Nadav was out and no one answered. So he went back to his own place to get a few hours of sleep. It was his turn to do guard duty. Two or three men did it every night, taking separate routes, by foot, around the perimeters of the kibbutz living quarters, the dairy, chicken coop, fish pond, and orchards. They carried two-way radios and radioed back occasionally to the guardhouse. They also carried army-issue automatic rifles. The schedule for guard duty was a rotating one, like kitchen duty, and after serving your night of guard duty you had the next day off from work. Zvi was looking forward to it. But side by side with his feeling of pleasant anticipation was a kind of terror. He didn't understand this, and wanted to talk to someone, a friend. Still, he went back to his place and set the bedside alarm clock, stripped naked before sliding into bed. He thought he'd have trouble sleeping, but didn't.

Kessem was curled up inside Hava's place. She woke to hear the dim meow. Then she switched on the bedside lamp and squinted to read the gently ticking clock. Still before midnight. She hadn't been sleeping long.

"Hava."

It was a whisper sounding through the door. She threw on her old cotton robe. Then she edged carefully around an enormous arrangement of scarlet anemones on the coffee table. It was a rare treat for her, this flower—one of her favorites. Raya Sapiri had brought bunches of them back from a recent trip to some *moshav* near Rosh Ha-Nikrah. She was tying up the front of her robe when she got to the door. Another loud whisper sounded through, plaintively:

"It's me."

She opened the door and Kessem tried to rise to all fours but couldn't. Zvi walked in, nodding at her. He crouched, briefly, to stroke the old cat's head. Then he turned and stood his rifle in a corner.

"Can we talk?"

Hava sighed. "Sit."

His head was half in shadow. When he sat, the part of it illuminated by lamplight was sheer white, but the part still in shadow was a dull, silvery gray. His expression was gentle. When he looked at her she felt stirrings of the old long-ago regret mingled with pity. She realized, for the first time, that she'd never really loved him.

Zvi kept his thick jacket on but removed his gloves. In the room's sudden warmth his face took on a rose-tinged glow. But the eyes looked tired and bewildered.

"Kessem's sick."

"Yes," she said, "he's dying."

"That's what the veterinarian said?"

"It's something with his liver."

"Ah."

They were silent a while. When he glanced around his gaze seized on the violent blood-red of the anemones. He looked back at her with tears in his eyes.

"From the north?"

"Yes. Raya brought some back for me."

"You know about the history of those flowers?" His voice was suddenly agitated. "The ancient Syrians called them 'the blood of Tammuz.' Because they say that every year the young god Tammuz died by the harvesting knife, and he sprinkled the earth with his blood to fertilize it. So when the flowers grew on Lebanon, they were stained the color of his blood. You know the rest of the legend?"

"No." She leaned back in the chair wearily, began to play with a lock of her hair.

"The legend says that Tammuz was the lover of the greatest goddess of all, the goddess of fertility, Ishtar. When he died, she grieved. Then she went down into the land of the dead to find him and bring him back. But she had to make a deal with the goddess of the dead first, because the goddess of the dead was jealous and wanted to keep Tammuz all to herself. So they made their deal. Ishtar would have him for the spring and summer. But as soon as harvest time was finished, he had to return to the other goddess in the land of the dead. Then after winter Ishtar could go down into the land of the dead again, and bring him back to life. You see? That's why they say he died each year. You think it's a nice legend?"

Hava shut her eyes. "I don't know."

"*I* think it's a nice legend."

"Listen, Zvi, you have to leave now. I'm tired."

"Okay."

But when she opened her eyes he was still sitting there looking at her. In a corner, Kessem licked his paws and yawned.

"So, Hava. You're marrying David? In the spring?"

She nodded.

"Tell me something—he knows who he's marrying? He knows he's marrying Shimoni's widow?"

"Shut up, Zvi."

"Shimoni's virgin widow. Except that I fucked you first. But at least your heart is pure."

"Please, Zvi, get out."

"Okay." He stood. "What are you going to do about the animal, Hava? You'll take him with you on your wedding night? Maybe he can suffer to death while you're fucking your new husband."

"He'll die before then." Her eyes were filling but the tears didn't spill. Behind was protective armor, a stiff unmelting reserve. "I'll just try to keep him comfortable until he dies. You have some other suggestion, maybe? No? Then get out."

"Give him to me!"

"Okay, then, take him!" She flung out her hands in exasperation. Now the tears were falling. But maybe it was frustration, not sorrow, that made them fall. "Take him! You think I care any more? You think I care about either one of you?"

He turned and went to the corner, checked the safety on the rifle and then strapped it carefully to his shoulder. His gait was stiff, the legs very long and oddly clumsy tonight, as if he was an adolescent still growing into his own bones.

Kessem was purring as Zvi knelt before him. The copper eyes glimmered with pain, but still the purring sounded. Zvi crouched close to the floor and put his long arms around the cat. Carefully, easily, he lifted him. And stood there a moment, cradling Kessem against his chest. Then he walked to the door and tapped it open with a shove of his boot. Cold air drifted in, heavy with dampness. Halfway out he turned to Hava. She was still sitting in the same chair, her chest flushed pink around the borders of her robe.

"Can't you?" he asked, a hopeless plea.

Her eyes were tired. "What, Zvi?"

"Can't you love me?"

"No."

He stepped into the night, let the door close by itself behind him.

"Come with me, Kessem. Let's go."

The cat shivered a little with cold. Zvi opened the front of his jacket, closed the flaps as far as they would go around the frail white body. Kessem's nose nestled against his shirt.

Carrying the cat this way, he made his rounds. The dining hall, the post office, the clinic. Here and there a generator hummed. But most lights were off for the night. The windows of every little boxlike home were black, sleeping. The animal's weight was nothing. He was an easy burden, wasting away. After a while, Zvi thought he slept, could feel the sick heart pumping, breath purr through the old white throat. Above, stars were out in full cold splendor. But there wasn't any moon.

At the north end of the children's quarters he and Dodi Kinderbach crossed paths, and Dodi raised his rifle in greeting.

"What's new, Zvi? You brought a friend?"

They both laughed, then, at the sight of Kessem's tail falling from the folds of Zvi's jacket. Then Dodi headed for the nursery. He was a big, barrel-shaped man. Walking away, he looked like a dark bear moving through the night.

Zvi went in the opposite direction, toward the orchards, the fish pond and factory. There wasn't any wind tonight. The air sat, damp and heavy with cold. He moved through it as if through something tangible. It seemed to him that the substance, whatever it was, was very difficult to penetrate, that his legs were becoming tired, that now and then his eyelids sought to roll down forever and leave him in darkness. But he glanced up at the stars and felt revived. They were spectacular, glittering, a carnival of icy white flame searing the black permanence of the sky, a constellation of torches.

"My good, good Kessem."

The tail curled.

"My magic one."

Zvi walked downhill toward the main road. Just before the turnoff was a path through bushes and pines, and he took it. Then the stars overhead were obscured by trees, the night pressed in all around. Wading through it, he felt enveloped. He walked carefully, toeing ahead for potholes and stones. He reached under his jacket now and then to caress the cat. Once, Kessem made a faint gurgling sound.

"It's all right."

He peered ahead toward the clearing.

"It'll be okay."

The trees were behind him and stars reappeared, dimly illuminating the graveyard of Mayan Ha-Emek. They cast faint shadows on the cool, smooth surface of old stones. Zvi walked among the overgrown mounds, where here and there a dried bunch of flowers rested against some inscription. At the grave-yard's end he stopped.

Carefully he knelt, swinging the rifle from his shoulder and resting it on the ground. Kessem's tail curled again as he began to open the folds of his jacket. He thought better of it and simply removed the jacket one arm at a time, making sure to keep the animal wrapped and warm. As he did, a putrid odor filled his nostrils. Kessem had fouled the jacket. There was a flat, dark stain on the lower part of his shirt. Slowly, he unbut-toned the shirt and pulled it off, dropped it.

It's okay.

He tore a clump of hard earth from the ground, smeared it across his naked chest and belly. The cold raised tiny bumps along his back. He sat, then, next to the fouled shirt, the old white cat wrapped in his jacket's folds. Kessem's head poked from one end of the jacket, the tip of his tail from the other. Zvi stroked his head.

It'll be okay.

He leaned close, gazed into the glowing animal eyes.

"Good cat."

He reached for the rifle, undid the safety.

"Sweet Kessem. Good one. I know, my friend. I know how hard you tried."

The cat's tail twitched once more, twice, feebly.

It's all okay. Come with me, magic one, good one, my white beauty, white like snow and ice. My one, my love, my white cold love, love of my life. My love. He aimed. *My love.*

It was nearly dawn when he patted the last clump of earth onto a small, fresh mound. Zvi's skin was faintly blue with cold. His arms, scratched and bleeding, were caked with dirt to the el-bows.

Later people saw him wandering up from the direction of the main road, shirtless, the rifle strapped to one shoulder. His eyes were wide and gentle, like a child's.

Steel

THE RAIN STAYED AWAY ALL THAT DAY, AND ZVI SLEPT. ANOTHER night came, sheer black and cold, and for a while rain threatened but never fell. Morning promised to be clear—another sunny winter morning north of the Jezreel, south of Kineret. In his bed Nadav tossed uncomfortably. He was awake, and thinking of Ramat Alon. Of the things Avi'd told him. Of Miriam Sagrossa.

An hour before sunrise, Avishai the demented rooster began screeching and wouldn't stop. This stirred the entire chicken coop. Across the turnip and sugar-beet fields, a chorus of panicked clucking blew with the wind. In the coop itself, feathers swirled as hundreds of misguided birds rose to the roof and landed, over and over again, in mindless terror.

Aside from this, nothing marked the day's beginning as extraordinary. Avishai often crowed before dawn. So often, in fact, that when Zvi had returned from the last war he'd threatened to gun the bird down. No one took this threat too seriously.

That morning a slight breeze gusted over the fields, through the grapefruit orchard, the oranges, the plucked dark cotton field and the olive grove. Around the core of the settlement, trees clustered thickly. The night guards began their final round.

Raya Sapiri inched from under a blanket at the edge of the grapefruit orchard and shook the shoulder of the naked man beside her. For a second, she forgot his name. He seemed almost dead to her—anonymous, motionless. But he began to mumble and move around, and a brief tenderness overwhelmed her. That's when she glanced up and saw, through the twisted trunks of the grapefruit trees, the figures of men she didn't recognize moving silently and swiftly. She saw the shape of at least one dark rifle. Her fingers tightened around the upper arm of her companion until the nails drew blood. She clamped her other hand over his mouth, and when he glared up at her she nodded. He followed her gaze, froze. Then, flattened close to the earth, he and Raya began to slide away from the orchard on their naked bellies. When they were far enough away, torsos streaked with the dirt of the field, they stood and ran. In the rivulets of morning light spreading down the eastern face of Mount Gilboa, over the orchard trees, they were a strange sight: a young woman and tall sunburnt man, running naked across the lands of Mayan Ha-Emek.

"Here," said Yigal Kafner. "Look." He handed the binoculars to Sasha Levy.

"It's Raya Sapiri again."

"Sure. But who's the guy?"

"Wait. Wait. Ah. It's that bastard from Eilat—what's his name? Something Gittelman. Dodi's cousin. He's visiting. A real snob, you heard him at dinner last night? He complained about the chicken."

"He complained? But the chicken was good last night."

"I know, idiot. Everyone knows. He's a stupid snob." Sasha looked through the binoculars again, focusing on Raya's breasts, which bounced freely as she ran. He smiled with longing. "Still, maybe he's not *so* stupid. I wouldn't mind running after some of that. What about you?"

"Give me the binoculars."

"One last look."

"Give, Sasha."

Watching, Yigal got nervous. He was a pale, freckled boy who'd scored low on each of the army's intelligence tests, and spent his years of military service at a supply base slicing tomatoes. Social nuance eluded him. Instinct didn't. The morning chill dampened his face, a slight breeze lightened the chill as it gusted across their hillside vantage point at the northern boundary of the kibbutz. It occurred to him that they were still supposed to be on guard duty. And he'd left his automatic rifle leaning against a wall in the tiny guardhouse near the main road, next to Sasha's old guitar. He shook Sasha's shoulder.

"Let go, you fool."

"Sasha. The rifle."

"So?"

"I forgot it."

"Well? So? I have *my* man." And Sasha patted the semi that hung at his side.

But Yigal began to sway from foot to foot. Finally he gave a desperate growl and took off downhill. Muttering Arabic curses, Sasha wrenched the binoculars from his eyes and followed. The thuds of their thick boots echoed behind them.

Staggering naked and breathless into the center of Mayan Ha-Emek, Raya Sapiri and the Gittelman kid were surrounded by people on their way to breakfast. Soon the entire dining hall had emptied to gather around, some still chewing bread and eggplant. Gittelman clasped both hands over his dangling genitals. Then he fainted.

"*Terrorists,*" Raya gasped. "*In the grapefruits.*"

"Hello, Raya!" called a man's voice from the crowd. "Why not give some to me, too?"

Raya stood naked in the center of the circle of people. Morning sun gleamed along her breasts and thighs. Her skin was brown from summers of hot sunlight, and even in the pallid winter it glowed, reminding everyone that she was still young. A hiss sounded between her lips. Then she spat.

Someone whistled shrilly. Someone else told him to shut up. Adolescent boys gazed and placed concealing hands across the crotches of their trousers. Shlomo stepped into the center of the circle, blankets draped over one arm. He gave Raya a brief bow. Then he eased the blanket over her shoulders, covering her body to the knees. He squatted on the grass to put another blanket over the body of Gittelman and calmly took his pulse. He glanced up at the waiting crowd.

"Someone, please. Get the key to the clinic. And help me take him there. He'll be okay."

He stood to face Raya. She stared at him, eyes seething, the only sound she made the measured inhalation of breath as her breasts rose and fell beneath the blanket.

"Raya," Shlomo said kindly, "you're all right?"

Raya's nostrils flared. For a moment, her face was extremely beautiful. In that moment a tiny flame of desire surged through him, then dissipated, but before it was gone she noticed and laughed. It was a mad laugh of taunting and rage. It was a laugh aimed at the entire male species that loved her, entered her, then went off to fight wars with other men and die. She hit him hard across the cheek, leaving a single nail mark that bled. Then she turned and stalked away. She passed through the thickest of the crowd, which had fallen utterly silent and parted for her now without a word, as the waters had parted for Moses and for God.

In the dairy Jolie was finishing her shift. The dairy night shift rotated—like guard duty, and peeling potatoes. When Dodi Kinderbach showed up to take over she was hosing down each stall with blue disinfectant. Dodi had put on a clean pair of coveralls, gloves, rubber boots.

"So. How's everything?"

"Fine," Jolie said.

He was a big man, with a handsome face and large fumbling hands. Recently he'd left his wife of one year—they'd lived on another kibbutz, somewhere in the Negev—and he walked everywhere slowly now, with the same fixed half-smile that said he was both weary and puzzled. Rumor had it that she'd refused to sleep with him for months because she was terrified of becoming pregnant. She was obsessed, they said, with the thought that any child she had would be murdered. No one knew why.

Jolie handed him the hose and he unlatched one of the gates, parading cows back into stall after stall while the sound of loud moos echoed everywhere. He stepped quickly into each stall, attaching siphons to each set of teats, turning on the milking machine. Jolie watched fresh milk swirl in the great canisters for a few minutes. Then she stepped outside into pure damp air. She peeled off her dung-spattered coveralls and rubber boots before heading for the adjacent shed to shower, feeling tired but also very awake and nervous. It reminded her of the way she'd felt just before the outbreak of war: the sensation that something irrevocable was going to happen. But there wasn't any reason she knew of for such a feeling this morning.

Jolie dressed in clean work clothes. She was filled with self-disgust this morning. Her breasts were pale, and imperfect, and she was not beautiful, wasn't attractive enough, self-assured enough, intelligent enough, she was not particularly brave in the face of despair, she was too young, and unpracticed in matters of love. She brushed her hair back. There was no mirror—she was grateful. But she stepped back from a dim reflection in a section of window glass, a little alarmed. The most terrible thing of all, she thought, was that none of it mattered: her appearance, desires, her own small happiness. This, the war had taught her. None of those elements mattered in the vast scheme of things. Even her own death didn't matter. The inevitability of it, the acceptance of mortality—this was, maybe, the only profound concept grasped in common by every living human being on earth, because no one had any choice but to ultimately grasp it. Yet even the universal grasping of it did not matter.

Or did it?

On her way out, Jolie opened the small refrigerator in the shed and tore off a hunk of cheese.

That's when she heard it. Or rather, felt it, was enveloped by it—a sound that exploded and set the earth trembling, seemed to echo in her head and rattle through all her bones, then burst out again from some deep place inside. The shed door fell open and she stumbled out, off balance. From the corner of her eye she could see Dodi Kinderbach staggering out of a stall. Behind the shattering echo she heard, dimly, the faint sound of cows mooing in panic. The sun was rising, a blurred ball of orange heat. On the morning air came the unmistakable odor of smoke. When she could stand upright she looked across the turnip field to the orchards and beyond. A bright black-rimmed tower of flame rose up from behind the wall of trees. The factory was burning.

The echo of the explosion began to die and other sounds emerged: stomping hooves, from far away the panicked cluck of cooped chickens, a faint whine of breeze. The roar of flames. Then, from the grapefruit orchard, a single gunshot. And another. Then the drilling, agonized sound of an Uzi discharging, peppering the faded echo like staccato drumbeats, ripping a million holes through the fierce bright roar of fire.

In the grapefruit orchard, men hid in the trees. One held a rifle with Russian lettering on the barrel. The barrel caught a ray of sunlight and gleamed malignantly. But they were stalked, and didn't know it.

From the twisting branches of another tree, Zvi Avineri balanced near the trunk, singling out the one with the rifle.

"Hello, my friend!" he called in Arabic.

Then he aimed his handgun and took two shots, perfectly placed. Branches crashed. The body recoiled backward through leaves and tumbled. Mumbling sounds came from nearby and Zvi spotted the other man, in the same tree, whispering in panic. The man leaned forward on a branch until he was revealed, and held his hands up, palms open. His lips were moving with emphasis. His hands spread in supplication. He seemed about to say something.

"Speak," said Zvi, in Arabic. Then he aimed again, this time with the Uzi.

The round of machine-gun bullets aborted whatever the man might have said. He was thrown forward and down in a flutter of twigs and dirt. Blood burst across his gray shirt front. His legs flew backward as he pitched from the tree and the Uzi kept firing, great chunks of earth ripped loose around him. He landed on his face, blood-drenched and twisted like a broken doll. Dozens of ripe grapefruits fell on top of him.

When the clatter of bullets stopped there was a strange silence in the orchard. The hum of insects had ceased. Not a single bird sounded. There was only the scent of crushed grapefruit and flesh, the breath of breeze. And, traveling on the breeze, the hot smell of smoke, the crackle of flames. The bomb these men had planted in the steel factory had exploded, but neither of them heard it. It had shaken the ground. But they were too deep inside their own terror to hear it. Then they'd died.

Zvi dropped from his tree. He landed on his feet, sprang up with a cougar's grace, the Uzi cradled in his arms. He wore a strapped-on pistol, and various knives were strapped to his forearms with leather bands. From the waist up he was naked. His head was newly bald, scabbed here and there where the razor he'd used that morning had cut too deep, and his clean-shaven face had an innocent glow. He gripped the Uzi in firing position again. Then he approached the bodies and turned each over with a foot. Two punctured faces stared up at him, open-mouthed, dead. The faces of the factory workers Shoukri and Zaki Afafa. Zvi nodded.

"You see," he said.

Men had come down from the kibbutz. Someone was calling the authorities in Afula.

They converged around Zvi, and stood back a little when they saw the look in Zvi's eyes. Then, as if in the uneasy beginnings of a tribal ceremony, they circled him slowly while he stood there ankle-deep in grapefruit, staring down at the bullet-peppered bodies of Shoukri and Zaki Afafa. They thought, looking at him, that he hadn't noticed them at all. But he glanced up suddenly without a hint of surprise. And smiled broadly for the first time in years. He held the Uzi high in one hand.

"Okay," he said triumphantly. "It'll all be okay now. Everything's safe."

Nadav sidled forward, still breathing hard from his run. He held out a hand and managed to grin. "Give me the Uzi, Zvi."

"Sure." Zvi shrugged. "We're all friends here."

He handed it over. The smell of smoke and blood choked their throats. Nadav passed the gun to someone else. Then he opened his arms and pressed Zvi to his chest. The leather-bound points of daggers poked him.

"Zvi." Nadav held him as he would a child. "Don't worry, Zvi."

Zvi rested his head comfortably on Nadav's shoulder. His eyes were closed now, but he was still smiling.

The police and military authorities descended on Mayan Ha-Emek like wasps to a nest, searching the fields around the factory for more home-made bombs. But the specially gauged equipment and specially trained dogs turned up nothing. In the end, they were forced to cover the bullet-riddled bodies of Shoukri and Zaki Afafa and cart them off for autopsies— which, as Dodi Kinderbach pointed out, were quite unnecessary, since everyone could tell what had killed them. A special military unit was dispatched to their home in Nazareth to question members of their family. And the people of Mayan Ha-Emek were subject to questioning, too, but of a friendlier nature. Had they noticed anything unusual about the outside laborers lately? Or the volunteers? No one had. No one but Jolie, and sometimes Shlomo, had any contact with the Arabs who worked at the factory. And neither Jolie nor Shlomo could offer an explanation of why the Afafa brothers had done what they did. Jolie thought, once, of bringing up the political discussions she'd sometimes had with Shoukri. But it seemed pointless now. She didn't want to open a can of worms. And anyway, the man was dead.

News of the bombing swept the country. There were newspaper reporters to deal with, too, along with a temporary invasion of privacy which the people of Mayan Ha-Emek detested. Also, the factory had been a main source of income. Times were bad, now—at least until an emergency loan from the government could be rushed through—and the result was that, as shock receded and was replaced by impotent rage, people went into mourning. The general grief was exacerbated when, the day following the incident, Zvi Avineri curled into a fetal position in a corner of the room where one of the military attachés was questioning him and refused to stand up or talk. Shlomo had to arrange for an ambulance. Zvi was taken to a hospital in Haifa, where it looked like he'd be staying for a while. Nadav went along in the ambulance and didn't return until the next morning. When he did he spoke to no one, skipped breakfast and went directly to his own place.

Even Rafi came back for a visit that week. He slept on the couch in his mother's place, ate all his meals with her or with Jolie. He seemed polite and responsible, and uncharacteristically quiet. There wasn't any mention by him of America this time. He took a turn at night guard duty, too, without complaint. Everyone remarked on this.

But when he'd gone, and the reporters had gone too, the authorities wrapped up all their investigations and the people of Mayan Ha-Emek were left with the rubble of their factory, the job of making their way through mounds of critical red tape for loans, and the necessity of mobilizing a clean-up crew—for which everyone, in mourning or not, had to volunteer. This task looked like it would consume much of the month. Michael Kol returned on special leave, his young face tight and hard, and worked for nearly a week without sleeping. Then he rested a few hours, ate dinner, and left to return to Officers School. He'd graduate in the spring, he said, maybe as outstanding cadet.

One night in late January, after most of the cleanup was completed and a rebuilding loan had come through, seven people woke before dawn to the sound of feet passing quietly by outside. Several of them lifted the corners of their window shades to see who it was. Some saw nothing. But a few claimed that they'd seen the General walking, alone, among the houses, dressed in civilian clothes: workboots, old trousers, and an ancient flannel shirt that he'd often worn many years ago, one riddled with stitching and mismatched buttons. He wore no jacket or coat, they claimed, though the night was cold.

In the morning it was obvious that these people had either fabricated or hallucinated. The General wasn't on Mayan Ha-Emek. Still, the similarity of each claim was striking.

Breakfast was worse than usual. The eggs were barely cooked and oozed from the shell. The tomatoes were bad, the oatmeal thin. Jolie threw cucumbers, bread, and jam on her plate and sat at a far end of the dining hall alone. It was going to be a pointless day. With the factory gone, Shlomo had assigned her to pruning grapefruit trees. She felt her value slipping away.

In the mirror that morning, her hair had curled like frizzing rodent tails. Her breasts ached. She was reminded that her body, long unloved, could be oppressive. Reminded that Rafi had left her, that she was still inexperienced in matters of love. And she'd cried, for a few minutes, because she was not beautiful.

She poured hot black tea into a cup and dumped in too many spoonfuls of sugar. Outside it drizzled. The windows were streaked with mingled water and dirt, and a slight wind blew.

"Good morning."

A small paper bag dropped on the table. Shlomo sat across from her with a tray of food, and slid the bag closer.

"Nadav asked me to give this to you. He didn't have time himself, he left this morning."

"He went somewhere?"

"To Ramat Alon, he said. He'll be back in a few days. You want some juice?"

"No. Thanks."

Shlomo poured some into his own glass, and she peered in the bag. It was some coffee Nadav had borrowed. The smell rose, sharp and pleasing, evoking nostalgia for things she wasn't even sure she'd experienced. Mornings in cozy quilts before sunrise. Bright, leisurely days filled with hope. The odor of food frying. Unlimited life.

"How are you? You're sad because of the factory?"

"Well, sure."

"Why? What's with you, you liked the smell of steel?"

Tea burned her throat, hot and sweet. She felt tears in her eyes. Looking up, she could see the beginnings of tears in his. And nodded at him. "I liked the smell of steel."

He blinked swiftly. Then his tears were gone. "Good. So. I hope you'll stay. It's not so easy to find someone who likes the smell of steel. When you find such a person, you hope they'll stay. Even if there's no steel left any more." He abruptly shoved his plate away and leaned back in the metal chair, lighting a cigarette. Shlomo smoked kibbutz-issue cigarettes. They came in flat cardboard boxes and were stubby, foul-smelling, filterless, rolled in thin stale paper. The tobacco was brown, specked here and there with slivers of something that looked like sawdust. He inhaled deeply, reached to remove something from his tongue. When he exhaled his face was momentarily obscured in a cloud of yellowish smoke. Around them utensils clattered and conversation spun to an indecipherable babble, punctuated once in a while by the sound of vegetables slapping the surface of plates.

Someone walked by outside, a tall woman carrying a parcel

of fruit. Her head was covered by the kind of kerchief you bought in Arab market stalls, cloth rough and thick, the edges tasseled. It was Yael. She walked slowly, with a kind of grace, looking to neither right nor left. Shlomo watched intensely, until she passed out of sight. Suddenly he leaned forward and stubbed the cigarette out in his plate. The tip sizzled, died. For a second his face was twisted misery. But the features smoothed instantly and Jolie looked away. Then they sat a few minutes in silence, staring at the tall rain-streaked windows.

Shimoni's Lover

NADAV ARRIVED AT RAMAT ALON AFTER DINNER THAT NIGHT, SKIRTED the dining hall and the row of volunteers' shacks where he'd roomed with Galitzianer. He kept away from the lighted paths, not wanting to see anyone who would recognize him. The settlement was familiar to him now. He knew where he was going.

He knocked on the door of her place.

A light was on, but no one answered. The wind blew through his jacket, chilling him. He was about to turn away but hesitated, shuffling from foot to foot like a boy, then gently pushed the door open.

She was sitting at a small table near the window, smoking a cigarette. The ashes fell on the table. She turned to him and didn't seem surprised. Tears streaked her cheeks.

"You know something? I hate this country. You know what I hate about it most? This country cares nothing for her women. To the men of Israel, we're all milk cows." She flicked a thumb toward the cigarette pack on the table. Leaning back against the door he stared at her hand, then at the pack. Europa brand, menthol. "You know what a man told me once when I was in the army? 'The women in this army are good for one thing, and one thing only,' he said, 'and that's to fuck. That's why we want you here. There's no other reason.' Hah! Me, you know what *I* wanted to do in the army at first? I wanted to fight in the front lines. 'Wait,' they told me, and they were laughing. 'Wait until you have a son. Then *he'll* fight for you.' The idiots." She faced him and held up the pack. "See this? I bought this today. Years ago, I smoked a lot. I stopped. It's bad for the lungs. But today I don't care any more. Let my lungs rot away. Let the organs of my body dry up and die. What's it all for, anyway? For a man to use? To put his sperm into? Tonight, *no.* Tonight I hate you all. *All of you.* I hate all you stupid men who die."

She tossed the pack on the table. Then she laughed, loudly, without humor.

"I'll tell you something, my friend, I'm tired of men with big ideals. I'm even tired of men with big *ideas.* My husband, Sami, he was a man with big ideas. He thought he *needed* so much, so much money, so much sex, so many women. All his big needs exhausted me. He tried to beat me into wanting as much as he did—or into wanting *him* as much—and I tried once to kill him, but a land mine killed him first. And the others, they were all great *idealists.* Especially your brother. The great warrior Shimon! The perfect Israeli man! Peace fanatics, war fanatics, religious fanatics—you know how sick I am of fanatics? What I want in my life is a man who will consider *reality.* Like raising a child. Living a life, a human life, full of error. Loving *a little.* Hating *a little.* A little *moderation,* that's what you men need, the peaceniks, the warniks, all of you. Arabs. Israelis. Idiot Muslims and idiot Jews and idiot Christians, the whole stupid mess. What do you care that your women and children suffer? Or die? You know what we are to you? Vessels for your sperm. You think, that way, you'll become immortal. You think that with us as slaves to bear your children, you'll finally become gods. You use our misery as an excuse to go out and butcher each other some more. Well, me, I'm through with it, I'm finished."

She was still crying.

Then she stabbed her cigarette out on the table and bowed her head. "Why are you men so *different?*" she sobbed. Her tears made splotches on the wood. "So different from us? You know what I think? I think sometimes you don't really want to be. I think maybe you envy us—us women—you want to be *like* us, even, but maybe you're afraid. No one taught you how. You'd have to admit that you need us, too. That you want children, really want them, that you want to spend time raising your own children with us and living in peace. You'd have to admit that you're so afraid. Arab men, Israeli men, all of you. But you won't. Your bodies stand in the way. And so do ours, somehow. Our physical bodies stand in the way of peace, because in our bodies, in our sex, is a great difference, and a war that never dies." She glanced up, her face wet, her eyes red. He stepped forward by instinct and bent down to kiss her. Then she slapped him and slapped him, the blows hard, making his ears ring and cheeks burn, until he covered his face with both arms and backed away.

"Get out!" she screamed.

He did.

Nadav spoke with no one for a few days. The repair garage of Ramat Alon occupied his mornings and afternoons, and he cleaned dusty truck parts until the smell of grease nauseated him and his arms were chilled, smeared with black oil. Once or twice, in the dining hall, he saw Miriam. Sometimes she sat alone, sometimes with Rana. The child was acting more strangely than ever, throwing tantrums at all hours of the night and day. This gave both of them a haggard look.

Occasionally Schindler sat with them. Seeing him made Nadav's stomach churn with a hateful, desperate feeling. Once, she caught him staring at her from across the room. For a second their eyes met and held. He felt himself blush, then felt his face drain of color while he kept looking directly at her. He was utterly exposed and didn't care. But she turned away.

He was staying, temporarily, in an empty volunteers' shack.

That night after midnight someone rapped at the door. He threw on trousers and began buttoning his shirt. When he opened the door the wind hit him full force. He blinked with the cold, then caught her smell: cigarettes and a touch of perfume, a hint of cheap wine. Her eyes were red. She was bundled up, and her legs were jean-clad spindles sticking from the jacket folds, the old work boots she'd put on too large. There was something absurd about such clothes on her, the way they didn't fit reminiscent of the hospital to him. Or maybe she looked, instead, like some disheveled but still beautiful prison inmate. She was shivering.

"Please talk with me. I want to talk."

He motioned her inside. "Okay. I'll listen." He went to set up tea on the burner, but there wasn't any. So he just sat on the edge of his cot, she in the armchair. She kept her jacket on. He ran a hand tiredly across the stubble on his face, through his hair. It was late, he was weary, and maybe that was why her appearance didn't surprise him now. It seemed a brief pause in a dream.

She spoke about her men, about her life. Her parents had immigrated from Rabat, had gone through the usual delousing in some shabby absorption center. She'd grown up with a lot of brothers in one gray development town after another, trying to make ends meet with too few lirot and shekelim, moving everywhere in a cloud of mended clothes and cooking eggplant, watching her mother mourn the hours of a life lost and, in memory, idealized. She watched her father waste into death, her brothers fight with knives for money and drugs and the love of women, go into the army, get out of the army, marry, beat their wives, gamble and go to jail, and somewhere in there she'd entered the service herself, but in the end had married a man from another development town. That was Sami. Sami Sagrossa. Hopelessly handsome and violent, he owed money to bad people, drank too much, lost one job after another, and twice beat her black and blue. Once, she stabbed him in the thigh. She'd been aiming elsewhere. Like her brothers, she had a penchant for knives. She threatened to leave him. He said if she did he'd kill her mother, and brothers, too, and she believed him. But he went off to war one day, stepped on a land mine, looked down in shock when he heard the click. It was his last living gesture. They'd buried what was left of him in a humble grave facing east. It was a traditional funeral in the Moroccan style, the rabbi chanting wonderfully, each drone of the answering chorus more Arabic in quality than Hebraic, the women of his family veiled in mourning. Afterward she'd shed all traditional clothes for modern ones. And except for the name, she was free.

There was the Tel Aviv hospital where she'd worked nights cleaning. She had a tiny, run-down rented room somewhere and another job waitressing during the day, and she moved in a state of suspension between exhilaration and mindless exhaustion. There was a large closet in the hospital where doctors went to nap sometimes. In it was a cot, next to a stained table on which there always seemed to be half-finished Styrofoam cups of coffee, cigarette butts and amphetamines in the ashtray, lingering smoke in the air, deserted textbooks opened to pen-marked pages. Wounded soldiers and victims of traffic accidents bled down the hall. It was at some dead hour of night or early morning when, seeing the cot empty, she'd stretched out for a few bleary moments of sleep. And opened her eyes with a start to stare into a homely, humble face of the dark East. His young eyes smiled down at her through thick metal-rimmed spectacles while he explained in embarrassment, and in bad Hebrew, that he was Mohani Benjamin, from Bombay, and a Jew, yes, a new immigrant. He worked here as a night janitor. He studied during the day. And had come here, like her, to look for a few moments of sleep.

Studied? she'd said, in surprise. *Studied?* Yes, he told her, he had himself attended medical school briefly in Delhi, long ago. He'd considered neurology but wound up reading Dostoevsky instead, and failed. He'd found something more fascinating than all of those axions and dendrites, those quasi-electric impulses—he'd discovered brain fever, demons of the mind. *But, he said, they are all much the same thing, after all.*

They did their cleaning chores together that night, talking. He had the heart of an idealist. He was destined to fail. She knew this at once, by instinct, and what she came to know of him later only confirmed it. But soon he had her taking classes in the morning, reading, learning things. She found she had a good mind. This surprised her. And because he'd shown her this, and was gentle, she loved him. She'd never known male gentleness before. It was something exotic, erotic, utterly new. There was much of the feminine about him. Violence made him recoil. In many ways he was not like other men. For food he ate only fruits, vegetables, nuts and seeds. She teased him about it cruelly once, and he was hurt. After that she never ate meat in his presence. He had his own idealist's concept of the ideal way to live. It must be in a community, he said. He wasn't really sure that the kibbutz represented his ideal. He was searching for something more perfect. Again, she knew—but kept it to herself—that he was destined to find only failure. There was still his military service to be gotten through.

So he'd gone into the army. Like many new immigrants who spoke the language poorly, he'd been given a low-prestige job as some officer's driver. He was ecstatic, though, she remembered. Finally, he said, he'd experience the true rite of passage into his adopted nation's soul. But he was far away from her in basic training, stationed at miserable supply bases or outposts, too rarely with her in the rented rooms they shared in Tel Aviv. Without him she could feel her own despair more acutely. She could watch the fresh flowers she'd bought and set up in Moroccan vases wither too soon. Gentleness wasn't enough. She longed to do something to punish herself, and the entire country, and especially him. Something to puncture his equanimity and gentleness, to see if he was violent, like other men. Once she visited for an afternoon at the base where he was stationed, far to the north. She arrived there as he had arranged, weathered the stares and jeers and greasy appreciative whistles of the soldiers, waited for him in front of the makeshift mess hall while tanks and supply trucks went rumbling past. He'd driven up in a jeep, proudly at the wheel. In the jeep with him was his commanding officer, Major Uriel Lucero.

Eight months later he was driving on an errand, alone, down a northern dirt road. The jeep hit a bump full speed, lost a wheel and overturned. He fell out, snapping his neck. And died instantly. She was pregnant, but did not know it yet.

And Lucero? Well, she'd met him again at the funeral. He was the one, in fact, who'd sent the telegram.

The thing with Lucero was sudden and passionate. He was a beautiful man to look at, she said. Naked, his body was smooth and glistened like bronze, and he had the strong but finely formed features of the ancient Persians: pretty face, magnificent dark eyes. He was intelligent and volatile. Often he was very aroused, and finished too quickly to satisfy her. For all that, she'd felt more real passion with Lucero than with anyone else. She didn't know why. Maybe it was his physical beauty, maybe something more. He'd been through much to harden a man, being in Special Forces, had displayed courage and dogged will, had shown himself to be a leader. But there was in him a persistent kind of sensitivity. Usually it was a sensitivity only to himself, but he could also sense sometimes, as if by instinct, what she was feeling, or thinking, or doing. It was, she believed, an oriental trait, and particularly a trait of oriental Jews. It reminded her, at times, of herself. And though her feelings for Lucero were sweet, she'd always known that someday they would end. They would burn themselves out. Because he was too much *of* her. Really giving herself to him would rob her of the last vestige of power she had over her men—the knowledge that they did not really know what she was feeling, or thinking, or doing. With Lucero she was stripped, she felt her mystique slip away. He had too much of his own. Maybe that was why she'd betrayed him, in the end—and with another officer, his best friend. Someone he'd introduced her to at a party.

Because it *was* that, she said: a betrayal. Mohani Benjamin had loved her most humanely. But Lucero loved her the way men love fire, seeking it, desiring and needing it, possessing it, ultimately learning to control it and snuff it out. In the end there was only one final blow she could deal him, one way out of the trap she'd constructed with her own feelings, and his. Shimon.

A tear slid down her face, curious, silent, solitary. But there weren't any tears in her voice.

"Your brother was a serious man, a very powerful man. But of them all, he loved me the least."

She'd been conscious of others back then, she said, only in relation to herself: how much they loved her, or if they did, and how well. Having a child changed all that for good. But she basked now in the glow of her memory, because even the agony of it had been all hers and no one else's. Despite the difficulties of her life she'd remained, for many years, a child herself. Rana had forced her to make choices. Her breasts, her life's blood, her time and her love were now all inextricably bound to another, one who was flesh of her flesh and utterly dependent. With Benjamin gone, and Lucero believing, no matter what she said to convince him otherwise, that the child was really his, she had to protect her daughter from as many mistakes as possible—theirs, hers. She chose a safer man: Shimon. It was as simple as that.

He was safer because he knew her the least. Because he cared the least, away in the north, always, with his men. With him her mystique would remain intact, and with it her power. This power was all she had to give her daughter. But it fractured something inside Lucero that never really healed. He insisted that the child was of his own seed. And only went away, finally, when she threatened him with medical tests. She'd realized, then, that he didn't really want the truth—what he'd really wanted was to lay claim to a living possession, a legacy. She licked a tear from her lips, glanced tiredly at Nadav. He stared back.

"You loved Shimon?"

"I loved them all."

"One more than the others?"

"I don't know. Each was special to me. But the truth is that I loved them all. Maybe one loved *me* more, or less. Still, each loved me in his way, as he was able to love a woman. Sometimes I think maybe the truth of love is that it's a lonely thing, anyway, it doesn't have connection so much with the other person. *I* love, *you* love, he or she loves. But we're each alone with our feeling. Because we can't be two bodies at the same time—only one—and not for long enough before we die. When I think of loving I think of my daughter now, and only of her. I love *her* in a different way, a protective way that has no end to it. You understand? Shimon wanted a woman to instruct and possess, to show to others. The child came with the woman. He knew Rana wasn't his. That hurt his great pride. But he never really had time to love either one of us. He only *required* me. A woman was part of the necessary background for his greatness. Still, *I* loved *him*, because—" she stopped, something choking her throat. He stared at her coolly.

"Because?"

"Because he left me alone with her. And by then that was all I wanted from a man: That he'd leave me alone with my child."

"You know, Miriam, you're a terrifying woman."

She shook her head until long dark strands of hair fell from her jacket collar, swung over her face. On the front of the jacket, tears dripped.

"I'm a woman," she said, "just a woman."

She moved the strands behind both ears and leaned forward, meeting his eyes. Then, quietly, she reached for his left hand, laced her fingers in his. A kind of terror pounded through him.

"You see me?"

He nodded.

"You hate me?"

No, he tried to say, but no sound came out. Beneath the terror was a coldness in him, a kind of clinical objectivity. She was a beautiful woman, he thought. But he thought it without the slightest twinge of desire. Her female presence did not stir him. After a while she stood and removed her jacket. She folded it onto the chair.

He watched as she removed her clothes. The light was dull and unkind. Without clothes she was much older. Her breasts were stretched and marked from feeding, her belly had never regained youthful tone after giving birth. She stood there, swaying a little, as if uncertain for the first time that night, but she did not seem in the least ashamed. Then suddenly, beneath the coldness and the fear, he wanted to hold her. But he reached to turn off the light instead. When his eyes got used to the dark he could still see the dim shadow of her, standing there. He stood too and turned away from her and took off his clothes. When he looked around she was in bed, under the blankets. The terror left him then and he was cold and limp approaching the bed. He lay there on top of the blankets. Their skin didn't touch. The air's chill made his flesh prickle, and in the dark he could see the kerosene heater glow. He wondered what would happen and broke out in a sweat. But she reached to touch his face.

There was no coyness or artifice on her part. She'd been through too much to waste time playing games. And if her own desire seemed unfocused, her need was direct and real. He realized that it was a need, not for passion, but for tenderness. She was tired of pain. Distance was going to be impossible to maintain, and, anyway, the bed was too narrow. He put his arms around her.

"What do you want, Miriam?"

"Hold me."

"Okay."

He maneuvered himself under the blankets, too, felt himself enveloped by the warmth. In the dark it was hard to see her, but her body was soft like a wound. He caressed her a little as if observing by touch, more a doctor than a lover. Sometimes, very earnestly, she took his hand to guide it—*here*, she said, and *here*, as if showing the source of hurt. She had an odor of salt, musk, sweat, the smell of a woman in full maturity. She was imperfect and beautiful. He told her so.

"You think I am?"

"Yes."

"It's hard to get older. You're left with your body. You see it desert you a little, every year. You know someday you'll lose everything, your life, all the love inside you, it's like a stream drying in the sun. You don't want to be alone at night with such thoughts."

"So you came here."

"Yes. It's okay?"

"It's okay, it's good. But you talked about all your men tonight. You talked about love. So maybe you won't lose the love inside you. Maybe it will stay."

"You think so? Very nice. Then love me."

He tried, asking her to show him how. Her pain, he realized, was as real as she, and she was close to the edge of it, isolated up here in this tiny northern settlement with her own loneliness and loss. He didn't want to hurt her. But his fear was a constraint, too—all their wounds, combined, ran so deep. He was a stranger to her, if not to all of her pain. He let her guide him, felt the heart inside him thudding loudly through the walls of his chest. *Here,* she said firmly. *Here.* Utmost care was required. Her body was a long hotbed of taboo. Any invasion was forbidden. She'd been adored and tormented, desired, mauled, pleasured, violated by the men she loved, and now her guidelines were exacting. She knew how she wanted to be touched. She'd come from some kind of warmth and patience he wasn't sure he knew how to provide, and a maximum of gentleness. She would not be penetrated. He couldn't have, anyway.

He touched her as she wished. His own fear fought back each swell of sensation inside, so at times he felt like a surgeon performing a delicate operation—meticulous and caring, and, if he'd dropped the protective mask of concentration, full of love, of pity. Then she arched against him, and again, quivering, clutched at his hand, at his face, everything damp and slippery warm.

Finished, she said, *I'm finished*. But what ran down her cheeks were tears.

She pulled him on top of her, then pushed him to the side. She asked him to hold her again and he did. Relief filled him, mixed with a kind of sadness.

"Miriam, what is it?"

"I didn't know if I could do this."

He stroked her hair while she cried. She pressed her face against his and he could feel her temples throb, could smell her hair, a sweet smell, like perfume mingled with oil and smoke. But he felt weighted by his own exhaustion. He was limited, neither strong nor tireless. And after all, he told himself, she was the wife of Sami Sagrossa. Lover of a little Indian Jew. Of Uriel Lucero. Then Shimoni's lover. Not his.

"It's okay if I stay?"

"It's okay. But, Miriam, I want to sleep now."

Holding her, he did. It was a hard and sudden sleep, motionless, without dreams. He woke in the dark to see her face close to his, her eyes wide and dry. She blinked. And reached to touch his cheek, smiling. It was a gentle expression, giving her face a motherly look.

"Tell me, Nadav. You like to make love with women?"

"I don't know. Before—yes, always. But something happened with me, after the war, the hospital. In my head maybe. I don't know."

"Ah. You asked the doctors?"

He sighed. "No. Because I think *I* know—I think I *do* know what's wrong with me: I just don't care any more. You know something—well, in English there's this phrase: to be *in love* with someone—" She nodded in recognition, a slow breeze of flesh and hair in the dark. "You understand? So maybe I'm waiting to live long enough and care again, and be in love—"

"And maybe then, with time, you can."

"Maybe. Yes."

"I'll tell you something." Glistening in the faint light, another tear traveled down her cheek, solitary, soundless. "Sometimes I wish for a life without sex. Maybe to be with a woman, a good friend, whom I loved. I'd take my daughter and live with her someplace far away from all the wars, and we'd raise her together, my friend and I. Then Rana would be fine, I think. But maybe that's stupid." She wiped the tear off. It hung from her fingertip, a drop of dim-lit liquid silver. "Maybe there's nowhere left to run away to. There's war everywhere. Around us. Inside us. I think that if you feel *in love* then you also feel *in pain* many times. When you love someone with your body you risk feeling this pain. So sometimes, maybe, you grow tired of the pain and need you know you'll feel. You hide from it. You want to rest." She shrugged. "You think you'll forgive me for this later? Maybe you'll be very angry."

He moved his head drowsily on the pillow. "Why, Miriam? I'm not in love with you."

"Ah. But I want you to be."

He understood, then, her need to seduce. It was her only power in the face of catastrophe and loss. But there was something about it that was heartless, terrifying. He turned his back and curled into himself like a baby. Again he was exhausted, wanting nothing but sleep. He knew he sought sleep as an escape. She wouldn't quite let him go and put her arms around him. Then he slept. This time, he dreamed.

In the dream there was a border between lands, and a tiny arcing bridge leading across the border from one land to the other. In the dream three of them were crossing over, heading into the northern land: Miriam and he, and Rana.

They passed through a city where a single golden dome with a golden spiral towered above all the other buildings, gleaming in sunlight. Around them, people moved through the city. They were an ancient people, with dark skin and hair, dark eyes downcast, clad in ancient robes and sandals. The three of them walked among these people to the end of the city, until they came to a vast dusty plain speckled with clumps of coarse grass. In the distance were mountains. They were alone. He knew, somehow, where they were going. They set out due north across the desert.

After a while they came to a broad road of yellow dirt. Military jeeps roared by. Ahead were bleak wooden barracks, gray tents, lines of soldiers in dull uniforms cleaning weapons, sneering as they walked past. They too were ancient people, like the people of the city. But their black hair was cropped close to the skull, their eyes flashed with cruelty and boredom.

The dust exploded around them. They were suddenly inside the barracks. And Zeigler was there too, in the dull uniform of a commandant. But he glanced at Nadav once, winked desperately, and Nadav knew then that he was playing some part to save their lives.

Is it time yet, Avi?

Oh, no. When it's time, they'll send a car.

He understood that they'd be driven off to some heartless prison and tortured to death. Understood that their time was limited. Miriam got to her knees and buried her head against him.

Don't worry about me. Take the child.

Zeigler swung a long knife over them, twirling it in the dusty air. *Okay.* He laughed. *You're free.*

Dust exploded around them again. Then Nadav was running, panting, along a straight path of yellow dirt past all the soldiers and military equipment, heading south for freedom. In his arms he held Rana. She was silent, wide-eyed. The only sign of life was that she trembled like a bird.

Nadav woke to the first gray hint of light streaming around the window shade. Miriam had buried her face against his back. He could feel her blink. The words escaped him, a drowsy whisper.

"Tell me, Miri. Who's really the father?"

She sighed. "Mohani Benjamin."

"You're sure?"

Against his back, she nodded.

They both dozed for what seemed a long time but must have

been just minutes. When he opened his eyes again the gray light was the same. She urged with her arms, turned him toward her.

"Nadav. You hate me?"

"No."

"Then love me," she whispered. "Love *me.*" It was more a command than a plea. She began to touch him everywhere, and while the light from the window-shade edges lightened he let her, knowing that he was probably giving too much, understanding too little. But he asked himself: In matters of love, what is too much, or not enough, except a state of mind?

He let her do what she wanted, feeling desire now and not stopping it. He knew they weren't lovers. That later he'd be angry with her. In a spurt of anger he was suddenly erect, hard and wanting as he hadn't been in many long months. As he'd thought he would not be again. She was speaking, but he lost himself in his own yearning and barely heard her.

"Let me love you, too. Just for now. See, I don't believe love lasts beyond death. But you should let me love you, now, because *you* loved *me.* Otherwise it's not fair. It's not nice."

He closed his eyes and kissed her neck. Then pulled her on top of him and entered her abruptly, wanting to hear her moan. She was forcing him, after all, into a corner from which there was no retreat, into a place where the love inside him would finally be pushed out. The love inside him would take shape and form, would have a face. Sometime, somehow, it would have her name.

That was what she did in the world, anyway—she forced men to love. To love her. It was at once her great power, and her great, unforgivable crime.

Later she touched his right hand with a cool, curious expression on her face.

"Tell me about this."

He fought away the urge to pull his hand from her. It had been the same when Rana gripped it with tenacious curiosity— he'd had to fight himself then, too, and it made him break out again in a fierce sweat. But he calmed himself. Then after a while relaxed.

"It was a few splinters from a rocket they lobbed our way. Up near Kiryat Shmonah. To tell you the truth I didn't even see the explosion, I didn't even hear anything. One second I was moving forward, with my Uzi, like this—" and he cocked his hands, cradled an imaginary submachine gun in his arms— "and the next second I was rolling over on the ground. Then I remember I sat up, straight up. And I looked down. I saw everything very calmly, very clearly, I had the feeling there was all the time in the world. And when I looked down I could see, very calmly and clearly, three black fingers there on the ground, and half of my hand with them. And I realized they were all mine. Well, so, then I picked them up, all three of them, in my left hand, and I held them very tightly, like this—" he squeezed his left hand to a fist, held it in front of her face— "and I stood and ran. I even knew to run in the right direction. Don't ask me how." He chuckled, surprising himself. For some reason it all seemed a little amusing. "I know I fell at least twice. Each time, I stood again. The strange thing is that I remember I was very careful to hold the fingers tightly, so they wouldn't drop. I don't remember anything else—not if there was a lot of noise, or if I was afraid, or anything. Well, so, they say I ran more than eight hundred meters with the fingers in my left hand. When the men saw me they panicked, I think. One of them was a kid, just a kid, fresh from his first jump. When he saw what I looked like he shit in his pants. Then he fainted. Then I did, too." He laughed. "That's my story. They let me out of the hospital, once, after the fourth operation, to go to Shimon's funeral. I had a great bandage on the hand, my arm was in a sling, and the sling was strapped to the body, like so, to keep it from moving too much. I looked like a corpse. The nurses helped me get into my uniform, they even laced up my boots for me. Really, I couldn't dress myself. It was a little ridiculous. If I hadn't been taking so many antibiotics and pain-killing drugs at the time I probably would have felt humiliated. Then, just like that, I went back to the hospital for more surgery. It was the anaesthesia that I hated most, after a while. The fifth time, I remember, I had a hallucination. I thought the doctor was Shimon! I was telling him he shouldn't be there in the operating room. 'Go away, Shimoni, please,' I begged him, 'you're a soldier, not a doctor!' Then I thought *I* was the doctor, and *he* was the man on the operating table, and I was looking down at him and crying because I knew he was dead, and there was nothing I could do—no surgery, no medication, nothing—to save him. He looked very pale, like blue or gray. There was green mold growing on his cheeks. Then everything changed, and instead of looking down at Shimoni I was looking down at my father." He reached for her hand and pressed it to his chest. "Well. That's what anaesthesia does. It gives you crazy thoughts." He heard himself sigh from somewhere far away, as if his ears were tunnels slowly closing. "Maybe that's why I don't think she's insane. Ranit, I mean. Maybe she just has crazy thoughts sometimes, like me."

He slept again, washed in gentle calm. When he woke the sun was streaking across his face and chest in cold yellow winter rays. Sheet and blanket were crumpled around him. He reached for her, but she was gone.

The Chicken Coop

SCHINDLER STACKED SOME PAPERS ON HIS DESK IN THE GENERAL Office. Sitting there he was a man of authority, fair and young, apparently calm. But his hands were trembling. This Nadav noted with a kind of glee. Each sheet of paper shivered like the wing of a butterfly when he held it. "She left. To visit her mother."

"Her mother?"

It was noon. He'd missed an entire morning of work. In other circumstances he'd have been ashamed, but this morning he felt relief, satisfaction, a kind of triumph. Her disappearance marred it all a little. But he couldn't help feeling an extra joy at Schindler's obvious defeat. Schindler knew. Somehow, in the intangible way of knowing that comes with living in a small community, everyone knew, or soon would know. There'd be a scandal. Then they'd adjust. Now, though—the beginning of scandal—was an exciting time. Not for nothing had Nadav spent his life on Mayan Ha-Emek. He knew how things would be, knew that now was the time for him to take joy in it, to press his advantage, lay claim to victory, and begin to set things straight between this man and himself. It wouldn't do at all to begin with apology. So he waited while Schindler fussed with papers, tapped anguished, frustrated fingers on the desk, finally glanced up at Nadav with hate in his eyes.

"Her mother's sick." Schindler spat it out steadily. "She goes to visit sometimes when things get bad. This morning, she got a call."

"Ah."

"And you, my friend. You missed work this morning. Is that what they do down there on Mayan Ha-Emek?"

Nadav shrugged. He met Schindler's gaze and, for a moment, felt a kind of pity for the defeated bitterness there.

"So she went." Schindler stood. His hands were big and blond, spread out against the desk top. He leaned forward until they were face to face. "She told *me*. That she'll be back at the end of the week."

A small victory for him. That she'd told *him*, and no one else. But Nadav felt no immediate threat. He knew, instinctively, that this man glaring at him had never had her. Only dreamed of it. And dreams are sometimes the cruelest goad of all. So there was more than a little sympathy in him, after all, for Schindler, and for what he must be suffering. Still, he must not give up ground now. The man would do his best to humiliate him, but he was determined to remain stoic in the face of it. At least until she returned. So he nodded slightly, barely acknowledging Schindler, and then smiled in a grimly friendly way, turning to go.

"Wait, my friend! Not yet. You're working this afternoon? Or do they take the whole day off down at Mayan Ha-Emek?"

Nadav stopped at the door but didn't turn around. He heard Schindler's voice whip savagely past him, almost a yell, though the words were mundane.

"If you decide to give us the great honor of your work, there's a change of job for you. We don't need *you* in the apples any more. After lunch, go to the children's quarters. Ask for Malka. The women need some help there, they said."

He spent the next several days playing tag with six-year-olds, building things with blocks, learning how to diaper infants. He found, to his shock, that he didn't mind it. Though surely any guy—Galitzianer, for instance—would have laughed to see him now. He didn't even mind the brief sadistic glances Schindler threw him at dinner, or the snide, knowing looks of the other men. On more than one occasion a man passing him in the dining hall would wink, inclining his head in the direction of wherever Schindler sat. Nadav ate alone or at one of the children's tables. Sometimes a female teacher or two sat with him. Otherwise he was the only adult there.

He found he had a kind of way with children, particularly the difficult ones. They liked him. With the exception of Rana, who made it clear from the minute he stepped onto her territory that, in her child's way, she despised him. Maybe she sensed something—smelled her mother on him somehow, saw the sexual triumph in his eyes. But in her way she tried to make his time there as miserable as possible. That she didn't succeed only increased her fury. She'd throw tantrums in his presence, shattering toys, tearing coloring books to shreds, shrieking obscenities until she couldn't breathe, until he was forced to leave the room. Twice she kicked him in the leg. It left his ankle black and blue. He wasn't ever anything but gentle around her, yet nothing he did seemed to please or calm her. *A shame,* said one of the metapelets, *but what can you do? They took her to all the doctors. She's sick in her mind.*

He was silent.

One night in the dining hall he filled his plate and sat across from Rana at the children's table. She threw a spoon at him. It bounced off his chest.

Silence blanketed the table. He realized that the rest of the dining hall had quieted too. Then, after a second, talk resumed. There was the slap of food against dishes, the clatter of utensils. The hollow walls amplified hundreds of voices to a dull roar. Near one end of the table kids tossed cucumber slices at each other. He poured himself some apple juice, held the metal

pitcher high so ceiling light gleamed off it. Rana watched suspiciously.

"You want juice?"

"No."

"It's good."

Cautious disdain lit her eyes. Her face was dark and animal,
the open mouth twisting to a sneer. "Go away."

"No, I won't go away, Ranit. And you—you will drink this
juice."

"I won't."

He seized her cup and poured, then set it in the center of her
empty plate. The eyes flashed from him to the cup. He saw
their wicked intelligence as they measured, evaluated. She
grabbed it with both tiny hands, and for a moment he smiled
in triumph. But she moved it deliberately from plate to table.
A few yellow drops spilled.

The kids had stopped throwing vegetables and were still
now, watching. He poked his thumb through the cup handle
and set it, again, in the center of her plate. Again, she moved
it. From somewhere close, a child snickered.

Nadav let his right hand fall across the table in plain view.
Deliberately, he hooked a ruined forefinger around the cup and
placed it on her dish. This time juice sloshed over the sides.
Rana's head lowered so he no longer saw her face, just the
thick, glistening black of her hair, the tiny shoulders vibrating
with resentment. When she glanced up their eyes met.

"I won't," she said.

"Yes. You will."

She smiled. There was a tiny gap between her two front
teeth. The smooth child's skin was a glowing bronze, her lips
full, the black eyes large and delicate. He realized how beautiful she was—a glowing, beautiful child. She threw the cup in
his face.

From somewhere came a howl of rage. He stood, dripping
apple juice, smashing his left fist on the table, realizing that the
sound had come from him. A pitcher crashed. Juice spilled on
plates, soaked into bread. The kids had started laughing but

now one of them screamed. Rana jumped up and down on top of her chair.

"I won't!"

He lunged for her, landed across a tray of steaming eggplant. Vegetable sauce burned his chest. She shrieked furiously and leaped to the table.

Her tantrum had a rhythm to it, punctuated by strange chanted wails, like the accompaniment to a primitive dance. He reached and she danced lightly away, taunting with her eyes. Nadav felt his face scorch red. He tossed a plate to the floor, smashing it.

"Come here!"

"No!"

"Come *here!*"

"Go to hell!"

He vaulted to the table, stepped in tomatoes, and she jumped down. When the table collapsed food spilled toward the center, and when he picked himself off the floor his trouser legs were covered with pulp and pastes. People were standing now, heading for him. He knocked a man aside, saw her exit, slipped and fell and picked himself up. Someone else tried to block him and he swung with his left hand, heard a pained grunt. His vision clouded. There was only one sight for him: the child's thick, black hair, bouncing away, her mouth spitting contempt. He raced along the dirt trail leading from the dining hall, footprints outlined with eggplant.

Sundown was over, the sky darkened to purple. Air chilled his forehead as he ran, his hair's stiff black ringlets pasted against skin permanently browned by the sun. Arab skin. His mother's skin. Skin like Shimon's. But Shimoni had dropped away here. Old men in guardhouses at night might conjure lost spirits, might mistake him at first for the big brother they'd worshiped. Even mothers, at first glance, might speak the wrong name. But this child knew the difference. And in the full flow of her contempt he felt suddenly free. There was only him now: Nadav, the second son, the not-so-handsome, not-so-bright Nadav, who was good enough, brave enough, worthy enough, but never spectacular, never charismatic, never Shimoni. Yet it was *he* who'd survived. And he knew now, as he ran, the bright spark of violence inside himself. It had smoldered through mine fields and death, through seven operations, driven him past despair and impotence and lit the murky way toward reclamation of feeling, this common, earthly flame dead heroes never possessed, the flame of survival. He knew as he ran that he hadn't come for Shimon but for himself. He'd come here for Shimoni's woman, and for her daughter. To claim them, mark them, change them. To take them as his own. Because he'd never be Shimoni, only Nadav, and this child knew the difference with every fiber of her being. He would twist her if he had to, he would force her, break her. But in the end she would be his. All his, knowing the difference.

"Ranit!"

She disappeared behind bushes. Lanterns lined every path now, leading to the children's quarters, the laundry, the mountain road winding south to Zfat. They hung from the tops of ground-driven stakes, swinging in the wind. Golden light brushed the earth. He saw a small figure bouncing through shadows.

"Ranit!"

"Fuck you!"

The figure crouched in a pool of light. Something flew through the air, a sharp stone thudded against his knee.

"Come here, Ranit."

"Go away."

He advanced into the wind, his kneecap aching. "I won't, you know. I won't go away."

"Go," she said, "I hate you."

She vanished again. But he could hear the rustle of bushes, then feet pattering against earth. In and out of shifting lamplight she ran, heading along a broad path that led past the warehouse and carpentry shop. He followed at a slow jog. Air froze right up into him, brought a cold aroma of pines and spruces and crushed apples. Sometimes he heard her gasp to breathe.

Wind slapped his face. He turned once and saw, to the north, the black shadow of Mount Hermon capped with snow. Something inside him sighed then, a gut-deep root of fatigue and loss. He wanted to stop. But he turned back to the cold instead, the sounds of a child panting along the road in darkness. Cypress trees swayed. Above one tapered peak he saw the glitter of a single star.

Rana turned onto the path to the chicken coop. He followed. Every step made the odor of feathers and droppings more pungent. Pale shapes stirred against the wire-mesh sides of the coop as they approached, clucks sounded. He saw her dart ahead, the door that marked the entrance to the feed supply room swing open, and now there was a pervasive, troubled murmur throughout the coop. Chickens raised their heads, blinking. One began to flap its wings. Nadav stopped. From inside came the thud of a feed sack crashing to the floor, and there was an instantaneous storm of noise as chickens panicked. He could see the flutter of soft down when they tried to fly, their shrieks high and loud. He yanked open the supply-room door and went in.

Through wooden slats dividing this room from the coop flew hundreds of feathers. He knew they'd be rising in a vast squall of stupid panic, that they'd continue to do so like the undulating waves of a blanket flapping in wind. Yet, with eerie instinct, they knew when they were going to be killed. On Mayan Ha-Emek he'd seen them, heading for slaughter, crowded into tunnels where hands would reach down to wring their slender necks. Their clucking, at such times, was chronic and feverish. A strange smell would hang in the air: meat traumatized by shock and excrement, spoiling early.

In a corner of the room feathers fluttered through the slats. He saw one sift down, catch on a bed of shining black hair.

"Ranit."

She crouched like an animal. The sounds she made were animal, too, a combination of whimpering and snarling. Then he realized she was crying.

Hundreds of stubby wings beat, birds screamed high-pitched strangling noises as they rose to the roof, sank in unanimous confusion and rose again. Nadav crouched low. His hands dangled between his knees, and a sensation of tingling, electric pain came to him from the missing fingers.

"Listen, Ranit. You know I was here before your mother left, you see that I'm still here. And I'll be here when she returns. You understand? I'm not going away."

She was suddenly silent. He could see the feather, resting sheer and white on her dark hair, could see the flesh of her face glimmer dully. Pity swelled in him. She was only a kid, after all. And he'd been a man for years, had killed other men, suffered, seen things too terrible to discuss. *Remember who you are, Kol. Remember where you come from. Big bad commando, eh, to lose control of yourself over this little kid. It's pathetic.* He stood and stepped forward and reached down, picked her up in his arms, patted her head clumsily.

"Relax, kid. Forgive me. It'll be okay."

She kicked him hard in the ribs and he lost his breath. Then she landed another good kick, this one high on his cheek. Blood beat into his eyes, and Nadav tossed her against a pile of feed sacks like an unpinned grenade. One of the sacks split open. Grain spilled. Grain dust swirled. He stepped into the cloud of dust spinning in darkness. In the coop the birds had gone wild.

He lifted her by the shoulders. She was screaming now, but the sound was lost amid the shrieks of a hundred chickens. Nadav squeezed soft flesh in his palms. He shook her until he was sure her teeth rattled.

"*Love me!*"

She kicked and missed.

"*Love me!*"

He shook so her legs dangled in the air, peddling furiously, still trying to kick but unable to reach. His thumbs pressed harder. He barely knew what he was yelling, could barely hear himself.

"*Love me, Rana! Love me!*"

She screamed. Tears glittered on her face.

"Damn you if you don't love me!"

Then he stopped and held her against his chest. Feathers sifted around them. The little body was suddenly without fight. Rana sobbed.

The tears trickled on his neck. He could feel her wet nose and lips there. He smelled her soft, soapy child scent like a single strand of pure incense rising from the clutter of feathers and feed, and mingled with it was crushed eggplant stew, his own acid sweat.

Holding her, he swayed from side to side. His cheek and kneecap throbbed. He found himself humming something, suddenly, some tune he thought he'd forgotten long ago. Maybe his mother had sung it once. Nadav shut his eyes against the child's black hair. No way of telling, really, whose she was—was she the child of Mohani Benjamin? Of some other guy?

Of Lucero?

Swaying with the old Eastern melody, he rocked her in his arms. Tiredness filled him. How exhausted he was from fighting. How weary of terror and pain.

"It's okay."

She sobbed against his neck. In the coop the noise began to die, the birds to calm, dumb order to reign for the night.

"It's okay, Rana. It'll all be okay."

Maybe no one really knows who is the father of a child. But one thing's certain: everyone knows who the mother is. You're the child of no man, Rana. The child of Miriam Sagrossa.

He couldn't tell how long they stood there, swaying. He was clean of thought and reason. But after a while they left the coop and headed back. With the child in his arms he walked slowly, sometimes limping. She'd thrown a hard stone.

Between pines and cypresses came the flicker of holiday lamps swinging in the wind. If he shut his eyes they bobbed against the sightless background of his lids, and then he'd envision the final expression frozen on a dead man's face: mouth open, eyes forever wide. Such faces hurtled toward you from pockets of fire. Even when you crawled away alive the memory of them weighed against you, fouled the sight of the world. You lived, feeling death inside.

Rana's hands softly clutched his shoulders. She'd stopped crying. He pressed her to him.

On their way uphill she turned in his arms, and he saw where she was looking. Then he stopped to stand for many minutes, both of them gazing north to the dull white peak of Mount Hermon glowing in the dark, splendid and cold. Fatigue rippled through him again. He wanted to close his eyes forever and sleep near the top of the mountain, covered with white that turned from ice to warmth, knees curled almost to his chin. The way he'd slept as a child.

He didn't want to continue, and sensed the same in her. Then he shrugged off the feeling and went on, and as they approached the central path lined with lamps he saw Yitzhak Schindler standing there waiting.

"Stop here, Kol. It's decided."

"What's decided?"

"You'll leave Ramat Alon. There's a general meeting now. Give me the girl."

Rana's hand twisted his shirt collar into a ball as she clung, and Nadav patted her back gently. "Fuck you, Schindler, I'm not leaving—you can tell them that at the general meeting. This is Miriam's child. Well, I'm staying here with her until her mother returns. And I'll tell you something else: When the woman returns, she's mine. I'm telling you now so there won't be any confusion. You understand? I'm the only real lover of Miriam Sagrossa. The rest of you don't stand a chance."

Malka Cohen was a stocky, brown-haired woman with tiny laughing eyes and a nose that had been broken in childhood. She was one of those rare women who are utterly unashamed, and so social that you couldn't help but like her. At the general meeting convened by Yitzhak Schindler, she'd spoken out in favor of Nadav. Now she watched Rana cling to his trouser leg as he walked. She watched the child disappear with him into the big linen closet in the hallway of the children's quarters while he rummaged for diapers, trot along beside him on his way to the nursery. She laughed.

"So. Yitzhak doesn't love you, but Ranit does. Don't you, sweet one?"

She knelt in front of the child, who stared at her with dark liquid eyes and ignored the question. Malka stood then and took the diapers from Nadav.

"Tell me something. You'll stay here until she comes back?"

He nodded.

"And then?"

"Then?" He shrugged. What did he know, after all? That he missed Miriam but at the same time dreaded her return. Somehow, he couldn't know beyond that. "Well, I'll see."

"Sure." She smiled, curiously but kindly. "No one can do much else, these days."

He spent the afternoon chasing kids. It exhausted him. Rana stayed with him and threw a tantrum when one of the metapelets came to take her to the playroom. There, she sat in a corner by herself throwing building blocks at the other kids. Later he was allowed in to play with her. Under her direction he built a monumental palace with the bright-colored blocks. It had mazelike rooms, exits, entrances, dead ends, miniature courtyards. She pointed to each place where another block must go. *There*, she insisted, a little petulant, *over there*. He glanced up once to see that the clock on the wall said four. She'd missed her rest period. The others had left—they were alone in the room.

He heard a laugh and turned to see Miriam in the doorway. Then a section of the palace collapsed as Rana kicked it aside and ran to her mother with tiny brown arms held wide. Miriam lifted her happily.

"My sweet one. So you're playing today. You're playing with Nadav?"

With Rana in her arms, she approached him smiling. "So. You're playing, too."

"Yes."

"I heard there were some problems here this week."

"Schindler told you?"

She laughed again. "Poor Yitzhak. I never liked him. But I talked with Malka, too. Tell me, you're okay?"

"I'm okay. How's your mother?"

"Very old. She had nine children, you know. All of them men except two, and my sister died as a child. I'm almost the youngest. When she feels bad I visit her—her life isn't easy. But no one's is."

"It's true." He fondled a red building block in his hand.

"Mine especially, right now." She was half teasing, half sad. "Maybe you want to say hello to me?"

"Maybe. Sure, yes."

He stood to kiss her.

It was a gentle kiss, on her cheek. Then another, warmer, longer one on her mouth, and he felt his thighs tingle. For a moment he felt he loved her, without pain or complication. She seemed welcoming and complete, holding the child in her arms. It was easy to love her absolutely, this way. He felt the warmth of them both flood and envelop him, and standing there he wanted nothing but to protect them always, to love them forever and keep them his, keep them safe. Then he pulled back a little and some of his clumsiness returned. When she set Rana down and leaned forward to kiss him, Rana screamed and he blushed.

They went to dinner together. The child ate with them, humming to herself the entire time, her eyes removed and dreamlike. Later Miriam put her to bed in the children's house. He waited on the front steps to her place, shivering in his jacket every time the wind struck, his one and a half hands shoved deep into the jacket pockets. There was in him, suddenly, a great panic. Maybe he wouldn't be able to do it again. But when he saw her walking toward him in the dark, desire filled him. Along with it, too, was a budding, unfamiliar tenderness that brought tears to his eyes. He blinked them quickly away. When she was close he stood with sudden force, hoping for some reason to frighten her. She stopped in momentary fear, then recognized him and smiled with relief. He spent the night.

He woke up long before morning, disturbed by restless dreams he couldn't remember. Studying Miriam's sleeping face in the dark, he realized that he wasn't really seeing *her,* now, but some part of himself, coldly, clearly. All his torments and desires seemed very remote to him, like things from a former life. And he wondered: What is the truth of any relationship? Or the significance? Maybe it meant nothing in the end. Each person was separate, after all, on his own, so what was the meaning of human relationship? Maybe the truth was that nothing more than invisible ties, figments of one or more imaginations, ever bound anyone to anyone else. Maybe the truth was that nothing existed but bodies moving through space and time, suffering, laughing, eventually collapsing in dust to be blown by winds across the planet, under the blank face of the sky. Relationships didn't bind and could not save. Why, then, had he ever felt desire? Or loss? Or love?

He tried to whisper her name silently. *Miriam.* But he couldn't. He imagined it echoing across desert chasms like falling rock, disappearing into air. The name had a meaning—it was *her* name, the name of the woman, *this* woman. Miriam Sagrossa. What had they always called her? *Shimoni's* woman. Shimoni's *lover.* As if her relationship to Shimon was what defined her, gave her meaning in their eyes, lent her life comprehensibility for all the little people peering in at it. As if it was the only way he could forgive her for existing with all her unpossessable female quality, her scent, the soft wet power of it. A thing belonging to Shimoni. Reducing her to that. When in fact that was so very little of what she was. Reducing her to that. A thing to be possessed. A thing to be forgiven by him, by them all—for her existence, for her power. For her child. For making him love her.

Tears rolled down his cheeks, causing her sleeping face to swim before him in the dark. But a part of him wondered vaguely why he was crying. *The tears are foolish, Kol, and you—you have work to do. Whether you want to or not. Whether the odds*

of success are good or not. Your task is survival. It's your only duty,
your only real talent and, whether you like it or not, your only real
secret. Everyone can know everything about you immediately, you're
a stumbling country boy, no good at hiding feelings, no great intel-
lect—let's face it, the only thing no one knows about you is what kept
you alive. What made you run eight hundred meters, bleeding and in
shock, holding fingers torn from your right hand in your left. That's
the big secret, just that: survival. You don't even understand it yourself.
But you know it, you feel it. And so it's yours—your secret. And maybe
that's enough.

Then a name flew at him, spinning out of the night. He
mouthed it silently.

Lucero.

What was a man, after all, but a body? A name.

And what would a man's name be worth at the End of Days?
Only what it signified. Letters. Numbers. An essence maybe,
or quality of wisdom. A destiny. Such things had supposedly
been unmasked before Babel—once, common knowledge. But
the tower had fallen, shattered into the pieces of a million
alphabets, God's name clear no more, never again anything but
a puzzle. Except to those few who could walk away from the
rubble, the false pride, the material wealth, and leave all the
wars far behind. To know clearly again the meaning of the
Word. Why couldn't a soldier walk away, too? Why not? A man
stained with blood. Who stood, maimed, in the rubble of the
world around him. Realizing all he'd fought and killed for was
nothing but illusion. Realizing that his worldly beliefs had
finally betrayed him.

Shimoni, he thought. And then:

Lucero.

The name rang in his head. It seemed to him nothing but a
sound. A word. Faceless, meaningless, the way it had been
before it was a name. Make it a name, though, and suddenly
it was representative of so many things: a man with a unique
smile, with a particular manner of speech, a way of gesturing,
and sitting, and eating. A black-haired man with delicate Persian features and enormous black eyes. Yes. He could remem-

ber. Slender, but with powerful arms and hands. A good wrestler. Natural leader. A soldier.

Rana's father?

Lucero, he said. The sound itself was nothing to him. But when he could attach it to the dimly remembered face, it sent his heart pounding furiously, each fresh image it conjured like another spoor on the trail that led inexorably to the man, the soldier, his rival. His enemy. Once, long ago, Shimoni's friend.

Where are you, Lucero?

Who are you?

The answer rocked back and forth in the dark, amorphous and giggling, just beyond his grasp.

Behind it was someone, waiting. A man waiting and alone. If he shut his eyes the shadow of the man fell away to reveal a woman. She, too, was browned by the desert. Her hair tumbled around her ears and neck, black and thick and lightly streaked with gray. The eyes were large and dark. She had a name. Miriam Sagrossa.

The blood of ancient kings flows in my veins.

In the dark he cringed, trapped in a kind of cruel terror he couldn't even define. He didn't know who it was at first, speaking to him from the place inside his mind. Not the woman. Who, then?

Ancient kings. They ordered the deaths of thousands. They did so by a glance, a gesture. They dipped their robes in the blood of slaves. They were carried through the streets of the capital on chairs of gold.

Who are you? he asked the silent voice torturing him. Who?

And kept a hundred whores for their pleasure. They built an army that conquered the earth. They wrote great poems.

Lucero, he said. *Lucero.* And the voice stopped.

He knew it was Lucero speaking to him from the darkness. It was the soldier Uriel Lucero, speaking to him from inside himself. At such times he felt almost an intimacy with the man, a man he'd barely met. He felt he could reach out and touch him, shake his hand in the night. The palm would be calloused, the fingers strong. They'd share water from a canteen and talk officers' talk. They'd decide when to send a driver somewhere for food. Check over a terrain map. Later they'd relax, and speak of women. Of Miriam Sagrossa.

But he couldn't conjure her any more, not even by name, because Lucero stood in front of her. He'd have to get past Lucero to see her clearly. He'd have to get through Lucero, finally, irrevocably, penetrate the shadow of Lucero—even if it meant the destruction of the man who cast the shadow—to see her at all.

Uriel Lucero stood before him in an old army uniform, wearing the stripes of a lieutenant colonel, pearl-white teeth showing as he flashed a weary, sunburnt smile of comradeship and compassion. *You and me, Shimoni, there's no one else. The more you can do, the more they give you to do. It's the way of the army. The way of this whole incomprehensible little nation of ours. But let's break for dinner. Then there's this new material I wanted to discuss—they're bringing in more tanks tomorrow.* Nadav grinned back and opened his arms.

Uri, my friend. Let's go, you and I, and speak of all these things that only we can share. Because it's lonely to be an officer, responsible for the lives of many men, to face your destiny time and again down the nose of a gun. And later, much later, we can speak of women. Of the only woman there is.

Nadav held his arms open in the night, tears of loss streaking both cheeks. But his arms fell to his sides, the tears dried. He realized with a sensation like shock that he wasn't Shimon but Nadav. That Shimon was dead, burned beneath tank treads after an explosion in the Golan. He'd died in agony. Been given a hero's funeral. Somewhere, Uriel Lucero had watched. His own eyes shut in pain, lying on a hospital bed himself, wishing for death—his own face destroyed, and with it, his name. His purpose. What had he experienced? What could he have experienced, but absolute loss? His best friend, blood of his blood almost—but they'd shared the woman, too. So had the loss of his friend been nothing but grief? Or had he felt a twinge of relief? That in some sense his honor was restored. That, in some way, the woman would now be *his*. His alone, whether he had her any more or not—because he was her only surviving lover. Because while he and Shimon had loved each other, they had also loved her. And, loving her, there must have been a spark of mutual hatred mingling with their love for each other.

Or a spark of hatred for *her*. Her presence had poisoned their perfect love.

Somewhere, in the jumble of love and poison, they'd given up all talk of women and gone off to fight wars. One had died. The other had changed, become something different from what he'd been before. Or maybe he'd just realized, for the first time ever, a hidden part of himself. It had taken him over, mutilated him in its own way, sent him running far north, to a little house, alone. And it sent him stealing back into the world, time and again, for a sight of the child he thought was his daughter. A sight of the woman his memory still loved. And hated. Whom he still, in his dark mutilation, wanted. Because they were all that kept him on the earth, now: a woman, a child.

"Shhh," said Nadav. Lying in the dark, he shuddered. "Shhh." Not so much to Lucero as to himself.

You and I, Uri, let's meet. Let's talk about things. I know you somehow. Yes. Even if I'm not Shimon—I was a soldier, too. I had pain, too. Some of the pain will never go away. Some of the scars never fade. You walk through life always with the taste of death in your mouth. We shared some things, you and I. Let's talk it over, like friends. Let's bring it all out and fight it all out, here in the north. On your territory.

And only then, the woman.

Because I can't see her clearly with you in the way. I can't put the illusion of the great war hero Shimoni from my mind, I can't bury my poor dead brother in the ground facing east, can't put him at peace or even sleep until I'm done with you, done with war, and can return here a free man, keeping death far from my heart. So that I can see the woman, and finally be worthy of her, and of her child. I'll offer myself to her then. When I'm worthy. When I'm free. Of the sound of war inside me. Of Shimoni. Of you.

So first you, Lucero.

Then the woman.

Daddy

LATER THAT WINTER, WHEN MIRIAM BROUGHT IT UP, HE'D TEASE HER by saying that it was an old tenet of Jewish law for a man to marry his brother's widow. Even though she hadn't married Shimon. Even though she and Nadav never really spoke about marriage, either, except in this joking way.

He drifted through the season in a kind of dream. People on Ramat Alon were beginning to acknowledge his existence a little now. Schindler had receded from his life, tacitly conceding defeat.

He went back to Mayan Ha-Emek a couple of times for brief visits. Zeigler'd lost more weight. His mother told him that Rafi was talking about going to America in the summer, but people were beginning to doubt him again. And Michael would soon graduate from Officers School—probably as outstanding cadet. Michael wrote a short letter to Nadav at Ramat Alon once, saying that he was doing all right, enjoyed the military, and had a girlfriend. They didn't mention Miriam.

The child's behavior continued to be erratic. She was quite lovely and enchanting at times, at other times nearly demonic.

Once, toward the end of that winter, he noticed her running off deep into the fields of the kibbutz alone. He wanted to follow, but stopped himself.

Rana heard the giggling voices of other kids playing behind her but didn't look back, just moved farther away. The spring field opened up to her, a cold weedy jungle of milk stalks, buzzing insects, pliant thorns, here and there a flower of astonishing pure scarlet. She walked into it willingly. The place of her dreams.

Sometimes she couldn't tell if she'd done it this way before or only dreamed it. The others insisted that it happened in dreams, at night—but why was the harsh, sticky taste of a bleeding weed stalk so familiar? Why did the sheer red of a flower petal fit between her fingers as if it had always done so, her skin accustomed to the buttery feel of it? She went forward with a growing awareness of the sensations blooming inside her, budding edges of anticipation and terror. Soon the voices of children and the deeper, older voice of the metapelet faded to a dim chant. They were far behind. And she'd disappeared from their sight, too, but they hadn't even noticed today. The tall grass and weeds that were heads above beckoned. She drifted deeper into the field.

There was no place he couldn't get to, nowhere he could not find her. When the time was right he'd appear in front of her, suddenly, silently, waiting. Towering over her, arms opened wide as a bird's, he'd blocked the sun sometimes and cast a shadow on the ground, over the stones, the weeds, over her. She'd run into the shadow he cast, his arms long dark wings that reached down to lift and carry her. When he carried her she nestled her face against his neck. Once he'd shown her his face: a monstrous face, raw and ugly, nearly featureless. Something terrible had happened to it. The sight brought tears to her eyes. So he never showed it again. When she cried he held her tighter, rocking her back and forth.

A flower bobbed against her cheek. She stopped to roll her

face in it. Scent filled her, lingering, honey-sweet. She looked up at the sky.

It was blue like pools of clear water, streaked by ribbons of thin white cloud. High up, no larger from earth than a speck, a dark shape passed across one slender expanse of cloud, entered the sea of air, passed on silently, heading north. A reconnaisance drone, but she didn't know it. The tiny darkness crossed insectlike over the face of what had always been there. Then an image came to her of her mother's eyes filled with tears. They were large, dark, shaped like almonds, and the thought of them made her crouch very low to the ground, her head sunk nearly between her knees, humming a song without sound. Her mother's pain was in the eyes, always. Because of the things she told them that they wouldn't believe.

Dreams, they said. They'd taken her to places with machines. Sometimes the light was shone directly into her eyes. *Look*, they'd say, *look at the pictures on the wall over there.* Then flash the light. Because her mother was in pain. Because he'd gone away. But it wasn't true—he'd never left, only changed—he said so himself. And one day, he said, he'd take her with him. Then she'd be part of a world that was righteous and true. And her mother would follow, would no longer be lonely. All this, he promised.

She stood and continued.

The voices had faded to nothing. The chirping of bugs rose around her in waves that hummed to a dizzying pitch, receded, then rose again, and she felt herself urged forward on the crest of each chorus. Behind the hum was a single sound echoing in her head—his voice, coaxing, promising. *Come to me*, it said. *Come to me, my child.* For a moment, another face floated behind the voice. Shimoni. She smiled and reached out to touch it, her fingers brushing air.

Behind Shimoni's face was someone else again, another man. The one who'd chased her, almost hit her, then held her to him so she could feel the beginnings of a sob rumble in his throat. Nadav. The sob. It had echoed in his chest—she'd felt it when he held her.

Wind ripped the stalks one way and their leaves turned upside down, the undersides silvery gray. The earth was damper here. The insect hum rose and fell faster now, making her feet slap the earth faster and harder. Among the stalks a shape unfolded, stretched, stood.

He wore old repatched khaki trousers stuffed into the tops of worn paratrooper boots. A broad belt, a canteen, two knife sheaths on each hip, an Uzi submachine gun. His naked torso was crisscrossed with khaki straps and bloated red scars. Wherever there were no scars the skin was a smooth, golden brown. The mask he wore was the kind you pulled over your head, with holes for the eyes and mouth. From the holes two dark eyes glittered. He held out his hands to her. Then opened his arms.

Come to me.

Daddy, she said, *Daddy.* And ran there.

Toward noon of the next day, Nadav skipped lunch and wandered out himself into the northeast fields, where weeds would grow up nearly chest high in the summer. Now, though, they were wilted and brown. He tried to head in the direction he thought he'd seen Rana going. He didn't know what he was looking for, really. Just that the germ of a notion had settled in his mind.

Some of the brown weedy growth looked crushed to him, as if a body had lain there. There were smaller patches of flattened weed, too, matted onto the frozen earth. He followed the vague trail until he came to the northern edge of the apple orchard. Land dipped down here into the wadi, littered with rocks and fallen branches. Across the ravine, set far back on barren land, stood the little house.

He watched it for a long time, expecting to see something— some movement, maybe, a sign of life. There was none. When he turned away he looked down for a second, then crouched quickly to claim his find. A child's shoelace. It hadn't yet settled into the earth.

That night he went to the phone outside the General Office.

He placed a call to Mayan Ha-Emek, and asked to speak to Zeigler. The voice at the other end was some kid's. Nadav realized the accusation of sin he faced, calling back there: he'd taken his brother's woman, and everyone knew it now. He'd exposed her, in a way. And because of that he'd exposed something about Shimoni—something slightly distasteful, maybe, or even dishonest. He knew it wasn't Shimoni they'd despise now, but him. And despite himself, he felt that he needed to be redeemed—in his own eyes, if not in theirs.

The crazy plan he'd begun to conjure in his head—well, if it failed, maybe he'd never be redeemed. Maybe he'd never really have her as his own. He'd never see the truth: Shimon as a real man. Then he'd never see himself. Or her. And then, he knew, he really might go mad.

He waited. After an eternity, someone picked up the phone, panting from a run. Zeigler.

"So?"

"Tell me something, Avi. You're my friend."

"For that, you called? Yes, I'm your friend."

"You won't betray me?"

"I won't betray you."

"Then help me." His voice cracked, finally. "Help me find out if it's him."

Behind the madness that had formed in his mind was the far-off image of a ruined man, praying, alone in the night. And behind the man, a child. Then a woman. Miriam Sagrossa. Something was driving him deeper into the image, the idea, the plan, deeper all the time, until he realized that in a way he didn't even care so much about betrayal any more. Hadn't he, after all, betrayed his own brother—taken his woman? Stolen his secret? It wasn't trust or betrayal that mattered in the end, but the truth. Maybe that was why he needed, so desperately, to *know*. Because he realized, now, that she was the gift he'd promised himself. The light at the end of his darkness. The promise of his return to the world of men, the land of the living. But he had to prove his worthiness to her first. He had to save her daughter.

Lucero

IT WAS SPRING AND THERE WASN'T ANY RAIN THAT NIGHT, ONLY wind that slapped at the car windows, blew up chunks of hardened earth in the unplanted fields they drove past. It drummed into Nadav like a merciless kind of chant. The plan in his head had become flesh and blood, and now, more than ever in his life, he was afraid. Zeigler drove, crouching over the steering wheel as if peering through a mist. The darkness obscured how thin he'd become. The loss of weight had changed even his voice. It was a sharper voice now, a light tenor, clear and precise. They'd met somewhere south of Zfat, something Avi'd insisted on. He'd shown up driving a car Nadav hadn't seen before, and when he asked where it was from, Zeigler told him not to worry about it. Worry about Lucero instead, he said.

"The guy's got a lot of decorations for courage under fire, he performed above and beyond the call of duty many, many times, et cetera, et cetera. And like I said, some of the things he did are still highly classified. Even the computers don't know. Or maybe they just won't tell. And a lot of those things he did with Shimon. They worked as a team—I'm telling you this now just as a point of interest. But Lucero was maimed in the last war, and the important thing to remember is that it affected his mind. So they like to keep an eye on him. Because he is sometimes a problem."

Exhaust fumes crept in at them through the crack at the top of the windows. Zeigler's hands were fixed to the wheel like a statue's. Then he raised one to wipe his forehead, and Nadav could see that it was trembling.

"The reason he is sometimes a problem"—Zeigler slapped his hand back on the wheel, almost angrily—"is because he's very upset with the way things worked out during the last war, the way that war was terminated. It's his belief—and to be fair, let's say that this isn't just the belief of one troubled guy, but of some of our other people as well, including me, for instance—that, given more equipment and a little more time, we would have taken Damascus. And that *then—then* there would have been a few more chips to bargain with, we would have gotten a decent settlement finally, instead of the meaningless little treaty negotiated *for* us. Anyway, you can understand his point. The real problem begins when a man like Lucero threatens to take matters into his own hands. See, the psychological profile in the dossier indicates he apparently decided a while ago that, for him, the war wasn't yet over. He feels it must continue to a more favorable conclusion, even if he has to make that happen himself. Well, what man would blame him? But the problem is that it's inflammatory talk. It's against government policy, such talk. And who knows what kind of troublemakers he's still in touch with? Arms dealers, mercenary types, a lot of sick people, maybe? Our guys like to keep an eye on him. They even thought for a while that he was training his own little commando group, that he was getting ready to take some guys over the border. But nothing like that ever happened. No real evidence materialized." Zeigler steered them around a clump of rock. For some reason a warning ripped through Nadav, and he glanced at his friend sideways.

"How do you know all *this*, Avi?"

"More research on the side." Zeigler never turned his way.

"Listen, one more thing, Nadav. In the psychological profile, it says that he thinks he has a daughter. After the war—in the first hospital he went to, and in the offices of every psychiatrist in every hospital he was sent to after that—he spoke often of finding out where his daughter was, and of going to get her. He was obsessed with the idea of laying claim to a family. Even though, officially, he's dead. So maybe he's trying to do that."

"Maybe," said Nadav.

"And what happens now, my friend? Now that we know all these things?"

"Now I go to meet him."

"And then?" Zeigler sighed, a long, unhappy sound. "What happens after that? You think he'll agree to leave without a fuss, pack a few suitcases and move? Or someone will take Mr. Lucero to a nice hospital somewhere to rest for a while, and everyone else will live happily, then, for the rest of their lives maybe? Like in a fairy tale? Is that what you think? And you believe that you—that *we*, because I'm in this now up to my neck—can go and do what we're doing on our own, and that no one will notice? Don't fool yourself. They notice *everything*, eventually—"

"You're on my side, aren't you?"

"Thanks," spat Zeigler. "Thanks a lot."

Nadav noticed then that his hands were shaking. They drove deeper into the night and the north, past dreary signs pointing the way to some small settlement or other. Again, suspicion shot through him and he glanced over at Zeigler. Then the thought occurred to him that he'd go crazy if he kept on like this. He had to trust someone.

"Forgive me," Zeigler whispered, "but I think you're deluding yourself, Nado. And maybe it's not the child you want to save so much, but the woman. You don't even know that any of what you think is true. Maybe it's just some crazy way you think you can get to her, free and clear, with no obstacles cluttering up the path. It's *her* you want, don't you? You do. Your precious Miriam Sagrossa."

Hot blood surged through Nadav at the mention of her

name, as if Zeigler'd committed sacrilege by daring to speak it so intimately. But he recoiled from his own anger, feeling weak and incapable of harming even a bird. The fear welled up again. He heard his own voice come out a plea: "Help me, Avi."

Zeigler smiled and turned to him momentarily, his friend again, the old Avi he'd always known. "You know, Nadav, I was afraid you'd ask." Then he tapped his forehead with one trembling finger and turned back to the road. "But just in case, I made a plan of my own. I made some contacts. Anyway, *you'll* do all the legwork. This stuff frightens me. It's highly irregular, like I said—not to mention against the law, and if anyone really finds out what I've done I'll have my ass fried by the King of Israel himself." He grinned. "I'd make some commando, eh? Lucky the intelligence guys got me first."

Zeigler drove on silently. After a while he talked again, and Nadav just listened.

"As we discussed, he's probably not particularly sane. And all those so-called commandos of his—the ones they were worried about his taking in over the border—well, they're nonexistent, a myth. But he *does* have this one little mascot who does everything for him, runs errands, buys water and food, shows up to collect his government checks once a month in Tel Aviv. And around *him,* I think, you need to be careful. So if anything begins to stink tonight, get away from there. He could kill for fun."

"Lucero?"

"No. No, he just gives orders. It's the little mascot I'm talking about. A really sick guy, you understand, and quite devoted to him."

Nadav rubbed a clear spot on glass and looked out, expecting to see something. What, he didn't know. Phantoms, maybe. Ghosts holding out hands, in some kind of supplication. Hands with the flesh burned off. But there was only dust and the dark night air, the wind pressing in on them.

"This guy—his assistant—he calls himself Goya, okay?"

"Goya?"

"Don't laugh. You haven't read the creep's dossier. He was discharged—a psychiatric case if ever there was one, a real clown—he had his fun torturing some prisoners from Fatah land. You don't want to know the details. He'll probably sing and dance for you, or stand on his head to try and keep you away from Lucero himself. He's very protective. But he probably won't try to kill you. Unless Lucero tells him to."

"Thanks. I feel much better now."

Zeigler grinned wryly. "Don't mention it."

The road ended abruptly in a rising wall of dirt and rock. Dark sky blended into the hills. Zeigler turned off the road onto an unplowed field, bumping over potholes and stones. When he stopped the car he also shut off the lights, and they sat together in silence a while. Until Nadav looked at his friend, and nodded quickly. Then he opened the door and shut it quietly behind him. He didn't look back, just started walking uphill alone.

Two hundred meters north of here. There should be a path. You follow it until you're there—it's about an hour uphill, if you walk at a good pace. Directly uphill. To the north.

It occurred to Nadav that he'd been feeling this mixture of unreasoning fear, tinged with disgust, for a very long time now. And he was sick of it. Of war. Of death. He wanted it all, finally, to be over.

He headed north, mentally ticking off footsteps and distance. A soldier's knowledge was good for something aside from killing. Good for something besides just dying. The ground began to tilt up sharply. When he judged he'd gone about two hundred meters he pulled out the pocket flashlight and turned it on dim, running the yellow beam over dry ground and rock through the unreflecting, starless dark. There was a little path that cut through the rock. He turned onto it, leaned forward as it got steeper. The ground came up toward his face as if it had been expecting him.

He shut basic-training days out of his mind. What he imagined were her eyes hovering before him in the night. Her eyes were a dark beacon. Sometimes he stopped to check the time by his wristwatch. It was passing slowly now, then quickly, no two sets of minutes the same. What was it she'd said to him, once, when they were making love? *The value of a thing is the time it occupies inside you.* And he thought too of Mayan Ha-Emek. He imagined a star hovering over the settlement, shedding on it a pale, icy light. Then the star broke apart, and in the center of it was a deep hole opening into the night. He blinked and the star was gone. He stood at the edge of a patch of ground, staring at the splotched face of a court jester.

That's what he looked like, anyway—with the patched combat fatigues worn at the knees, sewn together with string, the jacket held together everywhere with thick red and blue wads of cloth. The helmet was old, not from the last war but from some European war of generations ago, and its buckle strap hung uselessly below his chin. Nadav aimed the flashlight. The face was revealed: round, unshaven, malicious infant eyes and a tiny button of a nose. Goya grinned.

"Peace."

"Peace," said Nadav.

"You're the lieutenant? I'm waiting for Lieutenant Kol." Goya giggled softly. Parts of his two upper front teeth were missing. Sound whistled between his lips. "You—you'll turn the light down, please?"

"Yes, sure." Nadav flicked it off.

The giggle whistled. "I was a little worried. The note you sent up said twenty-one hundred hours. Twenty-one hundred—"

"Yes. I sent the note."

"Good! So we have no secrets. And *you*"—his beaten boots scraped sand as he rocked from side to side—"you are Nadav. And you want to see *him*."

"Yes." Nadav stood motionless, stared into the narrowed eyes that glittered back at him.

"Mr. Lucero is a genius. They say that your brother was, too."

"Thank you."

"Mr. Lucero is also a friend of *mine*. We grew up together—near Bet Yala. Did you know?"

"No," Nadav said softly, "I didn't know."

"So. Most people don't know. He's private about things. You understand that way of being? You do. Maybe you're a private man yourself—"

"Yes."

"*Of course.* Mr. Lucero and me, we were in school together. We enlisted at the same time. We even went to the same base for basic training. Coincidence, you think? Maybe. It was summer. Summer in the Galil. Your brother also was there."

Nadav waited while the little man watched through narrowed, tiny eyes. Then he suddenly shrugged. He pulled a filthy piece of cloth from a torn pocket and blew his nose meticulously. The cloth fluttered in the wind. He shook it. Then folded it, replaced it in the torn pocket. One eye winked.

"You have a cigarette?"

Nadav handed him the knapsack gingerly. "There's a carton in there. Marlboros, from America. I understand that you like them. Also a bottle of Arak. For Mr. Lucero."

"Good." Goya felt cautiously along the sack's bulges before grabbing it. His hand, Nadav noticed, was thick and short-fingered. The thumb was missing. He caught his own deep breath and silenced himself. They began to walk. The ground kept sloping up and leveling, sloping up again. Around them sand whirled, wind whipping it into their eyes. And they came for the final time to level ground. Goya gripped his arm in a friendly way. His voice was suddenly relaxed, almost confidential. "You were in basic training yourself—I mean commandos, the real stuff, eh? Mr. Lucero made lieutenant colonel, like your brother. Special Forces. That's supposed to be a secret. But you know all about it, right? In basic training—we were together, did I tell you? I did? Ah. It was summer. Heat of the summer, my friend. One of the drills that day—we had to crawl under barbed wire in the mud and at the end of the course do a hundred push-ups, then run back to the beginning of the course and start again. Each time you ran it, there were fewer men with you. They dropped like dogs. Bloody, muddy, exhausted. I saw him do it all day—Uri, I mean—he was *enjoying* it. While the rest of us grew closer and closer to death. But you know about that. You know all about it. He's tough!"

"Yes."

"No man is tougher."

They kept walking. Nadav went along with a sensation of nothing but numbness. There was the sense, also, that he'd let go of things, of essential things that moored him to the surface of the earth. He'd entered a world that smelled more and more strongly of disease. Boundaries might disappear. But Goya kept talking, and despite the numbness Nadav listened intently. It was, in a way, fascinating. In another way, a way that frightened him, what Goya said made perfect sense. He realized this sense was what he must fight against now. It called him, beckoned. It hinted at a mist of logic at the core of the layers of disease, saying that all rules were gone now, all things that bound you to a life of civilization and treaties vanished, and there was only this: forgotten warriors gone mad, alone in the night with their weapons and their pain, doing what they would. Nothing tied him to the world, after all, except a pair of woman's eyes. But in a moment of panic, he realized he'd forgotten her name.

"Summer," said Goya.

"Summer?"

"Yes. You know how hot it becomes. By evening there were a few of us left. We were more dead than alive. The drill sergeant was a hard bastard, a son of a bitch. He ordered us to strip and run the course naked. So we took off everything until we were naked and covered with mud. Our backs were pouring blood from the barbed wire. A couple of guys fainted. This didn't make him stop, though." A dull giggle hissed in the dark between broken teeth. "Why? Uri explained it to me later, and it made perfect sense. The old bastard wanted us to *survive*, that's why. Because he loved us. You—*Nadav*—I can call you that, can't I? You understand about those things. You went through it yourself. You trained your own boys that way, maybe. Sure. Uri told me all about it. But you understand how it is, and *what* it is—you want the kids to survive. You want them to make it. It comes out of your love for them. And Uri understands those things. *A hard love,* he told me once, *it's a love that spares a man nothing, like fire itself. But a beautiful love. A love of survival, and of war. The love of men for men. A perfect love.* What do you think, Nadav? He's got poetry inside of him, yes?"

"Yes."

"And he's tough! Lucero, he's not just anyone. Neither was your brother. They shared a perfect love, he said. Their friend-ship was a meeting of the gods—of the gods themselves—that's what he thought. So tell me: you want to see him now?"

"Yes. Sure."

"*Yes,*" mocked the voice, "*sure.*"

They stopped and faced each other squarely, squinting through the wind that whipped more strongly now around them. Goya's splotched face glowed like a moon in the dark. The eyes narrowed again, lips revealed broken teeth in a silent snarl. They were at the edge of a flat clear circle of ground. Below, to one side, was nothing. Uphill from them could be seen the outlines of a small house. Two windows, shades drawn. From inside faint rays of light streamed around the edges of the shades, cast arrows of yellow along the earth.

"Mr. Lucero," Goya said, "will sometimes receive visitors. But never uninvited. You understand?"

"Yes. I understand."

"*Yes.* He *understands.* This is a nation of mongrels. From the slums of Paris, Latvia, you name it. German scum with their stinking blue eyes and beer breath. Every pig from a Russian farm wants to make it in the land of God, eh? And now there's the riff-raff from North Africa. Why don't they just convert to Islam and leave the rest of us in peace? A bunch of darkies, that's what they are. Like those Arab scum. You know"—he whispered now, conspiratorially, one eye winking—"I could always make them cry. A little burn here or there, a punch in the right place—those child-murdering scum would crumble.

I loved to hear them cry. But Lucero, he's of Persian blood. Pure Persian blood. Some of the oldest blood the civilized world knows. His parents are dead now. But in Iran, they say, his father was an educated man. A respected man. And blood runs thick."

Nadav met the insane eyes glittering back at him, fury tinging their madness. He wondered sadly if he'd have to kill this man. It all seemed so pointless now. Then he remembered her name again and chanted it to himself, silently. *Miriam*, he said, *Miri, Miri, Miriam.* For a moment it seemed to him that it wasn't Nadav silently chanting the name, but Shimon. There was a core of Shimoni that ran through him, that was forcing him to endure this now—he wasn't just himself any more, but his brother as well. Goya didn't know it but he was hopelessly outnumbered. Two commandos faced him now. Maybe the little fool was a trained murderer with the soul of an infant, but Nadav and Shimon were trained murderers with the souls of men. They'd murder judiciously, at will. All the time, knowing the difference. Facing Goya, he smiled.

"You'll tell him I'm here?"

The broken teeth glimmered. Wind whistled between them. "He knows. He knows everything. And he's waiting. He's waiting—for you, Nadav—he's waiting right now." The round clown's head nodded emphatically. "Go on. In there. He *knows*, Nadav—he's waiting, just for you."

The wind blew harder, sounding with a slight moan. Walking slowly toward the cracked plank door, Nadav felt the hard ground underfoot and knew that it all stank to heaven and beyond but there was no retreating now. As he walked he could feel Goya's eyes boring into the center of his spine. But nothing happened. There wasn't any sound. Death would not be now.

A kind of despair filled his throat. *Shimoni, what have you led me to?* Goya. What was it, that name? Something Zeigler would know. Zeigler knew about all those things. A musician maybe? Or poet? No, no, a painter. Yes. Would he have to kill him, this little clown named after a painter? But why that painter? What was it Rafi'd shown him once, some book bought third-hand from an old shop in Tel Aviv? The painter Goya. Yes. And the plates had made an impression on him because the names, transliterated into Hebrew, were Ladino. *Spanish*, Rafi'd insisted with a weary grin, *the language is called Spanish, my dear brother*. And the plate he'd remembered most: *Saturno Devorando Su Mismo Hijo*. A gray monster-god eating the still-living body he'd seized in one enormous hand, sick eyes rolled heavenward in horror—Saturn devouring his own son. But why? Because the child's eyes had seen too much, maybe. What happened when a child's eyes saw too much? Did they grow malicious? Was there sanity at the core of the eyes, after all—at the core, even, of Goya's eyes? Because to go mad, you must first have been sane.

He climbed to the second step. Nothing sounded behind him. He hesitated a moment before knocking. The damp plank sent tiny splinters into his knuckles. He waited but there wasn't any answer. Then he knocked again, the alarm bell at the base of his spine beginning to ring. He thought it was a sound at first and tensed to whirl around, fling out his good hand and strike to kill, but it was just the wind rushing by. He smelled dry decay. He smelled his own terror. And knocked again.

From inside, someone laughed.

"Come in," called a man's voice. "The door's never locked. Please. Come in."

In flickering lamplight, Lucero nodded greeting. He didn't seem surprised. He sat on a stool, leaning back against a makeshift bookcase. Nadav noticed that the third shelf sagged in the middle.

"Come in."

Then he turned his fire-scarred face away, closed his eyes, and rocked slightly back and forth. Nadav sat on a box near the door, eased the door shut with his foot.

Finally Lucero shrugged and reached for a bottle of ancient Arak at his feet, pouring some into a crusted brown mug.

Nadav noticed the text he'd been reading, also on the floor between his feet, spine broken, book open, face down. Selomo Ibn Gabirol: *Las Ultimas Obras.* Then a shock of sorrow swept through him. It had been one of Shimon's favorite books, one he'd carried with him everywhere during his days of university study. For good luck, he'd joked once, and to ward off the Evil Eye.

"You're here," Lucero said finally, "because we both share the same thoughts. And, maybe, the same love."

His eyelids were lashless, corrugated as if eaten away at the rims by moths, crisscrossed with dozens of tiny scars. When they flicked open it was as sudden and immediate as the tongue flick of a lizard. His eyes, sunk deep in their sockets, were enormous, dark, bottomless.

"Shimoni was a great man. When he died the nation lost a guiding light. I lost a friend. And you a brother. You're his kid brother, Nadav—I know. Believe it or not, I remember you. So. Tell me. You met old Goya?"

Nadav nodded. The place was dirty, walls smelling of alcohol and old food, the stench of urine pervasive. The bookcase was jammed, papers folded in the centers of books, marking places. There were stacks of folders on the floor, a broken old file cabinet shoved over to one side, a desk, a tiny hot plate, the half-finished bottle of Arak set amid a few filthy mugs and slices of tomato. The kerosene lamp shone on the floor between them. Lucero leaned back against the bookshelves, an automatic rifle across his lap, and he was smiling.

His face was terrible. Nothing but red scar tissue, the remains of a nose, lips that looked melted. But the smile was somehow exquisite—a perfectly even and white expanse, with teeth like pearls. And the eyes were rich, dark brown. His hair was thick and straight and black, cropped short. His neck was scarred down to the Adam's apple. Then the real, undamaged skin began, a golden brown. Nadav's heart pounded in his chest, so loud, so hard, he was surprised Lucero didn't hear it. But he bowed his head in a sort of deference, and waited.

"So. You wanted to see me."

Nadav nodded.

"Why?"

It came as an instinctive gesture, without thought: he raised his right hand and held it out as if it were a gift, proof of some sort. Then he waited while Lucero gazed at it in the full glow of lamplight. After a while Lucero nodded slowly. The eyelids closed over both dark eyes for a moment. He seemed to be considering something with utmost care. Then he opened his eyes again and stared into Nadav's with a kind of amusement.

"But a lot of guys get hurt. Why, really?" The ruined mouth smiled, revealing the perfect teeth. "Think before you speak, my friend. You know the old saying: *A word in my mouth I am the master of; a word out of my mouth is the master of me.* A problem with modern governments, and especially with modern politicians—talk, talk, talk. Yet little is said."

Nadav waited, hunched over on the box. His sweat subsided and the frantic beat of his heart calmed a little. Now he was immobile, while the shrewd dark eyes of the other man regarded him. What Lucero discovered wasn't obvious. An imperfection here, a limitation there? It was impossible to say.

"Listen." His voice cracked the dull background beat of wind. "Why should I put you through an inquisition? You're Shimoni's brother. I should love you like my own." He reached for the bottle of Arak. He shoved two mugs in front of him with one foot, poured automatically. Half a mug for each. Then, with the tip of his boot, he pushed a mug across the floor to one side of the kerosene lamp for Nadav. "Let's drink, my friend. Little Nadav. I remember you marching with the other cadets. You were a good class that year, all of you."

"Thank you."

"Please. It's the truth. Shimon was very proud." He raised the mug. "What are you waiting for?"

Nadav drank. It was sickly sweet, powerful, foul, and sent a chill through him. But he drank again, a larger gulp. And Lucero leaned forward suddenly, nearly startling him.

"You're here, maybe, because you share something with me. A certain love. A certain pain. Because we both fought and suffered honorably for the future of our people. We fought against an enemy that knows no future and has no honor. And when our own people made peace with such an enemy, instead of crushing them like the insects they are, our own people dishonored us. They dishonored our comrades—the men we fought with, men who died with us, men left behind as prisoners of war in the hands of the scum of the earth."

Nadav nodded. Then he was absolutely still, staring down at the floor.

"Who should we be loyal to now? To meaningless peace treaties? Foreign dollars? To the *enemy?* Or even to our own people? No, no, no, and again no. We can't be loyal to our own people, even. They dishonored us, they degraded the honorable deaths of our brothers, of *your* brother, they threw us out with the garbage while they listened to the clink of foreign change rattling in their pockets. You know the old saying: the enemy is within? Well, it's true. They let fools flood the nation with their anti-Zionist slogans. In the end, my friend, they'll always disown us. They created us, expected us to fight for their survival, to die for them, be maimed for them—and then they expected us to forget all we learned, to swallow humiliation and throw our weapons in the trash along with our pride."

"That's true!" Nadav exclaimed, surprising himself with the force of his words. Against his back, the plank rattled with wind. Lucero raised his mug in approval and smiled.

"Well. So. I say that such a people is no longer *my* people and no longer the people of my comrades. Or of Shimon. I say that I have no people, I have no nation, and I have no family any more, except for the family of men I fought with. The dishonored ones. The discarded ones. The men of truth and courage. *They* are my people. *They* are my nation. *They* are my only family."

Lucero nodded, still smiling. "They created me, they discarded me. But they also expected me to disappear or die. The problem is, I refused. In some small part of me that still is a man, I refused. Who says a man must honor a lie? Who says, except liars themselves, that we should stop doing what we're born to do? The liars and the foreigners signed cheap pieces of paper that sold my blood to enemies and to dogs, then they sat in their chairs, with their hands clasped over their fat bellies, and told me there was finally *peace*. But I know there is *not* peace. Their peace is a lie. And I'm much smarter than I used to be, because suffering is like fire—it teaches a man many things—and no one can ever lie to me again. Because for me the war never ended. It's still going on. They can fool their own fat bellies but they can't fool me, or God. God himself knows that the war never ended. Shimoni knows, too. Shimoni and I, we're an army of two. But Shimoni's dead. So *I* am His army now. Only I. Me. I am *His* people."

Lucero wove softly back and forth, as if in prayer. The smile was gone now. The black hair bristled against his scalp, close-cropped, glistening sweat.

"I am the army of the righteous God. Who smiteth."

"Amen," someone said softly. Nadav realized, with a quick stab of pain, that the word had come from him.

They talked that night. Or maybe it was longer than night, into the morning, then afternoon, then another night. Nothing sounded outside to signal daybreak. No one knocked. There was only the stinking little house itself, poorly insulated, heavy shutters shut over windows so the only thing that got in was the wind.

"Little Nadav." Lucero poured endless cups of Arak for himself. "You were Shimon's favorite brother. Did you know that?"

"No."

"It's true. Everyone thought he loved Michael best—that's his name, isn't it, the youngest one? But it was *you*, Nadav—it was you all along. Can you live up to that?"

"Yes," said Nadav. "Sure." And he poured himself more Arak, too. It was important, he thought, important somehow, to be able to keep up with Lucero. In consumption of Arak. Endurance of sleeplessness. Women. Everything.

"Shimon himself—" Lucero gulped the whole mug down

without a shudder—"had a difficult time living up to people's expectations sometimes. Did you know that? No? I didn't think so. Most people don't. I'm not saying that he didn't fulfill his potential perfectly. He did, of course. But it wasn't always easy. He was a remarkable man, you know. I don't even re-member all the times he risked his life. More than once he risked his life for me. But being a hero doesn't become easier with practice, my friend, it becomes more difficult. You endure moments of real self-doubt, of real despair. You aren't a man, though, if you don't have such moments. Shimon was such a man. I know. We were friends—the best friends that could be. It was a perfect love. I sat with him, on some nights, when he wanted to end his life. Once I heard him weep. But he did what he did because he knew God had called him. Well, I always saw things in religious terms—*he* called it his 'destiny,' but it's all the same thing: he loved his people. Everything he did, he did for Israel. In the end there wasn't any of him left, he gave it all away, all the little pieces. Israel was to him like a woman, consuming him. He burned in her flames."

Lucero stood steadily. Nadav was shocked at the sure, steady walk. After how many cups of Arak? He didn't know, his own vision was blurring. But Lucero walked to the hotplate, pulled it closer and sat on his stool again. He lit it by holding a matchbox between his teeth and striking. One hand constantly gripped the automatic. His eyes never stopped watching Nadav.

I know, said the eyes.

I know why you're really here.

But Nadav kept his face immobile. It was hard, with all the Arak in him—the stuff made him want to talk a lot, made him want to tell everything. But he fought the urge away and fought away his own weariness. He'd have liked nothing better than to sleep. Here, in the filth, on the floor. Anywhere.

"Coffee," said Lucero.

"What?" Nadav blinked. His eyes had shut.

"I said *coffee*. To keep us awake, my friend. Okay?" With one hand he arranged a pot on the burner, filled with putrid black substance. "I'll tell you a story. Once Shimon and I were waiting—never mind where, it's still classified. In hell. We were over the border, waiting in the black night of hell. There wasn't any moon, no stars. There was only the sound of our breath in the night. Do you know that after a while we breathed together? As one man? Our bodies were synchronized, there in hell. We became one. Like lovers. You think that's odd? Maybe you do. But I've seen things in my life, I've felt things, that most men never feel. The symmetry I learned to treasure—of breath, of the constellations, of our settlements in a valley below, like checkerboards drawn in the colors of harvest—all these things I *knew* in my life, I *saw* them. And most of these things I knew with Shimoni. *We* saw them, together. Bleeding together, sometimes, sometimes nearly dying. But we did it in the same cause. And because of that, we knew them as one man. When your brother despaired, I did too. When I loved the woman, so did he. Because we fought, my friend, as one. I was his true friend. I loved him. I *was* him. And there isn't any rest for me now until the people *we* honored with our love will properly honor *his* death, and properly mourn the loss of him. I don't mean with stupid statues. I mean with victory. Because let's face it my friend, my brother, my lover—we don't have any choice."

Sometime in the night or morning, whenever it was, Lucero dozed slightly. It was for no more than a second. But he snapped immediately awake and glared silently at Nadav in a scarred red fury of suspicion. That was when he displayed visible madness, rocking back and forth quickly where he sat, crooning Persian lullabies. Nadav could almost see him depart his own body and the dark eyes become vacant, the posture mechanical and listless. When he returned, his eyes were ablaze with insanity again and he continued to rock, back and forth. The melodies changed: Arabic chants, French folk songs, even a few English rock tunes here and there. Lucero spoke many languages. Once, it had been his specialty.

Nadav sank into the background sound of foreign tongues.

Lucero's posture changed with each change of language. He was, in turn, a French Jew, German Jew, Moroccan Jew, Italian Jew, South American Jew, Yemenite, Israeli. Each shift was subtle and utterly realistic. Lucero's gift for mimicry, maimed as he was, was remarkable. He jumped from one variety of Jew to the next. None was quite *him*—but he was, quite perfectly, all of *them*. And in the midst of it he glanced directly at Nadav, commanding him in rapid-fire English:

"Keep your eyes peeled, kid!"

Then, in Hebrew:

"Nadav, little Nadav, you remember how it was? Your first night jump? You stepped into line and then it was your turn. You kicked yourself out of the plane, tucked your legs, and you counted. But for a time it was just you in the dark, the wind rushing up past you and all over you. There's nothing like it, eh? You, *a single man, flying. In the dark. Alone.* There's nothing like it." Then he shook his head, fingers tapping the rifle grip. "Is it morning yet? Morning? Maybe? Well, soon. Then, time to pray."

Lucero kept talking. Nadav pinched his own thighs to keep awake, poured himself a cup of coffee that tasted like liquid mud. But after nearly dozing off that one time, Lucero showed no sign of exhaustion. Nadav realized through his own haze of weariness that the man had been alone a long time and was hungry, now, for speaking—a man close to drowning in his own unspoken thoughts.

Sometimes he'd place a hooded mask over his face. Then pull it off. Nadav didn't know why. Momentary shyness? Or self-disgust? Lucero's face was horrible. Still, you got used to it. You got used to anything. He knew that better than many.

"Some guys go through wars, they come out insane at the other end." Lucero peered at him through narrowed eyes. "You know how it is, my friend, don't you? You get paranoid. Colors change in front of your eyes, things begin to taste strange. You forget what's right and wrong. Maybe it's the hundredth loose arm sticking out of mud near some bomb site that does it to you, maybe guts spilled on the ground—whose guts? Theirs? Or ours? You begin to think that it doesn't even matter whose. You return home and somehow things don't seem the same. But men like me, men like Shimoni, those things weren't supposed to alter our stability in the least. Men like us, we were bucking to be generals one day. Men like us don't kill for *fun*. And we don't go crazy, either."

Nadav thought he heard the wind outside. Then he heard his own voice, quiet, almost shy, saying: "Tell me. Tell me even the little things. Everything that you remember. About Shimoni. About the woman."

Suspicion and cunning flashed briefly in Lucero's eyes. The ruined lips twisted in a grin.

"Well, it's difficult, my friend. It's difficult to remember sometimes. I'm very sick, really, you know. I'm a sick man."

Nadav nodded gently.

"Things you remember can make you sicker. People get hurt—physically, and in their hearts. Personally I experienced a great and crushing pain. Even before the last war." The grin faded. But the eyes kept staring at Nadav, narrowed, mocking. "Women! Women and children! And they say that *war* is hell! So what do you want to know, soldier boy? What do you want to know about the woman?"

Nadav counted the thuds of his own heart, tried to speak, but could think of nothing in the world to say.

"God," said Lucero. He pressed a hand against his face. "God, I'm a sick man."

"No, Uri. No you're not."

"Brave commando—shit. Gutless wonder." The hand fell from his face then and he gazed openly at Nadav with eyes returned to a kind of sanity. When he spoke this time, his voice was soft and caressing, full of apology. "Forgive me, brother."

"There's nothing to forgive."

"You think not? Listen, I'll tell you the truth. When we— when I was in one of the hospitals, they tried to make a deal with me. Part of the deal was that I assume another identity. Bad for national morale, they said, if the truth came out. Oh, they didn't say it to my face—I mean, to what's left of my face!—but that was the message. And the implication was that I lose touch with the woman, and with my daughter. No more relationships for me! Such was the price of continuing to live. I was going to be honorably discharged, they said. And they told me, the idiots, that I had to look at it all as if I were starting over. I had to become a member of civilian society now, they said. The stupid, stinking lunatics. To think that *I'm* the one who's mad." Lucero rocked back and forth. "It's late? Yes? Is it time to sleep?"

"Maybe," Nadav said softly.

"God bless us. His chosen people. And what about *you*, soldier boy? You think I'm crazy, too?"

"No, Uri."

"Well, so. Thank *you*, brother."

"Oh," whispered Nadav, "it's nothing."

He hoped, then, that the tiredness gripping Lucero would take over, envelop him, grant them both a second or two of peace. But Lucero half-stood, spread his arms like wings, one hand securely gripping the rifle. His arms were sleeveless and when he stretched and yawned you could see the long, firm muscles rippling like cobra throats in the lamplight, expanding, clutching. Then he sat again, fully awake, utterly relaxed. And smiled.

"A lot of these kids in the army now, they're dirt. Some of them, well, they're good men. They make good soldiers. But a lot of them—see, if they could think that far they'd be in some African swamp, they'd be killing tribesmen for good money without a single moral qualm. Dirt. I don't delude myself. Not all our people are *good*." His voice was soft now, a tenor caress. "Shimon and I used to talk about it a lot. The quality of the kids, I mean. How to turn a group of pigs and mama's boys into fighting men. It isn't easy, it isn't. And the fact that I call them pigs sometimes, believe me, doesn't mean I did not love them in a way that hurt." He poured himself more coffee, offered the boiling pan to Nadav. His eyes, needling through the holes in his face mask, were alive and intent as he observed. "You think it's effeminate? To love another man? To love him deeply, deep down in the center of you, here, here—" Lucero pointed to his belly—"well, it's not. It's not like the love of a man for a woman. Not at all. Because why do we love *women?* They're so different. We're aroused by the novelty. They're soft and wet where we're hard and dry. A complementary difference. A different smell. A different strength. And what is their strength, anyway, but the strange strength of the weak? Strength to endure, and to outlast us, in almost every way? Well, so, but you have to admire it. It makes them arousing. It makes them our enemy too—but a deceptive enemy, because their form is like art, it's a music that draws you, it's the vacuum that sucks you in and makes you create new life. A loving enemy, maybe, but an enemy. Because before you know it they're carrying away a piece of you: your child. Then the two of you, lovers, enemies, you're wedded for life through the connecting factor of the child. And all the complexity and mess of society, of civilization, is due to this: this connection between men and women and the binding factor of the child. What do *you* think? You don't have to answer. I think about these things all the time. Here, by myself, I have much time to consider such things. To consider nearly everything, believe me. But listen, you want more?"

"What?" Nadav sat upright, blinking away sleep.

"Coffee. More coffee."

"Ah. No thanks."

"Okay. What were we speaking of? Of what?"

"Of love."

"Of *love.*" A savage smile slashed the mask, an amazing perfection in the desecrated face. "Of *men.* I was speaking of my friend. I had one friend only in my life. Some men have more. I never saw the need for more. Men can't be closer to each other than we were. When men love each other, it's not a love of opposites but a love of similarities. Shimoni was my only true friend, and the love of our friendship made me understand that I could love *myself.* We were the same—the same spirit, the same body. To love *him* was to love *me.* We were wedded in the spirit of our people. I mean the strength and power of a people who will fight for life, not go like stupid cows to the slaughter. *We* were the *real* Jews, not like these fat, pale-skinned whiners, these American rich kids and South American *yids*. They're the reason the Arabs think they can beat us, don't you know? Because what are Arabs, anyway? Fighters, you think? Hah! A few Syrians, maybe, or a Jordanian or two—but the rest of them? You think they stand a chance against an army of men like Shimoni and me? If we had such an army they'd crumble. Crumble and be crushed into the dirt like worms, like cow fodder. We'd take Amman, we'd take Damascus, and all of the Lebanon would be *ours,* the way it should be. You say: But what about the Soviets? And I say: Shit on them, too! What are a few hundred million drooling idiots compared to a million *real* Jews? It's no competition, my friend. We'll ruin them if we have to, so they'll never stand up again. This will be in the final battle. And you know what we'll call it?"

"What, Uri?"

"Operation Shimoni."

His head drooped, casting a larger shadow on the wall. Somewhere, Nadav thought, he heard a child crying. He stiffened, suddenly awake. But it was only the wind. And Lucero was falling asleep. Nadav reached to touch his shoulder gently.

A hand caught his wrist in a violent grip. Lucero snapped awake, grinning cruelly.

"No, no, no. You don't yet know the rules."

Nadav felt sweat on his forehead.

"No one touches the king. On pain of death." Then he released his grip and shrugged, and Nadav cradled the twisted wrist in his lap. He was careful to show no expression of pain, though he wanted to cry. "But this time," said Lucero, "you're off the hook. Just don't do it again." He leaned back in his chair. The rifle settled across his lap. Inside the mask the ravaged eyelids drooped. Then flicked open again like bandages peeled suddenly off twin wounds. And Lucero spoke calmly, entirely sane and whole for a moment, a gentle man. "I know you're here for a reason. You want to take away the pieces of me again. The woman. And the child. You want to stop me from seeing my child. But you can't, my friend. I'm the true spirit of Israel now, and my child must know it. Because I've been so hurt that I worship only the god of war and vengeance. The righteous God, who smiteth. You can't do what you mean to do—take my woman and my child, and live a quiet life of peace. I don't even think you *want* to do it. Even so, you can't stop me—or the spirit of God, or even your own love for *her*—I mean the *real* woman: Israel. And you can't stop *my* love for *you*. As the brother of Shimoni. As a soldier of my people. Such love is my only honor, now. And honor's all I have." He smiled sadly. "But never mind. Time, now, to sleep."

Nadav watched him sleep in a sitting position, pain shooting up and down his own spine. In the midst of the room's filth, he could smell himself. If he'd had a mirror he would have seen his eyes shine blearily from a dirty face like two bloody marbles. And now, when it would have been safe to sleep because Lucero did, he was too afraid to let himself. He watched the other man sleep instead, his breathing regular, his head drooping nearly to his chest. The rifle lay loosely across his lap and his finger twitched around the grip rhythmically, dreaming, twitching and twitching.

When he woke, it seemed to Nadav that hours had passed. Lucero pulled off the mask. His eyes were bloodshot now, his ravaged lips trembling. Was he sober now, maybe? For the first time in a long time?

Nadav's voice came out a whisper. "Please, Uri, listen to me. Please leave the child alone. For her sake. Let her heal."

Lucero raised the filthy mug and almost drank, then set it down between his feet. He stared at Nadav with watering eyes. Pain burned darkly through his eyes, unblinking, and Nadav felt somehow commanded. Not by words, but by something silent in Lucero himself. Or by something beyond Lucero that had merely used the man as a vehicle for its command, Lucero's eyes as the messenger of the agony. Darkness and light mingled in his eyes now. He was sober and disheveled, horribly maimed. Nothing more than a vessel. Watching, Nadav felt his own eyes water. He thought, then, that he was beginning to understand the message clearly—the command that burned in the depthless pain of Lucero's eyes. Something that became less a command than a plea. And, for a moment, it seemed to Nadav that someone else spoke through the eyes. Shimon.

End it, the eyes begged him.

End it.

"My daughter," said Lucero, "is in your care. Tell her the truth. All of it."

"Okay."

End it, Shimon begged him.

Lucero pointed the rifle tip at Nadav. Then he smiled faintly, swiveled it around and undid the catch, pressing it to his throat. "Help me."

Nadav nodded once, twice, without knowing why. Something screamed in his chest. "No, Uri."

It was a clean shot at zero range. Lucero's throat exploded and he flopped back like a rag doll struck by lightning. Bookshelves caved in on him. The head, chest, the destroyed neck spouting blood, were covered by cascading texts. Paperbacks flipped open and a dark, rich red that looked like it came from the earth's core bubbled onto their pages.

Lucero's legs straightened out before him so that he sat there like a child, chest covered with books and shattered wood, one foot twitching in its boot. Both eyes rolled open and stared at Nadav, lightless and dead. His close-cropped head tilted forward. The kerosene lamp was overturned, spilling flames everywhere. The heat seared Nadav's skin.

He leaped from the flames that pursued him. He fell down the steps and the bottom step tore completely away, revealing the space beneath the steps, beneath the entire structure of the house itself. Dry ground. An open cardboard box, filled with medals. He reached down for it but it burst into flames, so he ran as the house exploded, crumbling behind him, orange tufts of fire leaping at the night sky. There were other sounds around him now. The cracking wind of a rainstorm. Sirens. He heard it all as if he were far away and would never reach the source of the sounds, and while he ran he stumbled over something and looked down to see the dead body of Goya, curled on the ground in fetal position. Then someone held him in his arms. Someone hugged him hard, wrapping strong arms around him. Nadav covered his mouth with both hands and shut his eyes.

"Forgive me, Nado, I took care of everything," said a voice. "You're okay?"

"Finished," he sobbed. "I'm finished." And opened his eyes to Zeigler's face. Zeigler was holding him gently, kindly. Zeigler was easing him to the ground, telling him not to worry, everything had been planned and taken care of long ago, and it would all be okay. There were lights flashing around them and men everywhere, some in uniform, some not. Beyond Zeigler, Nadav saw the face of his father. He blinked and the face blinked back. Then he fainted.

Miriam Sagrossa

HE SPENT HOURS ON A TABLE IN SOME OFFICE, RECOVERING FROM shock and minor heat burns. His chest was bandaged lightly. The faces of men he didn't know swarmed above him, gently questioning. How had it been? What, exactly, had Lucero told him? He understood, after a while, that they were worried about details of certain undisclosed operations being leaked. Sometimes it seemed to him that he slept. And always, in the background, hovering among the swarm of faces when he opened his eyes, there would be the face of his father. Once, he thought his father smiled at him. And once—maybe, he wasn't sure—the General reached to stroke his hair.

Finally he was awake again, sitting up in an armchair in the waiting room of a clinic. The clinic of Ramat Alon. Everyone had left except Zeigler and a couple of others, men also dressed in dark, modest suits. One of them told him he could go now, a free man. He'd been debriefed.

It was morning, but a lot of people weren't working yet. A lot of them, in fact, stood around talking in urgent whispers, and when they saw him emerge from the clinic some pointed directly at him. He realized then that rumor would work everything out—the fire, the invasion of security forces, the death of a recent legend. Anyway, he was sworn to disclose none of it. For him, now, it must all be over.

He headed for Miriam's place, feeling the eyes of Ramat Alon on him. Maybe life had intended him for this: for taking part in what, aside from the skin seared on his chest, seemed almost to have been a dream.

But it was all over, and he sat in her little kitchenette with sunlight shafting across the tabletop like golden icicles. Some streaked her face and hair. Where it touched her hair, the gray and black blended to a pale shimmering hue. She wasn't looking at him or at the sunlight. She was staring down at her hands, clasped tightly in front of her. He peered to make sure and saw that her eyes were shut. When he looked again he saw that the tight-clasped hands were white at the knuckles, trembling with stress. She wasn't exotic to him any more. She looked tense and older this morning, without seductive quality, almost without mystery. Quiet, wrapped in something private, she was all there for him and she was just what she was, no more, no less. Just a woman.

Miriam Sagrossa—who was she, anyway? A woman who had done many things in her life, a lot of them foolish. She'd lacked education and made a living for a while mopping up the garbage of others. She'd married and suffered, erred with the men who loved her, had loved them all, differently, as she could at the time. She'd learned from life, the hard way. She'd made terrible mistakes. And borne a child. Had she wanted the child? No one would know. Now she was filled with love for her child. Maybe her child was the only real thing in life that would ever fill her with that, just that—pure and simple—love.

But who could say?

Even though she was without mystery this morning, there was still something in her that wasn't revealed. Something that he realized never had been, never would be. And she wasn't *his*, either, because she belonged to no one else. She was a world unto herself, a world called Miriam Sagrossa. To lay claim to that world was a violation of it and of her. What she demanded was revocation of ownership. She would not be possessed. Only given to, and shared, with herself, with her child.

Looking at her in the dry sunlight of morning, he felt that for the first time he knew her. And somehow knew himself. They were two simple people, after all, neither of them much at home with modern technology or intellectual sophistry, each of them full of ideal and of error. Both tender, both violent, filled with a knowledge of suffering and, in their way, of beauty. Both committed to life. He looked at her and for a moment saw himself. Then he gave up all the masks and saw her—just her, Miriam Sagrossa. He knew that she had made of her life a glory and a catastrophe, and everything in between. And despite it all, or because of it all, he loved her.

"You know what they say, Miri?" His right hand tapped the tabletop. He glanced down at it and didn't feel repelled. He was getting used to it, he guessed. "You know what a kid says at his bar mitzvah? 'Today I am a man.' Well, maybe it's not true then. Maybe he's too young. He didn't go through all the fire yet—I mean, the pain of being alive. He didn't. Not yet. Not really." He set his hand against a ray of sunlight. It made a distorted, hard-edged shadow. Then he smoothed it over with the left hand, both hands touching gently. One maimed, the other perfect—wasn't that, after all, a kind of symmetry? And he laughed. "Me, I thought I was a man long ago. I thought, after the war, 'There, that's all the fire there is and all the pain, I'll never feel pain again, I lost all there was to lose. And never mind *pain*, I will never *feel* again. I won't feel love. Or fear.' See, I thought that's what it is to be a man: never to feel or to love, really. Never to weep. But I was wrong."

Softly, she'd begun to cry. She kept her head bowed and her hands clasped tightly in front of her in the sunlight, and now and then her shoulders trembled.

"Anyway, Miri, today is *my* bar mitzvah. That's what I believe. It's strange for me, you know, it's a new feeling. Maybe men knew this feeling, or something like it, when they walked on the moon. I can't be sure. But I know that in some way I'm

changed. And you know what I feel *now*? Different from before. I don't want to possess you any more. I only want to be
with you. Because I'm worthy of you, finally, today. Today I'm
a man. Today I'm free."

She glanced up at him, tears streaking across the rays of sun
that split her face into light and shadow. She pressed a hand
to her mouth, once. That was all. No sound. He looked at her
and his own mouth went completely dry, but he spoke anyway.

"And I promise—" Then he swallowed something hard. It
was what he was about to say, he realized, that frightened him
now more than anything he'd said before. "I promise that you
won't ever lose me in military combat. I'll use violence only to
save your life or your child's. Aside from that, no. That's the
kind of man I want to be, a nonviolent man. I don't know how
to be one yet, but I'll learn. And we'll find a different way to
live. I don't know how or where, but we'll do it. This I can
promise. My days of war are over." More light came through
the window, flooding their corner of the room. It blinded him
momentarily, washed his face and chest while he looked at her,
so that for a second he had to look away. "What do you think,
Miriam? Will you marry a free man? I love you and I love your
daughter. I will take her for my own."

After a while she reached to hold both his hands. Her fingers
were warm around his. He watched her silently and time
passed. He could hear feet passing by outside on the grass and
stone, pans clashing, a far-off grinding of harvest truck gears.

The First Kiss

WHEN AVI ZEIGLER RETURNED TO MAYAN HA-EMEK, HE WENT directly to Jolie's place.

It was evening. He looked utterly spent to her, with an unhealthy, feverish color to his cheeks. Over the past few weeks, it seemed he'd lost all the rest of his excess weight. There was no more fat to him. This, then, was the essential Avi: slight, and surprisingly agile. But his eyes twinkled with a kind of malice, daring Jolie to question him. She knew better.

He sat there drinking endless glasses of water, as if there were a bottomless well inside that he was trying to fill. Sometimes a drop dribbled down his chin, which was overgrown with blond stubble. After a while he stood abruptly and headed for the bathroom. He was there a long time. When he came out he was a little pale, but his face had a scrubbed look and he'd dampened his hair with water, as if trying to revive himself. From what, she had no way of knowing. He sat again and dragged the chair in front of hers until their faces were very close.

"Tell me. It's true what they say?"

"What?"

"That the first time is the best time?"

She didn't like the cruelty in his eyes, and turned away. "What are you talking about?"

"I'm talking about *fucking*. Why don't you tell me—tell me all about it."

She searched herself for feeling now but didn't find it. "Why, Avi? Why are you asking *me*?"

"Because, *I*"—he was spitting out the words—"am a virgin." There was a barely controlled fury in his voice. She knew that it came from the loneliness of his life, that maybe he wanted vengeance for it all. But she could see only the cruelty of him now: he was pale and thin and mean, pared down, finally, to his most basic strand. Specks of spit hit her face. "And I thought that *you*—well, maybe you know. Something about sex, I mean. Maybe *that's* your big secret."

"My secret?"

"Sure!" He was sneering. "You think no one notices? You think they *like* loners around here? Everyone knows something happened to you that you don't speak about. And me, I'm sick of it, you know? So why don't you tell *me*? I'm safe! I'm a virgin! I'm nothing but your friend, right? And no one ever even let me kiss them—okay? So tell me, my friend. Why don't you tell me what it's like?"

Jolie blinked back a tear or two. It was strange, she thought, to be crying and not feel a thing. As if the lack of love in her life had prepared her exquisitely for this, just this: to show emotion, yet not experience it.

"Why should I, Avi?"

"Why *shouldn't* you?"

"Because you're cruel right now. And for all the sex I had with Rafi I might as well be a virgin too. Well, almost. And by the way, in case you're curious, only one person ever kissed *me* before—*one*—and it wasn't Rafi. Rafi doesn't like to kiss. He says it's too—"

"Too what?"

"Too *intimate.*"

His eyes bored into hers, unrelentingly blue and nasty.

"Then who was it?" he asked gleefully. "This great kiss of yours. Someone I know, maybe? Tell me, my *almost*-virgin friend—tell me who it was!"

Jolie said the name to herself, silently. Then formed the name with her lips. Until the sound came out, quietly:

"Shimon."

How stupid, she thought, how insignificant, really. A kiss. But Zeigler's eyes were clouded with confusion now, and he seemed almost to retreat, lurching back slightly in his chair. Then his mouth opened in undisguised surprise.

The knock on her door had sounded that evening in spring, weeks after Rafi'd left for good, and she was curious. No one she knew would have knocked. But she yelled for whoever it was to come in, then kicked off her shoes and toed them under the bed. When she looked up there was the dark figure of a man in the doorway, his form distinct but the features obscured. Then he stepped into the room's light like a moth emerging. It was Shimoni.

"So," he said, "how are you?"

Jolie set down the book she'd been reading and he stepped forward to lean over a little, peering at the title. He'd show-ered, so his hair was all damp ringlets. He had a smell of lotion about him, a kind of mint, and another odor that surprised her—a milky scent, like the smell of a child. A single drop of water slid from his hair down one unshaven cheek. She stared at it. He grinned and brushed it off, speaking in English.

"I don't know about this beard. I try to look like a professor. Maybe I need a pipe. Or some glasses—sure. So. I see you read seriously. It's a serious book."

"You've read it?"

In English, she thought, her voice sounded very small, ab-surdly demure. Almost pathetic. But he didn't seem to notice any difference and pulled up a chair, sitting in it elbow on knee and chin in his hand like the Thinker. Statuelike except for his smile, which was both weary and engaging.

"Sure, I read it. But in Hebrew. I don't know how good the

translation was. That's my favorite thing—" He looked away out the dark window, at nothing, and was lost for a moment. Then he returned and grinned again. "To study, I mean. Someday, when I finish with the army, that's what I'll do."

"When you finish?"

He nodded. Then he sat up and stopped smiling, suddenly uncomfortable.

Jolie felt apologetic. Also embarrassed, and full of a kind of fear she couldn't explain. She searched herself for something to say to this man she'd heard much of but didn't know at all.

"You like coming back here?" she said finally, reverting to Hebrew. "I mean to Mayan Ha-Emek?" Then blushed. But he relaxed again, and the smile reappeared like a curving white moon.

"I like it a lot, yes. But not to live on. Not any more. There's a great world out there to know. We need to decide for ourselves, each person alone, where to go and what to do—to follow our destinies, not to do what a group of others tells us we must. Even a group of others we love very much. Don't you think this is true? But, please, I need to ask you a favor. Can we speak now in English? If it's okay with you. I want to practice. I have some exams next week."

"Of course."

But Jolie felt a little hurt. He hadn't come to see her, after all. He'd come for her language. When she met his eyes, though, they were kind. Not at all the lizard eyes of the weary man in the truck. And there was mild apology in his smile.

"Don't be insulted. I want to learn, too. We're related by marriage, after all. Or we were. So at least we should know each other a little—yes? I want to learn from *you*. *I'd like* to learn from you. There. Did I say it right? I mean, correctly? Nadav told me to come visit you. He says you're his best friend." Then he laughed. "And Rafi says so, too."

"And that's funny?"

"Ah, no, no! No. Now you're angry with me. And I didn't mean to insult you. No, listen—I laugh because I think it's great. I *love* my brothers, even little Rafi, but I think Nadav's

329

a great guy. He has an open mind and an open heart. You see, most men wouldn't admit that a woman is their best friend. But Nadav will. And you know something? I think that he's the best man I know. I think he's a better man than me. Excuse me. Than *I*."

But she was still a little offended. After all, she thought, she'd had about enough of the whole family. She stood and tossed her book on the bed. She puttered around the burner, pouring out old coffee grounds and setting up a single cup with milk. Then relented and set up two. She noticed him watching with a solemn look. Being offended had given her back her power at last.

"And you?" she said finally.

"Me?"

"Yes, you. What about you? Is a woman your greatest friend?"

"No. Only my greatest lover."

"I'm serious."

"Ah. So am I."

"Well, then—why not?" A match burned down to her finger, searing it. She sucked the finger dispassionately, proud of her stoicism, and lit another.

He was watching with a curious expression, one ankle hooked over the opposite knee and his arms flung over the chair, which tilted back. It occurred to her how male a thing that was, that perpetual tilting back of a chair. Men were always testing to see how far they could go before disaster. And plenty of times they achieved disaster. But, at any rate, they'd discover some essential point of limitation—and if they and everybody else survived, they'd know just how far they could actually tilt the next time. There was something tiresome in it, but also something admirable. It occurred to her, too, that most women sat differently in their chairs. Some were just beginning to think of tilting back. Some never did. Yet there was also much to be said for simply sitting, in the moment and the stillness, and not testing nature past its breaking point. Both qualities, tilting and stillness, must be parts of a full human being. Both were part and parcel of fulfillment itself. But *bal-ance*—of all movement and stillness, all maleness and female-ness—was the most difficult thing to achieve. And she realized, watching him tilt particularly far back, then right himself at the last minute, that it was a balance she had also sought, without knowing it, all her life. A balance of male and female, of friendship, individuality, community, love. Because of that she'd married Rafi. And had not found it. Still, she was trying.

Now Shimoni sat completely upright, like a kid chastised at school. She could see him contemplate. He was attempting to answer the question.

"Why not?" he said softly, finally. "Why not? I don't know. Maybe it's because I'm in the army so long. Excuse me. Because *I've been* in the army so long. A strange dichotomy occurs—inside men, sometimes, I mean. A *friend* is defined as someone who will save your physical life. In other words, a man. But for tenderness, and all the civilized things, you go to someone apart from the men and the wars: a woman. So you walk around as a human being divided. On one side, your friend. On the other side, your woman. Probably it's not the most healthy—I mean, *the healthiest*—it's not the healthiest way to exist. But I see no way out of it at the present time. At least not until there's no war. Even then, I don't know! Because opposition is the way of nature, too. For example—" The chair tipped back, then he leaned forward so it jerked upright again, and spread his hands apart, palms turning away from each other like wings. "For example. If you have a pair of electrons in a system of two particles—well, this is difficult to explain, but just imagine two little dots moving. Let's say they are *spinning*. Well, the *spin* of one of the electrons will be *exactly opposite* the spin of the other electron. Exactly! And here, now, here's the amazing thing about it: if you take one of the elec-trons and pass it through a magnetic field alone, you will change the spin of it. But the *other* electron—the one that *didn't* pass through the magnetic field—will *automatically change its own spin until, again, it is the reverse of the spin of the other electron.* So nature insists on opposition! It insists on essential difference. Some even say that nature *herself* insists on war. She makes of it all a great symmetry. To fight, to be always opposite, even to be always opposite *nature*, this is our destiny." He grinned, a little hint of mischief in his eyes. And in that moment, she thought, he looked like Rafi. "It's even our destiny to fight *against* opposition, to fight against *fighting*. But maybe fighting is natural, too. When we're born we fight to breathe. The first act of our life is a scream of war. We wrench ourselves from a harmonious bubble into the blinding light and terror of an unknown immensity. Why shouldn't we scream? And fight? We fight for the first breath, we fight for the last breath of life before we die. And for every necessity in between. So maybe—maybe—is it more proper to say 'perhaps'? It doesn't matter? Thank you—maybe *I'm* like the original primitive man. A warrior."

His smile was broad now, a fierce white. The coffee boiled and she poured it into two cups, where it mingled with milk to a muddy brown. He stood. Suddenly he was leaning very close to her, and his smile was gone.

"And you? What do you think of all that?"

Jolie offered him a cup but her hand was shaking. He took it, set it down. She felt suddenly chilled.

"I think you should leave the army." She heard herself faintly, with a kind of shock. "Before it's too late."

"Too late for what?"

"For you."

"Ah," he said quietly, "but that doesn't matter."

When he looked at her, his eyes were gentle.

They took a long walk that night, away from the settlement, down along the road, and every once in a while he'd point out some little area between trees or bushes, where he and his classmates had hidden things as children, maintained secret meeting places, acted out imaginary scenes of battle. Always, he said, *he'd* played the hero. For some reason the others had just allowed it at first. After a while they'd demanded it. He'd felt compelled to fulfill this demand, even on days when he didn't really want to. And after a while it had seemed to him that he had no choice any more. The demand defined the role. He stepped into it automatically, to learn what he might become. The imaginary scenarios had grown more and more complex over the years, more filled with imaginary danger. Once, at the age of twelve, he'd crawled on his belly through the trees in a kind of aching excitement, so swept up in the drama of things that he fully expected to die that hour. When he stood to run for a clearing, his heart thudding doom and victory, he'd felt a stiffening between his thighs: an erection. Looking up, his face had been spattered with drops of rain. Then for a moment he'd thought of a girl he liked, and of his mother, but brushed these thoughts from his mind and attained the clearing in a triumphant climax, kneeling on the earth, staking an imaginary flag, bending down to kiss it while against his back the rain splattered down.

Did she mind? he asked. Did she mind him telling her all this? He hoped it was not embarrassing.

No, she told him, she didn't mind.

"You're strange. Not in a bad way—in a good way. You're not really like an American."

"That's good?"

"Yes." He laughed. "But please don't misunderstand me. I think Americans are great. They're big and loud and spoiled and inventive, and very friendly. They're the infants of the world. They eat, they talk, they *want* all the time—but sometimes that's good. Still, you seem different to me. Maybe you're just quieter. An excellent quality. Nadav says you have a good soul. And Rafi told me that too, once, in exactly the same words."

She didn't know about souls, and said nothing.

"The woman I love has a child." He bent down to pluck a weed stalk from the earth. Then he crushed the stalk, bit by bit, in his hands. "A daughter. She isn't mine—she came with the woman, in a way—a very pretty little girl, very bright, a little crazy. But whenever I look at her I feel a loss of pride. That's stupid on my part. A great failing. I hide this fact, the fact of the child, from many people I know. I hide it for a long time.

Excuse me—*I've hidden it* for a long time—even from my brothers. *Especially* from my brothers. You know why? Because even though I know I'm a man whom other men admire, I feel a little ashamed that the child isn't *mine*, I mean mine in the physical sense, she's not from my seed. Because of this great failing of mine I leave the woman and the child alone more than I really want to. I mean that I keep a distance from them both in my heart. I decided not to marry the woman. I won't allow myself to become a father to the child. She calls *me* by my first name, and her mother she calls *Mother*. This makes me unhappy, too, but it's my own fault. And my life is complex. It's hard and demanding. A man has just so much energy to give. The army takes up all my time now, and my studies take up most of the rest. I *choose* the army over the woman, even though I love her. My destiny isn't with her, but with my work."

"Your destiny?"

"Yes, sure. The path of my life. The nature of my death."

She felt a little sorry for him then—for his pettiness and self-involvement—but most of all for the way he had cut off his options. Or maybe the way choice had been taken from him by all the others wanting a hero, long ago.

A couple of stars had come out but no moon. Jolie knew what he'd told her were secrets, that she was sworn to keep them to herself without any oath being taken. He led the way, a weary prowler, moving with tired strength and grace. Once in a while he stopped to pluck aside a tree branch for her. They kept walking, all the way to the cemetery. Then he sat easily on a gravestone. She sat on one nearby.

"You know the history of this place? They lost six children the first two years here. The whole area was swampland, everyone died of malaria or yellow fever. Please correct me if I commit any grammatical errors. They were malnourished. They lived on bad milk and rotten tomatoes. And the cow they had died the second year, too. Then they had to exist on bread donated by a Zionist group in Jerusalem. There were forty of them at first, but after the second year there were fifteen and one surviving child. They built the whole place on the bodies of the dead. By the third year there were thirteen of them, and two surviving children. Things became better after that. They thought at the time that death was less interested in them, and that's why he left them alone. But they didn't know the worst was ahead—not the worst for them as individuals, maybe, but for all of us as a people. The bodies of their few dead would seem like *nothing* to them, by 1945. They'd yearn for the days of malaria. Well, maybe they would, for a while. Have I spoken it all correctly? Yes? Ah, that's good. I'll do well on my exams. You know what I think? I think this nation of ours is like a larger Mayan Ha-Emek. It was built on fever and dreams, and the bodies of the dead. I must respect that. I *will* defend that. Compared to all the death buried in this ground we stand on, what's a single death? Yours, even? Or my own? And if the death occurs while I'm fighting for the life of the nation, maybe that's good. That's what I think. That's what I think about *destiny.*" He turned to her. "What do you think?"

Jolie did something she'd never done before. Never, because she'd been too self-conscious, too aware that she wasn't beautiful. Now, though, it wasn't her own state of beauty that concerned her but the feelings swelling inside her: tenderness, pity. He'd consumed too many mottoes, fulfilled too many expectations. Something in him teetered near the breaking point, for all his grace and strength. For a moment, she felt he was her son. She leaned forward to kiss his forehead. It was a gentle kiss, utterly chaste.

"I think," she whispered, "that you should forget your *destiny* and marry her. Stop opposing nature. Just live."

He shook his head slowly. He was smiling now. In his eyes were traces of tears, but they weren't tears of sorrow. "My brothers can do that, maybe. Nadav can. For me it's too late."

"Why, Shimon?"

"Because," he said quietly, "I can't change any more."

Sometime in the night they lay side by side on the outskirts of the cemetery ground, still talking. America concerned him. He was both disgusted and enchanted by Americans. Once, he said, he'd visited there after his first stint in the army. He'd been sent there to see some medical specialists. And he'd hobbled around American cities—Los Angeles, New York, Chicago, Washington—on his worn crutches, hobbling far into the night, obsessed with seeing as much as possible, as if his eyes were containers he could cram everything into. Obsessed with the movement, the vastness, the filth and splendor and beauty, obsessed with all the lights. In America, he said, he'd finally succeeded in fulfilling a childhood dream: he'd lost all sense of time. Because of the lights—from windows, from street lamps, from cars streaming down the geometrically patterned highways—he'd lost consciousness of the difference between day and night. America was where all oppositions met, blistered, fought, sometimes blended, grinding loudly, never satisfied, never fully revealed. In Israel, well, that was a different thing. The Middle East was where opposition burst into flame. A place of little mercy. Of great dichotomy. And few compromises that did not leave a trail of fresh blood in their wake. People in America, he thought, had a terror of death—too few of them were willing to die for what they said they believed in—and because of that they would eventually stand little chance against all the world's poorer, hungrier people who possessed nothing *but* a willingness to die for their beliefs. He was afraid Israel would become like America in that way, worshiping life above all else. Sometimes, he said, life had to be sacrificed. Those who were truly of the Middle East understood that. And the people of the West must realize, he said with grim anger, that even if oil was precious to them, oil also burned.

She glanced over to see a mask of bleak violence on his face.

"Do you mean that?"

"Ah," he said, "yes."

Then he smiled again, kindly, and gave her a questioning look. "Tell me something. You'll say, maybe, that's it's private for you—I mean, that it's *none of my business*—I said that correctly? Good. But you—you grew up in America. I know that things are different there between men and women. Still, I hope you don't mind my asking, everyone on this place wonders what happened with you and Rafi."

She didn't feel threatened any more and told him the truth. "We hardly ever made love. We tried a lot, but—well, he never loved me in that way—"

"Never? Then maybe he loves men only? Maybe he's so inclined."

"Oh, sure. But I don't think you can say it was all his fault, or anything like that. Maybe I never loved *him* enough—I mean, accepted him as he was. I think we both just wanted to fit in somewhere. I wanted a husband, to show the world that someone somewhere *wanted* me. And he wanted to go to America. He thought he could go through with it all—marriage, I mean—if only it would get him to America. But he couldn't. And I wouldn't. I wouldn't take him there. So we were both disappointments, to ourselves, and to each other. But that's all over now."

He peered at her in the dark, saw that she wasn't lying at all. The gentle smile remained with him. It was calming, totally restful. Jolie couldn't imagine him firing an Uzi. For a moment he looked like a cheerfully contemplative monk, just finished with his prayers for the night. He reached to squeeze her shoulder gently. "So," he said, "you were tired of being alone. So was he. That's all."

It was true.

The stars were out fully, bright constellations backed by the hazy white of auroras, and behind that the night. He pointed out a flashing bright red streak, a meteor burning to oblivion.

"There. It's magic."

"You think so?"

"Yes, sure." He was quite serious. "A sign of good luck. Think of the universe as an enormous sea, burning with lights like that one. The future's very bright."

Lying there, he fell asleep. Jolie did, too, and woke up soaked with dew, shivering. She could feel herself moving toward him as if in a dream. His eyes were open, but the rest of him was washed in gray light, like a corpse.

"My friend," he said, in Hebrew.

He cupped a hand behind her head, opening his lips slightly against hers. It was new, tingling, a little frightening, his taste and smell so different. He unbuttoned his shirt and pressed her hand to his chest, then along his rib cage. She felt his flesh, dark curling hair, the lumpy raised ridges of scar tissue. There seemed to be no place on his body that was free of scars. They popped up everywhere, upper arms, chest, back, his entire torso. Her fear took over for real. She could see death blacken his face, bursting through the eyes on twin waves of fire and blood. Then she stopped being curious. She didn't want him any more.

"Don't worry," he said, "I'm tired anyway."

He pressed her hand against the biggest scar. "If you go back to America, tell them the truth," and he pressed the hand down harder, "like this. It's not pretty. But maybe you won't go. Rafi thinks you'll stay."

He fell asleep again and Jolie kept her hand against his scar, felt the fear inside diminish. She watched him sleep. His eyelids rolled wildly. His arms twitched. He was fighting in his dreams. Then panting, running. Then he smiled, a smile of exhaustion, even in the middle of deep sleep. His breathing became deep and regular. Just before dawn, she slept.

He was gone when she woke up.

At breakfast she was tired and thought maybe she'd been sleepwalking—something she hadn't done since childhood.

Nadav sat with her, Zeigler too, talking about something she didn't even listen to, and at some point Nadav mentioned to someone passing by that Shimoni had gone already. He'd taken a morning bus back to Jerusalem.

When she returned to her place after work that day there was a note, in a dark and foreign hand, thanking her for the English lesson.

Zeigler reached for Jolie's hands and held them, gently. She saw him with great clarity then. A thin but solid body. Blond hair, fair skin peppered with white-blond hair, tiny blue eyes.

Something about his mouth, though, was distinctly Jewish—maybe the soft, rounded, sensual lips. All his false flesh had melted away. He was the bud of Avi Zeigler, a kind of flower, actually, in the process of blooming for the first time. And it would have been nice to love him. It struck her as harsh and unfair that he should love her and she not return the love. Even though she was afraid and he was, too. Even though neither one of them had much experience in these matters. Maybe life would always be like that, she thought, for people like Avi and her—they would search, err, stumble. They had no tangible vision of the love that they wanted, that they would search out, that would receive them with grace. They had no Shimoni. No Miriam Sagrossa.

They were quiet for a while. Then Avi took one hand away and removed his glasses, squinting down at them.

"I wish I had perfect vision. Not just to see things clearly a few meters away, but to see things—to really *see*—things infinitely close and things infinitely far. If I had perfect vision I could see the molecules of your body. I could see through the walls of each cell. Also, I could reverse my perfect vision and see in the other direction—I mean the large things. I could see the beginnings of time. I could see time to its end."

She pressed his hand to her cheek. "But the past is finished. And the future hasn't happened yet."

"No! You're wrong! Listen, we see only with light, and light travels only at its own speed. But if the light doesn't reach our eyes soon enough, the image it transmits—what you call the thing that happened *in the past*—well, we see it happening *still* when the light finally reaches our eyes. What if the light continued traveling past us, beyond us? And what if it reached the eyes of someone else, in a place even farther away? Well, *he'll* see the thing happening right before his eyes *then*, even though in *our* eyes it's already happened. Because we don't have perfect vision, we don't see that everything really happens all at once, so we think that when we can't see something any more it's finished. But no one can prove to me that it's true! You can't! And until someone proves that our limited vision is true, and real, then *I* believe that *nothing* is ever dead, or finished. Because of the light!" His fair skin was flushed, his near-sighted eyes sparkled in a kind of triumph. She pulled both his hands into her own. "With perfect vision, you'd see everything happening all at once. And *then*, to see it *truly*, all the unnecessary details, all the illusions of the world and the universe, would be stripped away—and you'd see nothing but light. Energy. Inside us, outside us, it's all the same thing, my friend! We're only light and energy. Moving light. There's a universe composed of it, and we're part of the universe—of all the light. Dancing."

He was crying.

Jolie knew then that she loved him. Not a perfect love, maybe, but it was love nonetheless.

She knew also that the probability of peace, of anything working out—between nations, between them—was very slight. But the *possibility* of it *did* exist. And possibility could not be proved dead, or finished. There were no easy solutions in life. For her, for him, no perfect endings. But they could try.

She touched his face. His glasses slid down the slim wet nose. "Avi. Come here." When he looked at her the dark, sleepless half-moons under each eye were wet, too, and he shoved the glasses back up his nose quickly, as if to hide them. Then he held both her hands.

"I don't know how to begin."

"Me neither."

"What if it's bad for you?"

"Shut up and kiss me. If somebody doesn't love me soon, I'll wither up and die."

They were both clumsy then, and a little feverish, terror edging out pleasure. Until the terror receded and they were friends again. Then they both began to laugh, lying unaroused and still a little frightened beside each other on her bed, their clothes in various stages of disarray. But the terror went away completely, and they began to kiss for real.

———

When Jolie woke up she was covered carefully with the blanket. Avi had tucked it in around her. She wanted to ask him where Nadav was, and what they'd both been doing the past few weeks. But she didn't know if he'd answer.

From the bathroom came the sound of a shower. Then Zeigler's tenor voice singing—a nice voice—he was singing a popular folk tune and really hitting all the high notes. Jolie felt, through her haze of sleep, a kind of delight. She'd never heard him sing before.

Down in Dahav

RAFI HAD SOUNDED STRANGE ON THE TELEPHONE, AND JOLIE WAS surprised. But it was he who insisted she come to Tel Aviv and talk things out, and so she did, leaving one morning in late summer while the cotton was being harvested and everyone on Mayan Ha-Emek was walking around with white tufts in their hair and clothing. She pulled Zeigler's ears, rubbed his cheeks, scratched his head and kissed both eyelids until he growled awake, jumping up to pull on some clothes and tell her half-jokingly to leave him alone, he was awake finally, was she happy now? But he was tender, too, fixing her coffee the way she liked it, and when he walked her down to the bus stop she noticed he was regarding her with anxious looks.

"You'll be back tomorrow?"

"Early."

"Good," he said, and nervously adjusted the shoulder strap of her overnight bag. He was very thin now but had stopped losing weight—a good sign, she thought, since he had not gained any either. One thing left over from the days of his most stringent dieting was that he no longer ate meat of any kind, not even fish. An occasional hard-boiled egg, a daily glass of milk, and a piece of cheese were his sole concessions now to protein requirements. He'd become quite good, he said, at living on vegetables and bread, water, air, love. At this, he always blushed.

The morning was hot and they were both beginning to sweat. He left the strap smoothed across her shoulder. From down the road whirled a pale cloud of dust: the bus.

"So. Have a safe trip."

She kissed his chin and nose. "Don't worry, Avi. I'll come back to you."

The trip was nothing out of the ordinary: crowded, hot, miserable. The bus passed through lush summer hills and barren land, then along main roads to the highway, the traffic, the heat steaming off the rooftops of Tel Aviv. Before the bus pulled into the Tachanat Mercazit she saw Rafi—miraculously— standing in front of a crowd of waiting people, his hands shoved into the pockets of his blue jeans and no camera around his neck. He looked grim to her, and almost pale beneath the permanent brown tan. She saw him eyeing every descending passenger as the bus stopped and doors opened, and knew that he was looking, with some kind of strange desperation, for her own homely face.

"Here I am. I thought I'd meet you at work."

"I took the day off." He grabbed her bag from her. "Let's go. You never saw my place. We can walk there."

She realized, with surprise, that she'd spoken to him in English. But he'd replied in Hebrew.

The apartment was small but he'd fixed it up really nicely, she thought, with an oriental rug and big soft tapestried pillows decorating the simple furniture. He'd also been doing some interesting free-lance work, and some of his favorite photos were enlarged and framed on the walls. The bed had been freshly made, the kitchenette cleaned. Along one shelf she noticed small framed photos of people she recognized. The young and old of Mayan Ha-Emek. Yael. Nadav. Michael as a child. Shlomo. Shimoni, in uniform, with a major's stripes. Then, too, there was a picture of her. Rafi had manipulated the light and shadow a little. Her face looked almost pretty. *Well, you'd think, looking at such a photo, this woman isn't bad at all!* But she thought there was something about it, after all, that lied. And she wasn't in the mood for any more lies. She turned the picture around when he wasn't looking.

He was busy in the kitchenette, preparing iced tea and a salad. She watched him from the bedroom doorway, neatly dicing onions and tomatoes, sprinkling pepper and basil over everything, squeezing lemon juice, dripping on a little olive oil.

"Rafi, we have to talk."

"Sure, I know."

"I decided to become a citizen. I want a divorce."

The knife he was using clattered into the sink. But he didn't look up, or miss a beat, and when he retrieved it to begin slicing a cucumber the sound of the sharp edge against the cutting board had a calm, measured tempo.

"So you can marry that fat Mossad boy?"

"He's not fat any more, and he's *not* Mossad."

"You're sure? Remember, the security of the nation depends on secrecy—why would he tell *you* if he *is* Mossad? That's a thing with all those guys, all those great *Zionists*—excuse me, since you decided to become one yourself—never tell anybody anything you don't *have* to tell them. Israel before honesty."

She banged a fist against the wall so that it hurt, and the sound made him pause.

"*Stop* it, Rafi! Stop avoiding things."

"What things?"

"The divorce."

The knife clattered into the sink again, a piece of cucumber splatted on the floor and, turning to face her, he crushed it under a shoe.

"Go to hell! I *won't* give you a divorce!"

"You will!"

"I won't!"

"Stupid little queer!"

"Stupid ugly bitch!"

They were wrestling with each other somewhere between the kitchen sink and the front-room rug, trying to rip out each other's hair, and she was trying to hit him as hard as she could.

"You malicious little queer. Fuck *you*. All you ever wanted me for was an American passport. Well, you're *free* now, voilà! So *go!*"

"No, fuck *you*. You *never* loved me. All you wanted was a cute little husband to show to the world. To show the *rest* of the idiots that you fit in with them!"

"Go to hell!"

"No! You go to hell! You're just like all the others! All of you fools standing there, waiting to condemn me. Waiting for me to be *normal*—like *them*, like *you*—well, no thank you! Not if you *paid* me, even!"

He slapped her across the face and she punched him on the lip, drawing blood. He twisted her hair into his fist, pulled hard until tears came to her eyes and they collapsed together on the carpet, twisting and punching.

"I *shit* on your normalcy! You and your fat intelligence goon! And Michael! And Shimoni! And the whole country! *All of you, and all your stupid wars!*" He banged her head against the floor, and it hurt so much that for the first time she was scared. "Fuck *all* of you! Fuck you for casting me out! Fuck you for leaving me!" He sat up, rocking back and forth, covering his face with his hands. From between the splayed fingers came a sound—a bubble, a gurgle, a sob. "Fuck you for letting me go!"

Jolie lay there, blinking until her head cleared. She listened to him cry. It was terrible, as if everything would burst out of him onto the floor. After a while she reached over and moved closer, and they held each other. They were both crying now, and both of their noses were bleeding.

They had dinner in a Chinese restaurant off Disengoff. She hadn't had shrimp fried rice since leaving America, and the taste seemed almost aphrodisiacal until she realized that it wasn't the taste she'd clung to in her memory so much as the pain that went with it: the pain of being homely in America. She had been a masochist all her life, in one way or another. Once, maybe, masochism had been a survival tactic. And old habits die hard. But there was no more need for it now—and, she realized, shrimp fried rice was not her favorite food. Rafi might find his real glory in it, though—in America, and whatever he consumed for sustenance there might nourish him far better than either she or eggplant or Israel ever had. She toyed with some chow mein and watched him drink his soup.

"Do you have a lover?"

He shoved the bowl away and sighed. "I wish I did. The truth is, my friend, that I don't know *how* to have a lover. The truth is that I meet men in bathrooms for sex. If I bring a man home to my bed, all the faces of the people of Mayan Ha-Emek swim through my head, condemning me. So I can't do anything. It's embarrassing." He broke an eggroll in half, shaking shreds of cabbage out onto his plate. "And always, I thought: If I live somewhere far away, in another country, maybe, I'll live without this fear. Then I'll love someone, truly. In a place where men like me live more openly. Like New York City. I always thought that. But these days, you know—well, so, it's strange, the feelings I have. I have feelings that all the faces of Mayan Ha-Emek will swim through my head forever, no matter *where* I am. And that I can't stop that, no matter how hard I try. But the one thing I *can* change is the fact that, while they go swimming through my head, they're always condemning me. Someday what I want is that they'll swim through my head applauding. They'll smile, every one of them, and say to me: Good, Rafi, we approve. We approve because you're honest, because you went somewhere you wanted to go and did something you wanted to do. Because you didn't kill anyone, even in a time of war. And because now, you can finally *love*. That's what I want them to say—just that. I think maybe I want *you* to say it, too."

"But I do."

"Sure. Maybe." He grinned then, like a child, and covered

her hand with his. "So why are you so anxious for me to go, suddenly?"

"Because you want to. You always wanted to." She smiled then, realizing it was true. "Because—I *approve* of it."

"Yes," he said, suddenly serious, "and maybe, someday, I won't need the approval. It will be nice to *receive* it, maybe—but I won't *need* it." He twirled a chopstick in his fingers. "You want some more rice?"

"I'm not hungry."

"Eat. This is probably your last American meal, my wife." He spooned some onto her plate, grinning again. "You know, Jolie—I have a dream sometimes, usually the same one. In the dream I'm lying on a field, and all around me there are dead things. It's a terrible place, some place where bombs exploded and burned all the grass away and burned all the trees to the ground. I'm lying there. There's nothing wrong with me at all, but I can't move, I feel heavy in all my limbs, and as vulnerable as a baby. Then, from nowhere, a man comes walking toward me. He's dressed in some kind of uniform. A soldier. In the dream I know he's been fighting hard—his face is smeared with black, his eyes are tired—but he's still not injured. And his hands are bare. He lost all his weapons somewhere, long ago. I hear him walking toward me. Then he stands there, looking down at me. And then—then the wonderful thing happens! He takes off his uniform, and his boots, very slowly, until he's standing there naked. Then he sits on the black ground next to me. Suddenly, I can move a little. I reach up and touch his knee and thigh. He bends down to kiss me. But the strange thing is that neither one of us is aroused at all, there's not really any sexual feeling—yet, it's wonderful. He kisses my forehead and my cheek, almost like a mother. Then I curl up against him. He holds me in his arms. And in the dream, then, I understand something—it's suddenly very clear to me—this feeling of calm, and of, well, *peace.* I know then, in the dream, that what I feel in that moment is love. I know that there *is* love, and that *I* can love, and that if only I can keep feeling this way then everything will be okay." He tapped his glass of water with a spoon, smiling gently. "Then I wake up."

That night, sleeping on Rafi's sofa, Jolie had a dream herself.

She dreamed she was down in Dahav, by the Red Sea, in some palm-thatched hut on the edge of the oasis. Camels poked their heads through the open doorway. Little brown-skinned Bedouin kids ran by under the relentless sun, selling pita bread and well water.

She wandered in and out of worlds, dressed in dusty Arab robes. Up golden stairways to a chamber of sacrifice. Along ancient roadways, through seaports that smelled of all times past, over oceans tiled with dancing, gusting whitecaps. Across beaten deserts. Through Mesopotamia. The spice markets of Constantinople. Roman Palestine. Along barren Asian steppes, the riverbanks of Poland, the mosques of Spain. In the dream a chorus of voices accompanied her, mumbling sweetly so that the words became music, honey-sweet music, holy words. She wandered through worlds until she came back to Dahav, lying in a little sun-dried hut while oasis water splashed somewhere outside, staring up at a ragged Bedouin face. In the dream he was kind, and held a cup of rancid coffee to her lips.

Drink now, he said, in slurred Hebrew. One of his eyes was blank and blind. An ancient camel's tooth propped the eyelid open. *Drink. Such visions are good. Submission to the universe, to the will of Allah. But life is also good. You will choose it in the end. And leave the deserts to us. Now, here, you are under our protection. So drink. And live.*

Rafi had a good laugh over that one.

But he kept interrupting her attempts at dream analysis to encourage a little gossip about the wedding. All of Mayan Ha-Emek must be scandalized, he kept saying gleefully— Nadav had really gone and done it. He really was going to marry Miriam Sagrossa. Shimoni's woman. And Rafi, for one, was ecstatic.

"I'll tell you—you know all about us *Kol* men. We like to keep everything in the family."

Before she threw something at him he made her promise to come to Tel Aviv for a few days and help him close up the apartment later that autumn. Because he was leaving—he really *was* leaving this time, he said—for America. But before he did he would have to see the wedding. He'd also have to keep an eye on her for a while, her and her precious Zeigler, to make sure she wasn't doing anything stupid. And, he promised, after his brother's great scandalous wedding he and she would discuss the logistics of their divorce. She was right, he said, to want to be free. They must initiate the proceedings soon, because things could take a while and, if he knew anything at all about his native land, probably would. But he promised to go along with whatever she wanted now. All the way, with no turning back. The future was ahead for both of them. He must go, and she must stay. And it was time, he said, for both of them to find the truth. To find some love. Yes, he'd leave.

After all, he teased her, it would be a gesture of love for her in the end. And, maybe, for himself.

It would be a gesture of friendship.

The Secret

THE ANNOUNCED WEDDING OF NADAV KOL AND MIRIAM SAGROSSA caused plenty of rumor and scandal, of course, but that was only natural. Yael maintained her usual silence and dignity in the face of it all. Sometimes, now, she and Shlomo could be seen walking together in the evening. Sometimes they were seen together at breakfast, sitting across the table from one another, silently sipping coffee. Eyebrows were raised over this, but the truth of the matter was that no one was surprised.

One week, Yael took several days off and left for Ramat Alon. When she returned her face had a happy glow. For the entire week after that she looked exquisite, ruddy and polished, like an ancient queen of Morocco.

Shlomo seemed content too, these days. Hava had married David Yardeni a month before and moved to Tel Yonah. And it was Shlomo who, once a week, traveled to the hospital in Haifa to visit Zvi Avineri. Zvi refused to see anyone else from the kibbutz. But once he confided to Shlomo that Nadav also visited, traveling down from Ramat Alon at least twice a month, and they always had good talks. Also, he said, he was getting better. There would be no more Hava in his life. When he said this, he smiled sadly.

Rafi showed up at Mayan Ha-Emek one day to visit Jolie. Zeigler bore it all in a grim silence that lightened when he saw that things really were over between her and her husband. Rafi said he'd stay for the wedding. Then he and Jolie would petition for a divorce. Then he really *was* leaving for America. He had more money saved now. As soon as the divorce was in the works he would make reservations and buy his ticket.

For some reason everyone believed him this time—there was a new light of resolve in his eyes. Yudit Spira even invited him for tea one afternoon and said he'd been inoffensive, even polite and charming, and she'd be sorry to see him go. In the meantime, Jolie had Zeigler and no one was surprised. People were a little gleeful instead, even happy. They seemed so right for each other.

Nadav's wedding would be held on Mayan Ha-Emek. A rabbi had agreed to come up from Jerusalem.

Nadav traveled down from Ramat Alon two weeks early, worked in the grapefruit orchard, and spent a day in Afula getting blood tests and a physical examination. The results of one test he kept to himself. He'd requested the test specially, having harbored suspicions of his own for a while. The test confirmed these suspicions. Rana would be his only child.

As for the girl, her mental state had begun to improve a little. She still saw psychologists twice a week. They said she often seemed to forget entire incidents. She sometimes had no conscious memory of the hours spent with Lucero. The psychologists called this memory loss a protective mechanism. But she was coming out of her shell a little, playing once in a while, now, with other children. She still had tantrums, still drew pictures filled with images of blood and war and fragmented limbs. But no one expected immediate miracles. And her fondness for Nadav had deepened, as had his for her. A week before the wedding, Miriam brought her down to Mayan Ha-Emek.

She actually played with some of the kids there once or twice, and even went off with them, one day, on a field trip.

The General had been contacted, of course.

Still, everyone was surprised when he appeared two days before the wedding, sitting quietly in the dining hall at dinner as if he'd always been there, a small canvas bag at his side, dressed in unassuming work clothes smudged with dust. He was eating baked eggplant and bread, cutting everything methodically into bite-sized pieces before forking it slowly into his mouth. He looked dramatically older, and tired. His body was still lean, though, his gray hair thick and shining. When Yael sat across from him, he looked up to smile. Then reached for her hand.

On the day before the wedding, Nadav's family and a few friends had a picnic down near the grapefruit orchard. The General was there with Yael. Shlomo was there. So were Jolie, and Avi Zeigler, and Miriam and the child. Some of her brothers and their wives, and her own mother, would come for the wedding the next day. Rafi had gone back to Tel Aviv a few days ago but would return in the morning, to help set things up properly in the dining hall.

Only Michael would not be there. He had training maneuvers down in the desert, he'd said when he called, and duty came before pleasure. The truth was, people said privately, that he'd been a little full of himself since graduating from Officers School as Outstanding Cadet—he seemed to feel that he was the sole upholder of some family tradition. To feel that he himself was a worthwhile replacement for Shimoni—as if anyone ever could be.

The General lifted Rana in his arms, swung up and let go. She bounced in the air and giggled. When she dropped he caught her and swung her up again. As he did his fingers felt tough and nimble, his arms strong. Tiredness left him. He threw her in the air again and again, watched her glow against the pale sky, the burning white sun, catching her as easily as he would the feathers of a bird. Rana was ecstatic. Her eyes widened to circles. Her mouth opened, laughing. He tossed her one last time. She was a beautiful child, he thought, but never more beautiful than now. Thick hair streamed from her face like burnished black silk. Her skin was smooth, a light red-tinged brown. He caught her and held her. She twisted a gray curl of his hair in her fingers and tugged hard, laughing.

"Nado told me you send men to fight."

"Yes, that's true."

"Did you send him to fight?"

He patted her hand gently and she let go. The hand moved against the side of his face, tiny, soft.

"Did you? And they cut off his fingers?"

A hint of the old tiredness seeped slowly through him. He stroked her back. *No, no my child, you don't understand. It wasn't me. Men like me—other men actually sent him to war. I dealt with the intelligence, you see. It's hard to explain. Even if I dealt with the fighting end of things, it's against regulations to have your own son in your command. So you see, men like me sent him, but not me. How could I?* Her voice insisted.

"Did you?"

"Yes," he said.

"Why? You don't love him?"

"I love him very much."

"How much?"

"How much? As much as I can love, that's how much." Breeze rippled the yellowing tips of weed stalks. He felt some brush the legs of his trousers. No, the answer wasn't good enough. "I love him more than I ever loved any man, Ranit. I love him more than I love myself."

Across the valley rang a chorus of birds squawking. Then they appeared from behind a hill, flying west from Jordan, their formation a ravaged dark triangular shape moving rapidly. She fidgeted in his arms.

"I want to go play."

"Okay." He set her easily on her feet. But she clutched his thumb, pulling him with her.

"There's something—I brought it here from Ramat Alon. I hid it. I'll show it to you."

"Ah. A secret?"

"*My* secret. But you have to promise."

"What?"

"Not to tell. Not in your life or your death. You can't even tell God."

"Okay."

She stopped, staring up at him darkly. The breeze whipped strands of hair across her face. Next to her skin, the tips of weeds danced like specks of yellow sunlight. *"Promise now."*

"I promise." With his free hand he pressed his chest, kept a solemn face, felt the heart pounding quickly beneath shirt and flesh. "I promise now that I'll never tell."

"Good." She was pulling him along again, following a thin trail through weeds that grew increasingly taller and thicker. Soon they reached past his waist. They were taller than she was, and among them her head was a bobbing, shining black thing. He glanced down to see her brown hand dwarfed by his large white one.

Above, the birds flew. The black triangle passed directly overhead, momentarily blocking the sun. It threw a large gray shadow on the breeze-rippled grass. Rana stopped to look up for a second, then pulled him on ahead. She didn't notice the dull rumbling sound that he did, coming to them from far away. He recognized it immediately, casually glanced up once to spot it—a nearly invisible speck in the sky—just a reconnaissance drone, that Sampson VII model, he guessed, one of the new hotshot playthings those pompous incompetents in Jerusalem and Washington always got so excited about, and it was on a little routine outing, surveillance from the heavens, heading north. But he didn't break his stride. And the distant rumbling diminished, the tiny speck disappeared in a mass of puffy white clouds. The weeds around them grew taller, to his chest.

She was following a path she obviously knew well. A secret. Stepping carefully behind her, he smiled. Invisible weight dropped from him. He could feel his heart beating strongly now, urgently but silently pumping rejuvenated blood. Summer heat stroked his face. He could feel his sweat as the breeze cooled it. He glanced up at the sky again. Clear, calm. Light blue brushed by magnificent clouds that floated whiter than fresh-cleaned cotton. For a second, he was happy. It moved through him quickly: a second of happiness.

The orchards were far behind them now, a dark green thicket rising in the distance, and the voices of the others had dropped away. There were only the two of them. Only the silence of the valley broken by the crush of a child's feet against ground, then the louder tread of a man broken by the breeze, the disappearing calls of birds. Rana's hand was damp against his. He could see, ahead, a place where the weeds were shorter. He followed her along the thin dirt trail until it ended. Its end was marked by a large stone nestled in the earth. She let go of his hand and knelt to pat the stone with a faint whimper of excitement. Then she looked up at him, her face a mix of shyness and cunning.

"Remember, you promised."

"I remember."

He knelt beside her. Sharp stalks crushed beneath his knees. The hard shell of the earth was dry, unyielding. "Your secret, it's under this?"

She nodded. He could hear her breaths quicken with anticipation. He pressed a hand to his chest. His own heart was racing at high speed. He didn't know why. He could feel her excitement course through him, the core of private childlike fascination ripple through them both with a force that felt like pain to him, and he wondered what it was that thrilled him so—this simple unveiling of a five-year-old's secret hiding place. There was nothing she could hide here of value. Bags of stolen cookies, maybe. A few bright-colored stones.

She smiled and stood, clutching the rock firmly and pushing at it with concentrated effort that compressed her face into a red-tinged fury. For a second it seemed that the stone wouldn't budge. He thought to offer help, but better instincts prevailed and he didn't. Then the stone moved a little. Her effort increased. The large round eyes shut tight. A thrill shot through him again like pain, trapping his left arm and shoulder in a steel grip until he gasped for breath. Then it left him sweating, with a feeling across his belly like lead. He blinked, surprised. But his curiosity was peculiarly intense, as if he were a child again, and the revelation he'd been invited to witness the greatest possible treasure that could have been bestowed on any man. The rock moved up and over, rolling quietly in a small cloud of dust. Her eyes opened with triumph. She crouched beside him. He breathed hard, leaning over to look.

"See." She reached into the impression left by the stone. Looking down, light shot across his eyes. He squinted and saw her dark hand moving through the dust. "Here." She was holding something urgently out to him. He glanced up at the sky and forgot to close his eyes against the sun. It shot through him and the feeling of lead spread across his chest. He blinked desperately, trying to see again, and when the splotch of absolute white had faded from his eyes he massaged the pain in his shoulder and chest and gazed down at the objects she held in her hand. They were small pieces of stone, flattened, gray, roughly shaped into sharp-pointed triangles. He counted them. Several. Seven. Eight. More? Fragments of an ancient spear, maybe, or of old stone knives. Not an uncommon find for the area. Some claimed that archaeological findings in the land represented the missing link between *Homo sapiens Neandertal* and *Homo sapiens.* These little finds were in the earth everywhere. Every Israeli an anthropologist unto himself. A nation embedded in layers of history. A people stuck in time. His people. And despite everything it was his people that he worshiped still—not the earth, or God. The pain intensified. He looked at her young eyes, words coming to his tongue. *Where did you get them?* he wanted to say, and tried, but his throat had constricted and no sound came out. She smiled at him happily, oblivious to his discomfort. "From a place near Ramat Alon.

We went on a trip one day, my whole class." Her voice was light, musical, very young. "They took us to excavations. I found these and brought them back. They said it was forbidden. And I even brought them here with me. But, see—no one found out."

"Yes," he breathed hoarsely. "Thank you."

Then the sun flashed into his eyes again even though he was looking at the ground. The thrill shot through him, encasing him in bright white pain. He gasped for air.

Ranit, go back to the grapefruits and tell Nadav. Tell him to come here. Hurry.

No, forget it. Never mind. Stay, Rana. It doesn't matter. Stay.

He tried to speak but there was a block of lead in his throat. Breath trickled into him desperately—too little, like sporadic drops of water onto parched soil. His left arm and shoulder seemed to wither and freeze. He felt himself falling to one side. Then he was curled on the ground in a fetal position, his neck twisted strangely and eyes blinking straight up at the sun. White light blinded him. Like a dark blur against the sun, he saw her face.

"Ra—" he said. "Ra—"

Then he thought: *Shimoni.*

Her face blurred. Breeze washed him. The General shut his eyes, and slept.

He woke to the feeling of weed stubble scraping his back. His skin was chilled. When he opened his eyes the sun wasn't in them any more—it had shifted to the west—and he blinked up at a placid sky that glowed intense blue, empty of clouds. Then he half sat and saw Shlomo Golinsky crouching a few feet away. Old work clothes flapped loosely around his wiry body. He was mindlessly fingering the soiled ends of an old handkerchief, a white brimless hat sat cockeyed on his head. Shlomo stared back at him gravely.

"You're okay?"

He cleared his throat. Sounds came easily now. His mouth felt swollen and dry. He had the odd sensation of floating, though he knew he was on the ground among weeds. The feeling of lead and steely pain had vanished, leaving instead a naked, effortless feeling tinged with unreality. He formed the question deep in his belly, felt the words come from him in a detached way:

"We're dead?"

"Not yet, my friend." Shlomo grinned gently. "Not yet."

Not yet? I thought, for sure, it was the end. I threw my soul to the dogs of hell. So willingly. So easily. How easy—to die. Peace. Finally. And now, what do I feel really? Relief? Disappointment. Knowledge that I'm ready for it. I wait for it. No great general now, just another tired old man. He wiped dust from his forehead. He spoke softly, as if talking to himself—and, listening, Shlomo wondered vaguely why he spoke Spanish words.

"No hay esperanza, hermano. There's no hope in my heart."

"Listen, General, don't say those things. It's not important, anyway. We live. We live beyond the end of hope. We live not even for hope, but for life—it's your duty, you can't escape it, so don't try. See, General. *You* taught me that. So don't worry—it'll be okay. It'll all be okay."

Sure. Yes. If I tell them they'll want me to endure a thousand pointless tests. Lock me up with physicians in Tel Aviv. In Jerusalem. Political pressures. Afternoons spent wired to machines. And for what? A waste of time. When there's work to be done. Whether or not they want me to do it any more. So much work. He sat carefully, waiting for the pain to strike with its leaden weight. But it didn't. There was only the sensation of being still slightly detached from earth. A vague feeling of pins and needles in his left arm. He could breathe fully and effortlessly. Could feel a slight hunger in his belly. Along his flesh, the sweat was beginning to dry. *Interesting. A heart attack—well, why not? Never thought it would be that way. A thousand other scenarios, sure, but not the heart. Another old man, getting older. Warning signals. So it goes. Why shouldn't it be? All so arbitrary anyway. The truth is I don't so much care. I don't even care where they bury me. Or if they do.* Sitting there, he looked at Shlomo and grinned. *Heart attack. Why not? Good, Shimoni. Every day now, I know, I'm nearer to you. So it's all okay. After all, I've lived long enough. And the truth is my child that I've lived too long. Any man who outlives his own son has lived too long. Nearer, now. As it should be. Nearer, my child, to you.*

"Como gastando una broma, hermano. It's a bad joke."

"What, sir? I didn't understand."

"That we're still alive. Never mind. Help me up."

Shlomo stood and offered a hand. Then they were both standing. The General waited for a round of dizziness to hit him but none did. Even the tingling sensation in his arm receded to nothing, and he felt tired blood course through him, the pleasant cool of late afternoon mitigating the harsh heat of the baked earth. Suddenly he remembered, and turned to look at the large stone she'd upturned. It was back in place. It looked as if it had nestled there in that same spot for centuries, unmolested, settling deeper and deeper into the dust.

"The arrows! We have to find her."

"Find who, sir? What are you talking about?"

"The girl. *Rana.* We have to—"

"Don't worry! She's all right, believe me. I walked out here with her myself from the orchard, then she went back."

"She went back?"

"Yes, sure. She was tired and cranky. She wanted her mother. Well, what do you think, *General?*" Suddenly, Shlomo's voice had a cruel edge to it. "You think maybe we should go back also? They're all busy there, like chickens about to be plucked, all the members of your family. And one half-member. The truth is that you had *three* sons. Now you have two. Nadav was always mine." Shlomo's eyes narrowed bitterly. "I did exactly what you ordered me to do, didn't I? 'Take care of her,' you told me—you remember, maybe? Sure you do. 'Take care of them all.' Well, that's what I did. I took good care of her. The best that I could. Never mind that I'm left with the taste of dust in my mouth. It's what we're all left with, in the end. But you thought you could go off and arrange all the plots and the counterplots, and the wars—you thought you could be absent from all the things of life, then come back when you pleased and lay claims to them. While I stayed here with the

359

things of life, the women, the children, the land, and I knocked my head against a pillar of stone trying to protect them from the general insanity. So you thought you could return when you wanted and lay claim to them, and pay me nothing. But I took my own payment, *sir*. And today I have a son, a son who's a living man. Yael's other children are nothing in comparison. Not even your precious Shimoni. Nadav's a chip off the old block, in a way—he also struggled and suffered and learned while everyone else was busy praising another. He's quite a man, my son. I love him. There's no way *you* can claim him."

Shlomo stopped, panting. His face was flushed. Tears had come to his eyes. The General's face was drained of color but his eyes never wavered, only met Shlomo's with a weary pain. Then they just stared at each other for a long time. Finally, Shlomo wiped his tears away. His breathing became normal. Then he bowed his head, and when he spoke again his voice was kind.

"Listen, let's go back. Lucky they didn't miss a couple of old men. But there's this wedding tomorrow—"

"Yes, of course."

"So. Maybe we should go back now. Even if it doesn't matter."

"Okay." The General smiled quietly, painfully. "Let's go."

They walked through the weeds, making slow headway. Shlomo offered him an arm to lean on but he refused, trudging along to hear the crunch of sharp-edged weed stalks underfoot, pleased somehow that he could make it on his own. Gradually the stalks grew shorter, falling from his chest to his waist, then lower. They came to land where there was only short grass and churned earth, and across the field they could see the edge of the grapefruit orchard and people sitting, standing, some of them tossing fruit back and forth like large yellow balls. Once in a while came the faint sound of conversation or laughter, drifting on the breeze. In the west the sun had begun to set. They walked more steadily now across the field. Then a tiny shape came racing toward them. It neared, and the General saw it was she.

Her clothes were grimy from the day, her face tired but ecstatic. Black hair flopped along her forehead like a decoration. She was running toward them with open arms, her teeth a streak of pure white in the burnished face, and as she got closer he saw she was smiling.

"Grandpa!"

For a second he thought his insides would break.

"Grandpa!"

They stopped walking. He leaned over slightly to her and she hit against him softly, slowing, rolling into his chest and arms. As he hugged her she cupped both hands over his ears and whispered into one.

"You didn't tell, did you?"

"No! Never."

"*Good.*" She hugged him fiercely. Then she let go and was a sweetly energetic child again, soft fingers edging into his hand. She pawed at Shlomo's trousers, flashing a brilliant smile. "You brought him back."

"Sure," Shlomo muttered, tousling her hair. "No problem."

They went ahead to the orchard with Rana walking between them, suspended between their hands. She was a little dark glowing child, skipping along, sometimes dancing, sometimes leading, sometimes swinging briefly in the air.

The sun seemed to take a long time reaching the top of Mount Gilboa, sinking to touch it. But it was suddenly sinking lower and lower, its bright yellow darkening to orange and then a dull scarlet whose brightness rapidly diminished. Soon there was nothing left of the sun but a dim arc of red over a single hilltop. The sky around it glowed with strange gray light. Then spread itself out into a muddy blue, varying shades of violet, and, finally, a deep color of night. In the east twinkled a single star.

Yael and Miriam were bundling things together into the

large baskets, excess food, greasy scraps of paper. The child was with them. Everyone else was busy too—it seemed that way to the General. But he couldn't quite concentrate on what it was they were busy with. Sitting a little apart from them all on a straw mat on the ground, he watched them leaning over and rising like shadows against the vast shadow of the orchard, and it seemed to him like a sort of play, acted out with a combination of absurd and commonplace gestures in the limbo time of evening. He breathed easily, felt cool and comfortable and oddly weak, anchored firmly to earth but still somehow detached from it all. In the growing dark he examined the backs of his hands. He realized suddenly that they were old man's hands despite their remaining strength, spotted here, wrinkled there, beginning to sag and shrink. He looked up and saw a shadow detach itself from the shadow play, walking slowly toward him. He closed his eyes a moment, opened them and looked up again and saw Nadav. The figure loomed tall over him for an instant, dark and strong, and young. Then he sat facing him on the straw mat, his legs crossed easily like a meditating oriental's, the damaged right hand falling into his lap.

"So. How are you?"

"All right, really."

"Really? What happened out there today? I heard something crazy, that you fell asleep—tell me, it's true?"

The General gazed back at him a while in silence. Then he smiled, gently patting his chest. "Listen, Nadav, this heart I have is old enough. You don't know most of the things it's seen, and sometimes out of selfish pity I even forget some of them myself. It's old enough to protest a little. It's old enough to break if it wants. The truth is no one can tell it what to do any more—that's the truth. Someday it will throw a tantrum and break for good, and that's also okay. But there are many ways to tell the truth, and many ways to believe it, so if you want another way I'll give you one: yes, the truth is I fell asleep. I fell asleep for a while out there. Okay?"

Nadav stared at him without speaking. Then his shoulders

heaved in a silent sigh. He dropped his head and remained that way a while. Then he glanced back up at his father and managed a slight smile. "Okay," he said.

"Good." The General pounded the mat vigorously and stood. He offered a hand to Nadav, pulled him up, squeezed his shoulder. He noticed, for the first time, that they were the same height. Shimon had been taller. Not much, just a little. Not that it mattered. Sons were destined to be taller than their fathers in the end, to stand above them in youth looking down on their old age, to tower alone at the edge of a grave, gazing at death—or maybe, who knew, come running toward them at the End of Days, arms outstretched, ready to gather up their shriveled old fathers as if they were insubstantial sacks of moth wings ready to scatter in the wind. There was something he ought to tell Nadav, now. Before there was no chance to do it.

The truth is that I love you, more than I ever loved any man. More than I loved myself. The truth is I always kept a special place inside my heart for you. Not for Shimon. Because if I had a favorite son it was you, Nadav. No matter whose child you are. It was you.

But they bent to gather and roll the mat, dark stretched around them, the chance went away. They walked together to join the others. Rana's voice rose in a tired laugh. It echoed against the leaves on gnarled grapefruit trees, got carried off by the breeze. Then she laughed again and suddenly Miriam was laughing too—long, gentle, melodious laughter. Nadav trotted over to them, leaving his father behind. Miriam and Rana glanced at each other when they saw him approach. Then their eyes grew sly. Their faces burst with suppressed laughter. He stopped in front of them, grinning a little foolishly.

"What's the joke?"

But they wouldn't say.

Rana exploded in giggles. Impulsively, he reached for her and pulled her lightly from Miriam's arms into his own. He grumbled in a voice full of mock threat.

"You won't tell me, eh?"

She shook her head, laughing. "It's not for men to know."

"Sweet man." Miriam leaned forward to kiss his cheek. Her

lips left a moist warm spot. She was laughing, too. He realized that whatever the secret was, they'd never tell. Then he realized that his only way in on things was to join them, and suddenly he found himself laughing, laughing genuinely, though he didn't know at what, laughing long and hard. He pulled them both to him in a long, hard embrace. Then he released the woman, held the child up at arm's length, still laughing. Rana laughed with him this time. In the dark he held her firmly and swung her around and around.

"Fly," he said, "fly." She yelled with delight.

He swung her around until they were both dizzy. It seemed to him for a moment that they were all alone in the dark, spinning, their human sounds absorbed by the trees and sky and night. Nadav stopped slowly, easing her feet to the ground.

"You still won't tell me, eh?" he said, but he was breathless with dizzy laughter and sank to his knees.

"You're both crazy." Miriam ran a hand through his hair. "I'm going to help your mother, Nadav. You'll bring Rana with you?"

"Sure."

He watched her disappear in the dark, heading away after the others. Everyone had gone ahead to the kibbutz, carrying the remains of the day in picnic baskets. It would be time for dinner soon. Then more socializing. Friends would stop by to talk, to congratulate. To say good-bye.

And it was stupid, really, sitting by the edge of the grapefruit orchard when the sun had sunk completely and there were so many things to do, when there was tomorrow to prepare for, the day he gained a wife and a child. His wedding day. Rana crawled into his lap suddenly, hugging him. He sensed a fear in her embrace and patted her back.

"What's new?"

"I'm tired."

"Okay. We'll go back now."

He stood, holding her, stepping across the field, then along a dirt road in the dark. Ahead, through the trees, he could see the settlement lights. But no sounds, yet—no human sounds.

Only the breeze, the faint flutter of leaves, the steady crunch of his soles hitting earth.

"Why do people die, Nado?"

"I don't know."

Her breath was soft against his neck. "Then why do they live?"

His belly sank with a hard, dull knot of despair and he kept walking, turning past the pecan grove uphill. He felt her waiting.

"Everyone lives for something different, Ranit. Everyone has a different reason for his life. You don't always know what a person's real reason is—it's a mystery that way, like a secret." *In other words, I don't know, I don't know at all. The reason is each man's to discover. Your own reason is yours to discover. The mystery of your birth. The secret of your life, of the life of your people, my child. The secret of your birth and the secret of your death, and all the secrets in between.*

"What's your reason?"

It was dark but he carried her easily and walked surely uphill, his feet knowing the way even when his mind seemed to forget. For a minute he felt that moving ahead was his sole purpose, and he was light and clean and without thought. The lights of Mayan Ha-Emek shone ahead through the swaying shadows of trees. He noticed her glancing upward, followed her gaze once and saw that the stars were beginning to appear. They sparkled down like beacons of cold flame—dozens of them, hundreds, thousands. On earth, the clustered lights of the settlement glimmered back, a tiny mirror of the raw bright infinity above.

He leaned into the uphill grade and strode forward, lights looming brighter now through the trees. This was his child now. Answers were now important. So was the truth. *For you,* he thought to tell her, *for you, and for Miriam Sagrossa.* But he'd made his own choices, in a way, before he'd even loved them. She yanked his ear.

"So? What is it?"

"I'll tell you part of it. Part of it is that I want to learn about more things. I want to love you better, for one thing. Also I want to learn how to love your mother better."

"What's the rest of it?"

"Ah. That's *my* secret."

She laughed a little, twisting his hair around her fingers. "You won't tell me, eh?" she growled. Then she let go. "Okay. But what's *my* reason?"

"Well," he said, "that's yours alone to know. That's the secret you keep in your own soul."

America

IN DARKNESS THE PLANE HUMMED, OVERHEAD CABIN LIGHTS OFF FOR the night, an occasional reading light shooting solitary beams downward. Rafi roamed the aisles. He tugged the straps of his camera, feeling dried out inside. Maybe that was why his steps along the carpeted floor of the aisles felt so light to him, and airy. There was now somehow less of him. After all, he'd left his country. And he knew that he would not return. He was dizzy with fear, and homesick.

How did I do that? How could I?

When the fear began to spin too much in his chest he'd step lightly toward the restrooms at the rear of the cabin, press open the folding doors. He'd stand at a smudged mirror, stare into the image of his own dehydrated eyes. And sobs would shudder his shoulders, cracked dry noises busting up from his solar plexus.

What will I do without my people?

What will I do without my home?

In the middle of the second time zone he looked up to see his face blurred in the restroom mirror again. The plane bucked slightly. They were heading through minor turbulence, into another night. He fooled around with the lever on the razor-blade dispenser, plucked one out and peeled the white wrapper off until dull metal shone naked between his fingers. He gave the dry eyes gazing back from the mirror surface a wink.

I always wondered what it was like. Well, let's see.

He ran the blade edge gently across his left wrist, starting at the base of the thumb. But he applied little pressure and opened only a thin line of blood. Shallower than a cat's scratch. He ran the blade from wrist to inner elbow, trying for a straight line. Still too shallow. Just a pink little ribbon turning weak red. He crisscrossed the line, wove another one from wrist to elbow across the first one, from elbow to wrist and down again. The thin, pink designs swelled faintly with blood. He gazed approvingly.

—*Rafi, Rafi, what are you doing?*

—*I'm playing. A dress rehearsal, maybe.*

—*Now listen to me, Rafi—stop that.*

—*Shimoni?*

—*Yes?*

—*You want to know something?*

—*Sure, what?*

—*You're a real bastard, my friend. You were supposed to survive. Instead you left us all, you left us without you—*

—*But the tank was bombed.*

—*Listen, idiot, that's not my problem. When I was a boy I followed you everywhere, I thought you were God. When I went into the service and learned how full of shit it all was, I couldn't believe it, I couldn't believe that you, whom I loved and admired, were wasting your life leading other men into war—and don't tell me about Zionism and great ideals, all right? You know and I know that the important thing is survival—a human being should do anything to live. It's not my problem if the stupid tank was bombed. It's your fault, you know! It's your fault for putting yourself there in the first place!*

—*Listen, Rafi! Listen to me! I never wanted to die, not ever in my life did I seek death. I went into war to protect the things I loved in my life. If it wasn't me in the tank, it would have been some other man. And what is the difference between me and another man? Nothing.*

We're part of the same body. *You understand that? I was a man who planned to live. I always wanted to survive. It's just that, for certain things, I was willing to die if necessary. So. I wanted to survive that day. And the tank was bombed. And I didn't survive. Things happen that way, you know! You plan and hope, you have many great talents, you have many good intentions, but things happen that you can't control—*

—Oh! Well, excuse me for even bringing it up. The great Shimoni, stopped by mortal men, eh? The great soldier, the great scholar, the handsome one, the idealist, the great lover—Saint Shimoni, Our Hero. And what happens? The stinking Moslem hordes throw a weapon your way, and you're up in smoke for the rest of eternity.

—Go to hell!

—Thank you! That's what I'm trying to do!

—Listen, Rafi, stop it! I couldn't help it, do you understand that? I died when I did because I couldn't help it.

—Hah!

—It's true.

—I suppose you lived your life that way too, eh?

—Yes.

—Yes?

—Yes. Everything I did was because I had no choice. I was the way I was because there was nothing else I could be. It's entirely a matter of destiny. We're born with our destinies inside us. I did everything I did because I couldn't help it.

Rafi bent over the tiny sink, sobbing.

—Rafi, Rafi mine, stop crying. Always, since you were a child, I hated it when you cried—it hurt me—stop it, please. Throw that razor blade away. Throw it down the disposal slot. That's right.

—I want you to be alive.

—I can't be. Not any more. But I died because that was the way things had to be for me. Things are different for you. I want you to be alive now, too. And you will. Run water in the sink. Yes. Now, put your arm under the water. Good. Wash off all the blood.

—Shimoni! Help me! I hate blood!

—It's okay. It'll be all right. Take a paper towel, Rafi. Put it under the cold water. Good. Now wipe your face with it. There. Doesn't that

feel better? That's good, isn't it, to feel that? Now wet the paper again and press it to your neck.

—*What will I do, Shimoni?*

—*You'll put some dry paper towels on your arm and stay here a few minutes, until the bleeding stops.*

—*Always the practical one, eh? And then?*

—*Then you'll throw the paper towels away and you'll put some Band-Aids on your wrist.*

—*I will?*

—*Yes. Then you'll go out the door—*

—*How?*

—*What, Rafi?*

—*How?*

—*How do you go out the door? First you take a few steps. Then you hold out your right hand and turn the handle.*

—*But what happens then?*

—*Then you go through the door.*

—*To what?*

—*To whatever there is.*

—*I don't know, Shimon. I don't think I can do this alone.*

—*No problem. I'll be around. We all will. You'll feel us—*

—*Us? Who?*

—*Never mind. You'll feel me.*

—*I don't know. I'm nothing but a little queer running away from everything. Maybe back home they're right to despise me. Maybe it's right for God to despise me.*

—*Nonsense. The entity you call "God" is much too busy to care about your sexuality, or where you happen to live out your life. And it's the same for everyone else in the world, so stop pitying yourself. Now, listen. How are you feeling? Better? You can take off the paper towels now. Good, Rafi. You can throw them away. You see? Just a few scratches. Now, go to the Band-Aid dispenser. Push the lever down. Good. Do it again. Two Band-Aids. Unwrap them and put them on your wrists.*

—*Okay.*

—*Good. I'm proud of you.*

—*Ah! I can't stop crying!*

—You will.

—I will? I will? And then what?

—Then you wash your face and take another paper towel and dry it off.

—Okay. All right, Shimoni.

—Very good. You don't even know how proud I am. You're a man of courage, Rafi. You don't know it yet, but you will someday. Now turn around. Go to the door. That's right. Only two steps, you see? It's not that difficult, really. Even all the things I did in my life—they were little in a way—

—They were?

—In a way. Everything was just a single step at a time. Everything. Even dying. Even breathing. You still have to do the work, step by step. Even when you have power on your side, or destiny. The work must still be done. Now reach with your hand, Rafi, and push the lock.

—I'm afraid.

—It's okay to be afraid. I was afraid all the time.

—You were?

—Sure. You get accustomed to it after a while. Then you forget that you are, and you can do brave things. There. The lock's off? Good! Now. Open the door.

—What will I do?

—Live.

—Why?

—Ah. Because I want you to. And because you can't help it.

—So what?

—You know something, Rafi? You're a real schmuck.

Rafi stepped out into the darkened aisle. Somewhere, a child groaned in sleep. Somewhere someone snored. More reading lights had flicked out. The plane was nearly black inside, flying through night air.

He felt his feet ache with every step, absolute fatigue settle in every muscle and bone. He touched the flesh of his face and thought for a second that it had changed, leaving him puffy and aging. He came to an empty row of seats, slid in from the aisle and settled by the window.

—Push up the shade, Rafi.

—It's dark outside.

—Push up the shade.

He did, and met a reflection of himself shimmering dimly across the multilayered porthole. Beyond that was darkness, unbroken by a single star. Rafi pressed against the tired reflection until it blurred more and disappeared, and his nose met the pane with abrupt chill. He gazed out into pitch-black night. Then down.

At first he thought it was a constellation, reflected below as if by a vast mirror held up to the sky, displaying glittering seas of many-colored stars and comets. But he realized after a second that those weren't star formations he saw below but man-made lights—stretching suddenly across a black world in a long oval formation, winking, shimmering like a mirage, each light emitting its own aura, each aura blending with another to create a riotous haze, an island floating brightly in a dark sea. He blinked sudden tears away, pushed his lips against the pane and breathed out a cloud, blinked through more tears at the misty city of lights below.

—Nice, eh?

—Thank you, Shimon. I forgot about those things.

—What things?

—I don't know. Work. Art.

—Ah. You mean love, Rafi—it's the same thing. Like magic.

Shimoni left and Rafi leaned his forehead on the porthole pane, utterly drained. His eyelids felt weighted again as if by lead and, closing them, he slept.

Rafi dreamed of Shimon. The two of them were somewhere off the road between Be'er Sheva and Ein Gedi in the boiling heat of midday. Shimon was still in the tattered, gut-caked remnants of the uniform he'd died in. But his face looked wonderful, handsome in its rough-cut way, dark hair curling over the ears, the large eyes looking straight into Rafi's with indescribable tenderness. Rafi opened his arms to his brother. The sun blasted down.

"Shimoni! How are you?"

"Okay."

"You should visit Mother."

"I do, Rafi. All the time."

"Ah. Well, that's good."

They were silent. Then: "Listen," said Shimon, "how are *you?*"

"I did it. I actually did something I wanted to do. I'm really proud of myself!"

Shimon grinned broadly. Specks of dried blood peppered his large, white teeth. "That's good! You're going to America?"

"Yes."

"Congratulations, Rafi. I know how much you wanted it. Good luck."

Sweat dripped from his forehead to the ruined collar of his uniform. Rafi ran a hand through his own hair and perspiration clung to each finger. He wanted to embrace Shimon but knew it was somehow forbidden. Words sobbed in his throat. Under the sun, along the road lined with crumbling desert mountains, he held his face in his hands and wept.

"Rafi, Rafi mine. Why are you crying?"

"I want to be with you."

"My little Rafi." Shimon's voice was a melodious baritone, very gentle. "You can't yet, you're not old enough. Not yet. Where I am is too far away. You need to prepare. You need to experience a lot of things, and to grow old in life."

"You didn't!"

"Ah. That's different. I was a hero." Shimon held out both hands to him. Rafi pulled immediately back. The hands were on fire. Shimon smiled sadly. "When you search so hard for something, it means you're really waiting to be found. Live to work, Rafi. Real love will find you." A five-fingered torch waved. "I'll see you."

In his seat Rafi woke with a sore throat, half-startled to hear the pilot's voice over the intercom announcing descent into New York. NO SMOKING signs flashed on over each row. He sat, turned, and saw that the porthole shade was up. Then he stared for a while at the night. The plane was circling, beginning to descend, tilting, bucking winds.

I'll find work in America, he thought.

I'll find love in America.

I'll lose myself, and my people, in America. Or become something different. Transform. And leave them all behind. That's what it's about down there, where I'm going to—a land of transformation. As only in my dreams.

His ears popped as they flew lower, leveled, and descended again. He glanced out and down and was riveted. Tears he'd cried years ago—since then, only in dreams—made him gulp with surprise and joy. A sea of light glittered up from the dark, dark earth.

Epilogue

In the end there were more treaties. Not that it was really the end of anything in particular, just a continuation of something lurking beneath the surface of all the wars and all the uneasy cease-fire declarations that had gone before. What continued to evolve was a sort of inert hostility. Borders were grudgingly respected. There were occasional outbursts of gunfire, occasional terrorist attacks, top-secret military excursions into this territory or that, trespassing by one side or another, the occasional death of soldiers in the line of a duty that stretched dully, perpetually, into whatever future there was.

The Mediterranean rolled onto the western shore. At night, patrolship lights blinked up at a Middle Eastern sky spectacular with stars. In daylight soldiers on board waved to the children on coastal-settlement beaches. The children waved back, their hands tiny and brown in the distance. Akko shone dull white in the sun. Its Arab buildings were sheer and beckoning, blue or green trim along windows and doorways to ward off the Evil Eye.

South was the desert: sparse and colorless, crumbling mountains breaking the flats, wind whipping sand into chilled mounds overnight. Here, too, were settlements. Here, too, military outposts. Their observation towers poked up from the sand like dark silos in the American

Midwest. From each tower soldiers observed the area with broad sweeps of telescopic lenses. They zeroed in sometimes on moshavim where, at midnight, cotton was harvested, to avoid the heat of dawn. Cotton bouncing in the meshed walls of a truck appeared snow-like, flailing white specks against darkness. Through high-powered telescopic lenses they could see men and women working the trucks, knee deep in clouds of white. Their shirts were sweat-stained in the night.

Along the eastern border settlements clustered thickly. Here, each valley was so dotted with buildings it was impossible to distinguish civilian settlement from military outpost. This was intentional. Indeed, some served as one and the same. But farther north things changed. Here were mountains, permanently snow-dusted. Here everything hid in pines, among rocks, across ice-cold streams. Here was a border of constant wind. Even in summer, chill clung to the air.

At one spot along the northern border, a dirt road ran from Israeli territory into Syrian. A chain strung across it between opposing military establishments marked the border, and on either side of the chain a guard was posted. In the middle of the chain, someone had hung a pair of black mesh panty hose. Neither Syrian nor Israeli disturbed it, so it hung there unmolested, fluttering delicately with each breeze.

The soldier standing guard on the Israeli side was a paratrooper, newly assigned to the Golani Brigade. He was fresh from Officers School, and looked it—his boots were clean, his body fit even after the sleepless night. A dark shadow of morning beard peppered his young face. It was a face cut from a rough, stony mold: ruddy skin, strong nose and chin, thin lips, dark hair curling over small ears—and if it wasn't exactly beautiful, it had a certain appeal. The eyes were large, pale European eyes. Their sudden pallor was striking. They were old and cold, and didn't at all match the face's obvious youth.

Michael looked suddenly at the sky.

It was sunrise. Light spread across the predawn gray. He felt a little warmth sprinkle his forehead and lips, and blinked. Then a lump crept into his throat, he didn't know why. Looking skyward he blushed.

On the other side of the chain the Syrian kid shifted from foot to foot. He too was armed with automatic and semi, a pistol, knives, miniature detonator, radio transmitter and receiver, canteens, helmet. He cleared his throat, embarrassed. When he spoke, it was in French.